PENGUIN BOOKS

TILL DEATH

Or a Little Light Maiming

DO US PART

Also by Kathy Lette

Kathy Lette

TILL DEATH

Or a Little Light Maiming

DO US PART

PENGUIN BOOKS

PENGUIN BOOKS

UK | USA | Canada | Ireland | Australia
India | New Zealand | South Africa | China

Penguin Books is part of the Penguin Random House group of companies whose
addresses can be found at global.penguinrandomhouse.com

Penguin
Random House
Australia

First published by Vintage in 2022
This edition published by Penguin Books in 2023

Cover photography: legs with flippers courtesy of Jacobs Stock Photography,
Getty Images; hot air balloon by Samuel Acosta, courtesy of Shutterstock; island with
sharks by maconda, courtesy of Shutterstock; lifebelt by 3dfoto, courtesy
of Shutterstock; vintage suitcase by Oleg GawriloFF, courtesy of Shutterstock; plane by
Holly Polygon, courtesy of Shutterstock

Cover design by Louisa Maggio © Penguin Random House Australia Pty Ltd
Internal design by Midland Typesetters, Australia
Typeset in 12/16.5 pt Minion Pro by Midland Typesetters

Printed and bound in Australia by Griffin Press, an accredited
ISO AS/NZS 14001 Environmental Management Systems printer

 A catalogue record for this
book is available from the
National Library of Australia

ISBN 978 1 76104 868 5

penguin.com.au

Penguin Random House Australia wishes to acknowledge that Aboriginal and Torres
Strait Islander people are the first storytellers and Traditional Custodians of the land
on which we live and work. We honour their continuous connection to country, waters
and communities. We celebrate their stories, traditions and living cultures. We pay our
respects to Elders past and present.

To B . . . (or not to B.)

PART ONE

1

Why is it that just when you think you have all the answers, life starts asking all the wrong questions?

The last few months have taken me on a hair-raising ride – a parachute-free plunge from a space shuttle re-entering Earth's atmosphere barely comes close to describing their intensity. So, adopt the brace position and please remain in your seat until I've brought this story to a screeching halt. And, once the smoke has cleared and the warning bells are silenced, you can pick your way through the wreckage to the carousel to collect your emotional baggage.

The whole surreal saga I'm going to tell you about kicked off one perfect Sydney winter morning. The crisp, cloudless July sky was electric blue, the spotlight of the sun turning everything golden and sparkling with promise. It was the day before school holidays, the winter break. I should have been planning HSIE assignments to hand out to my recalcitrant high-school students. Instead I was driving along mentally packing lingerie for a scuba-diving holiday with my husband. Yes, lingerie. I may be sixty, or 'sexty' as my silver fox prefers, but Jason and I had only been married for three years and Jason, well . . . he was a veteran Ironman competitor, meaning the bloke was agile in places other men don't even have places. Imagine Chris Hemsworth, Hugh Jackman, Regé-Jean Page, Lord Byron and an army survival expert blended with a soupçon of poetry then sculpted into a six-foot, muscled mass of sensitive charm in R. M. Williams riding boots. And then you'd have Jason.

Velvety-voiced but craggy; brooding yet beguiling; capable but passionate; a bulging Mr Incredible with a novel in his back pocket; sensitive, emerald eyes but a beaming, cheeky smile, his look was kind of rugged, outback explorer-cum-English lit professor who played guitar in his spare time. It was hard not to imagine the sound of a revving Fender Stratocaster heralding his arrival wherever he went. Many times, the mere glimpse of him, fresh from the sea in his tight Speedos, had caused a high-speed pile-up at my beachside Pilates class. I sometimes thought he'd been brought to life by a bolt of lightning.

I'd never got over the fact that Jason Riley had fallen in love with me, Gwendoline Brookes, a high-school teacher, mother and bookworm, average in most ways – 167 centimetres, size 10, mousy hair – as ordinary as he was extraordinary.

My heart had just started beating faster at the thought of the salted caramel tang of his skin, when a news bulletin came blasting out of the car radio. 'A Sydney man is believed to have been taken by a Great White near Shark Island around seven o'clock this morning. The Ironman competitor was on a regular morning training session with a local swim team across the bay but did not make it back. Police are asking witnesses to come forward with any information . . .'

The air curdled. Panic sluiced through me. That was Jason's swim team. Blindsided by a queasy swell of dread, I hit the brakes. The jolt lurched me forwards into the steering wheel but it wasn't the bump to my head I was worried about so much as the emotional impact. Where was my psychological airbag?

'The remains of a swimming cap, a flipper and a scrap of torn, blood-stained wetsuit were found near the island.'

Could it be Jason? I pictured him before his swims, wind-milling his arms to get his circulation going, chiacking the other guys, cursing his slight hangover, betting his mates a bacon and egg roll that he'd still make it back first.

As I clutched the wheel, my dazed eyes focused on a squall of dry leaves on the nature strip, fluttering like tiny frantic birds. On automatic pilot, I turned the car around and headed back towards the beach. My phone rang, pinging plaintively from the depths of my handbag in the back seat. It kept time with the drum solo my heart was beating out against my bra.

Swerving off the main road towards the southern point of the peninsula, I clocked the heavy swell rolling languidly towards the shore without a care in the world and drove towards a convoy of police, ambulance and rescue vehicles at the end of the thin prong of land between the bay and the sea. Lurching to a halt again, I scrambled out of the car, leaving its door flapping. I saw men, ten or so, huddled, draped in towels, one or two in those emergency silver foil blankets, talking to a police officer who stooped, head bent over his notebook. My eyes raked the crowd for Jason, searching for his loose-hipped, supple gait. Surely I'd see his head rising above the pack, flashing that smile that lit up my world . . .

'Gwendoline.' It was Harry, Jason's friend, a doctor and part of the swim team. He broke away from the sombre huddle and strode towards me. 'I've been trying to get hold of you.' He was using his caring voice, the one woven from gauze and cotton wool and Savlon, with sorrowful cadences and a puppy-eyed frown. I felt a squirm of nausea in my throat. I felt sure he only used that voice when he was about to make some devastating diagnosis.

My eyes ransacked the crowd once more. The fact that I couldn't see my husband wouldn't sink in; it just floated on the surface of a mind still buoyant with hope. 'Jason? Harry, where's Jase?' I called. Why couldn't I see him? It was ridiculous. Any minute now I'd spot his twinkly eyes and playful mouth, a mischievous laugh bursting like a tiny explosive before he scooped me up into those strong swimmer's arms.

Harry seemed unable to answer me, but he was pointing at something. Behind a stretch of blue and white police tape lay a towel. And on the towel was a ripped swimming cap the same colour as Jason's and a flipper, a flipper with the letter J painted onto it in my pink nail polish. When I saw that my heart plunged into an abyss. Next to the flipper was a bit of torn, bloodied wetsuit.

'Jason is missing,' Harry said. 'It doesn't look good, Gwen.'

My psyche was instantly incinerated by the hot flash of a nuclear blast. I became a shell of the woman I'd been just moments earlier. Heartbreak minutes are a lot longer than normal minutes. They stretch on for miles – an infinity of awfulness. I drew in a breath but the air didn't reach my lungs. I must have swooned because strangers were now mosquito-ing around me, offering tea, blankets, a camp chair, mouthing at me like earnest goldfish. Police were telling me things: a search and recovery operation was underway; divers, helicopters, drones and rescue boats were combing the bay – with no trace so far. A great white shark had been spotted heading for the open ocean and Surf Life Saving had closed all beaches in the vicinity.

I ducked under the tape and snatched up Jason's flipper but an officer immediately wrested it from my trembling hands. So then I just stood there, stupefied by the power of death. The earth seemed to be having doubts about revolving. The thin chill of the sea breeze cut through my silk dress. My cardigan was in my bag on the back seat. I looked back at my car, at my former self who had been happily driving to school a million years ago. An imaginary camera slowly panned across the wasteland of my emotions. No man's land. Dumbfounded, I stared at the sky, waiting for an incoming asteroid.

And come it did – in the shape of a Boom Trike Mustang screeching towards us; a trike that mounted the pavement and skidded to a halt among the scattering crowd. A short, curvaceous, tattooed woman in sequinned purple jeans, leather jacket and high-heeled biker boots came barrelling towards the police, her face fierce.

'Where's my husband?' she shrieked.

When a policeman tried to calm her down, this sabretoothed bikie chick charged towards him with cyclonic impact. 'It's my husband, ain't it?! Answer me, you maggoty mongrels!' The woman screeched as though she was on fire then dropped to the ground and writhed as if being tortured.

I automatically went into school-teacher mode, kneeling down on the grass and putting a reassuring hand on her arm. 'Calm down, it's okay.' Shell-shock had rendered me icy cool. 'It's *my* husband who's missing.' I could hear words coming out of my mouth as though from a ventriloquist's doll.

The writhing woman spotted the torn flipper on the towel. 'Sweet Jesus, no!' Again, the air was cleaved by her wailing.

'No, that belongs to *my* husband,' I told her, biting back a sob. 'My darling, darling husband ... He swims here most mornings.'

'But look at the name tag, for chrissake! J for Jason.'

'That's right. Because Jason is my ... hus ... band,' I choked.

'Whatchaonabout? Jason's *my* husband!'

'*Your* husband? What on earth do you mean?'

The howling woman unzipped her leather jacket to reveal a bejewelled bustier. She yanked it up to expose the inky topography of her abdomen. Emblazoned there in an upwards sweep towards a pierced navel, a calligraphed flourish spelt out the name 'JASON'.

Still kneeling, I rocked back on my heels, wondering what the hell was going on. 'Look, there must be two Jasons. But it's *my* Jason, my darling husband Jason Riley, who is ... who is ...'

'Jason Riley's *my fuckin' husband*,' the woman reiterated between moans. 'Jason *Riley*. He's been trainin' with his swimming mates.'

I gawped at the woman like a goggle-eyed bather about to swim the English Channel. It took a moment to actually comprehend what she was saying, because her words suddenly seemed to be in Klingon. All I could hear was a kind of fizzing in my head as if a swarm of bees had flown into my ears. There was a long pause. Cogs turned in my brain. 'Why are you saying these dreadful things? Who the hell are you?'

'Who the bloody hell are *you*?' the wild woman spat back in my face.

'I'm Jason's wife.'

'Well, that's friggin' impossible. Because *I'm* his wife.'

My eyebrows were now in my hair. 'What? We've been married for three years – as everyone here knows.' I gestured across to the swim team, who were looking back at me from a distance with shocked compassion.

The interloper's face crumpled like a paper bag. 'Are you for friggin' real? That two-timing sonofabitch! That lowly worm!'

As this fiery high-heeled terrier spewed out these words, my astonishment grew. I tried to take her in – her whisky-drenched voice, her muscular arms, her huge breasts encased in that diamante-studded bustier, the abdomen tattoo, her long, pointed fingernails with the purple painted tips, her earrings shaped like little champagne bottles. Her eyes were flecked with green and fringed with thick spikes of dark mascara; her gaze was challenging, unwavering and furious. Was it possible to pull an eyelash muscle, I wondered, over-burdened as it was with all that make-up? Her hair looked as though it had made a forced landing on her head. The whole maroon-red mass was swept back from her forehead into a turban of tendrils. I didn't know who'd made her jeans but suspected there was a seventies surfie's shaggin' wagon somewhere missing its seat covers. The whole look could be summed up as Vampire Barbie.

But what kind of scam was she playing at? I drew back. Clearly on her tax return the woman listed her occupation as 'Crazed Loner'.

The police were now speaking to the media. An officer's voice cut through the melee. 'In a tragic accident, it would appear that a man identified as Mr Jason Riley has been taken by a shark. We're using all assets available, including sonar, to locate Mr Riley.'

'Look,' I hissed to Vampire Barbie, 'I don't know who you are, or what you want, but if you don't leave now I'm going to have you arrested for harassment.'

The woman yanked her phone out of her jacket and thrust it into my face. Her screensaver was a photo of her cuddling a man who looked remarkably like my husband. They were smiling contentedly. My heart scrambled and foundered. I tucked my hands into my armpits to stop them from shaking.

Laser-eyed joggers and jaunty skateboarders wove around us, not a worry in their sunny lives. The crowd had now been swollen by reporters, all jostling for comment. My head throbbed with the measured insistence of a bass drum. It could not be true. My Jason was the sort of hero who volunteered for the surf lifesaving club. If he had any spare time, he'd be rescuing seals from clubbings. Or orphans from burning buildings. Not scraping the bottom of the biological barrel with a woman like this. My husband looked positively under-dressed without a halo. In fact, he'd haloed me in happiness ever since we'd met. His love shone like a sun god, benignly warming and brightening my every waking moment.

I snapped out of my romantic reverie and steeled myself. This leather-jacketed lunatic must have stolen Jason's image and photoshopped his head onto some other hunk's body. But why? For what warped reason? Media attention? Money? Fraud? Was she a deluded psycho of some kind?

A police boat passed by the choppy point, heading towards Shark Island, its engine coughing smoke. The noise startled me out of my trance. I let out a harrowing, blood-curdling cry and threw myself at the woman's throat.

Harry and the rest of Jason's swim team immediately swooped down and scooped me up, cocooning me in their embrace. My voice, when I spoke, was scratchy as sandpaper. 'Get that woman away from me! Leave me to mourn in peace, you maniac!' I spat out syllables at the intruder like watermelon pips.

Just send her back to whatever sulphur-scented depths had spawned her, I thought as my heart cracked. My beloved Jason would never, ever deceive me . . . Right?

2

Wrong.

The coroner entered and the court room rose as one then sat again, as though obeying an invisible conductor's baton.

The coroner had a powdering of grey hair and a kind, world-weary face. She smiled sympathetically at me. I wanted to reciprocate but I just couldn't smile anymore. Since Jason's death, whenever I did, it was as if a ghost was flitting across my face.

'In the matter of Jason Riley,' the coroner began.

At the mention of his name, I felt a familiar love-pang pierce my heart.

'Without a body, the inquest relies on evidence provided by the police about a presumption of death. The coroner's court finds that the circumstantial evidence overwhelmingly supports the belief that, on the balance of probabilities, the individual is deceased. I hereby direct the registrar to issue a death certificate to bring the family some closure.'

'*Families*,' a voice hissed into my ear. I turned to find *that woman* sitting behind me. A cold wave of disbelief swept over me. Through the school holidays I'd been lost in a fog of grief. It was one long blur of kindness – my two children hovering, Julia dispensing hugs, Max, endless cups of tea; girlfriends cooking casseroles; neighbours commiserating around the kitchen table; Harry and a couple of members of Jason's swim team loitering, trying to find jobs to do around the house or chasing the odd journalist off the premises with the garden hose. Even cocooned thus, it was impossible to forget this unhinged hustler, no matter how hard I tried to dismiss her as a fantasist. What the hell did she want? And, oh god, was she dangerous? A jolt of anxiety zapped through my body.

'I would also like to extend my commiserations to the widow,' the coroner concluded, looking my way.

'*Widows*,' Vampire Barbie corrected. Her neon striped top made her look like a traffic light.

I shushed her with a glare – which had as much effect as dropping a feather into the Grand Canyon.

It didn't work. 'Proof,' the traffic light said, extending a document my way. She was chewing gum and a strong smell of spearmint was coming off her. 'My weddin' certificate.'

I took the piece of paper and scanned it, eyes on stalks.

On this day, and before these witnesses,
Patricia 'Tish' Delaney and Jason Conner Riley
took each other by the hand, joined their lives together
before God, family and friends, and declared themselves to
be married unto one another, and vowed to love, cherish,
honour and support each other as husband and wife.
In confirmation and celebration of their union, they set
their hands below.

And there on the dotted line was Jason's unmistakable hiero-glyphic in bold black ink.

I dropped the document as if it were burning hot. The winter sunshine streaming through the court room windows was warm, soft and lemony but my brain had iced over.

'Hello!' said the woman I now knew to be Tish Delaney, clicking her fingers in my face, 'Hey, you still in there?'

'No,' I said.

I felt as if I'd been pushed on stage in a play where I didn't know the lines.

'Believe me, I never would've got hitched if I'd known about you. Jason Riley, that mongrel we've both wept buckets over, was nothin' but a bloody bigamist.' A guttural explosion of gunfire, which I finally realised was laughter, ack-ack-ed from her mouth.

In my shock and confusion, my mind was seized by that one word: bigamist. I gasped. I think I even flung my hand over my eyes like the heroine in a silent movie. As the coroner summed up proceedings with a lot of legalese, I reread the wedding certif-icate lying in my lap. The whole scenario made no sense to me, probably because I don't do hallucinatory drugs and have never been bludgeoned over the head repeatedly with a blunt instru-ment. Since Jason's death, I had just lain on our bed and looked at the ceiling, which had been the sky of our world. The house, normally buoyant with Jason's charismatic presence, had shrunk to a weirdly dead, quiet place, like a school yard in the winter holidays.

I missed being twined together, our bodies warm and luxu-riant beneath the sheets, me running my fingers through Jason's hair, which was the colour of ripe wheat, with gun-metal-silver streaks at the temples. The warmth the man radiated could melt an igloo. Oh, and the way he could channel a smile through his voice ... Whenever I closed my eyes all I could see was a tableau of our happy life together – little glimpses of domesticity: dancing around the kitchen together to Fleetwood Mac, the day we were larking about getting leaves out of the pool, and both fell in ... And those emerald-green eyes which glimmered and glittered, full of a mystery I couldn't fathom. Well, now I knew why. Or did I?

I realised I was wearing my shoulders as earrings. What was the correct dress code for a coroner's court, I suddenly wondered? I wasn't sure, but felt certain that sequinned jeans and a striped halter-neck top revealing breasts that resembled two watermelons glued to your chest was probably not it. The woman looked like a Belle Epoque courtesan.

'This document could be a fake, for all I know,' I stage-whispered, smoothing my black sheath dress demurely back down over my knees. 'For starters, you're erring on the side of mentally unstable. I mean, who wears sequinned jeans to her beloved husband's inquest? You look like Tina Turner.'

'Zactly. And "What's Love Got to Do with It", eh?' Tish Delaney said before, much to my horror, humming the hit song.

'Desist!' I barked. 'In case you haven't noticed, we are in a court of law.'

People were looking at me curiously now, as if my nose was bleeding or I had a disfiguring facial scar I'd forgotten about. Had they overheard that my husband had double-dipped on his wedding vows? My twenty-seven-year-old daughter, Julia, mouthed to me, 'What's going on?' In social situations, Max, my shy son – a couple of years younger than Julia – often looks like an astronaut who's crash-landed on an unexplored planet. But his whole attention was focused on me now.

I wondered what the eye semaphore was for 'I'm being stalked by a tattooed female bikie who might just have proved to me that your stepfather's a duplicitous bigamist?'

The coroner called for quiet, threatening to remove from the old Victorian court room the next person who interrupted proceedings.

'Please don't make a scene,' I sotto-voced to Tish. 'I don't want anyone to get wind of this mess until we work out exactly what the hell's going on.'

The interloper's heavily mascara-ed eyes narrowed. 'All right, matey, but only if we work it out together. Startin' with the will. That'll prove for sure which wifey Jason loved the most. Where is it?' she hissed.

As the coroner continued, I whispered indignantly, 'That's all you're interested in, the money? More proof that you're nothing but a common con artist. Most of Jason's money is mine, anyway. I invested heavily in his projects. My whole inheritance, in fact – every penny my dear parents left me.'

'Join the club, sister. The charmer got my dosh too. Jason's investments seemed to be cookin'. I mean, the bloke was always minted,' she said, then added under her breath, 'No doubt on your bloody moolah.'

I felt myself heating up, as if I were straight out of a steaming hot bath. I immediately texted Jason's lawyer to say I was on my way over. I'd never met Martin Cash but he'd been in touch about winding up Jason's affairs. He'd be able to ascertain how exactly this vile woman was scamming me.

A low hum of voices filled the room, indicating that formal proceedings were over. I stood up but couldn't orientate myself. Lurching towards the courtroom door, my discombobulation was so great I was worried I'd stumble over the pattern in the carpet.

In the foyer I stared into the mirror and tried to remember where I'd seen that face before. After catching a glimpse of the deathly white pallor reflected back at me, it was clear that whoever it was should audition pronto for the lead in a Halloween movie. Respectful of my grief, friends and family kept their distance. Only Tish Delaney barrelled towards me, gums flapping.

'And take this.' Tish shoved her marriage certificate into my handbag. 'I made ya a copy.'

'Wait. How long were you married?'

'Two years.'

'A year less than me – making your marriage legally void,' I said, triumphantly.

Her hard face softened for a moment. Tears glittered in her eyes and great rivulets of mascara were suddenly coursing their way through the thick foundation caked across her cheeks. 'I reckoned I might cry myself to death over this bloke I loved so much. But now all I wanna know is, who exactly *is* this bloody bloke I loved so much?'

I looked at her, a five-foot sequinned mass of sass. Despite our differences, what we had in common was clear – we'd both thought Jason Riley was the catch of our lives.

'I'm going straight to Jason's solicitor's office,' I replied curtly. 'Give me your number and I'll let you know the outcome.'

Tish Delaney shot me a venomous look. 'Are you kiddin'? You think I'd let you go there alone? I'd rather nail my nipples to a wasp nest. Where there's a will,' she wise-cracked, 'I wanna make sure that I'm in it.'

3

'A bigamist?' Julia exclaimed, duly horrified and swerving lanes recklessly.

'That's what she says.' I heaved a strangled sob into a giant handkerchief. 'But I don't believe her.' Had I really walked by Jason three years ago and accidentally set off a Gullible Chump detector?

'Emoting is a waste of energy until the facts are established,' Max, normally monosyllabic, opined from the back seat.

Emoting? I was doing more than emoting. If a nurse had been present asking how much pain I was in out of ten, I'd be crying out, 'Twenty! Thirty! One hundred!' Most painful of all was this question: had I been studying for a degree in Idiocy for three years without even knowing it?

'I'm fine,' I lied, closing in on myself like a pond swallowing a stone.

'Fine? You haven't been *fine* since you fell for that A-grade douchebag,' Julia trumpeted.

My daughter is a dentist – she knows how to drill straight into a nerve. 'Don't hold back, Julia, darling. Tell me what you really think of Jason.'

'You know I couldn't stand the creep. I could never believe you'd fallen for an egomaniac like him, not after Dad.'

I flicked down the sun visor to stop the rays from slicing into my eyes, and caught sight of my face in the mirror once more. It was ravaged with despair. My peepers were so pink I looked like a lab rat.

'Another wife!' Julia shook her small, perfectly highlighted head. 'It can't be true, can it? Didn't you notice anything?' She sounded impatient, but not as surprised as I'd have liked.

'No, I did not,' I replied defensively. 'Mind you, I don't have a "Bigamy for Beginners" manual – do *you*?'

I chug-a-lugged a gulp of Rescue Remedy, wishing it came with a whisky chaser, and delivered a complete account of what I'd gleaned so far, concluding between sighs that it all just seemed so out of character – no matter what they thought of Jason, surely they had to admit he'd been a wonderful husband to me?

Minutes as thick and slow as molasses dripped by, then my brusque son said, 'He was never nice to me, Mum. Coupled with this new evidence, Jason's possible psychological profiles appear to range from antisocial personality disorder to narcissistic personality disorder. Alternatively, the man may simply have had a split personality.'

'Yes, and I hated both of them,' my daughter said firmly, leaning on the car horn.

Julia could be fluent in first-degree takedowns and I was definitely getting the double whammy today.

Tears of confused fury brimmed at my eyelids. My facial muscles flinched uncontrollably. I felt a squirm of nausea in the pit of my stomach and an acid taste in the back of my throat. Don't throw up, I thought. Not here in this spotless hybrid eco car of Julia's. My daughter would have conniptions. I loved her dearly, but she could inject a penitential flavour into any conversation. Since I'd met Jason she'd looked at me like a science project gone wrong.

A stubborn streak of acne had kept my son at his bedroom computer all through high school and uni, and turned him into a full-blown geek. Even now, in his twenties, Max still didn't socialise all that well. I sometimes wondered if semaphore might be the most effective means of communication with him; it was often tempting to have a whole conversation with signal flags – except for the fact that I might accidentally land an aircraft. But monosyllabic Max now piped up to voice a clearly long-repressed detestation of Jason's preference for 'processed animal corpses'.

This triggered the entire kingdom of woke – ka-BOOM! – from my vegan daughter, who felt compelled to deliver a lecture on how often she'd had to correct Jason's language – it was the 'developing world' not the 'third world'; not 'mixed race' but 'dual heritage'; not 'gay' but 'bi-curious' – and other misdemeanours such as his confusing her non-binary pals with sexually fluid flexitarians.

I needed an emotional fire blanket to protect myself from Julia's scorching commentary when it came to Jason. As she ranted on, cataloguing his many shortcomings, I couldn't help wish that just occasionally the woke would take a little nap.

I derailed the diatribe by calling Martin Cash to warn him about Tish Delaney. The rest of the ride to Jason's solicitor's office was without incident, the only interruption to the silence Julia's nasally Google Maps, which brought us to a halt outside a row of shops in a nondescript high street near the industrial port area of Botany Bay. Our car shuddered as a loaded coal truck whumped past.

A narrow door indicated the way to Martin Cash's office above a betting shop – more *Better Call Saul* than *Suits* or *Boston Legal*.

It must be a century, at least, I thought, since people had to turn up at a lawyer's office for a will reading. It was like being in a Jane Austen novel, minus bustle and bonnet. The prospect filled me with prescient fatigue – but Julia frog-marched me towards the frosted glass door.

The sound of a trike idling throatily alerted me to the fact that my nemesis had followed us. Max and Julia turned to take in the dyed red chaos of curls, leather jacket, traffic-signal halter top with half a boob hanging out and black jeans embossed with sequinned snakes, which coiled their way up powerful thighs and slithered into denimed nether regions.

My daughter speared Vampire Barbie with a reproachful glare. 'Oh god, is that *her*? You've got to be kidding me. Yet more proof.'

'Of what?'

'That Jason Riley must have hired someone to trepan your head and suck out your frontal lobe, the day you agreed to marry the maniac.'

Conversing with my daughter could be like ringing a complaints hotline, but today she seemed somewhat justified. I was as perplexed as my progeny – how could Jason have been involved with a woman like Tish Delaney? Crass, dim – I was pretty sure it would take her an hour and a half to watch *60 Minutes*. On forms where it said 'Sign', she'd probably write 'Aries with Gemini rising'.

A rust bucket pulled up behind Tish, and two teenagery types clambered out, whom I presumed to be her unfortunate offspring. My daughter canted one perfectly plucked eyebrow then looked away with disdain. Max pushed open the smudged glass door and we climbed the steps to the solicitor's reception. Greenish carpeting ran through the office like creeping mould. The glossily lipsticked receptionist advised us, between pink bubble gum explosions, that Mr Cash was expecting us and to 'scoot down' to his office. She ushered us into a room of bad modern art, flat, polished surfaces, pot plants so shiny they seemed plastic, cheap walnut panelling and rust-coloured carpet. It was all pretty predictable apart from a spindly-legged antique desk, poised on tiptoe, as if about to sprint from the room in horror at its surroundings. I knew just how it felt.

There were two gangrenous-coloured sofas at 45-degree angles to the desk. After a reluctant exchange of introductions, Tish and her offspring took one and I sat down with my children on the other. Our kids were clearly just as opposite as Tish and I. Whereas my son's short, dark coif resembled a smooth, shellacked wave breaking across his head, Tish's son's waist-long, blond dreadlocks appeared to have been groomed with salad tongs. Whereas my daughter's hair was blow-dried to perfection, Tish's daughter sported a buzz cut, dyed astro-turf green. Perhaps she was planning a game of miniature golf up there? While my son, suited and booted, sat rigidly beside me, Tish's son slumped into the leather banquette, knees apart, head down, arms wrapped around his mid-section. He pulled up the hood on his sweatshirt, completing the look of urban terrorist.

My daughter's wit is as sharp as the points on her vertiginous heels, but Tish's daughter's vocabulary seemed as plain and flat as her Doc Martens. 'Yeah, duuuuuuude', 'lush', 'frothy', 'totes awkie' and 'triggered' seemed the extent of her lexicon as she gas-bagged with her brother.

Tish Delaney and her offspring looked us up and down with the same dismissive attitude, a sarcastic manner which said loud and clear that they thought it might be time we buried our secret ambition to be fashionista influencers.

The door swung wide and Martin Cash swaggered into the office. With immense willpower I managed to compose my features into a semblance of dignity and fought to project an attitude of detached irony. Tish and I rose simultaneously, as though doing a calisthenics class.

'Well, this is a bit of a shit-show, ain't it?' The man's voice sounded like two jackhammers mating. He grimaced, offering us a full-frontal view of his terrible dentistry. Julia and I exchanged an appalled glance – we'd seen better teeth on a comb. Although sporting eyebrows so bristly they could clean the stove in *Train-spotting*, his hair was prematurely thinning. The wind had blown the remaining wisps into a kind of hirsute halo. He was wearing a nose-clagging quantity of aftershave.

The solicitor patted my shoulder avuncularly. 'Sorry for your loss, Mrs Riley.'

'*Our* loss,' Tish corrected him, gruffly chewing each word.

Jason's solicitor made a lip-fart of disapproval at Tish's interruption but extended his hand. 'Marty Cash,' he said with wheedling nasality. His eyes locked halfway down Tish's chest, where a ruby pendant, visible through a peekaboo window in her striped top, was being molested between stupendous breasts. 'I take it you're the woman Gwen mentioned on the phone?'

Tish looked at the solicitor's extended paw as though it was contaminated. 'No shit, Sherlock. We're here about the will. Some of that moolah's mine. In fact, a lot of it. And if he's left it all to *her*, I'm gonna spit the dummy.'

Her voice sounded distant, as if it were coming from the bottom of the sea, even though she was sitting right opposite me; I could hear sounds tumbling from her rouged mouth but there was a delay in my deciphering of them.

The solicitor puffed out his cheeks and, as he exhaled, lowered his bulk into a small, ergonomically correct chair, which gave a groan of protest. He then examined the marriage certificate Tish had thrust under his nose.

'Is that document legitimate?' my daughter asked haughtily.

'For chrissake,' Tish eyerolled, shaking her electric mane of red hair. 'Who do you think I am? Mata Bloody Hari?'

Marty Cash perused the document for a full five minutes, before finally glancing up. He had so many rolls of neck fat that he seemed to be looking at me over a stack of crumpets. Expectation weighted like a thick blanket over the room.

'I'm sorry to say that it looks legit, yes. But . . .'

The man might as well have pulled the pin on a live grenade. Reflexively I reeled back in my seat. As did my daughter.

'Surely you need to check at the Registry of Births, Deaths and Marriages?' Julia asked, suspiciously.

'Just cut to the chase – where's the will and which of us gets the dosh?' Tish demanded.

'Julia's right – I want that document checked.' I kept my face impassive, somehow managing to suppress the shocked incredulity coursing through my frame.

'It's neither here nor there whether it's a legitimate certificate or not because, ladies, the thing is . . .'

As one, all six of us leant forward, concentrating on Marty Cash as though he were Moses about to read from the tablets of stone.

'There is no will. And there are no assets for you. Jason recently transferred everything in his accounts to a business partner in Egypt.'

Marty Cash, having pulled the pin, now tossed his stun grenade into the room, where it detonated. How many more Molotov moments could I take, I wondered.

'Everythin'?' Tish's eyebrows were arched and full. They had a lot of personality. And they were certainly expressing themselves now – and not in a good way.

'*What*?' Julia exclaimed, leaping to her feet. 'Jesus, Mother. How much money did you lend the creep?'

'It wasn't a loan. It was an investment,' I explained. 'Mr Cash, that money is mine! Surely, legally, they must return it?'

'Do you have paperwork?' he inquired with the grim demeanour of an undertaker. 'Did you sign an agreement with Mr Riley?'

With those words, the solicitor sealed my fate like an envelope. My daughter read my expression fluently. 'Oh, Mother! How could you?' she said in a stentorian tone.

Jason's treachery cut into me like razor wire. 'Who exactly is this business partner?' I asked. 'Surely we can appeal to their better nature?'

'Well, strictly speaking that's classified information,' Marty Cash slimed.

'A *female* business partner, no bloody doubt.' Tish, fuming, was on her feet too now, pacing the office.

My life had become like an onion – the closer I got to the truth, the more it made me cry. The bitter taste of betrayal flooded my mouth once more. 'There must be some mistake. I simply can't believe you.'

Tish leant across his desk, her huge pendant swinging hypnotically across her creamy cleavage. 'Surely a little teeny, tiny peek wouldn't do any harm?' she purred.

Marty Cash, entranced, slid a document across his desk. As if magnetised, Tish and I moved as one, bumping heads in our eager pursuit of it. My eyes scanned the bank transfer to a Ms Skye Cavendish before jumping to the moniker at the bottom of the page – Jason's inimitable signature. Reality was a cold bucket of water in my face.

I flashbacked to the day Jason proposed, the way his eyes searched my face for my answer. It had felt so tender, so poignant, so perfect . . . Now, I suddenly saw his eyes differently – as the eyes of a soap opera actor looking into the camera in the seconds before an ad break.

'Who the hell's this Skye chick?' Tish demanded, her flirty mood extinguished.

Marty Cash clammed up again, saying that he wasn't at liberty to divulge any of his client's information, even if his client was deceased.

'Can't we get a court order for disclosure?' I asked.

'On what grounds?' he said, with granite indifference.

'There must be *something* you can tell us?' my dentist daughter drilled down.

The solicitor's silence made it clear he'd rather stab himself with a quill while eating his horse-hair wig than divulge details about the mysterious Egyptian recipient of my life savings.

The three of us – Tish, Marty and me – stood in a bleak triangle staring at each other. Then I started laughing. It was as if someone had turned on a tap. I couldn't stop guffawing. Finally, when I was looking seriously under-dressed without a strait-jacket, Tish also let out a sharp, contemptuous bark of a laugh.

'He played us both. That prick,' she said.

As Marty Cash droned on about winding up some small property items, Jason's car and motorbike, his guitar collection, etc., etc., all I could think was – a *female* business partner – in *Egypt*?

I racked what was left of my brains, trying to join dots that weren't there. Jason's job as a fly-in, fly-out mining engineer gave him plenty of excuses to be away. And his sports addiction saw him competing in Ironman events all around the world. He loved the camaraderie and excitement, and he often used the trips to go sailing and scuba diving in exotic locations. Most recently in the Red Sea, I now remembered.

'Mr Cash, I urge you to be less parsimonious with the facts,' my sombre son insisted. 'If you can't tell us any more about Jason's mysterious business partner, can you at least tell us exactly the nature of said business?' he probed.

'Something in mining. Sorry. That's all I know.' The solicitor blinked like a rat that had just crawled out of a drain.

'That story's so abridged, you should pay a toll,' I replied, coldly.

'Bloody oath!' Tish agreed, cracking her knuckles menacingly.

Jason's four stepchildren, although initially wary of each other, had, it appeared, found common ground – namely that their ridiculous mothers had been scammed. They were now commiserating in a huddle. Julia's face was taut, her lips thinned. Tish's daughter, Sienna, was cussing explosively. Tish's son Zack's dreadlocked head was nodding in agreement at something Max had said: 'Too right, duuuuude.' My son's head was shaking in disbelief and there was a wet moon of perspiration visible under each of his armpits.

As our offspring bonded over our gullibility, I found myself swapping an unexpected look of commiseration with Tish Delaney.

'Ah,' I sighed, through half-closed lips, 'if only I were young enough to know everything.'

This comment raised a reluctant eyebrow from my caustic companion. 'Never forget that a mother's place is in the wrong.'

'Next time you're looking for a new husband, Mother,' Julia said, overhearing us, 'why don't you kick over a stone and see what crawls out?'

'Yeah,' Tish's daughter drawled her agreement.

'Oi! Just can it, kids, and let me think,' Trish groused in reply.

Marty Cash cleared his throat and looked at his watch, uttering platitudes about how sorry he was that he couldn't be more helpful but he had another appointment. Like hell he did. I was just contemplating some kind of charm offensive when Tish thumped his desk so hard I thought it might crack.

'Listen, you diseased cocksucker, I want the details of that Cairo cow. And I want them now. Otherwise I'm gonna be tempted to nail your nuts to an ant nest,' she thundered. Apparently a career in diplomacy didn't beckon.

'Time is money. One more minute and I'll have to charge,' Marty Cash jabbered in that nasally voice of his. Tapping his watch continuously, he slammed shut Jason's file, ushered us all out the door, which he locked, then slithered away down the hall like the snake that he was.

As we traipsed after him towards reception, our offspring continued their quartet of maternal criticism.

'Ignore 'em. The first rule of motherhood – never negotiate with terrorists,' Tish said, turning to face me. 'But you and I need to talk. Thing is, I'm not buyin' any of it, are you? I don't trust that slimeball. I've got a gut feelin' *he's* stolen our money. Doan cha reckon?'

There was no doubt that Jason's solicitor was straight from Sleazebags-R-Us, right down to his acrylic suit and stained tie. His office was the whole clichéd shark's den, from the dodgy location to the dyed blonde receptionist with store-bought boobs. Why would Jason have done business with a bottom-feeder like Marty Cash? What did that say about his character? I watched out the window as Cash climbed into a Porsche, before roaring away from the kerb. How, I wondered, did a second-rate solicitor in a Botany Bay backwater, get that loaded?

'We need to find out if that Cleopatra chick's for real,' Tish continued. 'Which means we gotta get that file.'

'How? Break back in? No thanks. I hear that prison libraries are chronically short of the works of Proust.'

Even though Tish was at least five inches shorter, she always seemed to be looking down on me. 'Not with a crowbar, you idiot. I just had a manicure. You've been watchin' waaay too many crappy cop shows. Watch *this*.'

Loitering in reception, Tish extracted an e-cigarette from her pocket. I stared at her as she waited till the phone rang and the gum-chewing receptionist was vocally embroiled, before saying to a secretary sitting quietly typing, 'Oh god! I'm such a bloody fool. I've left my bag in Mr Cash's office. And I need my Nicorette . . .' She held up her vape, 'Urgently. Or I'm gonna crack and smoke a real ciggy. Don't bother gettin' up, hon. Could you just lend me the key for a sec?'

As the secretary absentmindedly handed it over, Tish winked at me. 'Back in a jiff. Wait here.' She flung the words over her shoulder before sashaying back down the hallway. All that was missing was the saxophone solo.

I felt an urgent urge as well – to get the hell away from her as fast as humanely possible. I summoned my kids and made a dash for the stairs. The only good thing about Jason not leaving a will was that I wouldn't have to spend any more time talking to Vampire Barbie. Using vernacular a woman like Tish could best understand, I'd rather nail my nipples to a wasp nest than be in her odious company ever again.

4

'So, what would you say if I asked you to fly to Cairo with me?'

'Nothing.'

'Why?'

'Because I can't talk and laugh at the same time.' I checked my watch. It was 4.30 p.m. and I'd just started a big pile of marking. 'How did you find out where I live?' I half-closed the front door in her face.

'It was all in the file. I stole it from fuckface.'

Of course she did.

'Drink?' Tish Delaney said, brandishing a bottle of whisky.

'No, thanks. I'm not feeling that sociable.' I pointedly closed the front door to a crack.

'I don't wanna drink to be sociable, you idiot. I wanna drink to get drunk.'

The fact that Tish had successfully managed to purloin the documents from under the nose of Jason's creepy solicitor might have buoyed my opinion of her, if she hadn't then shoved open the door, pushed past me and barrelled down the corridor to the kitchen, her lacy skirt swishing.

I followed, flummoxed, to find her flumping down onto the sofa by my conservatory window. I watched thin-lipped as she twisted open the whisky and took a husky slug. 'Trouble is, I can't get bloody closure. How can I when there's no body?'

'Yes, if only we could have a normal cremation . . . we could have brought marshmallows,' I said, sarcastically.

Tish snorted. 'Yeah . . . and got the deposit back on the urn. I started out with nothin' and thanks to that bloody mongrel, I still have most of it left.' She let out a peal of bitter laughter, and just as suddenly the animation evaporated. 'How could that sonofabitch have done this to me?'

'And to me.' I looked at the interloper squarely. 'What's left of my mind boggles.'

When Julia had dropped me home earlier, her lips compressed to the width of a paper cut, I'd called Harry. Had Jason ever mentioned a woman called Tish Delaney? Did Harry know anything about Jason's life when he was at the mining site? Did he know what had really happened during those overseas Ironman competitions?

'Gwen, you know guys. We just shoot the breeze about footy and fishing, with a lot of teasing about beer guts and bald spots and little blue pill overdoses – Vitamin V and so forth. Why, is something wrong?'

'No, no.' I hung up, too crushed to elaborate.

My girlfriends from book club, Pilates and water aerobics had rallied around after Jason's death, but I couldn't bring myself to discuss my husband's bigamy with any of them; I just couldn't think of the correct conversational opening for that topic.

'Hi. Well. You know that man I wed? Turns out he's a marital kleptomaniac.'

The fog I'd been in had now thickened into a real pea-souper. Not even Sherlock Holmes could find his way out of this one. What blew my brain was how Jason could have been in love with two women possessed of such polar opposite personalities. The truth pressed in on me like a low ceiling – he'd never really loved me at all.

'If only we'd been able to donate Jason's corpse to medical science, at least we'd be able to see what a body with no heart looks like.' I kept standing so that Tish would get the message that brevity is the essence of unannounced visits. 'So, good luck in Cairo,' I said pointedly. 'Let me know how you get on.' I made a move back towards the hallway.

'No need, matey, cause you're comin' with me.' She handed me a plane ticket. 'Non-refundable, by the way. Bought 'em with Jason's air miles. I mean, it's not like he'll be needin' them, right? Not where he's goin'. I hope Satan's rolling out the welcome mat as we speak. We're gonna confront this Skye chick, explain that Jason married us both and that he has responsibilities – meanin' the Queen of the Nile must cough up our cash or we'll take her to court. And if she doesn't comply, I'll point out what a big hole a bullet would make in her social life.' Tish growled before taking another hefty slug and smacking her lips. 'I've still got my roo-shootin' gun, ya know.'

I suddenly knew how my son felt a lot of the time – as though I'd been plunked down on a planet to which I wasn't native. 'Um . . . generally speaking, I think customs officials take a rather dim view of armaments in airline luggage.'

'Yeah, but nobody would ever search *your* baggage. I mean, look at you. You dress like a Mormon librarian. Oh, by the way, the nineties called. It wants its hairstyle back.'

I patted my hair defensively. Yes, I'd been sporting my Jennifer Aniston *Friends*-era shag for a few decades but that's because it suited my face. I glanced askance at Tish's unruly red pagoda of curls, lacy skirt, fishnet tights and biker boots. I couldn't believe she had the temerity to criticise my appearance when it looked as though she'd got dressed in front of an industrial fan that had blown random clothes onto her frame while electrocuting her hair follicles.

'There's no way I'm going with you to Cairo. So, thanks for asking, but . . .' I gestured towards the front door.

'Come on. Think of it. Egypt. The Pyramids. The Sphinx. How old are you?' She extracted an e-cigarette from her bag. 'Fifty-four, five?'

'Actually, I've just turned sixty.'

She looked surprised. I might dress like a Mormon librarian but my face cream was obviously working well.

'Jeeeesus? Really.' The woman was now pluming vape smoke. 'Well, I just turned fifty. Hard to believe, I know.' She hoiked up her boobs in their gilded bustier. 'J'know the best way to stay young? Be photographed in front of ancient monuments. Many of which are in . . . oh yeah, that's right – Egypt!'

'It's a wild-goose chase. As you heard, I trusted Jason to invest my money. Because we were married, I didn't insist on paperwork. You did the same. We have no legal leg to stand on – not even a wobbly prosthetic.'

'My missin' money's drivin' me mental. I mean . . . did my marriage mean nothin' . . . What the actual fuck is this all about?'

'I wish I knew.'

'Well, what are you gonna do to find out?'

'I don't know!' I said, exasperated. 'It's not as though there's a self-help section in the book shop on "Husbands Who Got Eaten by a Shark While Owing You Money – and How to Handle It". I'm thinking of seeing a grief counsellor who's supposed to be good. I could give you her number.'

'Grief counsellin'? Lemme just pop that on my to-do list . . . right below a DIY clitoridectomy.'

'I've read that you don't move on from grief, you move forward with it. I'm sure it'd help you.'

'No bloody way. Sittin' on a vinyl armchair near some noddin' woman with a box of tissues is not the cure I need right now. The cure I need is to track down this Skye chick. The greatest mistake in life is to live in the constant dread of makin' one. You know you wanna come. Follow your heart.'

'My heart says yes, but my brain says . . . Absolutely *no way*.'

'Jeez. What about your liver? Have you heard from any other of your internal organs?'

'Well, Tish, I'm riveted by what you have to say. I could just stand here and talk to you for, oh, *second*s!' I folded my arms defensively, nodding towards a pile of unmarked homework. 'But igneous rock formations await.'

'Oh look! What's that big white line across your bum? Is that from sittin' on the fence your whole bloody life?'

'No,' I said defensively. 'There are no splinters in this pert posterior, thanks very much.'

'Then why won't cha come with me?'

'I . . . I . . . I have to sort out Jason's clothes for charity.'

She looked at me with incredulity. 'What? *Now*?' She sent another eruption of vape smoke ceiling-ward. 'Jason hasn't even been fully digested by that shark yet and you're recyclin' his clothes? What's the real reason?' She narrowed her eyes shrewdly. 'Doan gimme any of your bullshit. What do you know that I don't?'

'Nothing,' I said ineffectively, all the time wanting to wring Tish Delaney's neck.

'Well, I'm not leavin' till you tell me.' She sank back into the sofa and crossed one fishnetted leg over the opposite knee.

'The truth is . . . if you must know, I hate flying,' I blurted.

'Crap. Your Facebook profile says you're a history and *geography* teacher, for chrissake.'

'Yes, and I like to stick to *terra firma*. For me the firma the ground, the lessa the terra. Okay?'

Tish gave a glottal bass bark of derision. 'Wait. You're a geography teacher who doesn't travel?'

'Flights of fancy are a very agreeable mode of transport,' I replied stiffly. 'And cruises. I do go on cruises. New Zealand, Fiji—'

'You really don't fly? Okay then, when *was* the last flight you took?'

'When I moved to Australia from England. Thirty-five years ago.'

'Jeez. Thirty-five years? Then why haven't you lost your hoity-toity accent? You sound like you were raised by Queen Victoria.'

'I moved here after meeting the Aussie father of my children in Cornwall. The flight over here was so awful, I vowed never to go in a plane again. Well, not until the law of gravity is repealed.'

'You're shittin' me?' she scoffed, theatrically. 'Flyin's safer than car travel.'

'Oh really? Do you know the actual statistics? How often does a plane crash?'

'Ah . . . just the once, I'd say. But it's bloody rare. Your fears are completely groundless.'

'Exactly! No ground! That's my fear.' I couldn't keep a smugly triumphant note from my voice. 'I get altitude sickness just licking an airmail stamp.'

'You never went with Jase on his jaunts?'

The grim freight of Jason's betrayal weighed heavily on my heart once more. 'You . . . you went with him?'

'Wanted to, but his trips always seemed to clash with my gigs.'

'You're a musician?'

'Yeah, a jazz singer.'

I felt as if I'd been holding the map upside down all this time. 'But Jason hates . . . hated,' I corrected myself, 'jazz. He liked classical.'

'Clearly we're not talkin' about the same bloke. Jason loved Oscar Peterson, Miles Davis, Ella Fitzgerald, the Montreal Jazz Festival—'

'That's ridiculous. He loved opera. Wagner and Verdi. And crosswords and books. He was the only man allowed into our book club.'

'Doan make me laugh. Jason's readin' material was limited to the racin' guide.'

'Racing? He abhorred betting of any kind.'

'What? He loved racin' nearly as much as he loved racin' me off.'

I looked at her curvaceous body. I have all the lanky ungain-liness of a woman who wants to be shorter, the exact opposite of Tish's voluptuous, compact, confident form.

'Actually, he did like readin' the occasional book. But only sci-fi.'

'Now *that's* an alien concept. We read all the Booker and Miles Franklin winners and discussed them at length. He couldn't get to sleep at night unless he'd read himself down.'

'Sleep? Jason was a night owl. We danced till dawn. And what a mover. It was like his feet had taken steroids. That's why we chose to live in the CBD – he hated the 'burbs – everyone went to bed so early.'

'He *loved* living here by the beach. He said the sea was the same colour as my eyes – cornflower blue.'

'Blue? He loved my dark, chocolate eyes . . . That's it. We're *definitely* not talkin' about the same bloke.'

'Six foot one, green eyes, sandy hair, with a sliver of grey at the temples?'

'Yep,' she nodded.

'A succulent bottom lip, broad shoulders.'

'Yep.'

'A warm smile lighting up his whole face, especially his eyes, which sparkled with wit.'

'A huge cock.'

I stared at her in awkward silence for a beat. 'What?'

'Darl, no wonder we married him. His cock was so big the tip of it entered you at 8 pm and the base of the shaft about half past ten.'

Her words caught me off guard. Who *was* this appalling woman? 'Do you have to be so vulgar?'

'Do you have to be so prissy? I can't believe my Jase married a tight arse like you.'

'And I can't believe he married a gauche philistine like you.'

We glared at each other, grief, anger and bewilderment shuddering through both of us.

'Jesus.' Tish got up and started pacing across my living room, her heels clickity-clicking. 'How could this bloody well happen to me? I'm street-smart. I mean, I grew up in the bush. I've worked as a roustabout on a sheep station. I've been a mill rat. I've been an offsider for a professional roo shooter. I've worked down mines, drivin' trucks and loaders – the only woman with a gazillion fellas . . . I'm in a band, for fuck's sake. I have a finely tuned crap antenna.' Her face was a balled-up fist of fury.

'How do you think I feel? I'm a teacher. I can spot a lying teenager from a hundred paces. I'm a human polygraph.'

Tish paused in her pacing to gaze at the magnetised fridge photo of Jason and me on honeymoon in Byron Bay, then spun round to scrutinise me. 'You never noticed anythin' suspicious?'

I cross-examined my memories for a moment. Had there ever been a time I felt that something wasn't right? No overheard clandestine phone calls? No new sex manoeuvres suddenly introduced into our R-rated repertoire? I studied my reflection in the mirror behind the kitchen table. Had I deliberately blinkered myself; eyes half-closed to blur my vision? Did I have the wide-eyed look of a joey or a bilby or pademelon or some other helpless, defenceless creature that gets eaten by a dingo in one bite? I shook my head. 'No. You?'

Tish's wavy mass of hair fell onto her face. She picked up a strand and chewed on it as she was thinking. 'Nope. Nuthin'. Not then or now. I've sniffed round my house like a bloodhound – but no clues. And it's not as though he left much of a digital footprint, either. He hated Facebook and Instagram, and he sure wasn't in Wikipedia.'

'Or *Who's Who*.'

'Nah, Jason was in Who's *That*? The bloke was so insanely hot. I couldn't believe that a man that good lookin' wanted little ol' me.' She smiled thinly.

'Me too,' I said absently. I thought back to the day we'd met. I'd joined other volunteers on a beach clean-up. As I retrieved plastic detritus along the shoreline, I'd felt his gaze brush warmly across my face. Looking up, there'd been a pulse of recognition. Even though I'd never encountered the stranger before, I had this uncanny feeling that he could really see me, without even realising that I'd been feeling so invisible.

'Do you want to join us for a drink?' I'd asked at the end of that beautiful day, 'Or . . .?'

'"Or" sounds good,' he'd twinkled.

He was wearing a white T-shirt that showed off his chiselled physique. Coupled with the cultivated perma-stubble, it made him look as though he'd stepped off a men's calendar. And then, when he decided to go for a surf and stripped off – well, an underwear advertisement clearly beckoned. His swimmers were so tight that *I* could hardly breathe. While drying off he said he was interested in saving the beach from developers. As I signed him up to our campaign group, I found myself jelly-legged with longing for the first time since the death of my dear husband twelve years earlier. I soaked up the attention Jason gave me like a rescue puppy at the pound on open day.

Later, in the sunset bar, his firm hands around my waist, pulling me into his warm body, I could feel the pulse of him, and then that hot, spicy kiss. When he touched me it was like liquid gold being poured through my veins. And now those happy memories were booby-trapped. I felt a hot prickling sensation behind my eyes, as though I'd walked into a stinging nettle, face first.

'I'm gonna ring the minin' company.'

'What? Now?'

'Yep. It's time we did some minin' of our own – minin' for info.'

While Tish was on the phone, I rifled through a kitchen drawer and extracted Jason's business card. It read simply, 'Expert' and on the back, 'I.M.O.M.' I'd once asked him what it stood for, thinking it was a qualification of some kind, and he'd replied, with a wink, 'International Man of Mystery.'

Tish solved some of that mystery a few minutes later.

'The rat,' she growled, tossing her phone onto the sofa, 'Jason hasn't worked at the mine for two years.'

That was when another part of my world humpty-dumptied, never to be put back again. 'So,' I finally said. 'All those times I thought Jason was working, or competing in Ironman championships, he must have been with you.'

'And all the times I thought he was workin' or in Ironman comps, he must have been with you.'

'What a nightmare.' I put my head in my hands. 'I just want to go back to my old life and pretend this never happened.'

'Yeah, well, I can't go back to my old life. I'm broke. Broke and friggin' furious. And confused. I need closure. I need sleep. I need dosh. Are you sleepin'?'

'Yes.' I lied. In truth, if I did manage to drop off before dawn, I'd wake with a jolt, as though a bomb had gone off – the white-hot, bone-jarring explosion slamming through my body over and over again.

'I'm also drinkin' waaay too much.' Tish took another hefty slug. 'I always plan to exercise first thing in the mornin' . . . and then, like clockwork, I'm out the door by three p.m. and straight to the bar.'

'Have you tried Rescue Remedy?'

'What, heroin? Not yet. I'm eatin' myself to death, too. There's a friggin' elephant in the room, as in – yours truly. Nobody's mentioned it, but I can see from the raised eyebrows of the boys in the band that I've piled on the kilos. Put it this way – they're installin' traffic lights in the green room to hamper my trips to the minibar.'

'I read that if you eat kiwi fruit an hour before you go to bed, it has pretty much the same effect as a Valium. Plus, it's slimming.'

'Oh, gee, well, I'm really torn now. I dunno whether to have a fruit salad, or just top myself. No, the only thing that can make me feel better is to find this Skye gal and get my dosh back. With or without you.'

But still the thought of abandoning my home and hemisphere to track down the lost money of my dead husband by confronting his possible paramour seemed as plausible as Trump winning a cryptic crossword competition. 'I don't even know you. And even if I wasn't terrified of flying, jetting off into the unknown with a complete stranger . . . Well, I'd be an idiot.'

'Exactly,' she countered, flippantly. 'So go pack a bag.'

'I'd have to get compassionate leave. Besides, I just can't abandon my kids at a time like this. They're very confused and angry.'

'Hey, I love my kids equally – as in, each is equally friggin' annoyin'. But I'm no good to them right now. And neither are you.'

I arched my back, hands pressing into my lower spine, and yawned theatrically. 'Safe flight. God, I feel like I need ironing.'

'Speakin' of which . . .' Tish flicked at the freshly laundered tea towels draped over the oven door handle. 'You iron your tea towels? Fuck me. Ironin' tea towels is God's way of tellin' you to get a life. You're so bloody unadventurous.'

She was right on that score. A glass of white wine at parent-teacher night is my idea of living dangerously. Suddenly drained of all energy, I sighed and sank down onto the sofa once more. I felt as though my world had been put on hold, as though the universe was saying 'Your call is important to us . . . Please hold the line . . .' All that was missing was the plinky-plonky musak. And the only person who understood what I was going through was currently sashaying down the hallway, out of my life.

'Just make sure you tell this Skye person that Jason had responsibilities to me too,' I said, trotting after her.

Her eyes suddenly glittered, 'Yeah, sure. You'll just have to trust me. The sisterhood and all that. We've been done over by a man, so we wouldn't do that to each other. Right?'

5

Wrong.

'Fuck a duck! What the hell are *you* doin' here?' Tish asked as I stood in front of her table in the airport bar.

'Perusing the fine wines, obviously.' Sarcasm seemed the only way to disguise the raw terror coursing through my veins.

'So, it's got nothin' to do with the fact that you don't trust me?' Tish mocked.

'Well, I know you keep saying you're on my side, but so is my appendix and it could burst, so . . .'

'Good point, kiddo.' She laughed. 'Take a load off.' She gestured to the empty chair opposite her. 'So, seriously, all trust is kaput, then?'

'Let's just say it sauntered out the door with fidelity,' I admitted sadly.

'That's true enough.' Tish downed a shot of something. 'We've both been scammed by a bigamist . . . It's nearly as bloody disturbin' as those shoes you're wearin'.'

I looked down at my Birkenstocks, then across at her diamante-studded high-heeled biker boots. My eyes moved up her bare legs to a sequinned miniskirt and a fluorescent boob tube. I felt pretty certain she was the one who'd forfeited her go at the annual Best Dressed Award.

'You know what, Tish? If you didn't have that ruthless look so common to hardened criminals, you could be a *Vogue* pin-up.'

The stare Tish Delaney gave me proved she was equally convinced that my minimalist, stone-coloured clothing palette of understated chic, ranging in shade from black to taupe, with a beige pashmina thrown in for 'fun', was the ultimate fashion faux pas.

'What do ya wanna drink?' she said, signalling the waiter with a lift of her brows.

'I don't know. What cocktail goes best with fingernails?' I held up my nervously gnawed nails, then pulled out a chair and lowered myself into it. 'What's your tipple?'

'I'm very choosy about what I drink. It's gotta be alcoholic.'

'I don't normally drink this early in the day but I'm so jumpy it's going to take me two martinis to get up the courage to open my Valium bottle.'

'Ah, your flyin' phobia. Ya need a whisky, then. Make it two,' she told the hovering waiter. 'Neat. And make 'em doubles.'

'No! A single is fine,' I informed him. 'How many have you had? Don't you listen to the news? More than two standard drinks a day is detrimental to your health.'

'Yeah, well, so's listenin' to the news. "*It's now been scientifically proven that drinkin' to excess is one of the leadin' causes of statistics*",' she enunciated in a posh newsreader's voice.

The woman wasn't stupid, I realised, just obnoxious. 'Anyway,' I changed subjects, 'what's wrong with my shoes?'

'You look as though you're headin' off to weed a rookery. Or maybe clean a fish tank. And that dress makes you look like one of those mums who buys wooden educational toys for their goody-goody kids who aren't allowed to watch TV.'

'You know, being lectured about fashion by you, *Patricia*, is akin to being lectured on, I don't know, veracity by Vladimir Putin. We're heading to one of the world's most historic, tantalising cities. How do you expect to go sightseeing in that ludicrous footwear?'

'I'm not in Egypt to go sightseein', *Gwendoline*. I'm there to kick arse.'

A steaming pile of hot chips and a burger oozing neon-coloured cheese was plonked down on the table before her.

'Um ... Would you like the name of a good heart specialist with that?' I asked her, appalled.

'J'know what? It took a lot of self-control and determination, but I've managed to give up dietin'. I have one simple rule. If you ain't in the obituaries, order dessert.'

I watched as she devoured her meal. Tish Delaney ate like a fourteenth-century serf fortifying herself for a day of toiling in the feudal fields.

'What are you gonna get?' she asked between mouthfuls. 'Some organic, preservative-free flaxseed tofu burger, no doubt.'

I decided to keep quiet about the small Tupperware container in my backpack that held a concoction of quinoa, oily fish, pulses and proteins.

'So,' she barrelled on, between vigorous bouts of mastication. 'What made you change your mind?'

I got out my passport and pretended to be busy checking in on my phone because I didn't want to tell her the real reason – that it turned out my terror of staying at home was greater than my terror of flying. Since Jason's death, all I felt was an emptiness, a withering, a fading away. I loved my daughter, but she was as sanctimonious as my son was remote – especially after discovering I'd lost not only my own but their inheritance. All I'd get from now on would be Max's most sombre Easter Island countenance and Julia's high horse act. And Julia would be mounting that high horse so often it'd need a nosebag.

Paranoia that people were finger-pointing and gossiping about the poor woman widowed by a Great White shark made every excursion a trial. Even taking the dog for a 'soothing' walk quickly became a commando course. Trying to elude sticky beaks meant ducking and darting and diving into undergrowth with the dexterity of a Special Branch operative. I spent every excursion throwing myself up behind bus shelters and plunging down laneways and sometimes into the path of oncoming vehicles in order to avoid busybodies. I would invariably finally crawl up the street on my elbows, like an invading marine dodging enemy fire, then bolt the door and lie in a darkened room shaking from PTSD.

And if people were already staring at me as if I were some rare Amazonian creature behind glass in a zoo, imagine how the curiosity would intensify once news of Jason's bigamy leaked out. The scandal would catch fire from friend to friend, from yoga mat to surfboard, from hairdresser's curling tongs to bikini waxer's spatula. I shuddered at the thought and had kept coming back to Tish's pronouncement: 'The greatest mistake in life is to live in the constant dread of making one.'

Out of the wreckage of loss, I knew I had to rebuild – but what? I felt trapped in a block of ice – disconnected from my old life with Jason but unable to envisage a new one without him.

So I'd taken compassionate leave, tagging on some long-service leave, and made my decision.

'I want to try to get my money back. But I also want to get away, until people forget about me. Don't you?'

'I couldn't give a toss what other people think about me,' she said, mid-munch. 'You should try it some time. Sweet Jesus!' She snatched my passport from my hands. 'Your passport photo! Are you sure you're well enough to travel?'

'Isn't it lucky that I now no longer care what other people think?' I retorted, snatching it back.

I soon found out that Tish and I were so incompatible we couldn't even agree on what to fight about ... And the woman picked fights with everyone. Having been made to wait at the check-in desk for a full five minutes, she barked at a passing supervisor, 'Excuse me, but did the check-in person who served me leave any next of kin, do ya know?'

'That's one way to make sure we're seated by the toilets,' I reprimanded her.

'And I'd like an upgrade, too, because I've been made to wait. Plus one for my emotional support animal.' She hooked a thumb in my direction.

'So is it okay if I urinate on your leg?' I shot back at her.

The closer we got to the gangway, the more I regretted my impulsive decision to accompany this madwoman. I had no doubt that our time together in Cairo was just going to race by – as though it were only a decade or two.

As I unloaded my backpack at airport security, Tish was surprised at the number of books I was carrying. I retorted that was because reading must make her lips get tired, to which she replied that only dull people spend their lives with their noses buried in novels. 'Jeez, Gwennie baby, you're so dull you couldn't even entertain a doubt.'

Tish's essential holiday item proved to be a solar-powered vibrator. I blushed as her phallic pink pleasure enhancer clanged into the plastic tray and disappeared along with her phone through the rubber curtains of the scanner.

While I was a passionate campaigner for the environment and female equality, Tish firmly believed in the two-party system – a party at lunch time and a party in the evening. A policy she immediately enacted on the plane, ordering drinks before take-off.

'You know you don't have to drink to make yourself more fun to be around,' I said, trying to stop my hands from trembling as I dabbed sweat from my terrified face.

'Hon, I'm drinking to make *you* more fun to be around,' she retorted. 'Clearly the old Valium's not doin' the trick, kiddo. Try this.' She produced a pill the size of a hubcap.

'What am I supposed to dissolve that in? Shall I ask the flight attendant for a soup tureen?'

Tish expertly cut the huge pill into four little pieces. Pure terror made me meekly swallow the quarters with my gin and tonic.

Not long afterwards, I was flying, in more ways than one. As we rose up above Botany Bay a surprising calm washed over me. The vast expanse of the sea was dotted with pleasure ships and, far out, fishing boats and a passing tanker. The city in the distance looked silky and soft, as if it didn't have any edges. After the seatbelt sign was switched off, more alcohol materialised. We drank it as though there was a timer on our lives and we wouldn't survive if we didn't down it all before the buzzer. Stories were soon pouring forth almost as easily as the liquor.

Tish told me how she met Jason. 'I was posin' as an artist's model for this painter pal of mine. Anyway, Jase said he wanted to paint me in the nude, and I replied that he was more than welcome to take his clothes off. He laughed at that and then . . .'

'Wait.' I nearly choked on an ice cube. 'Jason was doing an art class? Where? He's a terrible drawer. He can't even draw the curtains,' I punned. 'The sun wakes us up every morning, peeping through a chink . . . *Woke* us,' I adjusted, feeling the familiar lump rising in my throat.

'True, his artwork was bloody awful,' agreed Tish. 'I suggested he donate it to a charity – most likely the Blind Society. Well, he laughed again at that and we got talkin'. Feelin' cheeky, I told him that I liked his shirt – and asked whether he'd mind if I ripped it off with my teeth. After that he came along to hear my band and . . .' She lost herself for a moment in sad ruminations. 'Jase just made me feel so sexy. He used to make love to me in front of the mirror, to show me what he saw—'

I flinched. 'Okay. Stop there. Before I'm forced to wash my ears out with soap.' I quickly moved the conversation away from her raunchy reminiscences on to how I'd bonded with Jason over the importance of recycling and ethical farming.

That startled a laugh out of her. 'Jeeesus. In so far as I'm aware, no one has ever used "discussing compost" as a come-on.'

'I was picking up rubbish, not men! On the beach. With my volunteer environmental group.'

'Of course you bloody were.'

'I sat on a rock to take a rest and this man appeared, perched beside me, smiled . . . and my life changed.'

'That smile. Jase had a smile that could ripen bananas.'

'And those eyes. I just felt he could look into my heart – as though he possessed romantic X-ray vision.'

Tish sighed. 'Every woman who ever had milk in her tit would melt at the sight of that man. I wanted to mother him and fuck him at the same time.'

'And there was his voice, those seductive, molten chocolate depths.' The liquor was making me loquacious. 'We had so much to say to each other, until he kissed me. Who would want to talk then? I wanted to catch that kiss and keep it in a jar, like a firefly. And when he ran his hands over me there was a starburst of sensation . . .'

'Yes! Yes! Yes!' Tish's baritone boom trumpeted throughout the plane. 'He made my heart go *snap, crackle, pop* as well. Not to mention other parts of my anatomy.'

'Although I'm sure you will – mention them, that is. And why not!' I enthused tipsily. 'You were right about his appendage by the w– w– way,' I slurred. 'I can't believe airlines didn't take one look at the trouser department and make him pay excess baggage.'

'Fuck yeah. If he took a dick pic it would have to be taken by satellite.'

'Maybe that's why we turned a blind eye to other things? I mean, if your man has a big . . .'

'. . . cock, it makes you overlook those other things.' She finished the sentence I coyly couldn't. 'Although never IT. A gal really couldn't see anything *but* IT.'

I giggled like one of my students. 'I can't believe I'm having this conversation!' I made a fleshy megaphone with my fist. '*Good gentlemen, evening and ladies* . . . I'm god, aren't I, sloshed? I mean, oh god I'm sloshed, aren't I?'

'Dunno how. We've only had twee martoonies.'

'And a couple of grin and tunics.'

I heard bubbles of laughter floating down the aisle then vaguely realised they were coming from us. The ice now broken, we even talked about our first husbands. I told Tish about Jack – and how I'd been married to the world's most perfect man.

'We met in Cornwall. He was a Bondi boy, working as a surf lifesaver. My parents had both passed, so I came to Oz with him. Jack worked for the Fire and Rescue Service. Died doing it. Fighting bushfires.'

'Shit. That sucks. I'm sorry, matey.'

'I thought I'd never be able to love another man. But after I met Jason, little by little grief loosened its grip on my chest. Jason made me smile again – like a creaky front door opening up and letting in the sun. He brought colour back into my sepia, grief-stricken world,' I added, poetically.

'Too much bloody colour as it turns out. Tech-ni-bloody-colour.' Tish drained her glass.

I felt a painful buzzing in my ears. 'I lied to you. I also have terrible insomnia.'

'I thought you said you were sleepin' like a baby?'

'Yes. Waking up every three hours crying my eyes out. I'm not coping at all,' I admitted. 'I feel vague. Unmoored. Drifting. Anxious. If I already mentioned this, it's because often I'll complete a sentence and then repeat it few minutes later – see vague . . . And kiwi fruit's not going to cut it. Nor can Rescue Remedy or grief counselling fix me. I'm trying to grieve, but who for? Did I even know him? Who the hell was this man I married?'

Tish now also let her guard down. 'I come from a big family– all nine of us in a tiny fibro shack. I didn't know what it was like to sleep alone till I got married first time round.' She barked out a harsh laugh but there was no comedy in it.

'What? Why?'

'After kickin' around with shearers and cowboys – rough and ready fellas – I finally found a gorgeous, sensitive bloke. Trouble is, his boyfriends thought the same.'

I was so surprised I nearly spilt my G and T. 'Your husband was gay?'

'I should've guessed. After Zack and Sienna were born I told Brendan he'd become really effeminate and he replied, "Compared to you I am, yeah."'

'Ah . . . Not so sensitive after all.'

'His old man was very religious so I was an excellent smoke-screen. I tried to ignore it and just carry on, but I felt ugly.' Sadness pooled in her dark eyes. 'I started to think I had the sexual appeal of a bloody half-thawed rissole . . . After fifteen years of this I finally went to see a solicitor to draw up a separation agreement. Brendan's record label had really taken off and I knew I deserved a slice of that money pie. Anyway, the very next day I met Jase. After one night of laughin' and drinkin' he said to me, "Trouble is, Tish, whenever I meet a woman who'd make a good wife, she already is." Forget separation. I filed for divorce there and then, and pretty soon afterwards Jason moved in and we got married.'

I took a beat to swallow this painful information.

Once more I racked my brain for some evidence of Jason's duplicity. I must have sensed something? But whenever he came home, there was just this harmony – chords chiming. My body resonated first, sending happy overtures to my brain, and the next thing I knew we'd be back in bed, I'd be deeply satisfied and that would simply unplug any alarm bells.

'Oh Jason,' I sighed. 'My knight in tarnished armour.'

Tish gave me a shrewd look. 'You're still in love with the two-timin', red-bellied black snake.'

'Aren't you?'

'Yeah. Course I am.' There was an unexpectedly tender note of pity in her voice. Pity for us both.

I reached across the tray tables, knocking the pretzel packet floor-ward and grasped one of her hands. It's impossible to say which of us was more startled. And then we collapsed into each other's arms, sobbing at the loss of our sensual, exceptional, charismatic, enigmatic, hugely appendaged International Man of Mystery.

6

Cairo's early morning babel of sounds, fumes, odours and smog filled the baking air. After clearing Customs we hired a car and drove straight to the address Tish had secretly photographed from dodgy Cash's file. We acclimatised to Cairo traffic – basically an 80 km/h gridlock with everybody driving as though on crystal meth – as the sat nav guided us into the old city.

We pulled up in front of an Ottoman-esque, mosaiced building, pock-marked by time. Fighting a discombobulating mix of grief, jetlag and a pounding hangover, we waited until another resident buzzed open the ancient timber doors, then slipped in behind her and climbed the three flights of well-worn marble stairs to flat 5.

As Tish rat-a-tatted on the door, I dredged up the speech I'd rehearsed to confront this mystery woman about the financial injustice inflicted upon us when Jason had transferred our money to invest in their mining venture. I would then tearfully segue to the fact that now, with the tragic loss of his life, we widows (yes, widows, plural – complicated story) had come to beg for the return of our missing moolah. If necessary, I intended to give a dolorous tug on her heart strings by explaining the deep grief we were enduring, having lost the love of our lives (yes, *our* lives – as I said, *complicated*) and our life savings, which was not just impacting on us, but also on our poor, orphaned children. She'd no doubt melt like a marshmallow . . . Or call a psychiatric centre.

The heavy flat door creaked then flung wide open – and my world froze.

Jason's face was tanned except for a white stripe around his eyes from his designer sunglasses. He wore a bleached white T-shirt that made his bronzed skin shine like mahogany.

A shiver of ghostly shock ran through me. Not only was he alive but he also seemed to be sporting a full complement of limbs – not a shark-nibbled digit in sight. My heart hammered. Stomach flopped. Mouth dried. Tongue turned to mush. Knees buckled. Brain thumped. Eyes bulged. Overwhelmed, I instinctively threw myself on his neck with a sob. For a split second I felt like a rescued mountaineer clinging to a Saint Bernard dog with its brandy barrel. And then I thought, you *bastard*, and recoiled. I was trapped in an emotional accordion, being squeezed to and fro.

Beside me, Tish had spasmed into a coughing fit worthy of a TB ward. 'What the f– f– fuck?' she finally wailed. 'We thought you'd been lost in a death-spasm chomp; the fangs of a Great White shark affixed to your gonads.'

To be fair, Jason seemed as astounded to see us as we were to see him.

I pressed my knuckles to my ears to keep my brains from leaking out. 'Not only are you alive, but you don't look even vaguely injured,' I said.

54

'You lyin', lowdown mongrel,' Tish yelped, then punched him full in the face.

Jason reeled backwards. We lunged over the threshold to find ourselves in an elegant, high-ceilinged living room. The morning sun was shining obliquely through the window, shedding a misty amber light down onto an inner garden courtyard of Islamic medieval architecture. The sun cast everything in the room in a golden, fantastical hue.

'Jason, what's going on?' inquired a startled female voice from the shadows.

I swivelled back to look at my husband. 'Why?' I asked reasonably of the man who had recently detonated a nuclear bomb into my life, exploding it to smithereens. In my shocked confusion I post-scripted, ludicrously, 'You took art classes?'

'Who are these women?' the disembodied female voice asked from the fuzzily lit recesses of the magnificently opulent room.

'Turns out,' Tish answered, as calmly as you can when midway through a cardiac arrest, 'your business partner here gave his pallbearers the old slip-a-roo and took our bloody life savin's with him.'

'Business partner?' came a cool reply as the woman emerged from the darkness. 'My *husband*, you mean.'

Tish and I looked at her, stupefied. The woman sported short, straw-blonde hair, cut into a sheer knife-edge bob at chin level, high conical breasts, pouty pink lips, caramel freckles on her nose and a picket line of perfect white teeth.

'You cock-fondlin' maggot!' was Tish's response to this news, before launching herself at Jason with an animal roar, nails flexed, fists flying.

The shock of the impact brought Jason out of his stupor. He swore, vaulted out of her reach, squirted past me, then rattled down the ancient tiled staircase.

'Oi! Get back here, you cowardly pissant!' Tish squawked, giving chase, with me close behind.

Was it merely a hungover bout of delirium or had I really been jettisoned into a Jacobean melodrama? *Evil husband exits stage left, pursued by wronged wives who trothed their plights to a blaggard. Alas and alack!*

The old wooden door thunked shut behind Jason as he bolted onto the street. It took us a moment to locate the buzzer and we emerged to see him running towards a red sports car.

'Sonofabitch!' Tish screamed. We sprinted to our hire car, Tish scrambling to get behind the wheel as I hurled myself into the passenger seat. I fought the hysterical urge to laugh at how much this felt like a bad cop show as Tish careered after Jason through the cobbled streets of the old city, negotiating a maze of souks, bazaars, spice stalls and street vendors. Apart from sending up silent prayers for us not to end up as roadkill, my only other thought was that the man we were chasing was a clone of my real husband, who was clearly being held prisoner in the experimental laboratory on an evil alien's spaceship. I mean, there really could be no other logical explanation.

When Tish's acceleration through a red light triggered a horn-happy cacophony from irate drivers I snapped out of my reverie. 'Slow down!' I clutched the dashboard, white-knuckled in terror.

'In Cairo a red light's a sign to drive faster,' Tish boomed back at me. 'Have faith. I'm a bloody good driver.'

'Yes, you always look both ways before you collide with some-thing stationary!' I yelped back, as we dodged a donkey-drawn cart and bounced off a bollard.

'If people don't like the way I drive, they should get off the bloody sidewalk.'

'You could always let *me* drive.'

'Not if you drive like you park.' Another discordant symphony of carhorn honking followed in our wake.

'What's wrong with the way I park?'

'You drive a Ford Focus, right? I saw it parked outside your house.'

'Yes. So?'

'Well, didja catch a goddamned taxi back to the kerb?'

'Better than leaving a pedestrian puree down every pavement. *Watch out!*' I screamed, as Tish nearly took out a Coptic orthodox priest, who dived for cover and sent a shisha-smoking clique of men sitting outside a coffee shop falling face forward into their baclava.

'Am I losing my mind or did that woman say Jason is her *husband*?' I asked, through my fog of shock.

'Yep. The dingo-dicked bastard. Bloody oath! I've never seen a bloke move from one woman to another so friggin' fast! The guy's clearly got startin' blocks attached to his balls and racin' colours on his cock.'

Well, yes, I thought, that was one way of putting it. Ahead of us, Jason veered off down a dimly lit lane into the Roman quarter. A Coptic church, mosque and synagogue flashed past me in quick succession. I realised we were in the oldest place of worship in Cairo, maybe even the world. I'd read so much about this jewel of the Middle East, steeped in the early civilisations of the ancient Pharaohs yet blending in seamlessly with the history of Christian and Islamic culture. The whole area was a religious minestrone of faiths, nestled cheek by theological jowl. It felt surreal to have history strobing past me when twenty-four hours earlier I'd been defrosting my freezer in a quiet Sydney cul-de-sac.

'Saints Sergius and Bacchus! I can't believe it!' I gasped, pointing at the Coptic church. 'That's where Mary, Jesus and Joseph rested when they were fleeing one of Herod's hate-fests!'

'I can't bloody believe it either – a friggin' history lecture? Really? Now!? Um, in case it's escaped your notice, Gwendoline, we're in the middle of a life-or-death car chase here!'

'But look around you . . .'

'Just look ahead, for chrissake! Don't lose sight of that bloody car! Luckily, it's the only red vehicle on the road. The flashy bastard.'

And so we ducked and darted and dived our way through the throbbing city of a thousand minarets, breaking every road rule in our desperation to tail Jason's getaway car. With Cairo erupting around us it was a miracle that I only hit my head on the dashboard twice – once when we slammed to a halt as a donkey darted into the road, and again when an exotic belly dancer and a whirling dervish materialised magically in the middle of a dingy side road, full of closed cinemas and sleazy bars.

'Aphrodisiacal oils,' the dervish promised, banging on the car bonnet, while urging us to come into the perfume bazaar.

'More than three drops and you'll kill your husbands.' Undulating by my open window, the belly dancer curled a finger to entice us into the dank cavern behind her, where a dozen or so leering businessmen loitered menacingly.

Now that we'd found Jason alive, the thought of killing him was appealing. But Tish reversed, swerved around their gyrating forms, revved the engine then hurtled on at breakneck speed in pursuit of our reincarnated spouse.

When my knuckles had turned albino-white from dashboard clutching and I'd gone hoarse from hollering, I spied on the horizon a pile of what resembled huge cubes of Emmenthal cheese stacked in a triangular shape. It was only as we drew nearer that the triangle revealed its true magnificence. The proximity of these mighty religious monoliths hit me in the solar plexus.

'Oh my god, Tish. The Pyramids. They're right there! Egypt just haemorrhages history and mystery, doesn't it?'

'The only mystery is where that douchebag's bloody well off to,' Tish snarled.

'But seriously, to get your mind around the awesome majesty of this ancient civilisation – on history's timeline, Cleopatra is closer to *us* than she is to the *Pyramids*.' When Tish didn't react, I attempted to drive home the formidable facts. 'The queen of the Nile would have brought Mark Antony here sightseeing, to look at *old stuff*.'

'Are you for real? It's like being in *Thelma and Louise* but with Mary bloody Beard in the boot. Just shut your cakehole and keep your eye on our fraudulent friggin' husband.'

But I didn't need to take my eyes off the sights because we were heading right for them. Jason was speeding faster and faster towards the Giza complex.

'Wow!' I marvelled, as the largest structure on Earth loomed into view. 'Look at that pyramid. Nearly six million tons of stone. Just to put it into perspective, Tish, Stonehenge is a thousand tons. So, the Pyramid is like six thousand Stonehenges.'

'Yeah and I'm gonna entomb you alive in it, if you don't shut up.'

'Egyptians believe that the Pyramids are the petrified rays of the sun, did you know that? The king's soul used them as a runway ramp to ascend to the heavens, to merge with the sun god Ra.'

'You'll be mergin' with the bloody sun god too if you lose sight of that weasel.'

Far ahead of us, Jason executed a two-wheel screech into a parking area. A couple of minutes later we careered in after him, wheels spinning. I catapulted out of the car, head up, in full meerkat pose. 'Where is he?'

'Dunno.' Tish's eyes raked the tourist throng.

'There!' I pointed. 'Mounting a camel. We've got him, now, Tish. I mean he can't go far on one of those.'

'Are you kiddin'? The camel is a desert Ferrari.'

Tish sprinted towards the camel handlers, who swarmed around us, haggling and grinning and haggling some more.

Tish raised her voice and shouted slowly 'DO ... YOU ... SPEAK ... ENGLISH?'

'They're Egyptian, Tish, not deaf.'

I tried to communicate with the few phrases I'd learnt from my guidebook but it turned out that I also possessed Van Gogh's ear for languages. In the end we resorted to a Marcel Marceau performance, which we hoped would mime loud and clear the instruction to 'Follow that man!'

We could have been asking for a kebab for all I knew, but one handler seemed to understand our urgent request. After forking out enough in cash for a down payment on a whole herd of camels, I swung my leg over the saddle in front of him. As I clung to the pommel, the big beast unfolded itself to standing as though it were a piece of origami opening out. I watched as Tish's beast also lurched upright – an Anglepoise lamp with hooves.

Under normal circumstances I would have traded a few barbed comments with Tish about Cairo-practor bills and watching out for speed humps, and she likely would have made some crack about whether we could really trust anything that can last for two weeks without drinking, but these were far from normal circumstances. Tish and her camel driver were already trotting after Jason, astride his galloping desert Ferrari, set to soon vanish around the corner of a pyramid. My cameleer jerked on the reins, shouted a command and my furry chariot gave bumpy chase.

Ancient Egypt is beguiling and bemusing in equal measure – the architectural sophistication; the engineering impossibilities; the slavish devotion of the workers to their kings and queens, the bribery and corruption . . . No wonder Jason had found safe sanctuary here. And we were no match for his mastery of the art of deception, I deduced grimly, as he disappeared into the dust. The dry plateau had cracked in the relentless sun like a pottery glaze in a furnace. Rounding the corner of the pyramid my eyes were blinded by the heat haze. When Tish's camel pulled up short in front of me, I knew we'd lost Jason.

No amount of sign language could extract any further information from the camel handlers about his possible destination. With great reluctance Tish signalled to our escorts to turn around. Back at base, the camels' collapse into the sand epitomised our crumpled despondency. Dismounting, we slouched our way slowly back through the tourist throng and slumped in the shade of the Sphinx, catching our breath for the first time that day.

'Can you bloody believe it? The ratbag's alive! I mean, what the *fuck*?!' Tish said, finally. 'He double-scammed us.'

Since the moment of Jason's death I'd been thinking incessantly about the coup de foudre moment when we'd met – his smile, his breezy charm, his hair flopping into those mischievous sea-green eyes . . . Now the encounter played in my head like a scene from a horror movie on a loop – the moment just before the heroine sees The Creature.

'I've never thought of myself as stupid, but I clearly won't be splitting any atoms in the near future.' I wiped sandy sweat from my brow with a hankie. 'How could I ever have fallen for a liar like Jason Riley?'

'Ditto, darl. And the real question deepens – who *is* Jason Riley?'

'Methinks the Sphinx has the answer to it all, but she's not saying.' I gazed up at the ancient limestone lion, squatting on its haunches here in the desert, guarding secret tombs and temples. 'In fact, even the Sphinx is less of a mystery right now.'

'There's no bloody mystery, Gwen. We keep askin' how he could have loved us both when we're so bloody different, but we do have one thing in common.'

Jason and his fraud suddenly came back into focus for me, like a lens being turned. 'Money,' I said.

'Zactly. I imagine you got a pretty good whack of life insurance when your first hubby was killed in the line of duty, right?'

'Yes,' I sighed, dazed. 'And my parents left me money when they died. I'd been saving it for years, but Jason talked me into handing over a hefty chunk of it for "us" to invest in various mining ventures.'

'I got a pretty big whack of a financial settlement from my hubby two years back too . . . just around the time I mysteriously met Jason.'

'Do you think that dodgy lawyer has something to do with it?'

'What? Tippin' off horny fraudsters about merry widows and wealthy divorcees he's heard about through mates in the legal world? For friggin' sure.'

'If David Attenborough were guessing at Jason's species, he'd probably start with the categories of "werewolf" or "vampire". But Marty Cash is clearly of the vulture breed.' I rubbed my forehead as though coming round from a concussion. 'I feel like we're in an episode of *Dirty John*.'

'We've turned into those sheilas you see on docos who talk about how they were duped by some bastard and you think to yourself, "How could you be that stupid? It's your own fault, you gullible nincompoop." And then it happens to you and it's bloody mortifyin'.'

'Yup. I can detect margarine in a cake instead of butter, missed homework lies, plagiarised essays – all fakery immediately bleeps on my authenticity radar.'

'Me too, matey. *I* can spot a breast implant a mile away. Fake teeth, fake tans, hair extensions, fake orgasms . . . I can smell 'em. But not Jason. Why?'

'Our husband is operating in emotional hieroglyphics. We'll need a code breaker to decipher this mystery.'

'Or maybe just some pliers applied to his gonads. We've been outsmarted, kiddo. By an expert. Clearly, Jason could sell anythin'. Bloody hell. The man could sell nostril-hair trimmers to the Sphinx!'

I glanced up once more at the crouching stone lion with the inscrutable human face, the nose of the majestic countenance most probably blasted off by Napoleon's troops during target practice.

'The Sphinx is not givin' anythin' away . . . but I know who bloody will.'

'Skye Cavendish. Why did her parents name her Skye, and not some other air-related substance?' I wondered aloud. 'Smog? Spume? Belch?'

'Well, I reckon it's time we squeezed some hot air outta her and got some answers.'

Without the help of a handy Jason-shaped Rosetta stone, we set forth to try to decode this grotesquely implausible, preposterously fantastical scenario; to unlock the puzzle and make a few Howard Carter-type discoveries. We wanted to recover our treasure, yes, but we also wanted answers from this minx, while hopefully avoiding the Sphinx jinx. Besides, how could the curse of the Pharaohs hurt us now? Surely we'd been cursed enough already – the unfortunate day we met Jason bloody Riley.

PART TWO

7

'You don't have a gun, do you?' I asked Tish with alarm, remembering her talking about roo-shooting.

'Shit, no. I don't even have a penknife. J'have anything?'

I rummaged through my backpack. 'Nail clippers. Will they do?' I whispered, handing them to her. I felt ridiculous, as if I was trying out someone else's personality: one of those fearless, gutsy, wild and reckless women I'd read about in novels.

Tish pocketed my clippers with an exaggerated eye roll and knocked briskly. The door was opened by the same pretty, petite, leggy woman we'd met earlier. She was maybe forty. In a film, her part would have been played by a gazelle. Her fringe was snapped off straight at the eyebrows in a kind of blonde Beatles bob. She was wearing a white silk dress so skimpy the silkworms must have had anorexia.

Oiling the wheels in her usual smooth way, Tish boomed, 'So, where is the blood-suckin' maggot?'

'Jason Riley should be languishing in the outer ring of the seventh circle of Hell for what he's done to us,' I added.

'And if you don't tell us the whereabouts of that lyin' toe-rag, you're gonna *wish* you were immersed in a river of boilin' blood and brimstone 'cause I'm gonna kill ya. Slowly.' Tish clutched the nail clippers in her pocket as though they were a lethal weapon.

I was busy squinnying over Skye's shoulder, trying to take a sly peek into the apartment when Tish barged right inside, shoving Skye sideways in the process.

'Do you mind!? Who exactly are you?' The twang was Kiwi. Her baby-blue eyes were deep set in her delicate face, giving her an owlish appearance. Dressed all in white from her earrings to her sandals, the woman glowed with health. Skye was so luminous you could positively read by her at night.

'Sorry,' I interrupted in a tone of pained geniality, stepping more timidly over the threshold. 'You're Skye, aren't you? I'm Gwendoline Brookes and this is Tish Delaney – Jason's ... um ... wives. We were just wondering if you knew where he'd gone?'

Skye's cheeks sucked in and made valleys in her face. '*Wives?* Jason didn't tell me he'd been married before.'

'I bet there's a lot that scumbag hasn't told you.' Tish cased the classy apartment with an astute eye. Although elegantly furnished in Turkish rugs and low ottomans festooned in velvet cushions, there were also crystal lamps, a kombucha jar, yoga mats and on the coffee table books titled *Being Is Believing, Healing Is the New High* and *Chanting Your Way to Orgasm*.

'So, let me get this right. He divorced you both but then you two became pals?' Skye asked, screwing up her lightly freckled nose inquisitively.

'Not quite. I'm afraid he married me, then he married her as well and now it seems he's married *you* – so we're all his wives. Apparently.' I gave a pained sigh.

'Jason's motto? Never be unfaithful to your wife . . . except with another wife,' Tish drawled. 'Your typical A-grade, professional scumbaggery.'

Skye looked from me to Tish, totally bewildered.

I tried again. 'I'm afraid Jason has many altar egos,' I explained as gently as I could. 'As in not admitting that he had vowed true love to me at the altar before he married Tish, and not admitting he was married to us when he wed you.'

Despite her ethereal manner, Skye had sharp eyes, which she now narrowed. 'That's enough!' She folded her arms, defensively. 'You're talking about the man I love.'

'Yeah, yeah, we know . . . Those eyes, that smile, *blah, blah, blah* . . . One snog and it's all salty waves breakin' on a sandy shore and dolphins divin' and fun in the sun.' Tish's tone was a sarcastic sing-song. 'Spare us your tea-towel sentimentality.'

'The point is,' I clarified, 'Tish and I – and you? – got scammed by a bigamist who we thought was dead until a few hours ago. I suppose you gleaned from our first encounter this morning that Jason also staged his own death? And now we need to know why.'

Skye locked her eyes straight ahead then spun around and pointed a manicured talon toward the door. 'I'd like you both to leave now or I'll call the police.'

'And I'd like you to open your bank account and pay back our dosh before *I* call the cops.' Tish nodded towards the laptop sitting open on a dining room table that showed signs of domestic compatibility – half-drunk coffee cups, toast crusts, a newspaper open on the sudoku page, roses, a box of heart-shaped chocolates. 'Don't play dumb with me, kiddo. Clearly you're in on the scam.'

'Scam?' Skye's expression was amiably acquiescent. She raised a guileless brow and turned her shining eyes on me. 'What scam?'

'Don't act innocent, matey,' Tish fumed. 'We know Jason transferred all our moolah into your account just before he was "eaten by a shark". I took the bastard for better or for worse . . . and he just took me for bloody everythin'.'

'I don't believe you.' Skye flailed a bare arm in front of her face, as if she were being buzzed by wasps.

It did sound preposterous. I wouldn't have believed it either. I dug into an inner compartment of my backpack and produced our marriage certificates, which I'd packed as evidence of our claim. Skye snatched them from my outstretched hand and scanned them. As she did so, I added, 'When he came face to face with us earlier, why do you think he knew exactly what steps to take – as in *long ones*. But to where?'

'But Jason's the most charming, gentle, honest . . .'

'Yeah, yeah. You've got the most sexy and charismatic husband in the world,' Tish growled. 'Unfortunately, his other wives want him back so we can kill him.'

'How do I know *you're* not scamming *me*?' Skye's eyes, half-hidden by her sweep of fringe, narrowed once more with shrewd watchfulness.

'Just log on, kiddo, and have a proper look – you'll find that those money transfers came from *our* joint accounts.' Losing patience, Tish seized Skye by the back of the neck and propelled her towards the table. 'Just transfer the spondulix back and we'll bugger off. Okay?'

She shoved Skye down into a chair in front of her laptop. Clutching the nail clippers secreted in her pocket, she let the cuticle cleaner poke through the material so that it might be mistaken as the tip of a knife blade. Skye's keyboard immediately clacked like chattering teeth. At her elbow, Tish jigged impatiently from foot to foot like a Tahitian coal walker. Moments later, the Kiwi emitted a gasp so loud I thought she might be in need of an asthma inhaler.

'Jason's transferred everything out of our account. Today. Just hours ago.'

Her neatly manicured fingers clattered some more before coming to an abrupt halt. She stared at the screen, transfixed by the blinking cursor.

'What is it?' I asked, although I had an inkling. In any marriage contract with Jason Riley, the big print giveth and the small print taketh away.

'My personal account! It's also been emptied!' Her pretty face screwed up into a knot of despair.

'Jesus. You too? He's a monster,' Tish said furiously, spitting out a chewed fingernail. Jason's misdemeanours were piling on top of each other like a Chinese circus act.

Skye jabbed at her mobile phone, slamming it down when it went to voicemail. 'He hasn't answered since he bolted this morning.'

'And now you know why,' I said sadly, thinking, welcome to the Gullible Wives Club. Clearly a fool and her money are soon popular. Jason's duplicity was like a many-tentacled Jules Verne octopus looming up from the depths. I placed a pacifying hand on the woman's delicate shoulder. 'How long have you and Jason been married?' I asked solicitously.

'Six months.' Her eyes were brilliant pools of tears.

Tish let out a yelp of fury. 'This ain't bigamy, it's trigamy!'

I felt a prick of sympathy. Jason's betrayal was always with me, like background music. But of course for Skye it was brand-new. I knew exactly how she felt right now – as though she was tumbling through a timeless universe with no oxygen pack, gasping for breath. 'I used to think I wouldn't be able to endure the treachery,' I consoled her. 'But after what's happened today, well . . . now I'm just numb. And you will be too. Eventually.'

'But Jason loves me! I don't believe any of this. He must be under duress. If I could just talk to him . . .'

'Don't take it personally, kiddo. The man's a human vampire bat and you're just the latest body he's sucked dry,' Tish said bluntly.

'No!'

'It's true. The bloke's as crooked as the toilet piss aim of a football supporter on World Cup day.'

The evening call to prayer reverberated over the city's leaden domes and sway-back rooves. Skye crossed to the kitchen, opened the fridge and took out a bottle. She poured herself a glass of water, before remembering her manners. 'Would you like some?' she asked. 'It's got rose quartz to infuse you with positive energy.'

'Is there vodka in it?' Tish crossed to peer into the fridge. 'That would give me a surge of positivity, for sure.'

I too went over to the fridge, reading labels marked 'oat milk', 'almond milk', 'pea milk' – all the milks from substances that can't technically be milked. I accepted a glass of the botanically infused, positively charged water that had been filtered through rose-quartz crystals, or unicorns' balls or fairies' wings or whatever.

'J'have anythin' more substantial than poncey designer water?' asked Tish. 'I'm that hungry my stomach thinks me throat's been cut. J'mind if I graze?'

Skye nodded and crossed the room to gaze out of the window. I noticed she was shivering despite the heat.

Tish, her nose in the refrigerator, looked up at me and mewled under her breath, 'It's all just bloody salad.'

'Tabouleh or not tabouleh? That is the question.' I couldn't resist it, even if the reference was lost on Tish. 'And anyway, salad is good for you.'

'Pandas and manatees eat nothin' but salad and look at the bloody size of them!' she groused.

Despite her aversion to vegetable matter, Tish piled her plate high and started wolfing down food like a slave bolstering herself for a day of heavy Pyramid-building.

'How can you eat at a time like this?' I asked her, agog.

'How can you *not*?' she said between big, gaping mouthfuls, parsley sprinkling her teeth like lawn clippings. 'So, what we wanna know is this.' Tish sat cross-legged on the Persian rug, still forking food into her maw. 'A) J'know where the fuckwit's gone? B) Where can I get some weapon-grade plutonium?'

'I . . . I . . . I still can't believe Jason has done this to me,' Skye said in a tiny voice.

'We have to face the fact that we married a serial conman.' My tone was one of weary resignation. 'There's no more time to waste. I think we should call the police.'

'The Egyptian police?' Skye jerked her head away from the window. 'Egyptians have a saying: if you see a police officer . . . run.'

'Yeah, besides, j'know how far down the World's Most Wanted List Jason Riley would be? The cops couldn't give a flyin' fuck about a low-level conman. You'd get more reaction from a friggin' Madame Tussauds waxwork.'

Desolation crept over us as the reality sunk in that Jason was going to get away with it. We were now nothing more than a trio of side dishes he'd forgotten he'd ordered on some obsolete menu. We slumped in silence around the lavish living room. Tish took out the nail clippers and attacked her fingernails. Skye was too distracted with grief to notice that the 'weapon' she'd found so intimidating moments earlier also came with a tiny file and cuticle pusher.

'Any other ideas? What's the bastard up to?' Tish probed.

'Well, he does have mining interests,' said Skye. 'Egypt's trying to lure foreign investors. The country's mineral wealth is largely under-developed.'

Now I thought about it, I did dimly recall Jason talking about some kind of mining exploration he was interested in, but we were in bed at the time so I had other explorations on my mind.

Tish shrugged. 'We had an agreement. I never asked Jase about his business deals and he never asked me about my weight. But what have you got to do with any of that?' Tish asked the Kiwi.

'I'm a geologist,' Skye volunteered. 'Freelance. I met Jason on a diving holiday in the Red Sea. He was fascinated by my field work for an Asian mining exploration company. It was through my contacts that Jason started to make investments here.'

Her profession surprised me. I'd detected no obvious signs of a scientific nature. I reminded myself that people are not simply a bunch of hieroglyphic symbols, but an infinite pile of rocks with secrets growing underneath just waiting to be excavated.

I pressed her for more information but she replied, 'My mother says that if I could explain my job in a sentence, it wouldn't pay so well.'

After cross-examining Skye a bit more, we discovered that Jason had set up a little office in Aswan, only an hour and a half away by plane. Skye rummaged around on the table to locate his diary and discovered that he'd organised some appointments there.

The rose quartz positive energy juice must have really kicked in by then because she sprang to her feet, as if electrocuted, and began ransacking her apartment. Though she seemed the type to live in a yurt on a mountain with an aura-orientated guru who levitated while eating lentils, there was also something practical about the pert Kiwi. When she discovered a mobile hidden in an old sock at the back of a bottom drawer in their spare room, she gave a loud whoop of victory – a guttural sound, like car tyres on gravel.

Tish snatched it from her, turned it on then gave a disappointed sigh. 'Locked'.

'There must be a local mobile repair shop. Maybe they can unlock it?' I said hopefully.

While I went online to book tickets to Aswan for first thing in the morning, Skye took Tish to the closest phone repair shop to spin some story about having forgotten her code. I'm not sure whether the assistant succumbed to Skye's charms or Tish's bribe (in Cairo, bribery clearly pays off – you never reach a tipping point when it comes to tipping) but the salesman winked, smiled and told them to come back the next day.

I slept badly on Skye's oriental L-shaped sofa, with Tish's feet intermittently kicking my head, woke early and girded my loins for the next flight by popping another Valium. As we tore into the terminal, I thought, well, Jason's mobile phone may or may not hold the answer but at least, finally, I had his number.

8

A short plane hop later (during which a series of shuddering bumps made me gasp 'Did we land or were we just shot down?') we were striding into the Byzantine bar of the Old Cataract Hotel, which looked out on to the River Nile. It was here that Winston Churchill had swapped his signature cigar for a puff on a shisha and Agatha Christie had sipped her tea while brewing up the plot of *Death on the Nile*. The sinuous blue river dotted with darting white felucca sailing boats would have triple-curled even Hercule Poirot's famous mo with pleasure.

A small passenger boat, which resembled the *African Queen*, pulled into the hotel wharf and we climbed aboard. In amazement I watched the Nile slide by. Women washed clothes on the banks, bullocks grazed, camels sauntered off towards dreamy sand dunes, which hid the secret tombs of pharaohs. The scene seemed so biblical that every time the bulrushes rippled in the breeze, I found myself looking for Moses' basket.

But in truth, I was the basket case – chasing my fugitive husband across a foreign land with two women I didn't know. My natural habitat is a classroom; my idea of living recklessly an overdue library book. And yet here I was in the blazing, blistering sun on the cool blue waters of the Nile with a world-class New Age gobbledegook guru who dressed exclusively in white for the 'affirmation vibe', and a sabre-toothed jazz singer with a chin that jutted forward as if to say 'Yeah? You and whose army?'

We leapt ashore at a vibrantly painted Nubian village. I knew from my studies that Nubians came from Sudan to start farming near the Nile eight thousand years ago. The jumble of houses, built out of clay to keep cool in the scorching summer, were a rainbow spectrum of colours and festooned in bright mosaics of camels, palm trees and crocodiles.

A cornucopia of aromas tickled my nostrils – turmeric, mint, saffron, black cumin, ginger, cardamom, coriander. Skye led us through a street of stalls piled high with freshly harvested herbs and fragrant pyramids of ground spices – red, gold, green – then on past weavers pedalling ancient treadles to create intricate patterned garments from soft Egyptian cotton, all of which she captured for her Instagram account – after blocking Jason, of course.

We entered a whitewashed café, where Skye ordered hibiscus tea then summoned the proprietor. A tubby man in a fez appeared, flashing his snaggled gnashers. When Skye, who clearly knew the man, asked for the keys to Jason's office, he guffawed, 'Keys? Pleassssse, ha ha ha.'

The cause of the hilarity initially escaped me. Tish and I exchanged bemused glances. Then we saw that behind the tea-room was a small cabin with a flimsy sign tacked above the door – Down Under Diggers Pty – outside of which was the world's most ancient alarm system, a system narrowing its prehistoric eyes in our dismayed direction. Crocodiles are the oldest living species on the earth, excluding Keith Richards, and, judging by the way this one was straining at its chain and snapping at us, they also have some serious anger management issues.

'After you,' I suggested magnanimously to Tish, flattening myself against the tavern wall.

'Thanks, Gwennie baby,' said Tish. 'That's big of you. J'reckon it's domesticated?'

The crocodile's sinister yellow eyes sized us up from the shadows. Can crocodiles smirk? Because as the saltie prepared to use me as a chew toy, I felt sure I could hear it chuckling through its many razor-sharp teeth. 'Do you know why crocs haven't changed since the dawn of time?' she continued. 'Because they're perfectly evolved killing machines. Cows, kangaroos, sheep, tourists, duped wives – they're not fussy.'

As the crocodile's serrated jaws gaped greedily towards me, I thought with alarm back to the crocodile-skin handbag I'd bought from a second-hand shop a few months back. With matching shoes. What if this predatory reptile instinctively sensed my purchase and now wanted revenge? And the Egyptian sun was making my skin decidedly dry and scaly . . . Dear god. What if it wanted to *mate?*

If only I'd packed a few more useful vacation items in my backpack, like, say, a flame-throwing bazooka. As a teacher, the most daring part of my day is taking a quick sniff of a glue stick in the supply storeroom. But Jason had done to my temper what 200 tons of rocket-propellant kerosene will do to your average space shuttle. Fuelled with fury, I catapulted across the court-yard. The armour-plated carnivore waved its weird stumpy little arms, then lunged, snapping at my heels. I flung open the office door with seconds to spare, and prepared to vent my anger on my bigamist husband; although now that I was so close, I couldn't decide whether I wanted to vent my spleen or rupture his.

The small, dusty room was empty, however, except for a shredding machine that still had some half-eaten documents in it, and a confetti of strewn papers, which, at a quick glance, contained a lot of obscure information about iron, gold, manganese and phosphate gypsum – whatever the hell that was.

Moments later, Tish hurtled into the office too, slamming the door behind her like a cartoon character. Looking around at the chaos, she caught her breath then whistled through her teeth. 'Jeez. Jason shreds files faster than Ghislaine Maxwell.'

'Well?' Skye asked from behind us, having breezed into the office with nonchalant ease.

'Goodness. Weren't you scared?' My heart was still doing a fandango from my croc-dodging dash.

'I just zipped across the courtyard in a zig-zag. Crocs can only move in a straight line.'

If only I'd run for the hills in a zig-zag when I'd met Jason – but of course I didn't know then that he was a top-order predator.

Skye offered us a power infusion in the form of a sip from her bottle of 'Life-Optimising Moon Juice'.

'I'd prefer some death-optimising juice,' Tish grunted. 'A magnum of the stuff, to send our bloody husband's way.'

We watched as Skye chug-a-lugged from a bottle stuccoed in 'chakra stones'. She then omm-ed for a bit while caressing a crystal in an attempt to get some kind of 'reading' on Jason's whereabouts.

Tish and I were fast discovering that we shared little in common with Skye Cavendish – and not just because we lacked a tattoo of a unicorn in the small of our backs. The geologist's conversation revolved around soul cycles, whatever they were, antioxidants, 'mind–body' meditations, Manuka honey, bee

balm, kiwi seed oil, kale, quinoa, microgreens and free radicals –
by which she did not mean recently released Belarusian political
dissidents. I wasn't sure what I disliked more – her happy-clappy,
hippy-trippy optimism or Tish's toe-curling philistinism.

Later that day our pursuit of Jason led us even further afield,
to Luxor. While Skye followed up a lead, I used the time to
wander through the colossal columned porticos of the dramatic
temple of Karnak, transfixed by the timeless dignity and poise
of the stately, 10-metre-high giant seated sentinels, which stared
imposingly down at me through the centuries. Just as I reached
peak marvel, Tish popped a bubble of gum beside my ear.
I jumped out of my skin and wheeled around to face her.

'Can ya believe all these dumbass tourists payin' a friggin'
fortune to some beardy bloke to point at a pile of stones and
make up lies for bloody hours? Suckers!'

With great patience, I started to explain the epic archaeological significance of our monumental surroundings, but, clocking
Tish's bored face, abruptly gave up. It reminded me of the times
colleagues showed me cute pictures of their cats and I struggled
to respond correctly – like an autistic person who's been taught
to recognise human emotions from flash cards.

But Tish's cultural callowness became increasingly irksome.
Our pursuit of Jason next took us to the Valley of the Kings,
about forty minutes from Luxor. While Skye made urgent inquiries with her contacts about Jason's movements, blasts of cool
air coaxed me out of the blistering sun, down through a slit in
the hill along a descending corridor of brightly painted hieroglyphics. Of course, I knew all about the tombs from books,
but nothing could have prepared me for the colossal grandeur
that unfolded before me. Tunnels beneath the lunar landscape
led to brightly painted chambers whose walls told tales of the

Sun God, Horus and the Goddess Isis, Ramses. Awestruck, I stood gazing at the intricate hieroglyphics. But what I saw as metaphysical, mysterious and mind-blowing, Tish described as 'Just a bunch of early emojis, really.'

We entered the deepest vault in the tomb and came face to face with the shock of Tutankhamen, the teenage king, lying mummified in his coffin. I gazed agog at his three-thousand-year-old wizened face with its tuft of hair and grizzled tooth, which prompted me to think of the young man beneath the myth and reminded me of the humanity at the heart of this incredible archaeological story. Tish's response, however, was to blow another gum bubble. 'If you wanna see a well-preserved mummy, mate, why doan cha look in the bloody mirror?'

'If you keep this up, Patricia, it's going to be *Death on the Nile*, take two.'

As if the gods had heeded my words, turning to exit the vault Tish tripped on the steps and fell to the ground. As she clutched her ankle I made a move towards her.

'No bandages,' she recoiled. 'You can never be too careful in Egypt, right? The joint's crawlin' with wrap-artists.'

Floodwaters from the undulating Nile, which runs right through the heart of Egypt, brings silt to the soil to create a lush, green, fertile strip across the harsh desert. Temples celebrating life were built on the east side of the river where the sun rises; tombs where the sun sets. Egyptians don't die, they 'leave for the west', which is where I heartily wished to dispatch Tish Delaney. Spending time with my accountant, gynaecologist – hell, even a proctologist – would be preferable to another minute in her nerve-gratingly crass company.

'Well?' Skye asked as we emerged from Tutankhamen's tomb, blinking into the sunshine like newborn field mice.

'Oh god! Don't ask her. She'll just blab on with some long, dull story about dead dudes.'

Gritting teeth that were already ground down to stubs with annoyance, I did my best to ignore Tish. 'So, what did you find out? Where is Jason?'

Skye's investigations had revealed that we'd only missed our husband by two hours. 'He's been tying up various business deals to do with some mining opportunity that gets investors to encourage other people to invest—'

'Sounds suspiciously like a pyramid scheme,' I said. 'Which is weirdly appropriate, considering our location.'

'And he's now heading back to Cairo and then out of the country.'

'I don't know how Jason ever got a passport,' I added bitterly. 'I didn't think blood-sucking vampires were visible in photographs?'

'Too bloody right. On *reflection*, what the hell did we see in him?' Tish riffed.

But no amount of strained banter could hide the painful truth. Once Jason left the country, finding him would be harder than locating Cher's birth certificate. And not even Agatha Christie would be equipped to solve *those* mysteries.

On our flight back to Cairo from Luxor, the sky turned pink and gold above the yellow sand. We sat three abreast, Skye in her floaty white artisan fabrics hand-loomed in villages in Uzbekistan, which could no doubt only be reached by the riding of sacred llamas; Tish in a leather mini, fishnets and boots; and me in my sensible beige shirt-dress. Skye was as glossy and stylish as a racehorse, and with seemingly minimal effort. This mung-bean-munching, mantra-chanter's skin glowed with good health. Her teeth were white but not plastic-looking. She was slim but didn't look as though she spent hours in the gym. The woman just exuded effortless style. I also made an effort, taking at least thirty to forty seconds a day to whack on some lippy, eyeshadow and a half-hearted dab of blusher. Tish's make-up routine, on the other hand, was bordering on special effects. We couldn't be less alike. All we had in common was our conman.

'Is it possible to feel nostalgia for something that never really existed?' Skye asked quietly, her head pressed against the plane window. The ethereal geologist was clearly about three or four stages of shock behind Tish and me.

We sat in silence, watching the day slip into night, noting the wondrous tonal transformations of the sunset on its dimmer switch – blood-orange shading imperceptibly into ice-blue, on the knife edge of the sandy horizon.

'If it makes you feel any better, I wasn't exactly deafened by the sound of alarm bells ringing, either,' I said kindly, patting Skye's hand.

I felt the guilt crowding in on me again. Why *hadn't* I seen Jason's duplicity? Those last-minute 'jobs' when all the time he'd secretly given up work; the overseas trips running overtime; the missed anniversary dinners; the mutual dislike Jason and my children felt for each other; the constant borrowing of money as he waited for deals to come through or so as not to miss an 'investment opportunity'; and always the nagging, all-too-distant voice of reason in my head was drowned out by my amorous heartbeats. Jason had left me financially impoverished and, even worse, having to face up to the humiliation of my own naivety.

Not being adept at technology I wasn't even suspicious that my husband left no apparent digital footprint. When Jason explained that he preferred 'Faceless Book', not wanting to give any personal data to Zuckerberg to sell on to advertisers, I thought it showed integrity. He called his Facebook avoidance 'Nerd Immunity'. But why wasn't I more suspicious that his family tree was so bare? There were no branches – not even a twig. Distant relatives were his favourite – and the further away the better. Bar a very few such as Harry, his friends all seemed to live interstate or overseas, and his mining venture colleagues also remained elusive. I realised that I had no photos of him before our marriage; no phone snaps of former partners or bachelor buddies. In truth, I'd married a mirage. If Jason Riley walked across a sieve he'd completely disappear.

I now knew that when a man was described as a 'total charmer', it likely meant he was the type who says 'thank you' after a human sacrifice. When it came to Jason's 'charm' we'd paid a heavy price – literally, as he'd cashed in our life savings.

'We only saw what we wanted to see, that's the truth of it,' I sighed. 'Jason has raised the male of the species to a new low, so to speak. But we can't blame ourselves.'

'Bullshit. I bloody well can,' Tish exclaimed. 'Truth is, I was feelin' sexually rejected. My first hubby was last seen chasin' his toupee across a gay bar,' she explained to Skye. 'I was just so happy to find a bloke with a workin' dick who fancied me that nothin' else mattered. Especially when I realised that Jase really knew his way around a woman . . .'

All three of us looked wistfully off into the distance for a moment in tacit agreement.

'And, well, I'd have done *anythin*' to keep him then – like investin' in his minin' whatsits schemes.'

'Well, if *you* were sex-starved, I was emotionally starved,' I confided. 'My first husband, Jack, was killed in an accident – he was a firefighter,' I explained to Skye. 'I was still grieving, years later, solely focused on raising my kids. And then along came

Jason. He was so full of joie de vivre. I needed some kind of retraining program for widows re-entering the flirt space – and he was the perfect tutor.'

Skye sighed before coughing up her confession. 'My biological clock was, you know, *tick tock, tick tock*. Oh, sure, there are plenty of men out there, but they're married. Or single for a reason. Have you seen what's on offer?'

'Jeeesus, yes,' Tish grimaced. 'Tiny little trainspotters in grey shoes, pervy maniacs, drunks, or blokes who wear the same undies for a week.'

I too grimaced at the memory of the men my friends had set me up with on blind dates after Jack died. A *Star Wars* memorabilia collector; the tofu-eating eco-warrior who ran a puppet theatre for the deaf; an ex-crack addict now addicted to God; the wanker-banker corporate cowboy who over-exaggerated his tax appeal . . .

'And then I met Jason on that diving trip I mentioned, last year,' Skye swooned. 'Oh, to be wooed by such an attentive, attractive man . . .'

'Yeah, yeah, we get it,' Tish empathised, popping Nicorette like candy. 'Who wouldn't swipe right for a bloke with a perfect Body Mass Index who can jack up car tyres in the teemin' rain, execute a one-handed wheelie on his Harley Davidson while plucking his Fender guitar with his teeth. Plus all the rest of that whole flinty-eyed, buff-explorer, action-dude routine.'

'You're right.' I opened a pack of unsalted nuts and offered them to my companions. 'Jason always seemed ready for a spontaneous bout of jungle combat, where he'd fieldstrip an assault rifle, between one-armed push-ups . . .'

'. . . While drinkin' his own piss for survival,' Tish concurred.

'Well, yuk, but yes. Why do we women find that whole clichéd "surviving in the wilderness" trope so sexy?' I pondered.

'It's a hell of a lot sexier than the "*dyin'* alone in the wilderness", version.' Tish snatched the nut packet and tipped the contents into her mouth in one greedy gulp. 'Besides, if a bloke will drink his own piss, you have to ask yourself: what else is he up for? Sexually, nothin's off the menu, right?'

'Yes,' I said, dreamily. 'There was that.'

Once more we all gazed off into space for a moment, before a spate of turbulence jolted us out of our risqué reveries.

'Do you think Jason is working as some kind of undercover spy? Or for the SAS? That could explain his insane behaviour,' I mused. 'Maybe he's infiltrating an embassy siege and is right this minute lying wounded in a jet-ski pile-up after rescuing an imprisoned Saudi princess or something?'

'Could be,' Skye said, clutching at theoretical straws.

'Get real.' Tish hooked a thumb in her own direction. 'Sexually starved divorcee.' She pointed at me. 'Emotionally starved widow.' She flicked a finger in Skye's direction. 'And baby-hungry singleton. The perfect prey.'

Our row descended into a sad silence. As the plane touched down, we'd all come to the same conclusion – falling in love was easy. It's the getting up again that is hard.

9

The next morning, as I wandered around Skye's apartment touching Jason's casually strewn clothes and inhaling his scent from worn T-shirts, I tried to convince myself that getting over him would be easy. Yeah, sure – as easy as tying my own fallopian tubes. Blindfolded. Upside down. In a pitch-black mine shaft.

But breaking into his secret mobile was a good start. When Skye returned from the repair store with Jason's hidden phone successfully unlocked, I felt the same excitement as an archaeologist on a desert dig, except the treasure trove we'd stumbled on was information.

The mobile's history revealed several numbers dialled to the Maldives, as well as lots of downloads about offshore companies and tax havens. There weren't any incoming calls but there were links to dating agencies in Jason's search history, which caused Skye to slump back into her chair in a fugue of dismay. 'We've only been married six months,' she mourned, her face ashen.

'I could make a voodoo effigy?' I suggested lamely.

Tish gave a theatrical roll to her heavily made-up eyes. 'Really? *That's* your idea of revenge? *My* idea of revenge is to rip out his testicles with my teeth. We're in the traditional hot spot for revenge, right? All that smitin' and smotin' that goes on in the Bible. From now on I'm carryin' a vial of ricin on me at all times, just in case we bump into the bastard.'

Skye poured out three hefty glasses of her positively charged water, which she reminded us had been filtered through rose-quartz crystal, and Tish immediately topped it up with Jason's vodka. Thus fortified, we rang the numbers on his secret phone. One went to a hotel reception at a Hideaway Beach Haven in the Maldives. The receptionist only needed a little light flirting, maybe only a number five on Skye's charm dial, to confirm that Jason did indeed have a booking there. The other number that had been dialled more than once on the phone went to the voicemail of a perky-sounding American woman. 'Carly here. Hope you're having as nice a day as I am, y'all! Please leave a message!'

Skye's charm mode evaporated. She immediately filled a pink spray bottle with water from the kitchen tap before praying over it. With eyes closed and arms outstretched, she started making juddering movements that wouldn't have been out of place in an avant-garde dance company. Tish and I watched, intrigued, as she slowly moved from room to room chanting, reciting, humming and spraying. Nothing went unsprayed: the microwave, fridge, television, boiler and broom closet, even the loo. We followed at a discreet distance, exchanging bemused glances.

'Um, Skye, what exactly are you doing?' I finally asked, loitering awkwardly at her elbow.

'A space-clearing psychic scrubbing. Infusing the water with positive energy turns it holy so it can cleanse the apartment of Jason's negative vibrations.'

She then rang a brass bell which had apparently been 'blessed by a spiritual medium', and set alight some tied bundles of dried sage and rosemary. This was called 'smudging', she explained, as she continued to purify the apartment's energy. We trailed along as she waved her burning incense stick in each room. She did a lot of extra smudging in the bedroom to add a 'healing vortex' above the bed.

The apartment thus scrubbed and smudged, we slumped back down in the living room, staring at the secret mobile, willing it to ring. I waited for Skye's positive energy vibes to light up the room, but instead a pall of gloom, doom and despondency descended.

'Okay, that psychic shit's not doin' it for me,' Tish blurted. 'I think we should chase the douchebag to the Maldives. I need answers, goddamn it. I've got just enough dosh to last for the rest of my life . . .' her voice dripped with anger, '. . . unless I actually wanna buy food, clothes, petrol and provide for my kids.' She poked me with the tip of her boot. 'How much dosh do you have left in the bank?'

'I don't know . . . Let me just go give it a rattle.'

'Piggy Bank Limited, yeah? I'm bankin' with them too.' Tish gave a sour bark of a laugh.

Skye glugged down some more of her crystal rose-quartz water, then topped us all up, adding a generous slurp of Jason's vodka to her own this time. She curled her delicate feet up behind her on the couch. 'My main worry is how many other poor women he might dupe. Maybe you're right, Tish. We should go after him. Not just to confront him. But also to warn that poor Texan chick.'

'Um.' I hated to rain on their revenge parade, but one of us had to be practical. 'An assessment of our financial situation by anyone with even the vaguest grip on sentience would conclude that pursuing Jason is utterly impossible.'

'Well, yes and no.' Skye pulled a credit card from her purse. 'I've still got this. It's linked to a joint account, which in his eagerness to escape me, Jason's forgotten to block. Nothing would give me greater pleasure than to burn through his cash stash.'

Tish whooped with joy. 'I'm in. Let's go catch the anal polyp.'

I glanced from Skye to Tish, wide-eyed. 'You're actually serious? You want us to chase Jason to the Maldives? And what do you propose we do when we find him?'

Skye shrugged with one elegant, slim shoulder. 'Let's cross that bridge when we come to it.'

'Really?' I said dubiously. 'We've crossed so many bridges already, I'm surprised we haven't seen a troll.'

Skye kickboxed the air from the couch. 'We'll be like Charlie's Angels.'

'I'm a mum not a Mata Hari,' I interrupted. 'We just have to learn to forgive and let go—'

'What are you? *Switzerland*?' Tish looked at me with disdain. 'How can you act all neutral at a time like this?'

'Um, it may have slipped your notice, but I'm a *teacher*. Not a spy trained for surveillance and espionage. When I buy a pair of nylon stockings, I'm not thinking about how it will look over my head, bank-robber style.'

'Listen,' Tish said. 'My first hubby and I worked hard for our money. We were so broke when our kids were born, I had to leave IOUs for the tooth fairy. Brendan, startin' out his record label with loans; me out singin' in dives up and down the country.

I don't wanna go back to that kinda scrimpin'. That Jason bastard owes me, so why not be Mata Hari Mums?'

'Er, because we're not equipped. Jason's an experienced conman. It would be like standing up to a werewolf armed with a pavlova.'

'Actually, we *are* equipped. I heard on the radio that the British Secret Service is recruitin' middle-aged mums 'cause we're so adept at spyin'. Well, of course we bloody are! We've raised teenagers, right?'

That startled a laugh out of me. There was some truth to what Tish said. I knew how to snoop through a bedroom with the accuracy of a bloodhound. I could locate hidden diaries and memorise their details without detection. I could also sniff out alcohol fumes on Julia's breath at a hundred paces, and spot an 'I've finished my homework' lie by the flicker of her eyelash. Like all mums, no detail escaped my notice. If Max really had cleaned his teeth before bed, why wasn't his toothbrush wet? If he really did go camping with the Scouts then why did he have lipstick on his toggle? And those joss sticks in his room. Was he simply trying to camouflage the smell of hashish?

My French might not be up to the standards it once was, but I was able to speak fluent 'teenager', which had meant communicating by eyebrow only during Max's particularly monosyllabic years. Mums are excellent code breakers, too. What mother can't decipher 'Just having a few friends over while you're away' as a house-trashing Facebook party for the Satanic masses?

'Actually, biology backs up a mother's superior sleuthing potential,' Skye affirmed. 'Scientists have discovered that a surge in oestrogen hormones during pregnancy alters neuroplasticity, or the regrowth of nerve cells in the hippocampus, which is the part of the brain responsible for aspects of memory and spatial awareness.'

'Um . . . In English?' Tish requested, bemused.

'Basically, what Skye's saying,' I interpreted, 'is that an elite commando endurance course requires little stamina compared to a mother's legendary fortitude, including but *not* limited to going through the menopause while simultaneously teaching your daughter to drive.'

'You did that? What are you? In*sane*?' Tish grimaced. She turned to Skye. 'Mums and daughters have more wars breakin' out per day than in the Middle East,' then added in her typically blunt way, 'I take it from your tickin' biological clock comment yesterday that you'd like to have kids?'

'Well, I was trying to talk Jason into it. With his hot genes, you'd think he'd be desperate to become a dad. He said not yet, to wait a bit longer, but soon . . . So, I've been preparing my reproductive organs for conception with vagina mugwort steams.'

Of course she had. I exchanged another sideways glance with Tish. We weren't quite sure what planet Skye was from, but there was clearly an oxygen shortage up there.

'But I now know that Jason was just stringing me along,' she said, grimly.

'Yeah, well, kids are a pain in the bum at times, but you can't help lovin' the little squirts. Mind you, Zack and Sienna have probably turned my house into a meth lab while I've been gone.'

That said, I noticed she fired off a few quick heart emojis in a message to them before topping up our drinks once more and steering us back onto conversational track by injecting a note of frivolity. 'Think of the fun a life of spyin' offers. You get to smoulder in cocktail bar corners and reapply mascara from a cylinder that's really a long-range camera, and loiter on street corners wearing a slimmin' leather trench coat and a saucily angled beret under very flatterin' gas lamplight. Of course, death threats will be an occupational hazard,' she said tipsily. 'But most mums run a very high risk of dyin' anyway, namely by being bored to death while makin' dinosaur heads out of four egg cartons at short notice.'

'And we'd never give in under torture,' I laughed, feeling the vodka course through my arteries. 'We've given birth, for god's sake. What could be more painful than that? Except, perhaps, parent–teacher night. You know, now I think about it, Mata Hari and Ethel Rosenberg had to juggle kids *and* a career. That's a much more gruelling and heroic challenge than James Bond ever had the courage to face.'

'Bloody oath!' Tish enthused, toasting me. 'Thing is, Skye, once a woman turns fifty, she's gotta decide: "Shall I use my cape of invisibility to fight crime, or for evil?"'

'Cloak of invisibility?' Skye asked, lounging back on her velvet cushions.

'Yeah, sadly. Once you hit our age, you get served last in cafés. Waiters just look right through ya. A middle-aged broad might be chock-a-block full of life and energy, but rarely full of friggin' coffee.'

'It's true. Try to get a table for one in even the emptiest restaurant and you find yourself on one of the most successful diets of all time,' I concurred.

'Surely, if we've taken the time to age gracefully, the least someone can do is bring us a cup of bloody coffee,' Tish groused. She took my laughter as acquiescence. 'So, Gwennie, you in?'

I sobered suddenly. 'Wait. I thought we were joking?'

Skye turned her big, bright eyes in my direction. 'I've already texted my travel agent to book three economy flights to the Maldives.'

'Oh, and on our visa forms what exactly will we put for the purpose of the trip? *Espionage*?' I scoffed.

'Why not?!' Tish boomed. 'We'll be Vigilantes with Vaginas! Mums with Tough Muffs! Our muffs will be like Brillo pads.'

'I hate to break it to you, Tish, but *you* undercover? Going undercover requires subtlety.'

'I can be fuckin' subtle.'

'Ha! You might as well be wearing a neon sign saying "Psycho Husband Stalker" while doing jazz hands and high kicks in sequinned stilettos.'

'So, I'm a bit loud. Better than being a snob,' she grumped. 'You're so posh, Gwendoline, when your waters broke it was probably Perrier.'

'Just because I like culture, art and history doesn't make me posh or a snob. And there's no reason to raise your voice! Do you actually have a volume control, *Patricia*?'

'*Gwendoline's* a teacher,' Tish explained to Skye. 'She carries a placard at all times that reads "In case of emergencies ... Shhhh!" She won't even open a letter without knockin' gently on the envelope.'

'Ladies, ladies,' Skye relit her purification incense stick and waved it about frantically. 'Let the healing begin,' she said solemnly. 'We're on the same side.' Her voice was so soothing, like a big spoonful of honey.

'Well, okay, I'll stop raggin' Gwennie . . . but only if she agrees to help us. I mean, we've come this friggin' far.'

'Of course,' I replied, flippantly. 'Since when has abandoning your job, home, family and hemisphere to track a narcissistic psychopath conman around the globe, alongside a deranged bonsai jazz singer and a woo-woo psychic scrubber ever been the wrong decision?' I crossed my legs primly and folded my arms. 'I'm sorry. But no way. Count me out. Yes, I want my money back, but we'd be at each other's throats before you could say "lost luggage".'

There was a pause and then Tish said bleakly. 'Thing is, I just can't face my kids empty-handed. Can you, Gwen?'

A guilty pang made me check my phone right then and there. There were three text messages from Julia, wondering where I'd been for the last three days and wanting to know if I could pick up extra chlorine for her from Bunnings and when I might be available for dog sitting. I envisaged calling to explain how I'd like to help but was currently careering across the world chasing Jason in the company of his two other wives – yes, *wives*; as there were now three of us. 'You're *what*?' I could hear my daughter's voice spiralling up in my imagination. Her reaction to the fact that I'd not told her I was flying to Cairo would be so volcanic, I'd fully expect lava to flow forth from the phone and incinerate my earlobe.

There were voicemails and text messages from well-meaning friends inviting me on bushwalks and to brunches. I imagined them chatting their way round the orbital loop of Jason's death and bigamy rumours, with me desperately looking for the exit signs down a conversational slipway. I shuddered involuntarily. No, no, I was *not* ready for that.

'Well, I guess that between the three of us we must make up at least one working skill-set. But after we find him, how exactly do we get our money back?'

'We'll prod his moral conscience,' Skye said with firm conviction.

'You can't find Jason's moral conscience. You might as well be looking for El Dorado,' I sighed.

'I'm just lookin' forward to runnin' into the bastard again – preferably while *he's* walkin' and *I'm* drivin'.'

'The way you drive, Tish, that should be easy.'

'What the hell do you mean by that?' Tish bounced up on to her feet, fists clenched.

I rolled my eyes at her belligerent bravado and was about to hold forth on the brash, bar-room brawler's many shortcomings when Skye leapt in once more to apply her calming spiritual pawpaw cream.

'Come, come, sisters, we're in this together. All for one and one for all.'

The psychic scrubbing of the apartment must have started working because, at the thought of taking revenge on Jason, I suddenly felt reborn – and all without having to first entomb myself with my slaves in the Egyptian desert. There are eucalyptus trees whose seeds cannot germinate unless they're scorched and cracked in a bushfire, and there are men and women who crawl from the wreckage of a disaster not crushed but cracked open: open to truths and insights previously missed. Yes, we were unbelievably different but we were agreed on this – we would get our money back and stop Jason from ever deceiving another woman. I wanted to make him so toxic and untouchable that he wouldn't even be able to get a date on his tombstone.

We had a toast: 'To the Three Muffkateers!'

Hell, I realised, hath no fury, like three wives scorned.

PART THREE

10

The overnight flight from Cairo to the Maldives was uneventful, mainly because I'd sedated myself for most of it, and Tish was off having sex with an air steward in the crew's sleeping compartment – 'Because they're the rules of the Mile High Club: someone new, not the crew and not in the loo,' she told me, slipping back into her seat and ordering a post-coital martini. 'You should give it a whirl.'

'Casual sex is not for me.' My voice had a lip curl in it; I knew I sounded like a fastidious Victorian aunt but couldn't help it. 'I like sex to be as formal as possible – nasal swabs, thermometers, CVs, the works.'

'Really? More fool you. Where did formal sex get me? Married to a bloody bigamist, that's where. Nah, I'm keeping it *super* casual from now on.'

In reality, I was worried not only about ever being able to trust a man again, but also about ever finding one who was better in bed than Jason Riley. I could still picture the way Jason cupped my pudenda with both hands and then lowered his lips as though taking communion . . . I tried to dash the erotic memory from my mind.

The plane finally circled down out of the clouds and there were the sparkling Maldives – a necklace of 1190 coral islands strung across the turquoise Indian ocean. I knew from the airline brochure that the pristine reefs bustle with over a thousand species of fish. But we were fishing for one breed only – a husband-shaped shark. Careful not to tip off Jason that we were on his trail, we'd booked a shared room under a fake name. At Cairo airport we bought sarongs and thongs, and simply headed off.

The plane landed in Malé, the Maldives' capital. A sign at Customs and Immigration read 'No Pork Products Allowed'.

'Although they've let a chauvinist pig through undetected,' I pointed out to Tish.

'Too bloody right,' she grumped. 'My favourite meal – chauvinist pig roasted slowly on a spit.'

Next, we had to take a short flight to the tiny island of Hanimaadhoo. The plane took off from Malé with what felt like about as much control as a white-water raft in a category five hurricane. I jammed on my headphones and stared out the window at the spectacularly scenic world below, trying not to vomit up my Valium. After the longest forty minutes of my life, the plane started its descent, heading for a landing strip not much bigger than the ones you see in *Playboy* magazine. Despite my nail-biting misgivings, we landed smoothly and were soon being whisked by speedboat to the Hideaway Haven on a nearby island.

As our boat cut through the sapphire-blue sea, a pod of dolphins somersaulted out of the water as though dosed up on aquatic crack. I wanted to ask my accomplices if they thought the creatures were on an endolphin high, because, after all, who wouldn't be ecstatic living here? But Tish was busy applying waterproof make-up in the stern and Skye was chanting, cross-legged at the bow.

The water was so clear that peering over the side of the boat I could glimpse the pale corduroy of the sandy-ribbed sea bed. I watched the dolphins torpedoing back and forth beneath while schools of fish darted in and out of coral massifs in their own silent symphony. The blue skies above, with their curlicues of creamy clouds, made me feel so momentarily happy that I could have had my own cloud. But just as I was sinking into a sleepy, velvet torpor in the sun, the image of Jason gloating and floating in a jacuzzi full of my cash clouded my cranium and a wave of nausea washed over me.

This island was as flat as the buttermilk pancakes we'd had for breakfast in the airport café. The engine kicked back a notch while we skimmed towards the white silica sands of a palm-tree-fringed beach in a tranquil bay, semicircled by the foamy breakers of a coral reef. The vista was so exquisitely beautiful that I had to tilt my head backwards to prevent my eyeballs from falling out in amazement. It made me want to talk in exclamation marks. 'Wow! Oh my god! Incredible!'

Our boat glided into the dock and we disembarked. Blinded by the brilliant sunshine I stumbled through the hub of bars and restaurants that fringed the accommodation; an area enlivened by the odd knife-juggling teppanyaki chef. My gaze travelled from the sumptuous beachside bungalows to the private villas poised on stilts over the ocean, then on up to the opulent tropical treehouses poised above the lagoon.

On the beach, beautiful men caressed their chiselled abs with sunscreen, factor Lust, watched by bronzed women in teeny-weeny bikinis. This was clearly the kind of resort where a girl goes when she has nothing to wear. It was so exclusive I was amazed that the tide could even get in.

'Welcome to Hideaway!' the hotel receptionist enthused. 'There's no wifi on the island, but you won't find a better connection,' she chirped.

The cheapest accommodation on the hotel website was a garden suite, which promised to exude 'rustic charm'. What this meant was a thatched, open-roofed hut with an alfresco bathroom and walls covered in little green lizards. It was the first hotel I'd ever stayed in where the interior design was Art Gecko.

Swapping our leggings and trainers for sarongs and thongs, we Three Muffkateers started our surveillance operation at the beach bar. We didn't actually require a Le Carré training manual because the first person to whom we showed Jason's photo, a garrulous Canadian bartender, replied, 'Jason Riley? God. Now there's a guy who's got everything.'

'Yep – and what we wanna know is how to get it back.'

I jabbed Tish in the ribs and silenced her with my eyebrows.

'Well, it's bloody true,' she grumbled.

'When you say he's a bloke who's "got everything", in what way do you mean?' I asked, twirling my swizzle stick in what I hoped was a nonchalant manner.

The cocktail waiter placed an avocado dip, corn chips and a bowl of olives onto our table at the far end of the shady sundeck overlooking the lagoon.

'He's only gone and nabbed Carly – hottest chick on the island. And he must be, like, twice her age,' the Canadian babbled. 'They've just announced they're getting hitched.'

Rum punch shot out of Tish's nose. Skye immediately administered her version of Valium by chanting a soothing mantra.

A lobotomised grin was the best I could manage. I felt as though I was suffering from amnesia and déjà-vu at the same time – hadn't I forgotten all this before?

The air became very still, as if in anticipation of an incoming storm. Who the hell wrote Jason's marriage manuals, I thought to myself. Hieronymus Bosch?

'Carly?' I inquired, my smile still spackled into place on my frozen features.

'Yep.' The waiter hooked a thumb in the direction of the aqua sports area. 'Runs the dive boats. Lemme know when you want another drink.' He flashed his pearly whites before sauntering off, whistling. 'Her last boat should be going out shortly,' he called back casually, over one well-built shoulder. 'If you want to catch her.'

'Un-bloody-believable,' Tish hissed, vaping frantically. 'Three wives, with another in the wings. That's some classy husbandry right there.'

'He seems to have a kind of marital lazy Susan constantly spinning.' I was aghast and amazed in equal measure.

Skye put her head in her hands and let out a strangled sob.

I was beyond crying. My grief had no texture now – it simply cloaked me. I put my hand on the back of Skye's neck, comfortingly. 'Some people bring happiness wherever they go. Jason brings happiness wherever he went,' I commiserated.

'Poor Carly. I should be jealous, I suppose. But all I want to do is save her.' Skye's eyes were red-rimmed and pooling.

'Too right. We can't let the bastard ruin another bloody life.' Tish threw the rest of her cocktail down her neck then pushed up to standing. She strode down the beach, which was all palm trees and blue and pink hydrangeas, like a set from an operetta.

We followed, planting ourselves on sun loungers near the dive centre; our eyes on the door. I cracked open my paperback of *Middlemarch* and spent five minutes reading it from cover to cover. We knew who Carly was the moment she sashayed out of the dive shop in a pink bikini. Beautiful, sun-kissed, blonde . . . It was fair to say she'd have guaranteed our elimination in a Beach Babe contest.

Outside the shop, white dive tanks stood in a straight row, like giant milk bottles. She bent to examine them, showing off a brown bare back with a strong xylophone spine. When she stood up again she beamed a 100-watt smile. There was a high-spirited flick to her ponytail – the hair-do version of a cheeky grin. She looked like the kind of woman who has the Balinese words for 'love and serenity' tattooed on her inner thigh. She also looked in her early thirties.

'As Jason gets richer, his wives get younger – have you noticed that?' I pointed out, indignantly.

'Oh my,' Skye sulked. 'The woman could be a swimwear model.'

'Yeah, well, who wants to be a swimwear model?' Tish moped, embittered. 'You get sand in bloody everythin'.'

'I'm sure Carly's sun protection factor is higher than her IQ,' I added, in a futile attempt to make us feel a teeny bit better.

Carly smiled in our direction, her luminous dentition flawlessly white. 'Hi y'all! Can I interest y'all in a dive today?' she called, clearly thinking this was the reason we were gawping at her. She walked over with a confident gait and a bright, open face, her ponytail pinging up behind her like an antenna.

'Are you Carly?' I asked, tentatively.

'Dive master. At your service, ma'am. Diving in the Maldives is unsurpassed.' Her American twang gave the impression that her family's backyard contained oil wells. 'Y'all divers?'

'I dive, yes,' I said.

'Yeah, me too,' Tish added. 'My husband taught me.'

'So did mine,' I added.

'Mine too,' Skye said quietly.

'Wow. What thoughtful men.'

'*Man.* Thoughtful *man*,' Skye corrected.

Carly crinkled up her freckled nose with bemusement. 'Y'all married the same guy? Wow. That's like, totally weird.'

Skye, Tish and I exchanged a knowing glance; not nearly as weird as what we had yet to tell her.

Carly checked her watch. 'I'm due to take the dive boat out now if you folks would like to join me? You'd be the only guests today, so a private tour,' she winked encouragingly.

Tish, Skye and I performed a quick and subtle communication with our eyebrows. It seemed the perfect opportunity to talk to Carly, alone.

Ten minutes later the dive boat pulled out of the lagoon, expertly steered by a muscular young skipper. As Tish shrugged her arms into a dive vest, I watched her eyeing him up.

'Keep your mitts off the boat meat,' I warned her. 'We have work to do.'

'Ha! But there's always later. I'm not a sexual vegan, like you, Gwendoline.'

As we bounced over cheeky little wavelets, the wetsuits on the onboard rack waved their liquorice arms and legs as though dancing. The ocean was dazzlingly brilliant in the afternoon sun. Fluffy white clouds chased each other across the sky. Between them streamed golden rays, making the water sparkle with gaiety.

Carly handed out masks, flippers and wetsuits, talking knowledgeably about the diving conditions in the area. She told the skipper to avert his eyes and, 'as we're all gals together', coolly stripped off right there on deck. Before she pulled on her diving Speedos, we had a good opportunity to appreciate the fact that this was a woman with a masochistic penchant for the full Brazilian.

Tish followed Carly's laissez-faire example and started disrobing, brazenly flaunting an all-over tan and a rather elaborately bejewelled vajazzle. Skye sported the regulation Hollywood landing strip, which looked like a runway for mosquitoes.

Unlike my free-spirited companions, I do not like to get naked in front of strangers. My pudenda is the Greta Garbo of sexual organs – shy and reclusive. But not wanting to appear prudish, I reluctantly draped a towel around my waist and attempted a quick change beneath its terry-towelling screen. This manoeuvre was only half-accomplished when the boat gave a mighty lurch and the towel slipped, revealing what I can only call my 'Australian' – as in full bush.

'Jeez, your map of Tassie's so lustrous. What's it made of? Mink?' Tish chuckled, pulling on a lime green bikini, then stuffing her curves into a wetsuit. It was like watching a Great Dane trying to get through a cat flap. 'Whoa,' she panted, between hoisting-up movements, 'The last time I saw legs that friggin' pale, there was an identification tag tied to the toe.'

I wanted to hide my body as fast as I could, but it took forever to get on my Speedos then yank up the wretched suit – made, as they seem to be, from a fabric resembling recycled breast implants – over my posterior, allowing maximum amusement at the expense of my milk-bottle-white skin and wilderness area.

Once kitted up, Tish's laughter subsided long enough for Carly to go through a detailed description of the drift dive we'd be undertaking. She pored over the sacred dive charts with us as diligently as a Talmudic scholar, then concluded by asking if we had any questions.

'Actually, yes.' Tish took a big toke of her e-cigarette. 'Is your family rollin' in dough? Are they in minin'? And does Jason just worship the ground your father found gold, uranium or oil in?'

Despite Carly's nose crinkling in confusion at the sound of Jason's name, she illuminated. 'You know Jase?'

'Yep,' Tish replied, coolly. 'I'm married to him.'

'*What?*' This time Carly's nose creased; in fact, it creased so forcefully it nearly disappeared up its own nostrils.

'We all are,' I added earnestly.

Carly's javelin stare impaled me. 'That's impossible. I'm Jason's fiancée.' She was trying to remain cordial and polite, but obviously we were severely testing the limits of her hotel-trained hospitality and good ol' Texan charm.

'Well, be warned,' I said. 'Jason flunked the written exam for his marriage licence. And it's really such a simple, multiple-choice format. A) Have you ever been married? B) Are you still married? C) Have you already got three wives?'

Carly took off her designer sunglasses to examine us more closely. Her eyes were the piercing aquamarine of an ice queen.

'What the hell's goin' on here, ladies? Is this some kind of joke? Are you secretly filming me for my bachelorette party?' She looked around expectantly, then softened. 'Honestly, did Jase put you up to this prank?'

I extracted the three marriage certificates from my beach bag and thrust them under her nose. 'Let's just say Jason dislikes the formalities of the divorce court.'

As Carly stood gawping at the documents, Tish added, 'When we caught him out, he did what any self-respectin' rat would do under the circs – ran!'

Carly's face went taut and her lips thinned. 'Watch your mouth. That's my fiancé you're talking about,' the plucky Texan said.

'Your weddin' ceremony really should be conducted by an accountant, 'cause the scumbag's only after your moolah.' Tish was now blowing out vape smoke in industrial chimney quantities. 'I'm right, aren't I? Your old man's rich?'

'My daddy died six months ago.' It was Tish's turn to get the javelin in the eyeball. 'Not that it's any of your goddamned business.'

Tish leant into my ear to deliver her whispered diagnosis: 'Explains the age gap. Daddy issues.'

'And you're, like, totally wrong about my Jase,' Carly continued vociferously. 'There's nothing he wouldn't do for me.'

'Yup, and that's exactly what he'll do – nothin',' Tish shot back.

'You're totally wrong,' she repeated. 'In my book, Jason's one of the most lovely men I've ever met.'

'I'm afraid that book is a work of fiction,' I said gently. How to bridge the Grand Canyon-esque chasm between this girl and reality?

'Where did you meet?' Skye asked, looking shocked and blinking back tears.

'On a diving trip in the Seychelles. While I was there, my daddy died of a heart attack, and Jason took such good care of me. And well, like, you know, one thing led to another.'

'Your classic whirlwind romance ... Why? Because as soon as Jason knew you had money, the relationship picked up speed, which tends to happen when you're sliding downhill,' I explained dryly.

'And, lemme guess ... You've invested your inheritance into some dodgy minin' scheme of his?' Tish tutted.

'Why not? I totally trust him. A man like Jason is hard to find.'

'He sure the hell is,' Tish snapped.

Ignoring Tish, Carly thrust the three dog-eared marriage certificates back at us. 'These must be faked. Though I can't imagine why. Who are you bat-shit crazy broads?' Her eyes narrowed suspiciously. 'Are you, like, stalking him?'

'Carly, I'm so sorry to have descended on you like this. And I know it's a lot to take in, but Jason's stolen our money and we're on his trail to get it back. He's a conman.' I gave an involuntary shudder – despite the warm sunshine.

Carly looked furious. 'How do I know *y'all* are not conning me?'

'He's fake, Carly. He's faker than . . .' Tish groped for a relatable analogy, '. . . the silicone tit of a Las Vegas lap dancer.'

'The man should have a loophole named after him,' I added, gravely.

Carly surveyed us with a mix of mistrust and incredulity. Her eyes kept travelling from one to the other of us, drinking in our differences. 'Y'all clearly talking about a different Jason. My Jase spends most of his spare time on Ironman fundraisers for charity.'

Tish, Skye and I exchanged sceptical glances. When it came to charity, Jason Riley, it seemed, would stop at nothing – literally. Although of course he was also the charismatic type to be able to raise ten thousand dollars . . . without even having a designated disease.

Carly flicked her ponytail over her other shoulder with irritation. 'Jason and I don't have any secrets. In fact, I have the spare key to the safety deposit box he keeps at the resort. Right here.' She clutched a chain around her neck which held a small gold heart and a key. 'If he was, like, hiding something, would he entrust this to me?'

'Are all of Jason's important documents in that safe?' Tish couldn't keep the glee out of her voice.

Carly nodded, folding her arms across her chest defensively.

'Carly, I know this is a lot of negative energy to dump on you,' Skye empathised. 'And that it all sounds insane, but Jason only married *me* six months ago.'

'Okay y'all. That's enough.' Her ponytail boinged as she shook her head from side to side. 'Why don't we go talk to Jason. And then we can clear up this whole misunderstanding, 'kay?'

I felt a surprising rush of tenderness for this unknown Texan. She was in love. Why should she believe us? 'Good idea. Where is the marital mugger?' I asked.

She pointed to a smudge of land that we were heading towards. 'Coral Island. Just near where we're diving. Jason is entertaining a client for the day, snorkelling and paddle boarding. I'll call him now.'

'NO!' we Three Muffkateers shouted in unison – a chorus that could have been impressive but for the fact that we were in discordant keys.

'The point is,' Skye explained calmly, 'if Jason knows we're here, he'll vanish.'

'It's true. He'll just bugger off. Scarper. Vamooose!' Tish clicked her fingers. '*Poof!*'

'If you want to know for sure if we're telling the truth, we have to arrive unannounced.' I tried to talk evenly, as though addressing my students. 'If our drift dive is as close to the island as you say, why don't we simply scuba into the beach? That way he won't clock our arrival, affording him no time to escape by speedboat. Then you can see for yourself his initial reaction.'

We were getting closer to the end of Coral Island. The sea seemed to wake from its turquoise sleep and yawn with force. As the boat rocked, Carly chewed on the end of her ponytail then finally shrugged. "Kay. It's, like, your time and money. But I'm sure this is some kind of prank. Jason and I are gonna get married next month – we're even trying for a baby.' Her face became vivid with excitement.

Skye's, however, looked stricken. 'You're . . . you're going to have his b– b– baby? But Jason told me he didn't want children yet . . .'

'Carly, kiddo, don't bloody bet on it.' Tish's voice was vinegary. 'Truth is, your relationship with Jason has the life expectancy of a kid peerin' into a gas tank holdin' a lit match.'

'It's true, Carly. I'm sorry.' I was determined to cut through her complacency. 'Jason Riley makes the liver-sucking killer orca whales look harmless.'

Carly's lips set in cement. 'If he's really a conman, how come you three smartass ladies fell for him, huh?'

'J'a see that hole on the deck?' Tish asked, pointing to an open hatch.

'Yes.'

'Well, we didn't. But now at least you can.'

Carly chewed on her ponytail for a bit longer. All we could hear was the low murmur of the boat engine as the bow slapped through the water. Then she said, 'Fine. We'll moor here, where Jason can't see the boat, drift dive down the reef, then I'll give the signal to head into shore so we can sort this mess out. Dougie?' she beckoned the skipper. 'Can you hang around here, and pick us up from Coral Beach in, like, an hour? I'll call you from Jason's phone, 'kay?'

'Okay,' the skipper confirmed, giving a thumbs up.

Carly was by now perched on the side of the boat and poised to flop backwards into the sea. 'If we're lucky, we might even see a whale shark,' she enthused. 'They're as big as a double-decker bus, but don't be scared. They just eat, like, plankton.'

'Good to know there's only one man-eater in the near vicinity.' I kicked Tish lightly in the leg to distract her from honed and toned Dougie, then tied my GoPro strap to my wrist.

'Wait. You're takin' holiday snaps?' Tish demanded, incredulous.

'Of course.' I inflated my jacket. 'The Maldives is one of the richest biodiversity hotspots in the Indian Ocean, with over two hundred coral species, including fan and fire corals and the giant gorgonian.'

'Do you think we need a weapon?' a nervous Skye interrupted, defogging her goggles with spray. 'Like a spear-fishing gun or a stun-gun or something?'

'Why bother? No need for a stun-gun. We can simply deploy Gwennie here to give a lecture on marine life – that leaves victims feelin' drowsy within, oh, seconds,' Tish scoffed caustically.

'Ladies,' Skye soothed, preparing to follow Carly into the sea. 'No rancour, please. Positivity only. We are so close to closure.'

We three gazed at the low-lying tropical island with a mix of trepidation and excitement.

'The net's closing in, kids.' Tish skittered down the side of the boat, whooping with joy.

As I prepared to step off the back of the boat, one thought was on my mind – is the menopause a legal justification for homicide? Perhaps I could explain to the jury that I was going through my *Post*-Menstrual-Tension nervous-breakdown blue period.

If the jury was made up of conned, abandoned and cheated wives, I had no doubt they'd acquit.

11

I bobbed about on the surface in my inflated dive vest like a dumpling in a warm aquamarine soup. The wind had dropped and with no breeze the water took on a look of blank innocence. Placing the regulator in my mouth, I started dumping air from my BCD to begin my descent into the calm, clear water, holding my nose to pressurise my ears, the way Jason had taught me.

Crosscurrents of feeling were pulling me to and fro. My husband was here, right here, on this very island, a few flipper kicks away. It was time for him to explain himself. During the descent, I also thought about what I'd say when I did finally see Jason again. Perhaps I'd simply tell him that the difference between him and a cockroach was that one's a filthy, despicable scavenger ... and the other's just an insect. Or perhaps I'd just clobber him over the head with my oxygen tank?

By the time my feet hit the sandy seabed, memories of Jason's betrayal had left me as deflated as my dive vest. But when

I glanced around, the true majestic grandeur of the kaleidoscopic underwater world overrode my melancholy. I marvelled as a Mick Jagger impersonator (technically known as a bluestreak cleaner wrasse) whirled past me. A giant sea turtle stooged by at the same time as a huge stingray, with its theatrical cape and stage-villain grin, swooped by above. Entranced, I watched the colourful choreography of iridescent fish darting through coral, without a care in their weightless world.

When Tish and Skye were also kneeling with me on the corrugated sand, Carly curled her index finger to her thumb and made the international diving sign for 'Are you okay?'

I wondered what the international diving hand signal was for 'When they say the best way to a husband's heart is through his stomach, does that mean by an upwards thrust of a fishing knife?' But I made do with a reciprocal OK signal.

Reassured that her diving party was prepared, Carly made another hand signal to indicate our direction towards the reef. Finning after her, I took in the underwater topography, a sculpture park of atolls, Jackson Pollock-ed in coloured coral. The current was so strong all we had to do was drift along with it, marvelling at the spectacular reef, occasionally darting on a little detour through a coral-encrusted cave. Bursts of bubbles indicated Tish, Carly and Skye's tanks ahead. I scissored through the sparkling water in their wake.

The rhythm of my breathing and the gentle pull of the current lulled me into a meditative state, arms and legs in harmony, body and spirit in perfect synchronicity. But just as a warm sense of calm washed over me, I half-glimpsed something looming up from the shadowy depths where the reef dropped off dramatically into a deep, dark trench. Alarmed, I stopped swimming and looked downwards. The sunlight reflecting and refracting upwards in millions of silvery shards blurred my vision. Thousands of small black fish swarmed around me in a synchronised shoal. Then, with a swish, the scaly whirlpool evaporated and I found myself eye to eye with a humungous whale shark.

Moby-Dick and I looked at each other for a silent eternity, though my waterproof wristwatch recorded it as six seconds. My vision blurred and swam – the only part of me that could, mid panic attack.

What had I been thinking, hurling myself into a liquid environment known to be home to huge finned entities the same bulk as a cargo ship and with a maw the size of a garbage truck?

Until today the biggest beasts I'd ever encountered in the water were bloated Russian oligarchs bobbing about in Sydney Harbour aboard their ostentatious super yachts. Carly had said that whale sharks ate only plankton. But the rock and roll motion of the current was making me a little seasick. What if I turned green and Moby mistook me for a meal? Besides, did anything really get that big from eating algae? This massive creature could use me as a toothpick. Just call me Ishmael or, worse, Captain Ahab, I thought. Hmmm, did my travel insurance cover being eaten alive, digested, then expelled in a blob of whale faeces?

Panicking on dry land is uncomfortable enough, but in water what ensues is a surprisingly rapid decrease in buoyancy. However, the massive creature glided effortlessly by, giving me a look that seemed to say, 'You're new at this, aren't you?' The whale shark was studded with what appeared to be glimmering sequins, as if it were dressed for an underwater disco – and the way it whooshed by definitely gave the impression it was running late for the festivities. The sight was so awe-inspiring that I completely forgot to be afraid. I recalled a quote from Moby-Dick, 'Ignorance is the parent of fear', and calmed down.

It was then I remembered the GoPro tethered to my wrist. Emboldened, I turned back, swimming against the current to follow the whale shark, snapping away like an aquatic paparazzo before switching to video. If only there was a way to radio the others ahead to let them know what they were missing.

I was so entranced by the whale's streamlined grace that it wasn't until the creature powered back down into the ocean's depths that I thought to check my spare air supply. By the time I'd examined the oxygen gauge, the level was surprisingly low. Finning against the current had used up a lot of air. Not only was I now also quite far from the reef but I could feel the tug of another cross-current towing me further out to sea. Worse, there was no sign of my divemaster.

Clown, lion, parrot, puffer, butterfly and angelfish still flitted and nipped around me, oblivious to the fact that all I could hear was the sound of my own panicked breathing. In fact, my breathing was so rapid and jerky that I was using up my remaining oxygen. My mask filled with water, making me flounder more frantically. I cleared it but then my ears started giving me trouble. They wouldn't pop properly. I just couldn't find my equilibrium.

I felt a tug on my flipper and jerked around. It was Tish making googly eyes at me through her mask. She made the thumb-to-index-finger 'O' diving sign for 'Are you okay?'

I did my best to signal, 'A complimentary lung transplant would be good right now.'

A scuba diver who takes fright and gets flustered will end up regurgitating seaweed on a coroner's slab, so I pointed my thumbs upwards to tell Tish I needed to ascend. She checked her own oxygen levels and agreed.

Linking arms, we slowly finned to the surface, stopping at regular intervals to adjust to the change in pressure, inflating our jackets a little more at every pause. As I finally broke the surface, a wave slapped my face. Then another. They came at me again and again, as though conducting some kind of violent interrogation. During the half-hour we'd been underwater, the weather had changed dramatically. The sky was bulging grey, fit to burst. The sea had become snot-green and choppy. Through sluicing rain, I watched another wave hurtling towards me, hissing like a snake. I looked at the foaming, white-capped horizon with alarm.

The turbulent tide was dragging us further out to sea, no doubt towards the watery grave of other middle-aged mums who'd been stupid enough to attempt a drift dive in unfamiliar waters with an instructor who, it suddenly struck me, might be in criminal cahoots with her unscrupulous fiancé. Through the forest of white crests, I glimpsed Skye also bobbing to the surface, 50 metres away.

Tish shouted that we should swim to her. Rolling onto my back, I kicked strenuously in Skye's direction. Grey waves curled and arched up over us. Backstroking against a crosscurrent is a heroic feat requiring Olympic stamina, but it's even more arduous with a giant milk bottle strapped to your back.

'Where's our so-called divemaster?' Tish boomed, when I caught up to her. 'You know, the woman who is supposed to be protectin' us?'

I felt a tremor of anger fizz along my spine, too. Was taking us on a drift dive in the unfamiliar Maldives Carly's way of getting rid of us? A drift dive to where, exactly? *Sri Lanka*?

'You don't think she swam to shore to warn Jason, do you?' Skye's voice was pitched two octaves higher – Vienna Boys' Choir higher.

'Where's the bloody dive boat? Can either of you see it?' Tish bobbed in the waves beside me, her mask pushed up onto her furrowed brow. 'Gwen?'

I tried to answer but couldn't muffle the sound of my terrified molars grinding to dust. No sooner did I catch my breath than another wave crashed down on us, its white crest a malicious sneer. But as I rode up on the other side of the mighty wall of water, I glimpsed the dive boat. 'There!' I spluttered, pointing.

Skye began to wave frantically in the direction of the vessel, about 300 metres away, with Tish shouting in her big bass boom. Meanwhile, 'Gurrrrgle' was my only vocal contribution – I was too winded from whale-shark wrangling, general oxygen starvation and Carly's betrayal – a betrayal which might possibly lead to our premature demise – to contribute anything more substantial. Sea water was streaming from every orifice and both my ears were waterlogged, but through the gurgling I heard Skye yelling to Tish that she'd seen the whale shark behind her, alerted Carly and they'd doubled back. Skye had had to concentrate hard to swim against the current and then, like us, was so entranced by the majestic creature that by the time she'd turned around to make visual contact with our dive-master, Carly had vanished.

Miraculously, Dougie finally saw us and pulled up shortly afterwards in a spritz of spray. By the time we'd clambered back on board, I was more wrinkled and bug-eyed than an extra-terrestrial in a sci-fi movie; Tish and Skye, too. If David Attenborough had been filming us, he'd have declared us rare wetland habitats. When I shook my head, I could feel the ocean swishing around inside my cranium. 'Do you think Carly swam to shore?' I asked Dougie between sloshy head shakes.

'No chance. Carly would never leave her clients.' The skipper radioed for help and a nearby dive boat soon sped around the headland.

The second boat's two dive crew somersaulted backwards off the side of their boat and finned their way below, bubbles slowly disappearing as they sank into the deep.

'Carly's done a bloody runner with him. It's the only explanation.' Sea salt encrusted Tish's eyebrows, which were now puckered into a bristling, furious frown.

Why had we trusted the Texan twinkie? Why hadn't we learnt our lesson to be less credulous? Another of Melville's quotes dredged itself up from the murky depths of my memory. 'For there is no folly of the beast on the earth which is not infinitely outdone by the madness of men.' And women, Herman, sadly.

Peeling down the rubber arms of my wetsuit, I got stuck and just stood there, wedged, my stomach churning. When I thought of Jason slipping once more from our cuticle-gnawed grasp, the blood raced through my veins so fast I could practically feel the friction on my arterial walls.

The realisation that Carly was in on Jason's scam and that he was going to get away yet again made me want to curl up on the deck in a foetal ball. But if only I really *had* – because half an hour later the divers resurfaced, carrying Carly's lifeless body.

12

As a high-school teacher, there are some experiences you assume will never require your ingenuity – finding a cure for a pandemic, for example, or having to take over the wheel of an aeroplane because the pilot has collapsed mid-flight ... or dealing with the police in a foreign land after a diving fatality. Carly's death rocked me to my core.

A boat siren alerted us – and the entire Indian Ocean, for that matter – that the police were on their way. I was relieved, but also aware that we'd pretty much scuppered the old surprise element where Jason was concerned.

After confirming that Carly was indeed deceased, a policeman attempted to take my statement. I tried to answer but seemed to have a live sea snake wedged halfway down my duodenum. My attention kept darting back to Carly's outstretched body on the aft deck of the dive boat, lying gelid-eyed and cold as though on a fishmonger's slab.

Jelly-legged with shock, I staggered and had to clutch Tish's arm to break my fall. She passed me a Styrofoam cup of instant coffee, rustled up by the shell-shocked skipper, Dougie. I held it with shaky hands. Tish and I looked at each other, two shivering aliens beamed down from Planet Grim. At the back of the boat, Skye was balled up like a petrified echidna, sobbing. Behind her, the row of black wetsuits, arms thick as eels, writhed on the rack in the wind as though also in pain.

The police doctor pronounced the cause of death as drowning, most likely after losing consciousness in an unexplained blackout, but he said he wouldn't know for sure until after the autopsy.

As he spoke, a constant stream of bullet points ran silently through my head like the ones that run along the bottom of TV news programs . . . Carly is dead . . . Was it an accident? . . . Where is Jason? . . . Was he involved? . . . Has he gone full psychopath? . . . What will happen to Carly's money? . . . Did she give Jason access to her accounts? . . . Where is he? Back at Hideaway? . . . Is he right now clearing out his safety deposit box?

Tish's mind was clearly scrolling through an identical ticker tape. 'Listen, mate,' she snapped at the policeman approaching us. 'You don't want to waste time questionin' *us*.'

I wasn't sure growling at this law enforcement officer was the most effective method to get him on side, but Tish pushed on. 'The bloke you need to talk to is Carly's friggin' fiancé. Believe me, mate.' She now poked the trooper in the chest. 'Jason Riley's the kinda bloke who would kill his own parents just so he could get a sympathy screw by tellin' women he's an orphan.'

Now, there is one fixed rule when travelling in a foreign country – armed police are right about everything. Break this rule and you could find yourself unexpectedly bullet-riddled; I was pretty certain that poking a policeman in the chest rated high on the reckless rap sheet. The officer looked confused but showed his displeasure by twisting Tish's arm up behind her back.

'Seriously? Why the hell are you wastin' time talkin' to us when the culprit is gettin' away?' she reiterated, over her shoulder. 'Jeez, if you were any more moronic I'd have to water you once a week.'

The poked officer gave Tish's arm a more forceful yank. Her yelp of pain jolted me out of my stupor. 'She's right, officer.' I was slowly metabolising the shock, like you do with alcohol. 'Jason Riley's the kind of man who stabs you in the back, then tips off the police that you're carrying a concealed weapon.'

Bamboozled, the officer dropped Tish's arm and went to speak to Skye – a pointless exercise as her crying was still a rolling boil of noise. She was also shaking violently. The sun was sinking and though the rain had stopped, the wind off the dark water was cold. The police doctor diagnosed hysteria and suggested getting Skye back to the resort and into some warm clothes as soon as possible. So she was whisked off in a speedboat back to Hideaway, leaving Tish and me with the officers. I felt sure that it must be obvious, even to these obtuse policemen, that interrogation was pointless: I felt translucent, like those pictures of magnified amoebas you see on nature programs; or like a giant jellyfish – anyone could see right into me and all they'd find was a deep regret that poor Carly had ever got mixed up with our conman husband.

Tish had rolled her wetsuit down to waist level, the arms dangling by her sides like tentacles. She backed up the statement Dougie had just made, pointing to where she thought we'd gone into and got out of the water.

The whole horrible ordeal was a jigsaw I couldn't put together. There were missing pieces and no picture on the box, and any pieces I did find I had no idea where to slot. Only Jason knew the answers. And the question remained – where was Jason?

'Why would a divemaster – young, fit and healthy – stop breathing under the water?' I asked one of the officers.

'The prick must have tampered with her dive tank,' Tish answered for him. 'I bet we'll find Carly's bank accounts have also been tampered with and are now in his bloody name.'

I felt anger bulge up as big as a whale surfacing, but breathed it down. If Jason had murdered his fiancée to get her money, he'd no doubt beg for leniency on the grounds that he was bereaved.

The officer seemed to drift as slowly as plankton past the facts but finally gave an order for the dive boat to return to Hideaway, while Carly's body was taken to the police morgue. We weren't sure what was going on. The police conversed with Dougie in their language and nobody bothered to translate. Clearly we were considered mere collateral in the tragedy and not remotely useful any longer. We kept trying to ask questions but only succeeded in making the officers impatient and aggressive, so we backed off.

As our boat skimmed over the choppy ocean, I wondered how the hell this had happened to me. My preferred holiday activity is reading, during which there is not much potential for death.

Poor Carly had thought she was in a fairytale romance. Well, she was a fair maiden all right, but her knight had turned out to be a fire-breathing dragon.

13

As our boat drew up to the dock, Skye was pacing back and forth in the watery moonlight. Now warmly clad in a white track-suit, she no longer resembled Munch's *The Scream* but was still gnawing fretfully on the inside of her cheek, her face pale as milk.

'He's done a runner,' was her dismal greeting.

My spirits *Titanic*-ed. Jason was beginning to resemble some kind of nimble ninja phantom, the way he was always three leaps ahead.

'On the boat back, I did some mindfulness exercises and centred myself. Once we landed, I persuaded the guy at reception – he's a Dalai Lama devotee, like me – to let me into Jason's villa. It was cleared out; the safety deposit box open . . . and empty.'

We stood on the deck in a trifecta of gloom, staring at each other like the passengers on the Raft of the Medusa, before staggering back to our garden suite.

'How did the bugger know we were on his trail?' Tish moaned.

'Hmm. A hippy-trippy mineralogist, a tattooed jazzer and a beige bookworm – we are kind of hard to miss. Someone in the resort must have mentioned us.' I tried to shuck off my wetsuit but needed help. Slumping into the lounge I clung to the chair as Tish and Skye took hold of a leg each and yanked, finally freeing me from the suit's rubbery embrace. I hauled on some dry clothes and flumped back down. The room was awash with unspoken thoughts. Finally, I cleared my throat and said what we were all thinking. 'Is this our fault?'

'No!' Tish was adamant. 'We were tryin' to save Carly! Besides which, she was the divemaster – the divemaster who left us. In dangerous bloody waters. God knows why. Unless she was taken against her will.'

Silence fell like a thick blanket of fog across the room, despite the balmy tropical breeze. Tish emptied the minibar of miniature vodka and gin bottles and began necking them at speed.

'Do . . . do . . . do you really think Jason had something to do with Carly's death?' Skye's voice was juddery with angst.

I sank back even further into my chair. 'To be honest, I'm so disillusioned and jaded right now, I wouldn't be surprised if you told me Jason had just bitten the heads off newborn triplets, nuked a small country in the Outer Hebrides, grown cloven hooves and was now off smiting orphans.'

I saw Tish's shoulders slacken. 'We're waaaaay out of our depth, kids. It's time we cut our losses.'

I wondered for a moment if I still had water in my ears. 'Really?'

'We've gotta call off the chase. Things are gettin' too weird,' she concluded, crestfallen.

A ripple of relief went through my body. 'Oh, thank god. I totally agree. Face facts. We're just not equipped to stalk a murderous psychopath around the planet. We might as well try to climb Everest in stilettos.'

Skye shot up in her seat as though tasered. 'No! A woman has just died because of him. We cannot let Jason get away with it. It's bad karma.'

Tish handed Skye a little bottle of gin. 'We're amateurs, Skye. Hell, we couldn't track down a haemophiliac having a haemorrhage in a freakin' snowfield!'

'Tish is right, Skye – and believe me, I don't say *that* very often.' I picked up one of the little gin bottles, unscrewed the lid and downed it in one gulp. 'Despite the fact that Jason's ego's so big it can be picked up on every radar on Planet Earth, we have no idea where he's gone.'

'Well, I'm not giving up. I need to live my truth. That man stomped all over my chi. And got Carly prematurely reincarnated. He must pay.'

I looked at Skye, mystified. It was increasingly hard to believe that she was a trained geologist.

'Oh, pardon me, Sherlock friggin' Holmes, but what's your plan? To head off with a list of edible berries and a compass?' Tish pressed her hands into the small of her back, her huge breasts ballooning out in front of her. 'Half the time we can't even find our bloody glasses.'

'That's because we can't look for them until we've found them,' I elucidated, for Skye's benefit. 'I've got one pair of glasses for short-sightedness, one for long-sightedness and another pair to find those two.' I swigged back a distress-numbing vodka.

'Jeeeesus. Well, that just says it all, doesn't it? *Ophthalmic and Louise*.' Tish took a packet of chips from the minibar, tore it open with her teeth and began shovelling crisps into her maw, glancing askance at Skye, who looked disapproving. 'Some of us can't live on hot air alone,' said Tish.

'I'm not talking hot air. *I* happen to know exactly where Jason is.' Skye divulged this vital information in an almost casual tone.

I reeled around so fast, I gave myself whiplash. 'What?'

'I convinced my Dalai Lama friend at reception that we were spiritual soulmates and he gave me a copy of Jason's bill. Jason paid cash, so that didn't help. But he'd made numerous calls from the landline in his room – all to Tanzania.'

Tanzania? Were we about to make Stanley and Livingstone look like the stay-at-home types? Thank goodness Tish had finally seen sense and was putting the kybosh on our escapades.

I glanced her way to nod in agreement that it ended here. She was fiddling around with her phone when her face froze. 'Oh fuck. Do either of you have any drugs?'

'There might be some Nurofen in my make-up bag,' I volunteered.

'Positive Moon Juice?' Skye offered.

Tish tilted back her head and emptied another vodka bottle down her neck, wiping her mouth with the back of her hand. 'I was thinkin' more along the lines of ecstasy or opium, plus some kind of tool for a DIY lobotomy.'

'What's happened?' Skye stroked Tish's hand as though she were a cat.

Tish snatched it away. 'According to this email' – she held up her phone – 'the bank's foreclosin' on my mortgage in twelve months unless I catch up on my missed repayments.'

'Well, that's that then. We've got no choice but to head back,' I said, resolutely.

'Nah. You don't get it. I don't *have* a mortgage. But . . .' Tish went very quiet and screwed up her face in concentration. 'Jason made me sign some "insurance documents" one night, months ago ... after plyin' me with martinis ... The prick must have tricked me into remortgagin' my bloody home!'

'And the bank told you nothing about it?' I asked, aghast.

'Obviously they didn't tell me till now, so that I could have a heart attack at friggin' leisure,' she barked. Then her face contorted. It took me a moment to realise she was crying. It was such a surprise to see Tish vulnerable that I was momentarily speechless. I wanted to hug her but was too intimidated by her steely wariness that seemed to stand guard, like an emotional bouncer, at all times – even now.

'My financial situation is also on a solid foundation – as in, *on the rocks*,' I commiserated.

Skye then let out a sob of her own. 'What I didn't tell you is that I *also* let Jason remortgage my apartment to help fund some surefire cryptocurrency mining venture of his.'

'Cryptocurrency?' I queried. 'Could there be anything more dodgy?'

'That dingo-dicked lyin' piece of crap!' Tish ripped open another crisp packet and tossed a huge handful into her mouth, then chewed ferociously. 'Remember when I said I needed to fly with a support animal, Gwen? I was wrong. What I need to fly with is a support *bazooka*. Skye, I'm back in, goddamn it. Gwendoline?' she demanded, spraying crisp crumbs. 'Are you gonna wimp out and give up? Or fight the good fight and make the sisterhood proud?'

I looked from Tish to Skye and back again. I'm the type to watch SBS documentaries on Norwegian clog dancing. I attend seminars on inclusion and educational intersectionality. My downtime is spent alphabetising my canned goods and weeding my herb garden. I thought lovingly and longingly of my garden, the heliotropically lifted heads of my sunflowers, turning this way and that, looking for me. And what about my kids? I groped for my phone. There was a voicemail from Julia. I pressed the 'listen' button with trepidation. 'Mother! Why haven't I heard from you?' There was an unspoken reprimand in my daughter's voice, but I liked to think it was tempered by loving concern. What followed was a mini lecture mixed with requests to know where I was and whether I was looking after myself. It was sweet, but is there anything more annoying than being condescended to by your own offspring?

Julia concluded by saying she couldn't believe I'd gone away without telling her and that she missed my dog-sitting skills. I caught a glimpse of myself, slumped, round-shouldered, in the middle of Julia's domestic encampment of wet towels, dirty dog bowls and pooper scoopers. I loved my daughter, but she was freeze-dried and vacuum-packed.

Before hanging up, she asked me to come home immediately. Go home? I envisaged what else awaited me there: well-meaning friends in spangled leggings on their way to Pilates, or coming back from Ashtanga class, yoga mats sausage-rolled under lasered armpits, stopping to grill me for the gruesome details of Jason's 'death'. Peering over the rims of their over-sized sunglasses with feigned compassion and raw curiosity. Or beeping car horns to get my attention before screeching to a halt to lean across their steering wheels and ask how I was faring after the *terrible* news of my husband's rumoured resurrection and accusations of bigamy? I felt my chest tighten. No way – I still wasn't ready to face all that scrutiny, insinuation and explanation.

Tears of fury brimmed at my eyelids. A hard ball of outrage had lodged at the back of my throat. The thirst for revenge was spreading through my body like fast-acting poison.

'Give up? No! Skye's right. A woman has *died* because of Jason. I'm going to chase that man until I catch him or am too weak to blow out my birthday candles.' I looked around, amazed. Was this *me* talking?

'Before this tragic event, we were on the nursery slopes of revenge. Ladies, we are now on revenge's black run.' I couldn't believe how brave I was sounding. It felt like a long-lost skill from my past that I'd forgotten, like tumble-turning in the pool or doing a back bend.

And just like that, the chase was on again.

I emailed Julia and told her not to worry, I'd be away for a week or so more, leaving out any details. Well, there really is no good way to tell your control freak of a daughter that you're stalking a homicidal ex-husband halfway across the world with two strangers.

'This is now, officially, Carly's wake!' Tish shouted, popping the cork of the minibar champagne. 'We didn't know you, Carly, but your death shall be avenged! To the Three Muffkateers.' She raised her glass in a toast. 'TILL DEATH – *or a little light maiming* – DO US PART!'

She took a slug from the bottle, then passed it to me. I guzzled some bubbles then handed the bottle to Skye, who added a generous slurp to her Positive Moon Juice.

And with that, we were off once more, careering around the world on the trail of truth and financial retribution. Oh, and possibly the testicles of our traitorous husband.

PART FOUR

14

The curtain parted in the breeze and a wand of morning light fell across the bed. For a moment I had no idea where I was. My normally jam-packed brain had emptied faster than an embassy after a bomb threat. Through my mental haze I dimly recalled swallowing a fistful of tranquillisers. Why? Oh yes, for a flight somewhere or other . . . Dear god, was I really in *Tanzania*? As I lay listening to Tish's snoring, I pondered how the hell I'd ended up sharing a bed with a woman with a tattoo of Billie Holiday on her arm and one of my bigamist husband on her abdomen. It must be time to contact the European Space Agency and ask them to please locate my minuscule IQ with their Hubble telescope.

A muffled scream from the adjoining room snapped me from my reverie. I jabbed Tish in the ribs. 'Are you awake?'

'No.'

I sprang out of bed and careered into the living room at such speed I knocked my shin on the coffee table. 'Skye, are you all right?' I yelled, adrenalin coursing through my system. Carly's tragic demise had left my nerves shredded. 'What is it?' I looked around frantically, searching for attackers.

Skye was sitting on the lounge where she'd spent the night, her knees drawn up. 'There's a cockroach. In my make-up bag. How do I get rid of it?'

I sighed with relief. 'Gosh, I don't know. Suggest you start a monogamous relationship?' I advised gruffly, rubbing my grazed shin.

'For chrissake! What the hell's happenin'?' A bleary-eyed Tish staggered in behind me, brandishing an umbrella as a weapon.

'It's just a cockroach,' I explained, tipping the insect out onto the floor. 'Thwack it with your thong.'

'My G-string?' Skye asked, bemused.

Tish guffawed. 'Yeah. Just chase it round the room thwackin' it with your knickers. That I've gotta see.'

'Oh, do you mean my *jandal*?' Skye took a sip of her morning hot water with lemon.

'Jandal? Shit. Only a Kiwi would call a thong a bloody jandal. And no more bloody screamin'.'

'Must you spew out profanities first thing in the morning?' I chided.

'I don't "spew out profanities", as you put it, *Gwendoline*. I articulate them very clearly – like the fuckin' lady I am.'

'Why must you always be so argumentative?' I grumbled, re-boiling the jug for tea.

'I'm not argumentative.'

'You're so argumentative, you won't even eat *food* that agrees with you.' With pincered fingers I picked up her takeaway cartons from the night before.

'Oh ha ha ha. Let me just *digest* that remark.' Tish commandeered the kettle and poured the water into her instant coffee.

'It's bad enough you eat all this junk food, but can't you throw out the containers? They stink up the whole room.' I wrenched the kettle from her hand and added more water.

'I'm terribly sorry. But some of us actually like to eat a little more than the occasional sliver of raw friggin' salmon. You've eaten so much salmon on this trip you're probably gettin' the urge to go north and spawn.'

'At least my idea of a "balanced diet" is not having a burger in each hand.'

'Ladies, ladies, take a deep breath. Maybe this will help you channel your positive chi.' Skye whipped back the curtains and there, filling the window, was the majestic wonder of Africa's highest peak and one of the world's biggest volcanos. Mount Kilimanjaro jumped up from the plain before us, wearing a cheeky toupee of snow.

Resorting to impressive levels of subterfuge, Skye had purloined Jason's Hideaway bill. His phone record had helped us track him down to a hotel in a town called Mugumu. He'd also called a safari company that specialised in trips to the Serengeti National Park. While we were slumming it in a no-star motel, the rat was squandering our money on a luxury holiday.

Not only was the fifteen-hour journey from Hanimaadhoo to Tanzania exhausting, but also we'd arrived at the hotel by darkness, so we had no idea of the magnificent vista right outside our window. We moved as one to the glass and peered out in awed admiration.

'So, Tish, Gwen – no more fighting, okay? Disunity could put us in danger.' Skye's voice was leavened with delicate warning. She extracted a small spray bottle from her bag, took aim and squirted a jet of misty liquid my way.

I shielded my face. 'What *is* that?'

'Psychic Vampire Repellent – a protective mist that uses a combination of gem healing and deeply aromatic therapeutic oils to banish bad vibes and shield you from people who may be causing them. Like Jason Riley.' She gave another generous spray around my head, then dispensed a dose of her dubious elixir in Tish's direction.

'Whoa!' Tish seized the spray from her hands. 'What the hell's in it?'

'It's an essential-oil blend of lavender, rosemary and juniper. Its energy-refreshing scent conjures up positivity and safeguards your aura from psychic attacks.'

Skye's hippy mumbo-jumbo reminded me that our very own Dracula was once more within our manicured reach. 'Come on, girls. We have a runaway husband to catch.'

Tish checked her Swatch. 'Shit. Yes. Let's get a wriggle on. Doan wanna miss our next plane.'

As Skye paid the hotel bill, Tish's voice boomed out at me from across the foyer. 'You signed the guest book?!'

'So?' I replied, over my shoulder.

'We're s'posed to be travellin' incognito! You know. *Under cover*. You idiot.'

'Which is why you're SHOUTING IT OUT TO THE ENTIRE AFRICAN CONTINENT,' I scolded back. Tish blew her nose so loudly that for a moment I thought HMS *Foghorn* had moored outside the hotel.

'So much for not drawing attention to ourselves!' I chastised, heading for the foyer doors.

'Oh, I'm sooooo sorry, m'lady.' Tish walked backwards in front of me as though she were a fawning courtier.

'Come along, ladies,' Skye mollified. This was clearly to be her role – the ham in the frenemy sandwich, keeping the peace, and our crazy quest, on track. 'Let's take a moment to cleanse your auras.' The queen of psychic clean placed a hand on each of our heads – hands we shrugged off simultaneously.

'I'd prefer you to telekinetically transport us to Jason's side, armed with a breadknife,' Tish barked.

Our loathing of Jason briefly brought us back together again. But the truce lasted less than five minutes because Tish made a grab for the hire-car keys in Skye's hands then darted off through the sun-blistered metal tables scattered around a green swimming pool full of frogs and into the car park.

'Give me the keys. I'm driving,' I panted, catching up with her.

'No, you're bloody not. I'm the best driver.'

'Oh really? Last night when I pointed out that you'd driven down the street the wrong way, taking out a lamppost and a postbox, do you know what you said? "Oh shit. Am *I* driving?"'

'I was a little jetlagged, that's all. If we let *you* drive, Gwennie, we'll miss the goddamned plane.'

'But at least we won't end up in prison! You, Tish, drive in three speeds – Fast. Incredibly fast. And Guilty, M'Lud.'

Tish snorted with disdain and inserted herself behind the wheel. With bad-tempered reluctance, I flumped into the back seat and for the duration of the drive peeked out, terrified, through my fingers while simultaneously penning my epitaph.

'So?' Tish gloated, when we finally pulled into Arusha airport's hire car area without incident.

'Well, you are improving – I mean, you actually slowed down to go through that last red light. A first,' I said sarcastically. 'Congratulations!'

As we checked in, I looked with trepidation at the tiny plane we were about to board.

'Gwen, you're shaking. What's wrong?' Skye asked.

'Terminal illness,' Tish reported. 'Gwennie here hates terminals.'

This looked to be a flight to take your breath away – if you had any left, that is. I popped another tranquilliser pill and gritted my teeth – it was time to confront Jason, the man voted 'Least Trust-worthy Male to Marry' by wives worldwide.

Tish turned to address us both. 'Chin up. Tits out. Onwards.'

I followed her onto the tarmac to board the tiny four-seater mosquito, fully sedated, my aura cleansed and coated in Psychic Vampire Repellent, parroting our new motto: 'Yep. Chin up. Tits out. Onwards.'

15

The lodge in Mugumu was done out in colonial pith-helmet style with taxidermied animal heads on the walls.

'Jeez-us! Are they taking the pith?' Tish mewled.

I too had always been against hunting but suddenly felt an overwhelming desire to add to the collection of predators the mounted head of a certain husband. That would certainly give new meaning to the term 'trophy wives'.

When we showed the hotel receptionist Jason's photo, she beamed indulgently. Clearly the cad was indeed here, and had worked his charms – as usual. I was tempted to check her hand for an engagement ring. The 'gorrrrrgeous' Jase had left only an hour or so earlier – in fact, the driver had just returned. The receptionist rang his mobile and, after negotiating a suitable remuneration, he agreed to take us to the same location.

Moments later, we threw our backpacks into the boot of his four-wheel drive and clambered aboard. The driver drew to a halt on a grassy field half an hour later – in time to see a green-and-white-striped hot air balloon whooshing up into the broad blue sky.

'Follow that balloon!' Tish ordered a man in overalls who was securing guide ropes. She pointed impatiently to a huge pool of deflated canvas spread out across the field in front of us. 'Give it some Viagra and let's get up, up and away!'

My stomach churned sourly. 'Er, you do remember that I have no head for heights, right?'

'A posh Pom like you?' Tish retorted. 'I bet you're the goddamned Edmund Hillary of social climbin' – as you no doubt said to Prince bloody Charles just the other day.'

Flying in aeroplanes was terrifying enough but at least you were encased in a metal tube. Ballooning, of course, meant being borne upwards in the open air. I started to shrink back towards the vehicle. 'Why do I always feel as though you're trying to kill me, Tish? I mean, what do you have planned for me next? Cordless bungee jumping? Snorkelling with piranhas?'

Skye put a cool, comforting hand on my shoulder. 'Psychologists maintain that the best way to stay young is to try new things – to push yourself out of your comfort zone.'

Nausea rose in my throat as I watched the balloon being slowly inflated by gas jets fuelled from hissing propane cylinders. The balloon rose up off the grass like a huge, hooded cobra. The attached basket lay on its side waiting for passengers. I was a basket case just thinking about getting into that basket.

I glanced around nervously. I knew from years of devouring *National Geographic* magazine that Serengeti comes from a Maasai word meaning 'endless plains'. This place was basically 30,000 kilometres of prairie, and one big smorgasbord of thousands of zebras, gazelles, elephants, lions, hippos, hyenas, ostrich, buffaloes, impala, giraffes, jackals and other wild and wondrous creatures hunting and munching on each other – or trying to leap out of the way so as not to be lunch. It gave a new definition to 'fast food'. In other words, if our balloon went down out there, *bon appétit*!

'I am *not* going to crawl into a picnic hamper held up by a party balloon, inflated by a giant Bunsen burner to skim across herds of ravenous carnivores. Okay?'

'Jeez, Gwennie, you could propel this balloon upwards by your own hot air, j'know that?' Tish moaned, stowing our backpacks aboard. She climbed in next to Skye and whispered something to the big beefy pilot, who immediately scooped me up and stuffed me into the gondola, head-first. Before I could scramble upright and leap out again, there was a whoosh of hot flame up into the belly of the billowing balloon, the guide ropes were flung aside, the pilot leapt aboard, and we were off.

There are many reasons for sudden religious conversion – a particularly good one is hurtling skyward in a laundry basket. My scream was so loud I'm sure it startled a few oceanologists way down in their exploratory submarine in the Mariana Trench. By the time I dared open my eyes, we were 20 metres above the ground. Paralysed with fear, I wondered if the 'lump sum' promised in my travel insurance referred to the number of head injuries I'd sustain when plummeting earthward, post puncture.

A cloud lifted and my face was suddenly bathed in the sun's golden rays, which dripped down over the sweeping savannah like caramelised honey. The huge sky was now clear blue, bar a few curlicues of whipped cream, as though God had hit his shaving dispenser too hard. The warmth and wonder of it all meant I momentarily forgot to be afraid.

We whooshed gently downwards towards a herd of trundling elephants. They were so near I could practically feel the cooling flap of their huge ears – a kind of ear-conditioning. A family of giraffes hidden among the acacia trees periscoped their necks upwards at our approach. We were so close I was worried their long eyelashes would brush our wicker base, but the captain let loose another burst of burning liquid propane and we bobbed up out of their way. Moments later, the pilot pointed out a jam-packed pool of lugubrious hippos and, with astounding agility, steered the big balloon in another downward swoop so we could spy on their morning mud bath. The fifty or so big beasts stomped their stubby legs and flashed their foot-long canines in cavernous yawns of cantankerous greeting.

Tish, who was leaning next to me, whistled with amazement. 'Reminds me of you, in the mornin's, Gwennie.'

Before I could offer up Tish as a hippo hors d'oeuvre, Skye, who was peering through the binoculars, gasped. She shoved the field glasses into my hands and stabbed a finger at the balloon floating far off in front of us, towards the horizon.

As I focused the powerful lens, my eye closed in on a familiar face. The sight of Jason turning to smile at the woman beside him made my blood run ice-cold, despite the hot wind. Jason's smile was so dazzling it could blind you – especially to his faults. He was looking at his companion the way he'd once looked at me – as though I was salted caramel ice cream and he was the spoon. Little black dots danced in front of my eyes and sweat beads popped out on my upper lip. When Jason had wrapped his great arms around me, peering out at the world from the folds of his warm embrace, I'd felt secure and protected. This was the man I'd married. We'd chosen our china pattern together; left a cute joint message on the home answerphone; named our pet terrapins Sheldon and Shelly. Had that really all been a mirage, just like the heat shimmering up off the wide, sage-green Serengeti?

Hot air ballooning was not only the fastest way to get across the vast, untamed tundra, but also the most picturesque. So, who was this new woman Jason was trying to impress? And why, even after all he'd put me through, did I feel a pang of jealousy mingled in with my rage and grief?

I passed the binoculars to Tish, then turned my face away so that nobody would see the insubordinate tear crawling down my cheek.

An hour later, Jason's basket dipped lower and lower until it finally disappeared from view. Tish had instructed our pilot to make no more playful detours – which is why it was only forty minutes later that our balloon also lurched downwards towards the grassy plain. I jabbed Tish in the ribs. 'Has it crossed your mind that with all these prowling marauders on the loose, and us arriving in a giant picnic hamper, perhaps we might be on the menu?'

'If only you were a wise-crackin' quipster like me. I mean, the lions will leave me alone because I taste funny. You? Not so much.'

'Knock, knock . . . Oops. I'm sorry. I seem to be in the wrong joke,' I rejoindered. I was just contemplating which bits of Tish Delaney's anatomy to sacrifice first to any roaming, foaming incisors in the near vicinity, when our incorrigible dirigible hit the earth with a bump and we bounced awkwardly to a standstill.

After a quick pat-down to check all my limbs remained in their original location, I crawled out of the basket, which had tipped onto its side, and wriggled through the tall grass.

By the time I'd scrambled to my feet, Skye had located a safari guide named Berwani who, it turned out, had been chatting to Jason's driver, meaning he knew exactly which road they'd taken. Tish negotiated a fee for him to follow his trail. I noted with some trepidation that he wore a badge with 'Trainee' emblazoned on it.

Now, I often joke that the reason I don't like animals is because I went out with so many as a teenager, but jesting apart, I do prefer them in the past tense – as in, on a plate, soaked in gravy with a parsley garnish. 'Great! I presume we'll be travelling in an armoured vehicle of some kind?' I said, straggling behind this tall, khaki-clad kid with a cheeky face and a goofy grin, as he moved towards a thicket of trees. 'Possibly a tank?'

Berwani smilingly ushered us towards a side-less, window-less safari jeep – there wasn't even a windscreen to, you know, really afford maximum access to pouncing predators. There were just three rows of seats in ascending tiers, completely open to the elements.

'Are you kidding?' I gawped at him. 'What are we? Meals on wheels?' I pointed to the rifle lying across the driver's seat. 'I hope that's a tranquilliser dart . . . For me, I mean.'

'Well, we could always leave you behind, matey,' Tish suggested, gesturing to the wide-open plains around us – plains playing host to the entire cast of *The Lion King*.

The jeep engine spluttered into life and Skye vaulted up onto the highest seat. Tish slid in next to the young driver, batting her eyelashes so forcefully I was worried Berwani would mistake them for spiders copulating and promptly swat the woman.

Hmmm, I thought. Was hiring a trainee guide to hurtle across the African plains in an open jeep completely nuts? I wasn't sure. But chasing your dead husband across the world tends to recalibrate one's view of sanity. I reluctantly threw my backpack into the jeep and hauled myself up into the second tier.

At first, I sat in gritted-teeth terror. But as we darted and dived around and through the most extraordinary menagerie, I once more forgot to be afraid. We were glowered at by snorting buffaloes and laughed at by baboons who tumbled through the grass, babies on their backs. We swerved around warthogs scurrying comedically past nature's hoover – otherwise known as an aardvark. Everywhere I looked elephants contentedly munched on everything in sight, much like guests strip-mining the all-you-can-eat buffet on a cruise ship.

I watched grimly as a slinky jackal tracked a lost gazelle; scavenging hyenas salivating in the shadows. Yes, in Africa everything was trying to eat everything else, but to my mind, Jason, who was proving so strategic with his decoys and traps, was the true top-order predator. I wondered again what female quarry he was currently salivating over. I hadn't been able to see her face through the binoculars, just her expensive highlights, but, whoever she was, the woman needed saving.

Animals use a scent sat nav – all we had to guide us were the plumes of dust sent up by Jason's jeep tyres in the distance. Our one advantage was that he had no idea we were hot on his disreputable heels.

Skye climbed down over the seats and pointed through what should have been the windscreen, 'Can we head him off somehow?'

Berwani said he could try, and we immediately hurtled off the dirt track and bounced and jounced across corduroy country, dodging a city of beige skyscrapers otherwise known as anthills.

'You know they're made from ant excreta,' I volunteered, at full volume, teeth juddering from each jeep impact. 'They're basically poo palaces.'

'Thank you, Davina Attenborough,' Tish shouted over her shoulder. At least I think that is what she said. The jeep was now lurching so violently across the rough terrain it was like doing an Advanced Power Plate class, meaning that what she said sounded more like 'Th . . . k. youu, Dav . . . innnnaaaa . . . Atten . . . borrrrr . . . oughhhh.'

Tish then launched into song, each jounce moving her body closer to our driver. Berwani tapped out the beat on the steering wheel, smiling broadly as she blasted out 'Bumpy Ride' – something about roughing it up before taking it slow, rocking someone like a rodeo complete with a chorus about wanting to 'boom, bang bang with your body-o'.

I'd previously wondered whether Tish wouldn't so much carry a tune as stagger along under the weight of it, but her voice was surprisingly rich and resonating. As we crested a hill, several boom-bang-bang verses later, I zeroed in with the binoculars on our quarry.

Jason came into sharp focus again – sun-kissed features, akubra, khaki shirt rolled up to reveal tanned forearms, movie-star shades. Sitting next to him was a woman whose honey-blonde hair hung well past her shoulders. Detecting the sound of our engine, I watched as Jason signalled his driver to pull over. He swivelled around in his seat and hoisted up his own field glasses. My binoculars were still focused on his face, which is why I was able to see in precise detail the look of perplexed fury that flashed across his countenance when Jason realised that his three ex-wives were bearing down on him like a multi-headed gorgon from Greek mythology.

Seconds later, Jason's driver put his foot flat to the floor, as their jeep screeched off. Berwani upped his acceleration too. I clung to the jeep frame as if riding a bucking bronco, managing to stay in the saddle as we gained ground, bouncing up over the biggest hill in sight, just minutes behind Jason's vehicle. But we were not alone. There below us, galloping across the plain, was a lava flow of fur. 'Wildebeest,' Berwani shouted above the engine's whine.

I gasped in reverent wonderment. One of the greatest miracles of nature was underway right below us: millions of wildebeest were making their annual 800-kilometre migration north from their breeding grounds in the grassy southern plains. The long stampeding line was charging at full pelt from one horizon towards the other – and our road crossed right through their prescribed path. With their big shaggy white beards, and 'windswept and interesting' look, they reminded me of a herd of Billy Connollys galloping gaily by. The sheer mass of the migration was overwhelming. For predators, the wildebeest pilgrimage must be one giant conveyor belt of moreish morsels. But for us it was a hooved tsunami about to block our path and cut us off from our prey.

Jason's driver floored his jeep. It dashed forwards down the dirt road, his guide obviously determined to get through before the four-legged torrent cut off the route. We followed fast behind. Billowing black exhaust smoke, Jason's vehicle skidded across to the other side of the valley, just moments before the stampede thundered into full view.

Berwani drove faster. We flew over a bump in the road and I felt a sickening lurch as though we were hurtling downwards in a wayward lift. The trees cast long shadows which fell upon the road ahead of us like a net. My lying, cheating husband was within our nail-gnawing grasp. Tish made a fist and jerked her elbow back hard. 'Yes! We're gonna make it!'

For a fleeting second, I too thought we'd be able to cross in time. Berwani made a final and valiant dash, but the wall of wildebeest was bearing down too fast. We screamed in unison as our driver swerved hard to the right at the last millisecond, slamming on the brakes. The engine made an emphysemic sound, the jeep juddered and spun, then crunched to a halt and flipped onto its slide, flinging us out onto the dirt.

I saw Tish hit the ground beside me, landing right in a huge patch of animal poo a split second after me. I thought as I heard the plop of the poop impact, ah yes, this is why I joined you on this trip, Tish – I just couldn't resist the glamour of it all. And then I blacked out.

16

Winching open one eye, it took me a moment to realise that I was still in the land of the living. Dazed and winded, all I could do then was lie there, awestruck, watching the wall of furry flesh galloping and gambolling past in a permanent peak hour. My anger and pain evaporated at the wonder of nature playing out on the plains before me.

'We've lost the prick! I can't bloody believe it!' Tish howled, propping herself up on her elbows. She was wearing a buffalo poo patty on her head at a jaunty angle. 'Skye!? Hey, hippy chick, you all right?'

Skye wandered into view, her phone aimed at the cantering wildebeest. 'I'm filming for an Insta post. Brilliant footage.'

'Hoofage, really. For the *Hoofington Post.*' I barked out a laugh – a loud, slightly insane laugh, as in one-decibel-short-of-a-straitjacket. Relief at our survival had me teetering on the edge of hysteria. But I was soon sobered by an announcement from Berwani that the radio was smashed and the jeep, still on its side, undriveable. He tried the ignition a few more times but the engine gave the same croupy yelp.

'Does anyone have signal?' Skye asked, holding her phone aloft and moving about, optimistically.

Tish headed to the highest point at hand – a mound of earth not far from our stricken vehicle. She scrambled to the top and waved her phone about a bit but dropped it in alarm when the mound erupted. Ants. And when I say 'ants', I'm talking huge African ants – each one the size of a sumo wrestler on steroids and with the capacity to bench press 60 kilos. She ran, shrieking, into Berwani's arms, who brushed her down, although I noted that Tish made him check her *all* over. And over and over and over.

As he brushed, Berwani explained that normal procedure was to stay with the vehicle, but as the sun was so low in the sky, there was nothing else to do but walk to the main road, ten kilometres away. As he pored over the map, I noticed that he was no longer wearing his trademark goofy grin.

I wasn't finding much to laugh about either. 'Ten kilometres? Um . . . If you think I'm walking through the lion-riddled plains of East Africa, you don't need a map, Berwani, you need a brain transplant.'

Tish, a bushie by birth, took charge, nonchalantly shouldering her backpack. 'Anything we should know, before settin' out?'

'Yep,' Berwani replied. 'If an elephant charges you – pray.'

I felt helpless – like being stuck on a ski lift with a QAnon supporter. I looked around desperately. It was then I glimpsed a snake slithering from the rocks, probing our scent with a gossamer tongue. I really had no choice but to tag along, scouring the bushes for irascible pachyderms.

Now, the aim of every safari is to see the 'Big Five' – elephants, lions, buffalo, leopards and rhinos. If I'd been at my book club, which, I realised, was where I was supposed to be right about now, sipping a nice cold chardonnay and nibbling an olive, I'd be discussing the literary Big Five – Salman Rushdie, Margaret Atwood, Kazuo Ishiguro, Hilary Mantel and Chimamanda Ngozi Adichie. But no. I was traipsing, unprotected, through a carnivore-encrusted savannah.

As I trudged along behind the others, I couldn't help but notice the big sweeping wings of the vultures swooping and circling ominously overhead. The Serengeti is a time tunnel – it transports you back to the way the world was long before humans, when animals roamed freely and that great matriarch Mother Nature ruled supreme. And here I was, completely at her mercy. This was so far out of my comfort zone it wouldn't even register on my psychological sat nav.

But as we walked on, the warm wind silently moved through the grass, making the dangling branches of the sun-sequinned acacia trees dance, the rustle of dry leaves a murmuring accompaniment. The majesty of the sweeping savannah had just begun to work its relaxing magic when we rounded a thicket and walked smack-bang into a grazing rhino.

Unsurprisingly, my life as a bookworm had left me curiously ill-equipped to deal with a rhinoceros in the wild. My most arduous ordeal on any given day is teaching some recalcitrant pupil on detention the importance of civics and citizenship. The rhino stared at us with haughty disdain. Welded to the spot, we were close enough to see the heat rippling off its thick hide. Following Berwani's example, I backed slowly away, my heart beating like a jungle drum sending out a signal of distress.

Once we were at a safe distance, I turned to Berwani and whispered urgently, 'Okay, now we've seen a rhino, that must narrow our chances of encountering another of the Big Five, right?'

Tish put her hand on Berwani's muscled forearm. 'I know they reckon rhinos are the most endangered species but, I dunno, a non-predatory bloke in touch with his emotions – now, *that's* a rare breed,' she flirted, her eyelashes in overdrive.

'I mean it, Berwani. Tish is the only predatory feline I want to encounter out here.' I glanced around nervously. 'Lions, leopards, cheetahs – they really have too many claws for a supposedly friendly nature.'

'Much like *you*, after that catty remark.' Tish flexed her manicured talons and made as to scratch me.

My angry eyeroll must have been audible as Skye immediately sprayed me with an emergency spritz of something she called Psychic Calming Chill mist – because clearly, nothing prevents a cardiac arrest like a whiff of rosewater, right? Not to mention wild animal pacification. To say I felt a tad under-equipped is the biggest understatement since Wuhan medics said 'A few locals seem to have a touch of flu.' Especially when I glanced up and glimpsed some trademark spots in the trees. Too terrified to speak, I pointed towards the leopard lounging nonchalantly on a branch way above our heads.

Berwani told us to 'freeze', which was a superfluous command as I'd lost all movement in my limbs. 'I thought leopards were the Brigitte Bardot of the animal world – elusive and reclusive?' My voice was hoarse with terror.

'If she attacks, just clap your hands and shout, to look bigger.'

I shot Berwani a narrow-eyed sideways look. This advice sounded about as effective as standing up to Freddy Krueger with a fondue fork. The big cat stretched gracefully and yawned.

When it stood on all fours, I didn't want to clap my hands, I wanted to make like an ostrich and bury my quivering head in the sand. But the cat's elegance and poise were so captivating, I remained transfixed.

Casting a desultory glance our way, it insouciantly climbed to a higher branch and put its head down to sleep in the setting sun. Relieved, I turned to see Tish clutching Berwani's arm, her body pressed up against his, despite her cool and collected expression.

'Clearly a case of professional courtesy,' I said. 'I mean, a cougar is part of the cat family, after all.'

'I am *way* too young to be a cougar,' Tish growled back at me.

Skye's Psychic Calming Chill mist was to be in demand three more times during our impromptu sortie. The next nozzle-squeezing moment occurred an hour later. My heart had just calmed down when Berwani handed me the binoculars. Just ahead of us, fourteen or so lion cubs were playfully nipping and teasing each other in the long grass.

'Where there's a creche, there's a mum, right?' I was pretty sure that the face I turned to our guide had the look of a woman whose life support system has just been turned off. Before Berwani could answer, the lioness padded into view. My instinctive reaction was to climb the nearest tree and pull the trunk up after me. But all I could do was stand and gawp while my heart started up on its frantic drum solo once more. Oh well, a teenage dream come true: I was about to make the cover of *National Geographic* – 'Middle-aged Mum, Eaten in Serengeti'.

'Christ. I really don't want to get eaten . . . Well, not by an animal anyway . . .' Tish launched her most coquettish smile in our guide's direction.

I ogled her with astonishment. 'How can you flirt at a time like this?'

Tish shrugged. 'How can you *not*?'

Luckily, the lioness had just made a fresh kill of impala, so she showed little interest in us. She was busy taking pride in her pride. The more I watched the more she reminded me of any working mum on the school run, licking faces clean, chiding naughty ones, teasing shy ones, nudging them all on towards dinner – impala *plat du jour*.

In hushed tones, Berwani told us that while the lion is king of the jungle – 'the mane attraction', Tish interrupted, her eyelash-batting average now rivalling Don Bradman's – it's the lionesses who do most of the hunting and all of the cub-raising.

'It's the same in the urban jungle,' I told him.

In a reverential whisper, Berwani explained that the lion lives with a harem, servicing all the females in the mating season.

'No wonder Jason likes it here,' I muttered tartly to my fellow Mrs Rileys.

When Berwani spotted the patriarch, dozing under a distant tree, I noticed with alarm that our guide had shrugged his tran-quilliser gun off his shoulder and was now holding it ready. 'So, how many bullets are in that thing?' I whispered, dry-mouthed.

The lion was 'on his honeymoon', Berwani told us. Crouch-ing down behind a rocky outcrop, upwind of the big beast, we watched through our binoculars as a young lioness padded to his side, then, with a low growl, nipped his neck.

'She will now present herself for sex,' Berwani whispered. 'A lion mates every fifteen minutes during his seven-day honey-moon period. So, lucky for us, he's exhausted.'

Tish broke into a hypnotic, husky-voiced rendition of 'Fever' by Peggy Lee. While softly singing about fever all through the night as she stared straight into Berwani's eyes, she executed her pathetic mating-spider-eyelash-batting routine again. It made me long once more for my book club, exchanging views with literary lionesses, instead of watching her pathetic mating ritual.

Berwani signalled for us to move and we stole quietly away. It wasn't until the mauve tinge of sundown started creeping across the hills that we finally glimpsed a sliver of white dusty sand in the distance. With the main road in sight, my heart finally left my mouth. I stopped to wipe sweat from my brow and looked up to see a giant hat coming towards me. With their tall, skinny white legs and that mass of feathery hair on top, ostriches resemble super-models, strutting daintily about in the search of a piña colada.

'Lie down,' Berwani ordered.

'But it's only Kate Moss in a hat.'

'Ostriches run at a hundred kilometres an hour.' The guide tugged me earthward. 'They can run and kick forward and backward at the same time. One talon can rip open a car door.'

'Dear god, is there anything here that isn't trying to kill me?' No sooner had I whimpered this complaint than a blur of blond fur sprang out of the grass in the distance and accelerated from, it seemed, nought to eighty in three seconds, faster than a Ferrari, each stride about 8 metres long, in pursuit of Kate Moss.

'Ah, the cheetah is the fastest animal in Africa,' Berwani marvelled.

Bar Tish Delaney, I wanted to add, amazed at how fast she was putting her moves on our muscular young guide.

A hulking hyena also now skulked out of the shadows closer to us and cackled maliciously, saliva drooling from his massive jaws. With his huge shoulders he reminded me of a steroid-addled bouncer at a seedy nightclub.

When you're under threat, a lot of thoughts cross your mind. Mainly, the desperate hope that the Dalai Lama is right about reincarnation. Thank you, Jason. Thank you very fucking much for getting me into this mess. Anger suddenly shook me between its jaws like a lion shakes a half-dead gazelle, and I found myself hissing at the snarling creature, windmilling my arms with all my might. The hyena looked at me as if to say 'Take a chill pill, sis' and slunk away.

Utterly fed up, I thrust my head forward like the ostrich and ran flat-out for the road. When I reached the ribbon of dirt, I could have kissed it. Even better, there was a Land Rover approaching in a shroud of dust. Tish, Skye and Berwani caught up with me and we waved our arms in SOS semaphore. The jeep's driver slowed down then hit the brakes hard as a herd of zebras clippity-clopped across the road in front of him. Their perfectly rounded, striped bottoms, all peachy and plump, swung like fleshy pendulums on shapely little legs.

'It's a zebra crossing – literally,' I marvelled.

Tish snorted out a laugh. Relief at our survival instigated a truce. Skye linked her arms through ours and an unexpected camaraderie ensued.

'Should we get drunk tonight?' I asked my dusty companions. 'A) Yes. B) A. C) B.'

'A, B and C,' Tish cackled.

Even Skye agreed that after the day's misadventure, alcohol just might have the edge on her Psychic Calming Chill mist.

17

The Land Rover belonged to the manager of a nearby lodge and he took us in for the night. The timber lodge was all wafting, flowy white curtains, drapey mozzie nets, cushion-strewn hammocks and decorative native artefacts. Despite the luxurious comfort, it didn't take long for the euphoria of our survival to morph into despondency. Exhausted, we nursed our wounds and many gin and tonics on a spacious, elegant balcony overlooking a bustling watering hole, where monkeys chattered with cocktail-party volume and vivacity.

Tish slammed down her phone with such force that it made me jump. 'If I wanna make my next remortgage payment, we've gotta find that man,' she spat out grievously. 'Thanks to the fly-blown, two-faced sonofabitch, I've worked my way up from nothin' . . . to a state of destitution.'

This prompted me to log on to my own accounts, only to scowl once more at the gaping void that had also been gouged into my finances by my errant husband. 'Ditto. The only effective way I'll be able to keep my bills down now is with a paperweight.'

'Me too,' Skye sighed. Even our resident Ms Pollyanna had lost her perkiness. Skye had been hunched over her iPad since our arrival two hours earlier. The woman had spent so much time peering at her computer screen, I was worried she'd need to reboot her eyeballs and buy her brain some extra memory.

'Any luck tracking Jason down?' I passed her a plate of nuts, which she ignored.

'I've rung around the other local lodges. Nada. I thought he might be travelling under a false name, so I emailed his photo to all the nearby resort receptions too. But still nothing.'

'All I can say is thank Christ I haven't given up recreational alcoholism.' Tish chugged her Caipirìnha, then ordered another.

'I hate to say this, ladies,' I felt the warmth leave Skye's voice, like the cold drop in a summer's night. 'We may have to admit defeat.'

'No! There's gotta be a way to find the dipshit. What about online? I mean, even the friggin' *Pope* leaves a digital footprint.' Tish commandeered and downed my Mai Taị in one gulp. 'Come on, Gwen. You're the smart one, or so you keep tellin' us. Can't you go full Miss Marple?'

'I'd like to help track him down,' I added, flicking through a long list of emails from students and colleagues asking when I'd be back at work, followed by quite a few electronic moans from my over-protective daughter, who clearly wanted to ground me until senescence set in. 'But I'm a total technophobe. My computer has a sign on it that says "Abandon all hope, ye who press Enter here".'

'I just can't stand Jason getting away with this,' Skye lamented. 'If only we knew some kind of computer whiz. Don't you two know anyone? Tish, what about your kids – are they computer-savvy?'

Tish starting vaping, furiously. 'Nah. They're obsessed by TikTok and Snapchat and takin' pouty piccies for Instagram, but that's it. And my pals are all old rockers. They're more the type to send smoke signals and carrier pigeons, j'know?'

As Tish spoke I was scanning an email from Max, informing me that he'd installed a video doorbell that would send instant notifications directly to my phone. He went into detail – something about the 1080p FHD viewing, communications being integrated into the device and how the video recording triggered by motion detection would stream the live video feed via Google Chromecast and Echo Show, whatever the hell that meant. 'Well . . .' I said tentatively, 'There is my son. I think I could ask Max for help?'

Tish turned her laser-beam eyes my way. 'At what? Train spottin'?'

'Max is very intelligent,' I replied curtly. 'And he's working in some kind of IT, security role for the government, though don't ask me exactly what. He's not allowed to talk about it.'

Tish choked on an ice cube and spluttered out the next words. '*What?* And you're tellin' us this *now*?'

'My Max is on the spectrum . . .' I began to explain to Skye, but Tish interrupted.

'For chrissake. You have a son who works in cyber security and you didn't think to harness his help before now?'

'No, as a matter of fact, I didn't think of it. I mean, we've been hot on Jason's heels till today. Plus, the last person I want to involve in this debacle is my lovely boy.' My lips felt thin as a razor cut.

'Why the hell not?' Tish rolled a cold can of tonic water across her chest to combat a hot flush, although in truth she'd have needed a distillery to cool a chest that size.

I looked askance at my irksome accomplice. 'First off, it will mean breaking the news that his stepfather is not actually dead.

And secondly, I will have to tell him and Julia that their mother is spending what remains of their inheritance chasing said conman across the globe with a menopausal bikie chick and a psychic vampire slayer.'

Skye nodded. 'Right, yes. I do see your point.'

Tish snatched my mobile off the table top and plonked it into my lap. 'Call the kid. We bloody well need him.'

'Hang on, can we think a bit more about this? As I said, Tish, I *really* don't want to involve my son. Can't we just employ some International Hitman of Ambiguous Nationality? I've read enough Graham Greene and Le Carré to know those men are out there.'

'Sadly, even though it feels like it, we're not in a novel now, Gwen,' Skye patted my hand, consolingly. 'This is real life – our real life. And it's unravelling.'

'Come on, Gwennie baby,' Tish said, drumming her scarlet nails on the table top. 'Places to go, people to do.' She puffed some vape smoke in my direction. Coughing, I stood and walked away from her Krakatoan fumage to the side of the veranda. I sat on a swing seat overlooking a herd of elephants bathing in the watering hole, thought about our options and checked the time. It was late in Australia but my boy is a night owl, so I took a deep breath and dialled Max.

My unemotional offspring took the knowledge of Jason's resurrection and the reason for his mother's absence in his practical stride. 'Copy that,' was his response. He also explained that he should be able to locate Jason Riley without too much technical trouble.

'Apparently,' I told my cohorts, after concluding the call, 'with a little light hacking, Max can trace Jason through his credit card use. He's promised to get back to me in the morning with info.'

Tish looked suitably chagrined. She raised her hands like a teller in a bank robbery. 'Wow. I take it back. I underestimated that kid of yours. He could be our secret weapon of ninja kick-arsery. The manhunt's back on, mateys! Doan cha wanna strip naked and run around the resort singin' "Bang-Shang-A-Lang"? Or is that just me?'

The idea of spending any more time in Tish Delaney's obnoxious company suddenly filled me with prescient fatigue. Exasperation must have shown on my face, because Skye promptly said, 'So, the manager has organised two rooms. Gwen, why don't you take one and Tish and I can share the other? I know we're all very different but we do have a common goal,' she pep-talked. 'So, let's just try to keep things in a positive but neutral gear, okay?'

'Stalkin' your ex to use his testicles as maracas is not what I'd call a neutral activity, would you?' Tish chortled loudly enough to draw the attention of the other lodge guests, who looked our way with a mix of curiosity and mild disapproval.

'Excuse our friend,' Skye announced, her smile on full wattage. 'She's a little bit tipsy . . .'

'Either that or she's doing an impersonation of a speed bump,' I added, pointing towards Tish who had slid off her chair and was now taking a cat nap on the zebra skin rug by the campfire. We tried to rouse her but she muttered something incomprehensible and pushed us away. Skye slipped a cushion under her head and she and I adjourned to the open-air restaurant by a turquoise infinity pool. Having watched animals devouring each other all day, a ravenous hunger now came over me. We tucked into local dishes of tender, grilled meat called nyama choma, marinated beef known as mshikaki, a delicious fish curry named mtuzi wa samaki, and ndizi-nyama – plantains with meat and spicy pilau rice. We noshed in companionable silence until I lay down my knife and fork with a gratified sigh.

'Dear god, I've eaten so much I must now resemble our hot air balloon. I could attach a basket to my undercarriage and take you on your own escapade over the Serengeti,' I told her.

Skye gave a tinkling little laugh of appreciation. Despite her hippy-trippy inclinations, the pulchritudinous Kiwi was genuinely sweet and kind. The woman radiated such warmth you could positively tan in her glow – I needed psychological suncream just to talk to her. Skye's typical response to an inquiry about her wellbeing was, 'The question's not about how *I am,* but how *you* are?' In other words, the gentle geologist was the antithesis to Tish Delaney, who positively delighted in telling us *all* about herself in between bossing us around. Put it this way, the tattooed jazzer was so stroppy that when she walked through an airport metal detector, the security staff were tempted to take off their *own* shoes. Once more, I marvelled at how Jason could have married all three of us – it was like mixing oysters, custard and gorgonzola.

Gazing up at the velvet sky studded with diamantes, a cool breeze wafting up from the plains, I felt truly relaxed for the first time since I'd heard the news of Jason's alleged shark attack. Bone-tired, I was sure I would at last sleep deeply, undisturbed by nightmares. It was a relief when I finally unlocked the door to my room and kicked off my shoes in the gloaming. I was just exhaling a relieved sigh when I saw my bedspread move. My heart accelerated and I was instantly back on the Serengeti surrounded by marauding beasts. I approached the bed commando-style, as though confronting Boko Haram vigilantes. What could it be? A huge spider? A snake? *Jason*? I thought with a sickening thud – although surely that was a tautology. I flicked on the bedside lights while simultaneously whipping back the bedspread to find . . . Tish lying naked, entwined with our safari driver.

Minutes later I was banging on Skye's door. 'There's a creature loose in my room! Berwani's trouser snake.'

'Okaaaay.' Skye looked a little taken aback. 'Don't judge her too harshly,' she placated, ushering me in. 'Tish's had a tough time. We mustn't suffocate her aura.'

I clutched a pillow, menacingly. 'Fine, but what about the rest of her?'

For some reason Skye insisted that she had to sleep in an east–west alignment, which meant I spent a fitful night with her bum in my face. After tossing and turning and fuming in our plush double bed for a few hours, I abandoned all hope of sleep, crept out to the balcony and slumped into the hammock. But whenever I looked out into the bush, some exotic insect was blinking its 9,000,754,889,002 eyes at me. I slapped at my skin, having clearly become a pet for mosquitoes. African mosquitoes are the size of eagles. They're so big they probably have to file flight plans . . . but they were *still* not as nigglingly annoying as Tish bloody Delaney.

Pre-dawn, I came to the conclusion that for me this wild goose chase was over. I just couldn't take any more of the trike-riding, rough-and-ready jazz singer's selfish, crude and crass behaviour. I would make my announcement at breakfast – a breakfast for which Tish arrived an hour late, yawning luxuriantly.

'Tired?' I asked, testily.

'Nope. Not at all. Though I only got about two hours shut-eye.'

'You look pretty good on it,' Skye said, tactfully. 'What's your secret? I mean, you drink and smoke . . . How do you keep your youth?'

'On a tight leash, locked in her hotel bedroom,' I snipped. 'Sorry. *My* hotel bedroom.' I rubbed my shoulders to emphasise the cricked neck I'd got from all that mosquito-swatting on the hotel hammock. 'You are definitely doing the walk of shame this morning, Patricia.'

'Ya mean the stride of pride?' Tish said, strutting around the table to throw herself down onto the banquette opposite me. 'And, yeah, I bloody am. Not sure how it happened. One minute we were havin' a drink and the next thing I know he's gnawin' my knickers off. He even made cute little squirrel noises as he nuzzled my nether regions. He flipped around that bed as though performin' gymnastics at the Olympics. And let me tell you, kiddos, the boy was goin' for gold.'

'Berwani's a trainee ranger,' I castigated. 'Did he wear pyjamas with little feet?'

'He's twenty-one, actually. And who are you, anyway – the chastity patrol?' Tish griped. 'You know, life can be bloody wonderful – you should try not to miss it.'

Skye attempted to change the subject by asking if I'd checked my emails. I logged on and passed her my phone.

'Do you know what a cliché you are, Tish?' I continued. 'Lusting after a park ranger? It's probably not even legal. But no need for details. I'll just wait for the tabloid exposé.'

'Rack off. That's not a head on your shoulders, Gwennie, it's a giant chip you're luggin' around. You're just jealous. As you should be, 'cause it was a transformative shag.' She gave a Cheshire Cat grin. 'The bloke's got the stamina of a naval SWAT team.'

'I am *not* jealous of a meaningless one-night stand. Where is the romance in that?'

'Hey, at least there's no risk of discoverin' that the man you love has another wife . . . or two, or three,' Tish blurted resentfully.

I couldn't argue with that. 'Okay, but just because Jason's antics make Dante look like Disney doesn't mean you should—'

'Who?' Tish interrupted me, looking nonplussed.

'Dante.' Oh god, I mused. She probably thought I was referring to how Italians cook spaghetti. 'The great writer of—'

'See? That's your trouble right there. You spend waaaaaay too much time readin' and not nearly enough time gettin' laid.' Tish basked on the banquette like a lioness in the sun.

'Getting drenched in a stranger's bodily fluids is not my idea of fun. *Nor* is being chucked out of my bed at the last minute.'

'So, when's your vibrator due for its annual service?' Tish turned to address Skye over the fruit platter. 'Gwendoline's vibrator is so high-powered that when she charges it, street lights flicker and whole cities dim.'

But Skye wasn't listening. Her face was naked in its excitement. 'France!' Skye shouted. 'He's in France.'

'What?' we asked in unison.

'Your brilliant son has found Jason,' Skye explained in the hushed tones of awe usually reserved for Catholic miracles like weeping statues of the Virgin Mary.

Tish sprang upright, executing the kind of jubilant jump normally associated with winning the lottery. 'Yes!' She gave a bubble of a laugh and choked on her own vape smoke.

'Max has been snouting around and discovered that Jason got the last flight back to Kilimanjaro last night and leaves later today for *Paris*.' Skye showed us Max's email. 'So, Paris?' she asked, her eyes gleaming. 'Are you up for it, ladies?'

'Bonjour!' Tish ejaculated joyously. Her voice bore like titanium augers into my brain.

'Gwen?' Skye persisted.

'Um . . .' I glanced with disdain at the jazz singer. She reeked of sex while I smelt of soap and minty breath. I needed another adventure in that woman's coarse company as much as I required my own moon-landing module. I was not built for these kinds of escapades. My normal life was like a door with the security chain in place – I answered every knock by opening it a crack and saying suspiciously, 'Yes?' Living dangerously for me was running over on a parking meter and being late to write my students' report cards. In fact, marrying Jason and this deranged jaunt were the only reckless things I'd ever done in my whole life. Before meeting Jason, deciding what recipe to try out for my kids when I got home from school was about the highlight of my day.

That thought reminded me of my warm, cosy kitchen. I wondered if either of my offspring had watered the orchids on the windowsill? Would there be a primordial ooze in the salad crisper? Max would never remember to add salt to the dishwasher. And what if the rinse aid was low? I *really* should be at home digging the compost and tending my herbaceous borders.

Skye seized my hands. 'Please don't leave me,' she begged, all wide-eyed. 'I need you.'

'Come on, matey,' Tish added, 'Skye's right. As much as I hate to admit it, we do need you. I mean, for chrissake, Jason Riley is your *Mastermind* specialist subject. You know the mongrel better than either of us.'

'Don't you want revenge?' Skye asked me.

Revenge? I thought sarcastically to myself. I hardly ever thought of revenge . . . well, not for more than *twenty-four hours a day, seven days a week*. My need for justice was like a craving for chocolate after a 5–2 clean-eating keto diet. Looking from Tish to Skye and back again, I gave a world-weary sigh of resignation.

'So you'll come?' Skye clapped her hands together as if in prayer.

My phone suddenly vibrated. It was Julia on Skype, looking furious. Max had obviously brought her up to speed on my shenanigans. My darling daughter carries her responsibilities as carefully as Royal Doulton china, which is why she could not understand my recklessness. A technological glitch meant that every word she launched my way had an echo, so I got to hear twice over what an Irresponsible. Irresponsible. Gullible. Gullible. Mother. Mother. I. I. Am. Am.

Thankfully the connection fizzled out. My companions were looking at me.

'You'll come?' Skye reiterated.

'Well, I do have a needlepoint seminar to get to . . .' I replied flippantly before adding with verve, 'Okay. I'm coming!'

Actually, though, the real reason I couldn't give up the quest was because Max had gone to all this trouble to help me. I loved my son so much but I'd never been able to completely reach him. A solemn and solitary child, his dad's death had driven him deeper into himself. In truth, we didn't have a great deal in common. This would be our first real mother-and-son project since we'd made a crocodile from a shoebox when he was in kindy. Perhaps this man-hunt would bring us closer? And, I finally admitted to myself, Jason had often been offhand, even condescending to my son. I'd tried to deny it, but the niggling truth had always been there in the background, like the hum of a faulty refrigerator. His betrayal had forced me to enter the room of mirrors and take a good long look at myself – and what I saw was a woman tired of feeling distant from one child and judged by the other.

'There have got to be some new rules, though,' I said. 'No more strange men in my bed, Tish. No more getting spritzed by organic sprays, Skye. And if there's time, I want more culture. If we really are going to Paris, we might as well get our money's worth out of Jason's credit card. I want art galleries, museums, monuments, libraries . . .'

Tish gave an actressy shudder.

Of course, had I known what was in store for us, I'd have run straight down the hill and dived head-first into that watering hole, crocs and all. But my rage against Jason had cooled and solidified into a *Titanic*-demolishing iceberg, lying just under the surface in wait. I couldn't wait to destroy him.

PART FIVE

18

Arriving at Charles de Gaulle airport, my relief at being off the plane mingled with a nostalgic joy at being back in the northern hemisphere for the first time in thirty-five years. But these happy feelings were soon superseded by a fear we'd be arrested by the fashion police telling us, 'I'm sorry, mesdames, but you're just not chic enough to rub shoulder pads with Parisians.'

The only requirement I have ever made of my attire is that it be flame-retardant. I've always thought that haute couture is a big fat nothing – or a super thin nothing, really – with its nose in the air. But clearly that attitude was not going to cut the sartorial mustard in Paris. The French passengers in the passport queue were giving us a look that screamed 'Never darken my Dior again.'

I glanced down at my dusty jeans, sweat-stained T-shirt and trainers. I was wearing nice underwear, but had no doubt I'd still be deported – for wearing lingerie above my station.

Tish was even more of an eyesore in her khaki shorts, high-heeled biker boots and sequinned bustier. Skye's white linen trousers and pale silk shirt might have passed the French flared-nostril test, except for the fact that they were infused with safari dust.

Despite my misgivings, when our train arrived at the Gare du Nord and I caught my first glimpse of Paris, my spirits were riding higher than my fancy lace cami-knickers. I also began to wonder if French men had X-ray vision because as soon as we left the station, they began to flirt in earnest.

Living in Australia, England or America, a woman of a certain age gets so used to a lack of male attention she starts to think she possesses the sexual magnetism of a bit of limp lettuce. A woman over sixty begins to suspect that Interpol will put out a chastity alert on her – 'Not Wanted, Dead or Alive'. But Parisian men made me feel fluent in body language. Tish articulated it best. 'Wow,' she enthused, her eyes a-twinkle, 'these French fellas could pole vault around Paris on their own appendages. It's friggin' magnifique!'

'You speak French?' Skye asked hopefully, poring over her phrase book.

'Nah. My entire French vocab consists of five words: "rendez-vous", "champagne", "liaison", "lingerie" and "croissant". But I'm gettin' the feelin' I won't be needin' any more lingo than that,' she winked, coating on an extra layer of red lipstick.

We squeezed into the back of a taxi. I barely had time to close the door before the driver screeched away from the kerb, sending us flying backwards in our seats.

'What side of the road do they drive on here?' Skye, sand-wiched between us, asked, nervously.

'They're French.' Tish shrugged with her eyebrows. 'They drive on both sides. At the same time.'

'Well, *you'll* be right at home then.' I wound down the window to avoid her vape fumes.

'Oh, go drink bidet water, poodle breath.'

Two French words Tish and I would never master, it seemed, were 'entente' and 'cordiale'.

As usual, Skye aimed her nozzle our way, but we were spared a dousing because the taxi suddenly lurched to a stop outside a little hotel in the Marais. Skye had told us she'd found accommodation on some internet site at a knockdown price. Clearly this was because that's what the building needed – to be knocked down. Immediately. The crooked tenement was so old and rickety I suspected the only thing keeping it standing was the fact that the woodlice had their arms linked. But, I consoled myself, at least it did have wifi.

We staggered up a spiral staircase to a *La Bohème*-ish attic on the top floor. Here we found a saggy cot and a rickety double bed, which two of us were going to have to share due to budget constraints – the money we saved on accommodation we planned to splurge on fancy French cuisine. Exhausted from the flight, we draped ourselves across the bed, the rusty mattress springs moaning under our combined weight, and logged on to get the latest update from my supersonic, monosyllabic Max.

'Affirmative – Jason in Paris. Has adopted alias. Need time to locate,' was his succinct electronic missive. 'Sit tight.'

If only Julia could be so concise. Her email told me how saddened she was that I'd disappeared overseas without informing her; why did she have to find out through her *brother*? She concluded at length with her deeply felt concern that I was having some kind of breakdown.

When I relayed Max's message to my companions, Tish took a hit off her vape pen. 'An alias? We must've spooked the slimeball.

I mean, he was ballsy enough to marry all three of us under the same name. And get engaged to poor Carly.'

'I wonder what pseudonym he's using? Jason the Hun? Attila the Jason. Jason the Impaler? That's what he'd have been called in medieval, feudal times. We should bring that tradition back. Nominative determinism would save so much heartbreak.'

Skye's delicate brows knitted. 'If Jason's using an alias it means he's got smarter about covering his tracks.' She turned to me. 'You really have faith that Max will track him down?'

'My son can put fragments of info together so quickly, he makes Sherlock Holmes look like Inspector Clouseau,' I found myself bragging. It felt so good to be proud of eccentric Max instead of apologising for him. As we waited for his next instructions, we chatted convivially.

'How old is your boy again?' Skye asked.

'Twenty-five. He's moving out to live an independent life . . . just as soon as I wash and iron his clothes so he can pack them.'

Tish snorted. 'I hear ya. I send my kids an email every birthday remindin' them that check-out time's age twenty-one.'

'Do you know what I got for Mother's Day this year? Something I've always wanted. The keys to my car.'

Tish chuckled. 'Rule Number One. Never lend your car to anythin' you grew in your womb and birthed.'

'Do you think there's a statute of limitations on maternal self-sacrifice? Julia's got me fully booked on dog-sitting duties for the rest of my natural life. And once she has babies, I'll be the unpaid, full-time nanny, no doubt. What about *your* daughter? What's she doing this whole time you're away?'

'Sienna? Um, her hair and eyelash extensions, but no course-work extension, that's for friggin' sure.'

'So, what does she want to be when she finishes uni?'

'At this rate, a sexagenarian,' she dead-panned.

'What about Zack? What does he do?'

'As little as possible. His latest idea is to go find himself in an ashram in Bali.'

'What did you say about that?'

'I said hey, I have no idea who I am either, but I doubt the Balinese will bloody know.'

Just as we were starting to relax and feel a little more confident about our crazy quest, we were abruptly rerouted into a cul-de-sac when the hotel receptionist rang to say that our credit card had been declined. Either Jason had finally realised we'd been spending his money or we'd maxed it out.

'What now?' I asked Tish and Skye. Our heads swivelled like supermarket trolley wheels as we looked from one to the other, searching for a solution. Forget trolleys. With no money, we were basically in a reinforced handcart bound for financial hell.

Skye suddenly fluttered her fingers. 'Hmm. I could sell my engagement ring. It's a two-carat diamond Theo Fennell Athena. It's worth thousands – they'd fund our escapade for a while.'

'Jeez, kid. You'd do that for us?' Tish asked, incredulous.

Skye shrugged, sliding the ring from her slender finger and placing it on the faded bedspread. 'Using my ring money to track Jason down and get back what he stole is an investment in my future.'

'Are you sure they're not fake diamonds?' I asked, warily. 'Like everything else in these pathetic marriages of ours?'

Tish examined the ring with an expert eye. 'Those gems are real. It's the classic conman trick, you know, to splash out on jewellery. Gives the impression the guy's rich,' she elucidated. 'Helps quell any nigglin' doubts about the depth of his passion and pockets. Mind you, I'm sure it's me and Gwen that paid for it!' Tish wrestled her much less flamboyant ring from her finger. 'Don't reckon my ring's worth as much as my bloody manicure. Hell, come to think of it, my last shellack manicure lasted longer than my friggin' marriage.' She laid the ring next to Skye's. 'Gwennie?'

I gazed at my hands. 'Why not? This wedding ring's as useful to me now as a chocolate frying pan.' I wiggled free both my engagement and wedding rings and added them to the glittery pile.

'Let's find out where the diamond district is and go hawk these buggers,' Tish said, stifling a yawn.

I could also feel the fog of jetlag descending. (Jetlag, what jetlag? I always run a comb through my teeth and floss my hair.) 'Listen,' I said. 'It won't be long before the lag hits. Let's split up. Tish, you're the best haggler. Why don't you sell the rings while Skye and I go buy some fresh clothes? We can check out a few of the city's five-star hotels, too, en route. Maybe we'll luck out and stumble upon Vlad the Attila?'

After mainlining a coffee-bean plantation's worth of espressos, we headed off. Skye's phone app directed us to a nearby chi-chi boutique, which was way too expensive. Next door was a plush hotel. I eyed it with envy. There were no woodlice linking arms here, that was for sure. There was, however, a Parisian concierge who specialised in service with a snarl. We showed the epauletted flunky Jason's photo. He looked us up and down in all our plane-rumpled, dusty dishevelment, then gave a sigh bordering on disgust, as though he'd never seen anything quite so revolting in his establishment – certainly nothing alive. We found ourselves gazing up the infamous Gallic flared nostril for a moment, and then the back of his perfectly coiffured head as he turned away from us. When Skye tapped him on the shoulder to ask if he knew where we could buy some T-shirts and chinos, he told us that the hotel boutique didn't have anything in that genre – obviously we were far too downmarket to wear French fashions.

To lift our spirits, I abducted Skye on a detour into the Picasso Museum, where I devoured as much of the collection as I could in one greedy gulp, like a starving woman at a buffet. I knew the paintings so well from books, but never thought I'd get to see the actual canvases. When Skye finally tapped her watch in polite protest, I rewarded her patience with a refreshing citron pressé – which turned out to be quite a homage to Picasso, being nothing more than a deconstructed lemonade. 'Eyes to the right, nose to the left,' I joked as we left the museum, a comment that would have sent Tish into a blue period of her own.

Reinvigorated, we walked on through cobbled streets abuzz with bustling brasseries and sidewalk cafés. Soon the lanes opened out into a plaza surrounding the Pompidou Centre. I marvelled at the way the functional parts of this impressive building – the intestines of air conditioning, lifts, escalators and plumbing – pulsed away on the outside, leaving the vast interior spaces free to display even more paintings.

We continued on to the Île de la Cité, the epicentre of medieval Paris, known as the city's 'navel', past Quasimodo's Notre-Dame, with its majestic flying buttresses, which act like a giant bra for the cathedral. My spirits soared with joy to be standing before all these iconic buildings I knew so well from documentaries and movies. I snapped away on my phone, eager to share the awe-inspiring experience with my kids and students.

Skye could appreciate the city's attractions, but was much more interested in finding some French clairvoyant intuitive she'd read about. Also on her to-do list was a good acupuncturist and a colonic therapist for what she called a 'toxin-clearing coffee enema.'

'Someone who could have done with an espresso up his backside was King Charles IX,' I told Skye as we crossed the majestic courtyards of the Louvre, on the way to the Ritz. It was an awkward segue but I missed being in front of a classroom and was enjoying her attentive ear. 'He was rumoured to have sat on a balcony here shooting Huguenots with a crossbow. In those days the aristocracy often confused pheasants and peasants.'

Skye, however, had the maiming of one man only on her mind. Cutting my history lesson short, she asked me to check for a message from Max. With still no word from the super sleuth, and the queue for the Louvre unusually short, we were soon standing in front of the *Mona Lisa*. I shared the story with Skye about Napoleon commandeering the famous portrait to hang in his bedroom, only to return it to the museum a few years later. 'Perhaps her enigmatic smile proved too wry a reflection on his most intimate performance?' I suggested. 'Sorry. I'm rabbiting on too much ... Tish says I have nothing to say but spend all day saying it.'

'I kinda like what you have to say.' Skye smiled at me. 'Anyway, you're just being like the French. My mum used to take me to arty movies back in Auckland. I could always tell a French movie by the amount of talking that went on in it.'

I smiled at her now too. It was a relief to feel a sense of simpatico. I wondered if we might even kindle an unexpected friendship, despite the Kiwi's tendency to woo-woo-weirdness. We wandered through the Tuileries, pausing for a quick artistic plunge into the Orangerie's Monet waterlily ponds, which Skye snapped for her Insta feed, then sauntered back towards the Ritz.

Here, our Jason inquiries were instantly quashed by a predictable Gallic shrug. As the uniformed lackey practically pushed us out through the revolving door and onto the pavement,

I explained to Skye that the French don't need a traditional army. 'They can simply bore their enemies to death with a crack team of existentialist philosophers spreading ennui. The opponents they don't succeed in smugging to death they can just wipe out with passive smoke inhalation from Gitanes fumes.'

Skye gave a tinkly little laugh. 'So, what you're saying is that the French have a proud tradition of hating absolutely everyone?'

'Especially here,' I confirmed as we strolled across La Place de la Concorde. 'This is where all those aristocratic heads rolled.' I listed all the slang terms for the guillotine I could remember from my classroom lectures: 'The National Razor', 'the Regretful Climb', 'Wooden Justice', 'The Patriotic Shortener'.

'If only we could send Jason up to the scaffold.' Skye's sigh was world-weary and defeated.

'No. Gallows and guillotines are far too good for him.'

With hopes of finding our bête noir limbo-low, we crossed the threshold of the Hôtel de Crillon. While we waited to get the attention of the concierge, I told Skye how during the French Revolution, Monsieur Crillon had dressed as a maid and hidden in the attic of this grand palace, watching through trembling fingers as his posh pals got the chop. I warned her that despite its revolutionary history, we shouldn't expect the hotel staff to be particularly sympathetic to a couple of poorly dressed Antipodean plebs.

The concierge who finally turned to speak to us was a woman. Skye flashed Jason's photo on her phone and, much to my surprise, the gatekeeper nodded in recognition. In perfect English she explained that Jason and his companion had left that very morning. We pressed for more information, but she refused to tell us about Jason's paramour or give a forwarding address. Having exhausted all avenues of coercion and persuasion, I was about to give up when Skye unexpectedly launched into an improvised Academy Award-winning performance in which she played the part of an abandoned, pregnant girlfriend. With tears pooling in her big blue eyes, she explained that she'd lost her job and had no family to fall back on.

'How could he abandon his unborn child? If I could just talk to him, face to face, I know he'd see reason. At the very least I could make him take a paternity test.' The sob that shuddered through Skye's body was so raw and real that her tear-jerking tale even tugged at my heart strings, though I knew the story was faker than Donald Trump's tan.

The concierge's cockles were also well and truly toasted. She confided that she too was a woman spurned, concluding by telling us that she'd booked Jason's train tickets that very morning – to the Loire. He'd left only a few hours earlier.

We thanked her and strode out into the summer sunshine. I looked at Skye with new respect. I'd underestimated the geologist's ingenuity.

'That was a formidable performance,' I congratulated her. 'I think we've earnt a reward – a gastronomic reward.' For me, that meant some legendary French pastries. For Skye, it would no doubt involve her regulation mocha pea milk crappuccino and, maybe just to really make merry, half a gluten-free crouton.

Light of step, we strode off down the magnificent sweep of the Champs-Elysées towards the Arc de Triomphe. I could see why the Elysian Fields, the final resting place of Greek heroes, was the illustrious name chosen for this grand avenue. Feeling equally triumphant, we watched the well-dressed world bustle by from a table in a café I felt sure would have been favoured by 1930s French writers and artists. Day-dreaming of Colette and Simone de Beauvoir, I celebrated our success with a plate of creamy, dreamy éclairs, cinnamon-sprinkled palmier biscuits, macaroons and passionfruit and lemon meringues. The fluffy, marshmallowy meringue was soft as a cloud – a cloud I washed down with a bittersweet macchiato. Skye, meanwhile, logged on to the café wifi and booked three tickets on the next available train to the Loire, which left at seven the next morning.

Tish texted to say she'd sold the rings and had transferred the proceeds to Skye's account. I texted back for her to meet us under the Eiffel Tower for a celebratory glass of champagne.

Skye and I then wandered down towards the elegant, tapering Eiffel Tower. On the way, we bought crisp new T-shirts and coloured chinos in a cute little boutique. While we waited for the charming shop assistant to ornately wrap our rather mundane purchases in pastel-coloured tissue paper, I told Skye how Gustave Eiffel's tower was once described as a 'menace to French history' by a group of artists, including Guy de Maupassant, who famously ate his lunch every day beneath the tower. 'Do you know why?' I asked her.

'Um . . . the view?'

'No. Because it was the only place in Paris where he could avoid seeing it.'

Skye gave a gratifying laugh.

'Tish always complains that I talk five times as fast as she can listen, but you have no trouble keeping up,' I complimented her. Nor did she seem to mind my literary references. Just that morning Tish had complained that I could spend two hours 'denigratin' a semi colon'. 'Don't start Gwennie on grammar!' she'd moaned. 'Honestly, it'll kill you, *but*.'

While we waited for Tish beneath the vast iron legs of the Tower, Skye posted pictures on Instagram and I checked my messages. Max had written and confirmed some of what the concierge had told us: 'He's travelling under the name of Jason Jennings with a woman – I haven't managed to identify her yet. Nor an address but strong indications are they're heading to the Loire Valley. Can you get yourselves down there? Do you need help booking train tickets?' My taciturn son had even managed a sign-off that sounded warmer than the Max I was used to: 'Hope you're going okay, Mum. I miss your fish curry. Julia says you've thrown caution to the wind. But don't worry – she'll come round. Just concentrate on your mission – to make that creep freeze and assume the position. I'm with you, all the way. Over and out.'

Giving up on Tish, who wasn't answering her phone, Skye and I walked back to the Marais along the glittering Seine. I thought about my Mission Impossible. Julia was right to be worried. I hadn't just thrown caution to the wind, I'd chucked it into a tornado, strapped to a stick of dynamite. In emergencies, the drill is always 'Help yourself first before helping children'. Winding our way along the undulating river, past florists, book shops and brasseries, I pictured myself placing an oxygen mask over Max's dear, sweet face and then Julia's furious visage – followed by an end to all turbulence and happy landings.

19

Our room key was attached to a can-can key ring, one fish-netted leg crooked in the air. I turned the key and opened the door to find a pair of shoes splayed on the floor, as though they'd shot off the stockinged foot of the Moulin Rouge dancing girl in my hand. A trail of clothing led to the bathroom – the sartorial version of Hansel and Gretel's breadcrumbs.

I opened the bathroom door gingerly, not sure if I'd find witch, warlock or wicked wolf, and was relieved when only one tousled head emerged from the bath bubbles. With her hair pinned up in a makeshift chignon and her breasts bobbing about on the foam, Tish looked like a figure from a Toulouse-Lautrec painting.

'So, how was your day, possums?' She swigged from a minia-ture wine bottle balanced on the soap dish.

'Great. We found out where Jason is,' Skye enthused. 'The Loire. Train tickets booked for the morning. Plus we saw Notre-Dame, the Eiffel Tower and the *Mona Lisa*!'

'Christ. You wasted a whole day mooching from church to gallery? You must be wearin' stained-glass spectacles by now.'

'And how did you spend your day?' Skye perched her pert posterior on the end of the bath.

'Well, while you sad sacks dragged your weary arses around monuments and museums,' Tish replied, 'I got my arse spanked by a French saxophonist. Haggling made me thirsty, so after hawkin' our rings in Le Sentier – which was a huge success, by the way; youse can thank me later – I stopped for a drink in a café. The bloke sittin' at the bar next to me was a muso. I could see he was a saxophonist by his instrument case so I sang him a few bars of "Voulez-vous".' She launched into the famous Abba song, her velvety vocals bouncing off the walls of the tiled bathroom as she trilled joyously about nothing promised, no regrets and girls meaning business. On and on she sang, stopping abruptly on the line 'You know what to do . . .' before purring, 'And, boy, did Remy know what to do. I just can't resist a sexy bum in faded jeans.'

'Personality is also important,' I reminded her, while suppressing a cringe. Why did she always make me feel as though I had the facial expression of someone advertising a pill for indigestion? I wasn't a killjoy – she just killed all joy in me.

'Der.' Tish slid a razor across her armpit without looking. 'It wasn't just his cute buns . . . although they were oven-fresh.' She licked her lips. 'It was the bloke's pick-up line that proved bloody irresistible.'

'Really? What did he say?' Skye asked, eagerly.

'"What's got two thumbs, speaks French and enjoys cunnilingus?" Then he gestured with a thumbs up and said "*Moi!*" . . . I mean, ha ha ha. I just had to bring him home.'

Skye gave one of her tinkling little laughs, while I could feel myself reflexively pursing my lips in a kind of constipated librarian look. 'If you insist on random hook-ups, Tish, could you not have sex with strangers in our hotel room?' I said. 'Then at least Skye and I can go to bed without wearing bio-hazard suits.'

I stomped into the bedroom to turn the pillowcases inside out. 'And what if we'd got back earlier?'

'You could've joined in. There was more than enough to go round 'cause I brought back his fireman mate too.'

I turned on my heel, re-entered the bathroom and gawped at her. 'You also had a fireman in here?'

'Well, I'd never done it in a threesome before, so I thought, why the hell not? When in France, blah blah blah.'

'Let me guess? Your menopausal hot flush set off the café smoke alarm?' I felt a sudden urge to wash my hands vigorously.

'Actually, French firemen must spend all day puttin' them-selves out, 'cause these guys are smokin' hot.' I watched in the mirror as Tish lathered up her other armpit.

'How did you know what to do?' Skye was all wide-eyed wonderment.

'It was a bit confusin' at first – all those arms and legs comin' at me from every angle ... It was like wrestlin' an octopus. But then I kinda got to grips with it and I was ménage-ing and trois-ing as if to the boudoir born!'

Tish's varnished red toe stretched towards the hot tap to turn it on for a top-up.

With a martyred sigh I went back to the bed to flip the sheets over. 'Don't listen to her, Skye. Most men are better imagined in your bed than found there sprawled out and snoring.'

Tish leant out of the bath and peered around the door in my direction. She raised her brows in cheery bemusement. '*Some*body needs to get laid.'

'Really? I would say that *some*body needs to get her head out of her knickers. We're in Paris, for god's sake! Cultural and architectural capital of the world.'

I finished making the bed, tugging the sheets into tight hospital corners. It'd be impossible to get between them now without a can opener. 'You really aren't in any danger of breaking the old savoir-faire barrier, are you, Tish?'

She was about to reply but I quietly shut the bathroom door. As I was in the home of existentialism, if I didn't observe Tish, did she even really exist, I thought to myself.

She emerged some time later, stark naked, her hair turbaned in a towel. 'So, what time's our train tomorrow, kids?'

'Seven a.m.,' Skye said. 'I'll send the ticket to your phone.'

'A whole night free in Paree! Let's go paint the town red, or at least pink! Remy's taking me to a male burlesque dance show around the corner. Eight stunnin' guys; seven stunnin' outfits.'

'I'm sure Skye would rather come with me for a classic French meal. There's a little bistro next door. I've already looked at the menu – beef bourguignon with pearl onions and mushrooms; cassoulet; coq au vin; creamy, cheesy, garlic and thyme-flavoured potatoes dauphinoise; yummy buttery escargots . . .'

'Jeesus. Just because the French give snails a fancy name doesn't mean you're not eatin' pond life. "*Hey, garçon! Gimme a snail and a frog in a mosquito marinade, merci.*" Skye, come on! Wouldn't you rather put a man on your bloody menu? You've been stuck with the culture vulture all day. It's only fair you spend some time with me too, kiddo.'

Skye looked from one of us to the other – and then back and forth again, as though she were a spectator mid-match at Roland-Garros.

'And then for dessert we can finish up on profiteroles drenched in warm chocolate sauce.'

'Oi, I'm also pro cake,' Tish said, pulling on her fishnet tights. 'I'm pro-havin' it and pro-eatin' it, too!'

'Yes. Selfish in other words.'

'I'll have you know that I'm actually incredibly selfless. I give blowjobs, after all. And god knows, no woman does *that* for pleasure.'

'Yes, that's your problem, Tish,' I replied, sarcastically. 'Give, give, give. Oh, and thanks for using all the towels. I'll just dry my entire body with the face flannel, shall I? Honestly, sharing a hotel room with you is torture.'

'Shame,' Tish retorted. 'Can nothin' be done under the Geneva Convention?'

I watched as she added a flourish of eyeliner. 'Orgasms this good deserve my best make-up. Comin'?' She winked at Skye. 'I mean, stick with me, kiddo, and you soon will be.' She gave a lascivious chuckle and waited expectantly.

Unable to choose between us, Skye did her tennis tournament head-swivelling routine once more. Her solution was to offer us both an invitation of her own – to join her for a meditation session called 'Mind-Sound Resonance'.

'Concentrating on the vibrations in your skull is a good way of restoring positive energy and psychic balance,' she explained. She then bade us both partake in the supplies she'd bought for thin porridge with goji berries, nuts and cinnamon, made with hazelnut milk. I watched as she mixed up her meal. The brown milk made it look a lot like cat sick. I checked the price tag on the milk, which was not far off the cost of a bottle of burgundy, and was tempted to give Skye a skull vibration, all right – a quick whack across the head with the can-can key.

Tish and I exchanged a grimace. With a hearty 'Bonsoir!' she was gone. I headed out with her, but for my own rendezvous – with a cassoulet and crème brûlée.

'Just don't miss the train, girls!' Skye called out after us.

'Have faith!' Tish replied over her shoulder. 'I am, after all, accordin' to Remy anyways, the crème de la crème.'

Come morning, however, the crème de la crème had curdled. Skye and I waited on the station platform at 6.45. I was clutching a bag of brioche and croissants and steaming-hot croques monsieur. There was no sign of Tish, who hadn't come back to our room last night and was not answering her phone.

'Do you think we should call the police?' Skye's eyes fretfully raked the platform.

'And what would we say? Our girlfriend is guilty of Acute Lust in the First Degree? Last known whereabouts: the ham in a sexual sandwich, or rather the bedroom baguette.'

At five minutes to seven we boarded the train and found our seats.

At seven, the train pulled out of the station.

At 7.05, a bustle and a lot of 'bloody this' and 'bloody that' heralded the breathless arrival of Tish into our carriage. She was wearing the same clothes as the previous night and looking a tad more dishevelled, with the addition of a red beret. She flung herself down into the seat opposite us and whined jokingly, 'So, are we there yet? God, I *just* made it. It was like somethin' from a goddamn Rimbaud movie, gettin' to the station on time.'

I looked at her, stunned to learn that she'd watched films about the French poet, before realising she'd said Rambo, not Rimbaud.

'Oh là là, what a night,' Tish gloated. When Skye passed her a croque monsieur, she bit into it, oozing velvety bechamel sauce onto her chin, prompting her to say again, and even louder this time, 'Oh là là.'

'If you say "oh là là" for the rest of the trip, we really will be in an action movie because I will throw you from the train,' I replied.

'I'm starvin'. French tucker's so bloody yummy. My plan is to eat whatever the hell I like and just buy bigger jeans. That's my Jeans Therapy.' Tish snorted at her own little joke, crumbs spraying.

'Pleasurable night, then?' Skye asked, taking a delicate nibble of some gluten-free slab of Styrofoam.

'Oui, oui.' As Tish went into every dirty detail, involving a lot of positions I'd never heard of, such as the 'Cock Monsieur', I logged on to the train wifi. While the Parisian suburbs strobed past, I made my way through the usual electronic reprimands from Julia, but was relieved to see they also included a few kinder queries about the tourist attractions I'd seen. I wrote back about the delights of Paris, from the paintings to the pastries. By the time I looked up again the city views had given way to rolling green fields dotted with picturesque little villages and the poppy fields of Monet's canvases. And as I was drinking in the view, a ping alerted me to a very welcome email from Max.

'Jason's at a chateau,' I told my companions. 'Owned by the woman he must have been with in Tanzania. She's called Brigitte Dubois.'

Skye immediately got busy online, googling Brigitte, then looking at maps and searching out car hires. Tish took another bite of her ham and cheese croissant. 'Remy's arms were solid muscle and he had this peachy, perfect arse. It's just that when

I heard him sing with his band, well, out came this squeaky, counter tenor voice. I'm like, mate, have your balls actually dropped?'

'Um . . . it's called *youth*,' I said brusquely, brushing up the crumbs she was spraying all over our table.

'Hey, I may be fifty but I feel like a thirty-year-old . . . Unfortunately, there's never one in the near vicinity.' Tish threw her head back and once more laughed at her own little quip. 'And that's why they invented Tinder.' She extracted her phone from her back pocket, reading aloud from the screen. '"Allow Tinder to use your location". Yes.' She tapped the screen. '"Only show me people in this range",' she continued, scrolling through the options. 'I'll put down a twenty-kilometre radius, so it's only blokes in the Loire.' Moments later she was swiping through potential candidates.

'Is she always so . . . adventurous?' Skye asked me, intrigued.

'I'm beginning to suspect that Tish is to sexual shenanigans what the French are to macarons. Luckily, you and I don't share her sexual sweet tooth.'

'She's definitely starting to make me feel inadequate. I've only had about ten lovers in my life,' Skye confessed. 'How many men have you slept with, Tish?'

'That I remember?'

I stopped tidying the table and looked at her. 'You mean, there are some you've forgotten?'

'Well, you lose count, you know . . .'

'I don't! I don't lose count. Jesus. Four, that's my count.'

'Four? How humiliatin'! That's it. I'm settin' up a Tinder profile for you!'

'Don't be ridiculous. As I've said, a night of short-lived, meaningless sex is not my style.'

'Why not? There's heaps of short-lived and meaningless things that are also briefly thrillin' and fun.'

'Such as?'

'Rollercoasters, fireworks, cheese soufflé,' she said off the top of her head. 'And nobody feels guilty or ashamed of them.'

'That's preposterous. You can't equate sex with a soufflé.'

'Why not? On your profile I'll say that you'll only meet up with blokes in the crypt of some dusty, musty old museum. And that you like a lotta chat upfront. Hours of the bloody stuff.'

'Well, yes, I think it's always important to chat to your date first. That way you can discover not just what kind of sex they like, but what kind of sex they *are*.'

Skye nodded. 'Yes, it can be very confusing, all this gender fluidity.'

'Oh god,' Tish moaned. 'Who wants to chat? Then you discover his irritatin' voice. Or his irritatin' politics. That, girls, is when oral sex is your friend. Cunny is a very effective technique to shut a bloke up. I mean, it's impossible for a fella to talk with his mouth full.'

We all laughed then, hard and hearty. When Skye recovered her breath, she pointed at Tish's phone and said, 'Don't forget to write that Gwen is witty and entertaining.'

'I can't just blatantly lie,' Tish replied.

'But Gwen is witty.'

'Say somethin' witty then?' Tish demanded of me. 'Go on.'

'I'd prefer an app called Tender to Tinder, with an emphasis on intellect and emotional libido.'

'See?' Tish eye-rolled in Skye's direction, tapping her chipped nails on the table top.

'Well I for one wish I were more like you, Gwen. You're so cultured and clever. So passionate about literature and the arts.'

Tish's harrumph prompted Skye to quickly add, 'And I wish I were more like you too, Tish. You're so outspoken.'

I laughed so hard this time, I choked. 'Outspoken! Ha! I'd like to see someone try!'

'Oh, ha ha ha,' Tish growled. 'You're the one who never stops talkin'. *Gwendoline*, here, could talk under cement with a mouth full of marbles. And as for passion, her most passionate response so far on this whole trip was a disparagin' eye roll when a museum guide imparted a fact about a sarcophagus *with which you took umbrage.*' Tish laughed, imitating my voice to perfection. 'And what about . . .' She was no doubt poised to tease me some more about my general shortcomings when her face froze.

'What? What is it?' I asked, concerned.

Tish turned her phone towards me. And there was Jason's face. On Tinder. He was under another alias – Sebastian Sasse – but there he was, in all his heartbreakingly handsome, duplicitous glory.

'Oh my god,' Skye put a hand to her mouth in disgust. 'Poor Brigitte Dubois. He's already cheating on her. The man is a sex addict.'

'Dunno who this Brigitte chick is, but she doesn't deserve to get done over by a bastard like him,' Tish agreed.

'I think it might be time to award Jason Riley the Legion of Dishonour, don't you?' I proposed.

Lost in our own sad reveries, we all three stared out of the window in silence for the rest of journey.

How could any of us ever navigate a healthy relationship when our compasses were so clearly broken?

20

You know your day is not going well when you find yourself lost in an unfamiliar forest contemplating which of your two girl-friends to eat first.

Yet the morning had started so well. We'd caught the fast train out of Paris, changed in Tours and pootled along a branch line to the medieval town of Chinon. The whole trip had taken just under three hours.

Chinon was the town nearest to the map coordinates Max had sent me, which pinpointed Jason at a family-owned chateau 20 kilometres east, along the river. On the train Skye had checked us into a cosy hotel overlooking the cobbled town square, and when we arrived there we dropped our packs in our little room and went to nurse cafés au lait while we planned our next move. The busy market bustled around us, a medley of squawking chickens and caged birds on sale between pagodas of lush fruit, glistening oysters, pouting mussels and succulent prawns. The whole place was awash with the aromatic fragrance of freshly baked bread mingled with the pong of exotic cheeses. The twelfth-century Plantagenet fortress home of Henry II, Richard the Lionheart and Joan of Arc stood sentry above us, while the wide, shimmering river rushed by below.

In search of a taxi, we took a sortie through the town's crooked, wiggly streets, with their ancient churches and quaint, gingerbread houses. Skye's eyes were on stalks as she snapped endless vistas for Insta. But there were no taxis to be seen, and the receptionist in the only car-hire place in town explained why: the taxis were on strike, which meant all the hire cars were booked.

'Now what?' Tish griped.

'It's only twenty kilometres to the chateau,' Skye said, consulting her phone map. 'We could cycle?'

The look on my face must have registered more surprise than the congregation at Oscar Wilde's wedding. Tish? Cycling? While Skye was no doubt conjuring up images of us in berets, as we meandered through sun-drenched vineyards, strings of onions and garlic bulbs around our necks, I suspected the reality would involve me drenched in sweat, pedalling frantically on a tandem bicycle while Tish lounged back in my bike basket nibbling on petites fours while blasting out Piaf songs. No. The thought of us apprehending Jason by bicycle seemed as plausible a proposition as a Mormon with a bar tab.

Tish agreed. 'Forgedabout it,' she said, puffing on her e-ciggy.

'There's no other way to get there. Come on. It'll be fun!' our resident cheerleader enthused. 'You'll be cycling through what you'll be drinking later.'

Gliding through the rolling, sun-drenched, fragrant French countryside beside the soft flowing waters of the Loire without having to dodge SUVs burping exhaust fumes in your face on city roads did sound quite enticing. 'Why not?' I acquiesced. 'Anyway, the exercise will do you good, Tish.' I watched her hoover up the cream duvet atop her hot chocolate. 'Sharing rooms with you, I've come to know your fitness routine – up, down, up, down, up, down, up, down . . . And now the other eyelid. Repeat.'

'Oh, ha ha. Anyway, you're wrong. I do take exercise. I've been out two nights runnin',' she bantered.

'There's really only one exercise routine you need to master – restraint. Have you ever once exercised restraint in your whole life?'

'I'd rather take my exercise horizontally, thanks very much. Sportin' activities are just too bloody dangerous. In fact, I get plenty of exercise walkin' to the hospital beds of friends who got knocked off their bloody bikes.' Tish ordered another cake and coffee.

'Okay, think of it this way then,' I said. 'Guilt-free gormandising.'

'Whaddaya mean?' Tish licked chocolate from her spoon with a languorous tongue.

'Well, having pedalled off the pounds, no need to regret that baguette or not nosh that brioche. You can devour a gateau in every chateau.'

Tish's eyes lit up. 'I hadn't thought of that. I am gettin' kinda worried that next time I stand on one of those talkin' bathroom scales, it'll say, "One person at a time."'

A smile tugged at my lips. The woman was profoundly annoying but she could also be funny. We were both actually about to lose quite a lot of weight from laughing hysterically at the cycling shorts Skye had bought for us. After we struggled into these huge padded pants, I quickly realised that the only real danger of biking through the Loire was running into

194

lamp posts from guffawing too heartily at each other's well-upholstered posteriors. Clearly cycling pants were designed to prevent painful friction on those parts of your body primarily reserved for giving birth, but they also meant that our rear ends were arriving about five minutes after we did. Hell, they had their own arrondissement.

While I had no doubt that I looked like the progeny of a heffalump and a dirigible, Tish seemed to be labouring under the delusion that she now resembled a Kardashian and took to twerking at pedestrians as we whizzed on by. And of course I couldn't resist glancing over my shoulder to catch their incredulous Gallic expressions, which was why I kept colliding with inanimate objects such as cars, carts and cows that stubbornly refused to take evasive action.

Worse, it turned out that Tish cycled just like she drove – meaning she left a pile-up of startled ramblers in her wake. 'Hey, if you don't like the way I cycle, get off the pavement!' she was constantly yelling at promenaders as they dived for cover.

Besides multiple bruises from the consequential lamppost prangs, the main obstacle to finding Jason was the intermittent phone signal. An hour into our ride through the dappled forests and chateau-encrusted countryside of the Loire, I glanced up at the fluffy white clouds scudding across the azure sky and called out confidently to my companions, 'Next step the velodrome!' With the wind whistling through my hair, I felt sure we'd soon catch up with the Tour de France.

But the outing quickly turned into the Detour de France when our phones lost signal and we realised the true inadequacy of our French vocabulary. Cycling through a sleepy little town surrounded by orchards, I tried asking some people for directions, but once more found myself inhaled into a forest of disdainful nostril hair. Tish told me to leave it to a professional, tilted her beret to a rakish angle and, tossing her head coquettishly, exchanged a few words with a chocolate-eyed, laconic local who looked as though he'd sidled forth from the pages of a Flaubert novel.

She eventually glided back to us and jabbed a varnished finger towards a path that wound upwards through the woods – which is how our 20-kilometre ride turned into a marathon, bum-numbing diversion far, far off the beaten track. After an hour of cycling in a circle, I was no longer laughing. Nor was Tish twerking. Put it this way, I now knew that 'numb labia' is *not* a country in Africa.

It was the third wrong turn in the woods that had resulted in our current predicament – lost in an ancient royal hunting forest. As the afternoon sun moved west in the sky, I had a vision of us huddled in a ditch, blue from hypothermia and gaunt from malnutrition . . . which is how I found myself contemplating cannibalism.

Hungry, tetchy and tired, it wasn't long before a disagreement broke out. I'd been impressed by how lightly we were travelling between continents – washing our knickers, socks and T-shirts every night; alternating our one pair of shorts with our one other outfit. But there was no way of lightening our cumbersome emotional baggage.

'Jesus, I feel as though I've been sodomised by a herd of elephants,' Tish said, dismounting and massaging her buttocks. 'Whose bloody bright idea was it to cycle?'

'Well, bright ideas are clearly not your forte.' I pointed at her beret. 'I mean, riding without a helmet, you obviously need your head examined. And it will be, too, by a neurosurgeon. Any moment now.'

'Who cares about bloody helmets when we're clearly going to die out here in the goddamned wilderness.'

I glanced up at the tangled canopy of tree limbs eerily necklaced with freshly spun spiderwebs. The dim, filtered light of the forest made it seem alive and sinister. 'Oh, and whose fault is that? You clearly misunderstood that man's directions. You were far too busy waving your arms around, laughing and flirting and making out you could speak French.'

'I didn't ever say I could speak French!' Tish dropped her bike in a funk.

'Well, if you couldn't understand the man, why were you nodding and going, "Oui, oui, monsieur!" Wearing a beret does not make you Gallic, okay? You clearly speak French like a native – a native of, say, Argentina.'

'Let's all take a deep breath,' Skye beseeched. She pulled something from her backpack. 'I want you both to wear these bio frequency healing patches. They'll rebalance your electrical energy and will concentrate your minds on our mutual enemy. We are so, so close.' She slapped a patch onto my forearm. 'You teach geography, don't you, Gwen? Surely you can work out where we are by the clouds or the stars or the rocks or something?'

Taking a deep, calming breath, I unfolded the paper map the bike shop assistant had tucked into my panier.

'Gwen can't read a map!' Tish scoffed. 'She can't even locate her G-spot. Am I right?'

I promptly snatched another bio frequency healing patch from Skye's hand and slapped it onto my other arm as well. Did the French still have the law of *crime passionnel*, I wondered. If I could convince the judge that it was not a premeditated murder, but an understandable reaction to travelling in a foreign land with such an irritating imbecile, I would probably get off with a suspended sentence. Maybe even a medal?

Fortified with my bio frequency patches (whatever the hell they were) and half a slab of the emergency chocolate I'd secreted into my panier, I concentrated on the map. It was one of those huge ordnance survey charts, meaning it would probably take five minutes to locate the chateau and another two days to refold the map. I soon identified the shallow ridge to our left and the steep downward pitch into heavy forest. Then, taking my bearings from the sun, which was hard to do because of the tangled snarl of branches above me, I was able to lead the way out of the dark, dense forest and in no time at all we were pedalling back down towards the river.

The Loire Valley is known as the Garden of France. Cycling through its tapestry of strawberry fields, forests and vineyards was not only beautiful but beguiling. I began to think we'd hitched a ride in Dr Who's TARDIS and warped backwards hundreds of years. The countryside, casually strewn with medieval citadels, crumbling abbeys and enchanting Renaissance castles was pictur-esque, literally; the glistening Cézanne poplars, soft Corot-esque woods and serene Seurat waterways made me feel as though I'd fallen into one of the Impressionist canvases we'd seen in Paris.

Tish seemed less enthralled. She was grunting and groaning so much it was like listening to the soundtrack of a bad Polish porn film. 'This is the longest bloody twenty kilometres in human history.'

'Just remind yourself that cycling can add about ten years to your life,' Skye chirped encouragingly.

'You're right. I feel about ten bloody years older already,' she grouched in reply.

Rounding a bend in the river my good mood was punctured by the steep slope before us. Skye, who was the youngest, made a heroic dash upwards. Tish, meanwhile, made a noise like a bike tyre going flat and stopped so abruptly that I rear-ended her, bashing my leg on the bike chain in the process.

'Now that's what I call a "vicious cycle",' cackled Tish as I toppled sideways.

'Compassionate and sympathetic as always.' I scrabbled back to standing, rubbing my grazed knees, and looked up at the hill with dread. 'Maybe we should just call the paramedics in advance?'

Eventually, after a few deep breaths, we pushed our bikes to the top of the hill in silence and came to an awed standstill at the top, as we saw the chateau below us, backlit in a wash of syrupy sunlight. This jewel of Renaissance architecture rose up off manicured green parkland like something from a fairy tale – complete with turrets, Rapunzel towers, battlements, drawbridge and moat, the calm waters of which perfectly reflected the castle, which was set like a gemstone in the middle of a lake. The warm, honey-coloured, creamy pale stone seemed to have trapped the sunlight in its pores. We gazed down, goggle-eyed. Aussies and Kiwis go mad for castles, where Europeans will give a nonchalant shrug, remarking dismissively, 'It's only six hundred years old.'

But of course we were even more fascinated by what lurked within its walls.

Skye's blue eyes glittered. 'Ladies, the psychic vampire awaits!'

It was now a case of *vrooooommm*! I whooshed up and down the remaining inclines as though my bicycle had drunk an espresso. With the end of our quest in sight, it was suddenly as though I was sharing a tandem with Lance Armstrong.

If this was Brigitte Dubois' family home, Jason's attraction to her was crystal clear. A number of props increase sexual arousal – chief among these an opulent, aristocratic chateau in the lovely Loire. But the Three Muffkateers were riding to this deluded damsel's rescue . . .

If only we could think of some way of getting into the formidable fortress. After locking up our bikes at the entrance and finding a bush behind which to change into the smart gear we'd purchased in Paris, we peered through the gate's big bars to see a stream of people flowing from one of the castle doors and gathering in pools on the lawn around the moat. Waiters began to waft about, bearing champagne-laden trays.

'A party. Perfect,' Tish said, hitting the intercom bell. 'Bonjour! It's the chanteuse. For the party,' she ad-libbed, before breaking into her velvet-voiced, quaveringly heartfelt rendition of 'Non, je ne regrette rien'.

The huge wrought-iron gates magically yawned open.

Tish readjusted her red beret and beckoned us through with her eyebrows. 'If anyone asks, you're my entourage. Which means I want a lot more respect from you, *Gwendoline*, okay?'

But unlike Ms Piaf, I had regrets already. Sauntering up the gravel drive, I felt my mouth twitch into a rictus smile, as though a poisonous spider was climbing across my face. Because there, strolling over the lawn, with insouciant ease and not a care in his corrupt world, was Jason Riley.

21

Seeing Jason again up close, I staggered backwards in a fugue of shock. There it was – his Casanova smile, all impish insolence but with a hint of tousled tenderness beneath his bad-boy bravado. His charisma was set to 'stun' mode and his trousers left nothing to the imagination.

I felt an unexpected pang. Of what? Not love. Love for this mountebank? This ten-cent Machiavelli? I mentally slapped myself, but I could feel my anger melting like butter in the late afternoon sun. Obviously I needed to keep shielding until a brain donor was found.

I watched, mesmerised, as Jason bent down towards the woman on his arm – the same elegant blonde we'd glimpsed through our binoculars in the Serengeti – his smile showing off his perfect teeth; the toss of his head highlighting the luxurious-ness of his hair. But what hadn't come into focus through the binocular blur back then was that the woman must be in her late seventies. Her slim frame was elegantly draped in designer Dior and she had a dazzling string of pearls draped around her scraggy neck. The eyes she turned up towards Jason's were ablaze with girlish adoration. Watching my husband kissing this French doyenne on her puckered lips, I experienced a sharp stab in the pit of my stomach as though I'd been kebabbed.

'Shouldn't a grave-robbin', gold digger like him be carryin' a shovel?' Tish's teeth were more clenched than the portcullis of this posh French palace.

'I can remember where I got married and when I got married. I just can no longer remember why,' Skye said with disgust.

'That's it,' Tish fumed. 'Forget the money. Let's go kill the prick.'

I looked at her, not sure if she was joking. 'Sure, I mean at least in a French jail, in addition to your one phone call, you also get a nice glass of citron pressé,' I said, sarcastically. 'Plus, before a strip-search, dinner and a show.'

Tish cracked her knuckles and ground her molars. 'Right now I feel like Madame whatsername . . .'

'. . . Defarge?' I supplied.

'Yeah, her. Madame friggin' Defarge is my role model.' Tish made a slicing-off-his-head motion with her hand.

'Well, to bring about Jason's demise, all we need do is edge him closer to the moat. He'll be so distracted by the perfect mirror reflection of himself that we can push him in and he'll drown of his own accord,' I suggested, stonily.

'We have to warn the poor bloody woman!' Tish clenched her fists and made a lurch towards them. 'Brigitte! Brigitte!'

Skye stretched out an arm to restrain her. 'Stop! She won't believe you. In France, men rule. Plus, we shouldn't be here. You'll get us thrown out.'

'Skye's right,' I agreed. 'The 1871 Paris Commune granted voting rights to women, but they were taken away when the Commune fell and weren't reinstated until 1944.'

Tish stopped in her tracks. 'Nineteen forty-fuckin'-four! Are you kiddin' me?'

'You see the importance of facts?' I pointed out to her.

'Which is why we need to be stealthy. I have a plan,' Skye said. 'While Tish is singing, I'll slip upstairs, find Jason's room and nab his laptop. Gwen, you stay here and keep an eye on him.'

'What? No! Don't leave me alone with him.'

'Just call me if he's coming inside. Does your phone have signal now?'

I checked it and nodded. 'But what if someone asks who I am?' I started to sweat – a lot of sweat, more sweat than a Russian athlete taking a drugs test.

'Just think like Edith Piaf and improvise,' was Tish's blasé suggestion.

'I'm not an improvising kind. I don't like to do anything without a written invitation. I don't know what kind of small talk to make to French people, even if they could understand me. I mean, how long can I gush knowledgeably about Normandy endive?'

Just then a butler appeared on the side terrace and motioned for Tish to advance. She readjusted her beret, took Skye by the arm, gave a sanguine flutter of her fingers, and skipped up the stone steps, leaving me in solo, undercover spy, Nancy Wake 'White Mouse' mode.

I sidled to the back of the party crowd and grabbed a champagne flute floating by on a silver tray. When a bright-green soup bowl of what looked like slug pupae was placed into my hands by another passing waiter, I squinted at it dubiously. But I was so hungry after our intrepid cycling, I drank it down. One lip-licking minute later and now *I* wanted to marry Brigitte Dubois – for her gourmet fare alone. A rainbow of berries, displayed on a plate designed to look like an artist's palette, now wafted under my nose, followed by a selection of French cheeses, graded in order of pongability.

Guests were peering at me with appalled curiosity as I ravenously gobbled up each gourmet treat with gusto; washing down every mouthful with copious gulps of vintage Veuve. The stylish women, world-famous for living on one whiff of skimmed air a week, eyed me with a mix of envy and disdain. But my reasoning was this – by keeping my mouth full, I wouldn't be called upon to speak to anyone, thus revealing my gatecrasher status.

A glass was tapped with a silver spoon and a hush fell upon the chic gathering, who turned as one towards the couple ascending the bridge.

'Pardon, je ne connais pas le français. Parlez-vous anglais?' After a general smattering of smug nodding, my husband purred, 'It's often confounded me as to why men prefer their wine mature and their women young.' I felt his voice in the pit of my stomach. 'Touring Brigitte's estate cellars, where the champagne and wine are aged, so lovingly, for decades, I began to understand why it is that French men appreciate older women. The complexity, nuance, subtlety, fulsome flavour and delectable maturity of a vintage wine are so palate-pleasingly preferable to non-vintage.'

Brigitte laughed coquettishly, her bejewelled hand pretending to modestly bat away the compliment. I wanted to regurgitate the gourmet tucker I'd wolfed down moments earlier. With any luck, I could aim my projectile vomit in my husband's duplicitous direction.

'As Brigitte's sommelier described to me the differences between the '95 vintage and the rosé and Grand Cuvée we're drinking today, rolling the syllables around his mouth in the same way we are savouring this exquisite champagne, it struck me that we men should talk about mature women with the same passion and poetry. God knows, it can't be because they're not bubbly enough!'

His paramour gave a coruscating little laugh that tinkled and chimed.

'Which is why I am très excité to make Brigitte my wife.'

The guests around me cheered and clapped, and were given a dental hygienist's view of my tonsils as my mouth gaped open in astonishment. Clearly, where Jason was concerned, no woman was old enough to know better. Yet again he had found one he could really bank on. Yes, the wealthy Brigitte would fit the bill nicely. If only we could classify our men as the French classified wine, I thought bitterly, how much time it would save. *He's authentic vintage with a cheeky hint of mischief . . .* Or: *Beware! He's a dud batch of sour grapes who's matured into a vile vat of toxicity.*

'Do you take this woman to the cleaners, for fifty per cent of her income, from this day forth, for richer and richer? I now pronounce you Man and Mansion!' I muttered to myself. Except, judging by the sea of glaring faces that had now craned my way, I wasn't muttering it quietly. With a jolt I realised that I'd uttered these words out loud, and very loudly.

Jason must have heard the familiar voice of his actual wife because he too started, and turned. His eyes locked onto mine. He looked at me as though I were ticking, raised a glass to his fiancée, and started to walk rapidly towards a security guard. After he had whispered a few words into the guard's ear, the suited goon set off across the bridge towards me. Showing the courage of an imploding soufflé, I ran. Zig-zagging across the lush lawn I tried to find Skye's number on my speed dial but I was quickly collared. I steeled my nerves and turned to confront my arch enemy.

But Jason had vanished.

22

I was frogmarched through a side door in time to hear the dulcet tones of Tish's Edith Piaf warblings abruptly silenced by the same butler who'd ushered her into the chateau earlier. 'Arrêtez! Arrêtez!' shouted the angry majordomo. I heard a scuffle and looked up to see Skye being manhandled down the stairs by a security guard who looked as though he'd eaten one too many beef bourguignons.

Next, Brigitte arrived in a cloud of Chanel, demanding to know who we were and what was happening. I tripped over an antique desk of some sort, drawing all eyes in my direction. My lower limbs seemed to have undergone an acrimonious divorce from my upper body. I tried to struggle to my feet only to find they were not where they were normally situated. While Skye helped me regain control over my jellied legs by hauling me up off the floor, Tish was bundled to my side by a vexed valet, who glared down his nose at us. Since arriving in France, I seemed to have spent a great deal of time looking up the snouts of men who were shorter than me.

Tish, Skye and I exchanged complicit glances. I wondered what the French was for 'I don't want to sound like a heartless bitch by throwing your hopes and dreams under the bus, but you are engaged to a serial fraudster and bigamist.'

'Um ... that man, your pièce de résistance – you should resist every piece of him,' I blurted between hiccups, irrationally pleased to sound so French all of a sudden.

'Are you drunk?' Tish arched her eyebrow with amusement.

'Look, the thing is, a wealthy wife is quite a labour-saving device,' I continued, trying not to wobble as I addressed Brigitte. 'You and Jason clearly have so much in common – *you* have a chateau in the Loire, and *he* really, really wants one,' I drawled.

'Jason?' queried Brigitte, before she started prattling away to her butler. Our collective French vocabulary may have been minuscule, but the word *policiers* being loudly bandied about spoke volumes.

'Look, Brigitte,' Tish said. 'Sorry to break it to ya, but that bloke you're gettin' hitched to? His real name is Jason Riley. And he's married already. To us.'

Skye pulled up a photo of Jason on her phone, while I extracted the wedding certificates from my backpack – wedding certificates that were getting pretty dog-eared from the constant perusing by wronged women.

I looked at Brigitte Dubois. Now was our moment. I was dying to see the expression on Jason's face when we explained to his latest fiancée how he'd pulled not just the wool, but the whole worsted balaclava, over our eyes as well. I couldn't wait to see how he tried to wriggle out of the fact that he'd bounced back and forth between us like a marital shuttlecock. It was time for

Brigitte to know that the man was a rollercoaster that only went down. Rollercoaster? Huh! Who was I kidding? What Jason had put us through would make the Torture Tower of Terror Drop, or the Death Spiral Big Dipper look like the teacup ride. 'Jason's a grenade that always blows up,' I warned her. 'At least we can minimise the casualties and prevent you from feeling the full force of the explosion.'

Brigitte demanded to see him. Us three wives stood shoulder to shoulder, ready to confront our greatest foe; discredit him to his duped, chignoned meal ticket, and finally get our money back. Then the whole ordeal would be over. Meaning not only the sweet taste of revenge, but also that I could go home to my kids, leave behind his other crazy wives, and get my life back on track.

As the French woman studied our evidence with forensic attention, a security guard strode into the room and whispered to the butler, who then whispered into Brigitte's ear.

'Il est allé?' the mistress of the chateau exclaimed in horror.

'He's gone,' I translated as best I could. 'Cue Dracula chords and darken the house lights.'

While Brigitte was absorbing this perplexing information, Tish quickly showed her Jason's Tinder profile, under his Sebastian Sasse alias, looking for women in this area.

Another security guard entered to divulge that he'd seen Jason's car pulling out on to the road twenty minutes earlier. Further inquiries revealed that his bags were also gone. Brigitte looked flabbergasted, but we could have told her that Jason never chased a woman he couldn't outrun.

It was then we welcomed Brigitte Dubois into our Wronged Wives' Club.

What followed was much screaming and vase-throwing. We looked on helplessly, knowing just how she felt. She'd been charmed by Jason's silvery felicity and purred affections. Meeting his Dr Jekyll alter ego was akin to finding out that the nice Boy Scout organiser is really a paedophile; or that the vicar is actually a megalomaniacal murderer. Jason had performed cold, clinical surgery on us all, with the precision of an arthroscopy robot.

Within minutes Brigitte's tantrum had escalated from spectacular to nuclear. She was no longer throwing an engagement party but hosting a hurricane. As I ducked a flying silver-framed photo of them both, I realised that it's not so much the French are arrogant, it's more that they just do everything bigger and better, forcing the rest of us to suffer from delusions of adequacy.

23

There was no enthusiasm about remounting our chrome steeds. Tish sat slumped on the side of the road, head in hands. Despondency and despair were also battling for dominance in my psyche as Skye told us she'd managed to find Jason's room but had been rumbled and removed before she'd had a chance to nab his laptop.

Ignoring all scenic bike routes, we cycled straight along the main road back to Chinon, sucking up exhaust fumes from those speeding behemoth SUVs, and farm trucks. Finally the battered city walls whose crenellated tops once provided vantage points for archers loomed into view, but we'd already been shot, straight through the heart.

By the time we returned the bikes, we were not just crestfallen but also saddle-sore and swollen, and as bow-legged as Thanksgiving wishbones. 'It gives new meaning to the expression "read my lips",' I said in an effort to raise the spirits of my desolate companions. Things weren't improved when I tried to explain our cycling injuries to the late-night pharmacist who didn't speak English, meaning I had to mime the tender chaffing of my nether regions in full view of all the other customers.

Back in our hotel room, as I handed around great dollops of the soothing gel the pharmacist had prescribed, a fog of ennui engulfed us. Coating my crotch in the lotion, I thought about how the French had invented all the best in-between words – frisson, frottage, faux pas, ambience, nuance. But there was nothing subtle about our situation. Do you believe in nuance? Yes or no? Um, no. Not right now. Nor was there any word to describe how we felt, knowing that our bigamist cad of a husband was going to get away with his crimes. The trail had gone cold. Jason had escaped again. All that was missing from the scene was some Vincent Price laughter, a crack of thunder, a vampire bat, a bolt of lightning and maybe a sinister moustache twirl.

Forget Life-Optimising Moon Juice – Skye consoled herself with vodka, diving headfirst into a bottle she'd bought near the bike shop. With the restraint of an Exocet missile, Tish was out of her sweaty clothes and into the nearest music venue, and no doubt onto some jazz-loving garçon. I skulked down to a restaurant in the square for a bout of comfort-eating. A small group of drinkers was washing away the dust of the day with sips of sweet white Sauternes while bantering with the staff. Another top tip for a woman in her sixties travelling alone? Always ask for a table near the waiter. I was still waiting for my cassoulet, thinking, call me crazy, but it doesn't look like these French folk have got a handle on tourism, when a tipsy Skye appeared, waving my phone.

'I think it must be urgent,' she said, flumping down into a chair at my table. 'It's been ringing over and over.'

My heart lurched with anxiety. I hadn't given Julia or Max a thought all day. Here I was, off on this crazy, global goose chase, only thinking of myself, when my children needed me. I checked the missed-call menu and rang Max back immediately, mentally ready to hand over internal organs, the deeds to my house, bank codes, bone marrow – whatever he needed.

But Max didn't need me – no, he had something *I* needed. With his usual cool, calm composure, my son explained that he'd got his hands on a highly sophisticated piece of malware created by an Israeli cybersurveillance firm, designed to help law enforcement and intelligence agencies spy on a target's phone.

'The software,' my son clarified, 'allows hackers – although I'd prefer the term "security experts" – to break into a phone, extract all the data on the device, see incoming or outgoing calls, and access the phone's camera, microphone and location data to listen in on conversations. It works by manipulating any vulnerabilities in a phone's software or a particular app that developers, like Google or Apple, haven't yet spotted and fixed.'

'So, what you're saying is that this software does everything but jack up a car tyre and change a lightbulb?' I asked.

Max put on his patient voice: 'Mother, your grasp of technological terminology is truly tiny. Basically, I've tricked Jason into clicking on a web link on his phone that appears innocent but has activated my spyware. And the beauty of this software from our perspective is that when it starts running on a device, the user is unlikely to have any idea it's there: the phone just operates as normal.'

'Let me get this right. Thanks to this malware, from now on we'll be able to stick to Jason like pantyhose in a summer heatwave?'

'Once more, not the most technical description, Mum, but affirmative.'

My dear clever boy went on to explain that he could now determine whether Jason was stationary, or, if he was moving, in which direction. 'And right now,' Max concluded, 'he's on the way to Nantes airport, having bought a fare to Budapest. Also, Mum, what I've deduced is that he is running a cryptocurrency pyramid scheme, scamming unsuspecting investors.'

'He is? That *bastard*. And those unsuspecting investors include your mum, sadly. Without Jason I'd never be where I am today – in debt.'

'Don't feel bad, Mum. Thanks to this miraculous malware, your spirits need know nothing of Sir Isaac Newton and his absurd gravitational theories.'

I smiled at Max's whacky way with words, told my eccentric son that I missed him so much, and would keep him posted about our progress, passed on my love to Julia, then said goodbye.

I immediately called Tish. When she answered, out of breath and – I was fairly sure – mid-coitus, I summoned her urgently. While we waited, I plied Skye with coffee, convinced that if tested by a nurse right now they'd find only a small amount of blood in her alcohol system.

Twenty minutes later Tish shimmied towards us, waving goodbye to a Frenchman with arms like Parma hams and a slightly gone-to-seed musician's swagger. She lowered her leopardskin, mini-skirted derrière down at my rickety little table next to Skye.

'By the way, that ointment you got from the chemist, Gwen,' Skye said tipsily. 'I looked it up online. And guess what? It's not soothing vagina gel. From your miming routine, the pharmacist must have deduced that you were frigid. Which is why we're all now wearing aphrodisiacal lubricant, apparently.'

Tish snorted out a laugh. 'That could explain why random fellas, and even some farmyard animals, have been followin' me all evenin'. Forget Nordic Noir, this is Gallic phwooor!' she concluded, slapping her own butt while making a sizzling sound.

'Well, prepare to have your black sense of humour tickled, Tish, because what I'm about to tell you is surely a case of Loire Noir,' I said happily. In my excitement to impart Max's miraculous update, I was speaking as fast as a horse-racing commentator announcing the closing furlongs of a tight finish at Flemington.

'What the hell are you rabbitin' on about?' Tish asked. 'Have you inhaled a kilo of Colombian sherbet?' This was a question apparently shared by Skye, who crinkled her nose inquisitively.

I took a deep breath and slowed down, updating them on Max's malware and Jason's whereabouts, and asking if they were still up for the chase. I no longer had any qualms – I was doing this for Julia and Max; especially for Max as I was determined to make his heroic efforts worthwhile. But I realised that Tish and Skye may have had enough – and who could blame them? 'So, what do you think?' I asked.

'Halle-flipping-lujah!' Tish high-fived. 'The sun is finally out and the sky is blue. If choirs of angels were up for hire, I'd bloody well book 'em.'

Would Skye also jump at this new and improved opportunity to catch Jason? Yes, she would – like a weightwatcher over a cake-shop counter. 'Sweet as!'

And so, once more, we three most unlikely companions headed back into the fray.

Before we caught the train to Nantes the next morning, I looked over the information Max had sent me on the crypto-currency pyramid scheme Jason was running. Disgusted, I slammed my phone down onto the table. 'I still can't believe I fell for him. Why was I so stupid?'

'Because the bloke can play golf with his hands behind his back,' Tish replied. 'We've established that.'

'Oh god. Not this again,' I eye-rolled with a sigh. 'I got over his enormous appendage ages ago.'

'How? With a pole vault?' Tish wise-cracked.

We laughed and laughed, buoyed up with camaraderie and the thrill of the chase.

If only I'd had the foresight to think about hindsight, I'd have worked out that it was time to strap on my bulletproof bra . . .

PART SIX

24

As we chased our ex-husband around Europe, our Jason Geiger counter bleeping madly some days and dead as a dodo the next, we settled into a pattern. While I soothed all frustrations by broadening my mind with side trips to museums and galleries, Tish broadened her heterosexual horizons (her motto had clearly become 'Around the World in Eighty Lays') and Skye tried to keep us from decking each other. This mainly consisted of contorting us into an origami of calming yoga poses. Skye rarely even broke into a sweat, while I invariably ended up tied in knots with a knee wedged up one nostril, an elbow stuck in my ear and something alarming up my chakra. Tish, however, had no trouble taking to an exercise regime that allowed her to lie down and go to sleep.

But it was all to little effect. Tish and I had our moments – she made me laugh, and I seemed to amuse her, though half the time she was laughing at me. Mostly, though, we were still getting on like . . . well, like two Balkan republics.

Jason was always on the move and we were always one step behind him. In Budapest, while I marvelled at the way the blue Danube cuts through the heart of the city – a Cinderella city of turrets and towers, basilicas and battlements with the bustling boulevards of modern Pest – Tish bedded a hunky hussar.

'I thought you were going to check for Jason at the Raiffeisen Bank near St Stephen's Basilica while we staked out the Arena Plaza branch,' I queried crossly when she turned up back at our hotel two hours late.

We knew from the spyware Max had installed on Jason's phone that he'd made an appointment with the bank in Budapest, we just didn't know which one. As what Max called the 'spyware's tracking protocol' wouldn't kick in until Jason turned on his phone, we'd taken the precaution of staking out two of the main branches, in the hope he might turn up at one of them.

'Yeah, well, I was on my way, but I got hungry and stopped off for one of those yummy pogacsa biccies. Then this cute Cossack asked me to join him for a drink. It was just one Palinka brandy but next thing I know, I'm watchin' his silver chain slappin' against his sweaty, bronzed torso. As I raked an orgasmic scratch down his broad, chiselled back, I found myself wonderin' if "shagged to death" might be the official explanation on my death certificate?'

I fumed, furious that Tish hadn't stuck to our plan. 'Self-discipline – yep, that's what you're famous for.' I was practically levitating with vexation.

Sensing another tiff, it was Skye to the rescue. 'Gwen's been telling me all about the history of Budapest,' she placated.

'Yeah, Gwen charges nothin' for her lectures . . . and it's worth it.' Tish's vape smoke curled up into my cringing face.

I reminded myself that it's important to have your facts straight before you murder someone in a foreign country. For instance, do they have the death penalty?

The karmic Kiwi appeased and teased and just kept on administering large amounts of brain octane oil and green powder potions with added plant-based collagen and vegan protein to balance our positive energies.

In Vienna, with time to kill before Jason turned up at his pre-booked hotel, I took in the Schönbrunn Palace and the Spanish Riding School. The Austrian capital exuded culture from every nook and creative cranny. Opulence, elegance, palaces, pastries, schnitzel, apfelstrudel, art, music: the fin de siècle atmosphere of Vienna was right up my boulevard. When the liquid notes of Mozart spilt into the street from a cosy café, I half-expected to see a be-wigged Beethoven or even Strauss, in red frock coat and waistcoat, strolling through the elegant square towards the grand opera house.

Tish flippantly dismissed my enthusiasm as 'post-traumatic Strauss Syndrome'. When she turned up late to our café rendezvous on the Ringstrasse, where we were staking out Jason's imposingly luxurious hotel, Skye tried to break the tension: 'Apparently Vienna's a geographical hot potato, passed around from the Mongols to the Turks, the Prussians to the Russians . . . Gwen knows all about the city's history.'

'Yeah and I bet she told you all about it, too. Gwennie here has a terrible memory . . . she never forgets a bloody thing!'

Tish, it transpired, had spent the day with a foot fetishist she'd picked up in the Polkadot bar – a music venue with a punk rock twist. She brandished a photo on her phone of a skinny, pale, poetic-looking aristocrat with long hair and a goatee; the kind of guy who makes his own absinthe on weekends and could easily have a body or two stashed in his castle basement.

'He treated my foot like a friggin' holy object: kissin' and caressin' it. He smelt my shoes. Then I had to shove my foot in his mouth.'

'I hope you didn't give him athlete's tongue,' I said curtly. I attempted one more time to interest her in Vienna's cultural treasure trove, but the ensuing discussion went something like: 'Who the fuck cares? Beats the shit out of me. Hello, waiter? More wine, please.'

It was clearly time to send home a postcard reading 'Wish I wasn't here.' Comfort-eating our way through slabs of Sacher torte and hot chocolate, we whiled away a few more sulky hours. When Jason failed to appear, I FaceTimed Max, who reported that our husband's spyware still hadn't uploaded. This led him to deduce that our I.M.O.M. was turning off his smartphone when he got close to his destinations to avoid detection.

Before ringing off, Max gave me a shy smile. 'I like helping you, Mum. It's good.'

I was amazed and extremely chuffed. Before this escapade my son wouldn't even open the door for me . . . the door of the washing machine, that is. But now he'd become my trusted right-hand man. Yes, Tish Delaney was annoying and Skye was bonkers. But I'd buried a beloved husband, raised two children on my own, stood up to the thugs who bullied my son at school for being 'nerdy', watched my daughter veer towards anti-vaxxing with a bumper bar sticker that read 'My Body, My Choice', and remarried a conman husband. I'd survived worse things than travelling Europe with a New Age nut job and a nymphomaniacal jazz singer.

And so the Three Muffkateers continued to mime our way around the Continent, using hand signals and eyebrow calisthenics to make ourselves understood.

Max explained that as our husband's financial wheeling and dealing was borderline legal, Jason must be utilising every anti-surveillance tactic in the Ratbag's Handbook as he streaked his way across Europe.

In Cologne, when he failed to turn up yet again at a scheduled appointment – this time with a cryptocurrency wizard – I wandered through the cathedral, a masterpiece of high Gothic architecture with its filigree twin spires, the tallest in the world, dominating the city's panorama. Drifting inside, I stood over-awed by the stained-glass lozenges of light glinting in the sun like trapped butterfly wings.

Tish spent the day bedding a lederhosened lothario and jazz aficionado she'd met at some seedy basement venue. When she turned up late as usual, plonking herself down in a sloppy side-saddle on the bench at the beer hall table I was sharing with Skye, she speared a succulent sausage off my plate and elaborated, between mouthfuls, about how impressed Frederick had been by her singing career.

'Oh really?' I said, unable to help myself. 'So, tell me, did you play him a medley of your hit?'

Skye immediately started spouting advice on karma maintenance from psychotherapists and Reiki gurus about the benefits of positive thinking, suggesting Vitamin D, body-brushing and healing crystals. She'd taken to carrying around a little clear bottle filled with water, dish soap and glitter glue. She extracted this 'mindfulness jar', from her backpack and placed our hands on the bottle. 'This is a very powerful visual metaphor for expressing one's feelings.'

But, as Tish now forked up my sauerkraut without asking, my only feeling was – what the hell was I doing on a marital revenge decathlon with a tree-hugger whose elevator was stuck between floors and an indiscriminate, man-eating hornbag?

No doubt my companions were having the same allergic reaction to me, but we were bound together by our financial needs – Tish and Skye had remortgages to pay off and I had to recoup my kids' inheritance. Getting back our life savings was also the only way to save face. And so our unlikely trifecta pushed on.

Max's next call was to brainstorm a theory he had. As we hadn't glimpsed Jason through three cities, our husband was most probably making bookings and appointments then staking out the site to see if anyone was following him – cops, disgruntled investors, angry ex-wives . . . A shudder went through me as I imagined Jason watching us as we watched for him.

By the time we reached Czechoslovakia, I'd gained two kilos and lost two toenails. It was our fifth European country and our fortieth pint of that weird long-life UHT milk. I'd reached the point where all I wanted was to be air-evac'ed under heavy sedation to a sanatorium.

My tetchiness wasn't helped by lack of sleep. The ring money could only be stretched so far – Europe being no bargain basement – and as our finances dwindled, so did our accommodation. The rickety hotels we were now staying in were so decrepit they'd have had to be done up before they could be condemned. The rooms we shared were so small the cockroaches were hunch-backed and the dust mites round-shouldered. I was tired of ordering room service that was so slow to arrive, it was best to leave a forwarding address. I was also weary of Tish's peekaboo, crotchless and bondage-themed underwear drying all over the room. 'Wouldn't you like to keep Victoria's Secrets an actual "secret"?'

'Yeah, well, there are worse things,' she replied. 'For example, you could be the sort of wanker who uses their friggin' fingers in the air to indicate quotation marks around "ironic phrases".'

Jason, meanwhile, seemed to have embraced the full Eurotrash existence. Max sent us screenshots of the women our ex was now courting. They were invariably wealthy and 'of a certain age'; women with trust funds in tax havens and nasal reconstruction surgery from inhaling too much cocaine off the buttocks of toy boys. When their boats – well, their super yachts – came in these gals glided from a rock star's birthday party in Ibiza to a whipped cream orgy in San Moritz.

Our nemesis had branched out from low-hanging female fruit like yours truly to more exotic fare who flourished much higher up the social tree. But, with their old money and new underwear, these rich divorcees and widows gave Max a back-up method for tracking Jason. Face-recognition technology enabled my son to pinpoint Jason through the socialites' Insta posts. In every snap Jason was wearing his dazzling cat-that-ate-the-canary smile, and, judging by the backgrounds, was also speaking fluent waiter in every country on the continent.

Max's Sherlock-Holmes-ing revealed that Jason's risqué raison d'être was to recruit into his cryptocurrency scam rich women, who then recruited their rich friends, and so forth. This explained the globe-trotting, the wining and dining, the schmoozing and cruising. Basically, Jason was charming his way around the boudoirs of the world, building an empire on quicksand.

In Prague we nearly nabbed him. Thanks to Max's super sleuthing, we tracked him down to a Michelin-starred restaurant.

'When you wish upon a Michelin star, dreams really can come true,' Tish quipped as we sashayed into the swanky La Degustation. But Jason spotted us as we were blagging our way past the maitre d', and slid out of a side door with practised aplomb, leaping onto a passing tram, tipping a cocky wave our way.

In Copenhagen Max's undercover work ground to a halt.

'As Jason's using false identities with, I'm guessing, burner phones, there's a reduced digital footprint,' my son informed me on FaceTime. 'His cloned smartphone should still pick up this traffic. I suspect he's also using the dark web, which allows people to operate incognito. I'll need more heavy-duty software to tackle that weird underworld.'

Tish, Skye and I were sitting in a little café on the Langelinie promenade by the sparkling Copenhagen harbour. I looked at Tish, who was swigging Karlsberg in the sun, her legs up on the rickety table. Skye was sipping her usual Unicorn juice, twice filtered through a glacier. Ten metres from the shore, looking mournfully back at us, was the tiny bronze statue of Hans Christian Andersen's *Little Mermaid* – another female cruelly let down by a fella.

'I do know he's meeting some block-chain expert,' Max continued, 'but I don't know where or when. The answer might be in a weird message I picked up, though. Maybe you can work it out, Mum. You are a cruciverbalist, after all.'

The message pinged onto my phone. I read it out to my bemused accomplices:

Fear Hun, ask none 4, 6, 5
French but not French
Dammed by the Amstel
Ménage o'clock.
When? Don't beat yourself up. It's easy.

Tish looked baffled, ruminated for a moment, then blew a pink gum bubble, which she popped with a glittery fingernail while shaking her head. Skye shrugged, equally bamboozled. Before I could ask Max if he wanted to help out with his cryptic skills, he rang off. Jason was clearly taunting and testing me with this challenge – taunting me in that he'd always thought he was better than me at cryptic crosswords; and testing me by setting a trap to find out if I really was spying on his phone. The waiter was hovering. 'I'll take a cup of hemlock if you've got one,' I felt like saying despondently, but I ordered a double espresso instead, refocused and tried again, my fury with Jason packed tight as sardines.

'*Don't beat yourself up, it's easy,*' I mused aloud and thought for a while. The others were silent, watching me. 'Okay,' I said eventually – it had come to me in a flash. 'The Easybeats! "Friday on My Mind".'

Tish started to hum the famous tune as I scribbled out the second clue on a paper napkin.

'*French but not French.* Well . . .' This one was harder. Then it clicked. 'The Franks were an ethnic group from the Middle Ages covering France and other parts of Europe.' I scribbled down 'Frank?' on the napkin.

'*Dammed by the Amstel* could be . . . It's got to be Amsterdam?'

Only two more clues. In my determination to solve my adversary's riddle, I was channelling Inspector Rebus so completely I almost started talking in Scottish brogue.

'*Ménage o'clock . . . Must* be ménage à trois. So that would make it three o'clock?' Tish and Skye were looking at me with undisguised astonishment.

On I went: 'And *Fear Hun, ask none* – that must be an anagram.'

As the penny dropped as to this last clue, I looked at my scribbles with disbelief. Would Jason really choose such a poignant rendezvous for his shady dealings? Well, he was nothing if not ruthlessly unempathetic and tone-deaf to all sensibilities, so of course he would.

'Amsterdam,' I said, decisively. 'Anne Frank House. Three p.m. Friday.'

'*Really?* How?' Skye queried, peering dubiously at my inky workings-out.

'Yeah, you sure?' Tish raised a crayoned brown brow. 'If you're right, Gwennie babe, that's pretty bloody brainy, but I doan wanna schlepp all the way to Holland on a hunch. I imagine Amsterdam's just like the Tour de France – a lot of dudes on drugs, ridin' bikes.'

'There's a bit more to the place than that. Starting with the Van Gogh and Rijksmuseum,' I replied tartly, but secretly very pleased with myself for unravelling the strange workings of Jason's twisted mind. Bletchley Park clearly beckoned.

As the waiter hovered, I asked Skye for our kitty, doled out the right coins, then poked through the folds of her purse. Not only was the wolf at the door, but it would have to bring its own food. At the rate we were burning through Euros, we'd soon be so skint that if muggers stole our wallet, they'd put money in and give it back, out of pity. 'We need to talk about our budget,' I said, 'Pretty soon one of us will have to go.'

'Well, not me.' Tish swung her legs off the table and sat upright so suddenly, her metal chair squeaked with indignation. 'I've got nothin' to lose, now that I've lost everythin'.'

Skye nodded in agreement, placed her cool hands on our foreheads to administer an emergency aura cleanse followed by a meditation chant for positivity. And we were off again.

25

Gliding through Amsterdam by boat, I marvelled at this miraculous city, which floats and shimmers up out of the water like a mirage. Watching the sunlight dapple and dance on the canal as we eased our way along, I willed the Fate Fairy to wave her magic wand our way.

As 3 p.m. drew closer, we disembarked and made our way through medieval streets lined with golden age, gabled houses. The flower-bedecked canals and arched wrought-iron bridges suffused the city with an old-world charm that momentarily assuaged my anxieties. My shoulders had just dropped to somewhere around my ears when we rounded the corner onto the Prinsengracht canal and I recognised the supple, loose-hipped gait of the tall man walking into the entrance of the Anne Frank museum. Jason wore a new uniform – sockless loafers, Armani slacks and a cashmere sweater knotted casually around his big broad shoulders – but the physique was unmistakable. My face became so hot I was momentarily worried it would burst into flames.

Tish nodded at me with a mix of surprise and respect. 'You done good, kiddo. I never would've cracked that cryptic code. If I did, it'd be like,' she put a hand up to her mouth, like a makeshift megaphone. 'Call an ambulance! Jazz singer has freak accident! Struck by a thought!' She winked at me before tackling the situation with her usual trademark diplomacy, letting rip with the rebel yell of 'Oi! Fuckface. Gottcha, ya dingo-dicked deadshit!'

At the sound of Tish's broad accent, Jason wheeled around. He raked the sun-kissed hair out of his eyes. When he spotted us darting across the road towards him, his shoulder twitched, his head cocked and his eyes narrowed. Not missing a beat, he yelled 'Terrorists!' in his big bass baritone, pointing in our direction and ruthlessly deflecting the situation without so much as a blush.

Immediately two security guards barrelled into the doorway, barring our entrance. They stood firm, legs planted in an inverted V sign, patting ominous bulges in their pockets. Jason stood smirking behind them, watching the ensuing melee with cynical glee. Skye emitted an uncharacteristic lupine howl and sprang, as if from an ejector seat, towards him. One of the security guards put out his hand, traffic-cop style, instructing her in a chilly monotone, to please show ID. It was then that Skye spat out the worst word possible at the Anne Frank museum: 'Fascist!'

She was in an armlock within seconds as another hefty security guard galumphed through the door towards us. Things were going downhill faster than an elephant on a skateboard.

Then Tish did something truly inspiring. She burst into the Dutch national anthem. Her mellifluous, powerful voice rang out across the cobbled street with rich and sonorous purity. Passers-by paused appreciatively and sang along. One of the security guards saluted. Tish segued into Chevalier's 'My Old Dutch':

We've been together now for forty years,
An' it don't seem a day too much,
There ain't a lady livin' in the land
As I'd swap for my dear old Dutch.

The crowd was in the palm of her manicured hand. Coins were thrown, backs were patted, smiles rained down, Skye was released without charge. But Jason was long gone.

'You done good, kiddo.' I boomeranged Tish's compliment right back at her. But all she could manage was a queasy shrug.

'Honestly, you have a beautiful voice,' I persevered. 'If I entered a singing contest, I'd come second even if I was the only contestant.'

I looked to Skye for back-up, but she was downing a whole bottle of Rescue Remedy while pressing a rose quartz against her forehead chakra.

It might have been straight off to a cannabis café for the remainder of our miserable lives, if Max hadn't rung to triumphantly tell us that he had finally infiltrated Jason's dark web manoeuvres. Jason had another meeting scheduled at 5 p.m. at the private investment arm of the ABN AMRO bank. Did I copy that?

'Affirmative,' I said, in Max speak. 'Roger that. Over and out.'

This time, we would take no chances. Over pickled fish, savoury pancakes and bitterballen, the Three Muffkateers hatched our plan. Tish quickly made an appointment with an investment broker in the same bank branch at the same time, sending photo ID to secure her slot.

We found our (budget) hotel, dumped our stuff, and Skye and I set off to do a recce, leaving Tish to transform herself into a respectable-looking, wealthy businesswoman. As we left her she was applying liquid eyeliner with the precision of a surgeon.

Skye and I loitered discreetly near the bank's imposing entrance, glimpsing the interior – all dark wood like poured molasses, with flashes of gleaming brass and gold. I tried not to tie myself up in knots, but when Tish hadn't arrived by 4.55, I was fast resembling a pretzel. I stabbed at her name on my speed dial. No answer. At 5 p.m., a chauffeur-driven saloon swished up and Jason glided inside the building as though on invisible skis. I tried to call Tish again. Even the Zen devotee by my side was radiating anxiety – I could almost feel Skye's brain tightening and twanging.

At 5.10, Skye, who was the better dressed of the two of us, tried to bluff her way into the bank. But security proved tighter than a courtesan's corsetry in the nearby red-light district. At 5.15, my hopes were shrinking like a raisin. At 5.30, I felt the zig-zag of a migraine in my temples. At 5.45, my emotional thermostat was turned straight up to Hades. At 6 p.m. we rang Max and, sure enough, he told us that Jason was on the move once more. I scrunched my eyes closed and smacked the heel of my hand against my forehead. 'Tish had better already be dead, because I am going to kill her!'

But, bursting into our hotel room half an hour later, those harsh words came back to haunt me because there was Tish, spread-eagled on the bed wearing nothing but mint-green toenail polish and a mouth gag. Her arms and legs were tethered to the bed posts with her own stay-up stockings. As I sprang to her side, all my anger evaporated.

'Tish! Are you okay?' I pleaded, wrenching the gag from between her teeth.

Relief flooded through me as she licked her dry mouth then grizzled, 'Untie me, for god's sake.'

'What happened?' I unknotted her wrists first and then the ankles.

'Well, it was only going to be a quickie, you know, to relieve tension before confronting Jason. But turns out that Joah – he's the muso I picked up in the indie café downstairs, where I went for a quick nip of Dutch courage – is into Tantric sex. Jeesuz. I thought he'd never finish. No kiddin'. My orgasm took such a long time to come that it kept a diary of the trip.' She creaked to sitting, adding sheepishly, 'And then the prick left me tied up and stole my phone.'

I took a moment to absorb this information. Tish looked up at me with such rumpled embarrassment that I burst out laughing.

'It's not funny,' she yipped, pulling on a T-shirt.

'No, it really, really is.' I was now laughing with lunatic fervour. It wasn't long before Tish caught my infectious giggle and cracked up too at the ridiculousness of it all. Because, well, what else could a girl do? I told her, between chortles, that I would've ordered us a restorative drink from the bar but this was probably the kind of establishment where they watered down the water, which only made us laugh more – an unstoppable tsunami of hysteria.

That night the Three Muffkateers finally admitted defeat. Jason had out-smarted us. Confronting our lack of success, Skye was pushed to extremes – she actually ate a carbohydrate. I watched in astonishment as she lay on our saggy communal bed, munching her way through a plate of cannabis-infused Dutch delicacies called 'space cakes'. A subdued Tish spent the evening vigorously scrubbing her underwear then draping it around the room to dry. I took in the decor of drab brown furnishings and walls the watery yellow colour of leftover soup, the nylon sheets that would have my hair standing on end for weeks, and came to one conclusion. Did I really need to have this good a time?

An air of desolation hung above us like a wet tarpaulin. I missed home, with its cornucopia of beachy aromas and that big beautiful sky. And oh how that thought made me long to be curled up on my couch, watching animals mating in a David Attenborough documentary. I missed the daily routine of sock-sorting and ice-cube-tray refilling. What if the kitchen smoke alarm batteries needed changing? What if Max was using steel wool on my non-stick pan? Why had I put everything on hold to take off on this absurd and disagreeable pilgrimage?

We'd had one too many near-misses, and one too many nights in hotels that were so crummy the staff were stealing towels from the guests. It was time to throw in said towel; if I could find one that wasn't covered in Tish's fake tan and make-up or Skye's mindfulness glitter.

I rang Max to thank him for all his hard work and instruct him to stand down. But before I could explain that the shit had well and truly demolished the fan, my son leapt in. 'Jason's just booked a flight to Brisbane and a hotel in Noosa, the Seabreeze. Under the name of Fabio Beyonde.'

'Fabio Beyonde? It sounds like the starter at a gastro pub.'

Max gave a little chuckle once more and a warm glow suffused me.

'Are you sure?' I probed.

'I hacked into a server of the Encrochat encrypted communication service he's using for his cryptocurrency. It's how he's laundering money through all those dodgy mining ventures of his. Once I had his fake name, it was easy to do a little light digging and locate his booking via his new credit card usage. Some duty free would be adequate recompense, Mother, dear. Copy that?'

Before I could thank my idiosyncratic son with an 'Affirmative. Roger that', he'd once again hung up.

I turned to face my world-weary accomplices, with a smile this time. 'We're going home!'

Forget my fear of flying and needing to sit in the emergency escape aisle. To finally bring Jason Riley to justice, I'd fly back sitting on the goddamned *wing*.

PART SEVEN

26

Noosa is a cosy but cosmopolitan town nestled beside a national park of fragrant tea-tree woods, and chock-a-block with world-famous surfing beaches, where 'pod-cast' takes on a literal meaning as visitors broadcast dolphin sightings. There should be whiplash warning signs on its coastline: 'Tearing your gaze from the sparkling sea to the koalas canoodling in the tree tops and back to the sea again could do you serious damage'. Noosa is also plastic-free – well, not counting the boob jobs of the glitterati, who lie topless on sun loungers or dine by the shore on local kingfish carpaccio.

While we'd got used to staying in hotels where the staff go into a frenzy of indifference at every query, Jason's hotel could have had its guests hospitalised from hospitality. Jetlagged from our long flight in economy we stood in its marble foyer gawping at the ostentatious opulence of the gleaming chandeliers and manicured terraces which swept down towards the sapphire sea.

'Beyond sumptuous,' Skye whispered.

'If I were staying here, I'd never get up before the crack of noon,' I concurred.

'Too right. Especially when you're bein' served brekky in bed every mornin' by tautly buttocked waiters in crisp white jackets. Jeez, when I think of the tiny shitty shoeboxes where we've been bunkin' down, my blood boils.'

'And don't forget that *our* hard-earnt money is paying for all this poshness,' Skye concluded indignantly.

We'd hatched plan one thousand and ninety-eight (so it felt) on the plane. We'd devise a cunning ruse to lure Jason out of his room then finally gain access to his laptop so Max could hack into Jason's bank accounts.

As soon as we'd landed, we'd peeled off some precious dollars from our damp crumple of shrinking cash to purchase a ticket to a big football match scheduled that afternoon in BrisVegas. Though Jason was an Ironman fanatic, we thought the footy was a safe bet: all the codes blurred into one for me, but Tish said she'd seen him barracking at league matches on their TV. On our arrival at Jason's hotel, we sent the ticket and a note to his room – or the room of one Fabio Beyonde – which read 'From the staff at Seabreeze Hotel, in appreciation of your custom.'

We knew it would take Jason two hours to drive back to Brisbane. Kick-off was at 4 pm and, sure enough, around 1.30 we saw the porter bring round a hire car from the hotel garage, into which Jason stepped. After some surreptitious inquiries from Tish, the porter confirmed that Mr Beyonde was indeed on his way to Brisbane.

Just to be safe, we waited another few minutes before we decided the coast was clear. Tish and I continued to skulk in the foyer while Skye, pretending to be a delivery woman, took flowers to the front desk, asking for them to be delivered to Fabio

Beyonde's room immediately. After Skye sauntered away, Tish and I watched the bellboy being instructed to take the flowers upstairs. We followed, in the guise of guests, gossiping and laughing as though to the highlife born. When the lift pinged to a halt at the eighth floor, we followed the bellboy, strolling casually by as he entered room 8009. Now we had Jason's room number, all we needed was access.

Regrouping downstairs, it was decided that Skye and Tish would loiter on the eighth floor until a maid or minibar servicer turned up. After they had serviced Jason's room, Tish would distract the staff member with a faked fainting fit. Skye would swipe the key from the trolley, sprint to open Jason's door, prop it open an inch with her packet of bio frequency healing patches, sneak the key back before – hopefully – the employee noticed anything was amiss, and dash back to access the room. Tish would make her recovery, and, when it was safe, double back to join Skye. Max had instructed Tish to search Jason's room for his online banking double authentication key-code device, while on FaceTime he tried to help Skye crack Jason's laptop and banking codes to transfer back our stolen cash. If Max and Skye couldn't break into the software and accounts they needed to, the girls would simply have to steal his laptop.

This all sounded plausible until Tish decided that my job would be to wait in the lobby just in case Jason returned before we expected him to.

'Me?! Why me?'

'Because, Ms Goody Two Shoes, I doubt you're all that skilled at burglary or cyber-crime. I've spent my life breakin' into the hotel rooms of drunken drummers. And Skye's the youngest and most tech-savvy. I mean, *you* practically write with a bloody quill and ink.'

And so it was that, moments later, I found myself nervously crossing the hotel lobby, head down as though dodging enemy fire. I positioned myself on a squat couch half-hidden by a pot plant and lowered my novel – yes, still *Middlemarch* – an inch below my eyes, mimicking a TV detective on a stakeout.

Half an hour later, a shiver of ghostly shock ran through me once more because suddenly there he was, strolling cockily across the hotel lobby like he owned the joint. His akubra sat at a rakish angle, he was wearing an expensive-looking pair of Ray-Bans, his R.M. Williams boots clip-clopped on the marble floor and his peachy posterior filled out his Levi's with muscular panache.

'*Jason?*' I forced myself to utter his name out loud as he passed my couch.

When he saw me, my vagabond husband swayed as though he'd been buffeted by a gale-force wind. He gawped at me for a moment, then took two big steps in my direction. I braced myself for a punch . . . but instead he hugged me.

'Well, well, well – look what the tide washed in. How the *hell* did you find me this time? I've been playing pretty hard to get,' he grinned completely shamelessly. 'No cryptic clues this time. Although thanks for confirming my suspicions that I was still being tailed.'

My legs didn't shake or give way beneath me, nor did I wet my pants, so I deemed these opening minutes of my waylaying ruse a success.

Jason glanced around furtively, surreptitiously slipping his sunglasses back up his nose. 'Are you alone? I know you'll tell me the truth. You're the only person I know who's incapable of telling a lie.'

'Yes,' I said nasally, so that I could still honestly say that no lie had ever passed my lips.

Jason took a good long look at me, his eyes travelling down and then up my body. 'I've missed you, Gwen,' he said casually as though he'd just got home from work.

It took me a moment to regain my equilibrium. 'Oh really? Or do you just miss my bank account? When we got married I seem to remember you said you'd be eternally indebted to me. I didn't know you meant *financially*.'

'As quick-witted as ever, I see. I do owe you an explanation, I know that.' I smelt the odour of insincerity coming off him, a sour reek of selfishness and egotism.

'There's only one explanation, Jason. I took you for better or for worse . . . and you took me for everything,' I said, paraphrasing Tish.

I must have been speaking more emphatically than I realised because passing hotel guests glanced curiously in our direction.

Jason lowered his warm, velvety voice. It was a tone made to cast evil spells, charm deadly snakes and steal women away. 'Gwen, let's talk this through over a cocktail.'

'Yeah. Sure. As long as it's a Molotov. That kind of cocktail would make it a very happy hour for me indeed.'

He hitched a sardonic brow then steered me by the elbow into the bar, through swirls of cheery laughter, to a corner table at the back, en route issuing instructions to the waiter. As soon as we'd sat down on the plush velvet banquette, I extricated myself from his silky grip and groped for my phone to send an SOS text to my co-conspirators. 'So?' I demanded thin-lipped, stalling for time as I tried to furtively type. 'What are you doing here?'

'What? Today? Well, I was on my way to Brizzy for a footy match, but the traffic was horrendous so I decided to come back and do some work. I've got a few big deals in the pipeline.'

My blood boiled. 'Is that right? So you'll be able to pay me my money back then.'

Jason took off his sunglasses and hat and rubbed his hand over his head. He looked as fit as ever, and was now sporting a close-cropped haircut like a US marine. His face wore a shifting cocktail of moods – amiable, amused, remorseful, playful, sinister, cruel, contrite.

'Look, I've made some boo-boos—'

'"Boo-boos" doesn't even come close to describing what you've done,' I scoffed. 'That's like Hannibal Lecter excusing his behaviour by apologising for not being a vegetarian.'

Jason returned my fury with a sheepish gaze. 'What do you say to the woman you've stabbed in the back? "I'm sorry" doesn't really cut it, does it?' His melodious, ironical tones suddenly betrayed a tremor. 'How do I explain the financial shitshow that drove me to lead a double life? I just couldn't bear to see the disillusionment in your eyes. I'm a coward, okay? I was broke and took the coward's way out and buggered off. But I want you to know, Gwen, that you are the only woman I've ever loved.'

'I bet you say that to all your wives,' I retorted, bitterly. 'If you loved me so much you wouldn't have cheated on me and then vanished. Obviously we just didn't want the same things. I wanted "happy ever after" and you wanted a fifty-year-old jazz singer, a forty-year-old Kiwi geologist, a thirty-year-old American dive instructor and a septuagenarian French aristocrat.'

Jason extended his wrists upwards as if waiting to be hand-cuffed. 'Guilty as charged,' he said. 'You are my favourite wife, though.' He gave a roguish smile, apparently expecting me to take this as a huge compliment.

I looked at him, agog. 'That's the same as saying syphilis is your favourite STD.' Who *was* this man I'd once loved so passionately?

A bottle of champagne arrived. As Jason supervised the waiter's cork popping technique, I finally managed to type 'RUN' on my phone and press 'Send'. Jason poured two glasses with poised perfection, then raised his frothing flute, shooting me a look of contrition. 'I've behaved like a bloody idiot,' he said. 'Can you ever forgive me?'

'No.' I glugged the champagne in one mouthful to try to quell the murderous rage seething up in my breast.

'Oh, Gwen, I can't really explain what happened. Life with you was so good, and then, it's like my brain went . . .' he made a *pffffffft* noise.

I waited expectantly then finally replied, 'That's it? That's your excuse for stealing my money, committing bigamy – sorry, trigamy – breaking my heart and faking your own death? *Pfffft*?'

'Look, I was in debt. I didn't know how to tell you. I was disgusted with myself,' Jason said. 'I needed capital to put a few deals in play and an associate recommended investing in Bitcoin. With cryptocurrency, I thought I could double our money. Well, I soon found out that the best way to double your money is to fold it over twice and put it back into your wallet. I ended up in even more debt. Meanwhile, I was exhausted from my shifts at the mine and I wasn't thinking straight.

'All my mining ventures and investments started going tits up. I owed money everywhere. And I'd already borrowed so much from you . . .' He rubbed his eyes to show how long-suffering and misunderstood he was. 'And then I met Tish, who was crazy about me and kept saying how she'd just got this huge divorce settlement and wanted to share it with someone special. She said that if we got married we could have a joint bank account. It looked like an easy way out.'

I shook my head in disgusted disbelief. 'You're so in love with yourself, Jason, you really should just take your *own* hand in marriage.'

'I've got a problem, okay? I know that now. I think I'm an adrenalin junkie – addicted to the double rush of adrenalin and testosterone you get from running the longest race, leaping off the tallest cliff, wave or piste, swimming the most treacherous ocean, or juggling the most number of illicit relationships. I'm not proud of it. It's obvious that I need help.'

Words rolled so effortlessly off his tongue – silken words spinning a cocoon of lies around me. With a quiz-show host's smooth bonhomie, he levelled his gaze to mine, gave a quick downward glance, scratched a corner of his mouth with a casual thumb and inhaled a chuckle. I recognised the sequence. It's often deployed by a charming movie star right before he tells a disarming anecdote on a chat-show sofa. I cut Jason off coldly before he could say any more.

'You'll need a narrative sander to get the bumps out of that story. What about Skye? How does she fit in to the equation? Plus, I know you gave up working at the mine after you met Tish. You couldn't lie straight in bed, Jason Riley.'

He erupted into a baritone boom of a laugh. 'Ha ha. That sharp wit of yours – it can draw blood. It's one of the things I love most about you. God, I've missed you, Gwen.'

I let him have it with both verbal barrels, armed with ammo I'd been storing up for weeks. 'Love?! Don't talk to me about love, you duplicitous, treacherous, evil, vile, manipulative, Machiavellian, narcissistic sociopath.'

Jason gave his Cheshire Cat smile that in other circumstances could melt a woman at a hundred paces. He topped up my champagne, purring, 'Well, nobody's perfect.'

I launched into a litany of complaints that continued for a full ten minutes. But each loaded question was either batted away or rebuffed with confident fabrication. 'Can't you just stop lying!' I finally fumed.

'Okay, I admit, I am blustering, but only to cover up my mortification.'

'*Bluster*? This goes way beyond bluster, Jason. "Bluster" is merely windy rhetoric. You're suffering from epistemic insouciance – the state of simply not caring what the facts are. In other words, it's not bluster, it's bullshit – on a Trumpian level.'

His shoulders suddenly stooped and his head bent low, drained of all vitality. 'You're right. Make me eat my words. In fact, I would relish the meal.'

'Then, bon appétit,' I said coldly.

'Look, I think my behaviour is a cry for help. It must go back to my troubled childhood. There's a reason I never talked about my parents, you know. Because it was too painful to do so. And their physical abuse was nothing compared to the mental torture—'

'But you told Skye and Tish you were an orphan raised by a vicious aunt.'

'Ah, yes, well, I was . . . after my parents died . . . Of drug overdoses . . .'

'So, wait, let me get this right. You're telling me your being an unwanted child is the reason you're now wanted by the police in several different countries? Spare me!'

'Have you called them, by the way? The police, I mean?' Jason's breeziness was betrayed by his eyes, which darted surreptitiously around the crowded bar.

'No. Not yet. We've had our reasons. The main one being that I wanted to talk to you first.'

'Thanks, Gwennie. And the others? Macbeth's witches?' His eyes zoomed about once more. 'Are they lurking nearby with their cauldron?'

'We parted ways,' I said – nasally again, and feeling a lava-hot blush suffuse my face. I hoped he hadn't noticed or that he'd put my flushed countenance down to the vast quantities of champagne I was chugging.

'Amazing you found me this time. What happened to your famous fear of flying?'

'Conquered. You always underestimated me . . . and my kids. Especially poor Max. I tried to ignore the way he was around you, like a kicked dog. In fact, I look back in amazement at what I – and they – tolerated. You missed our wedding anniversary for three years running, Julia's graduation, my niece's baby's gender-reveal party. You didn't even vary the excuses you made up – shifts at the mine, Ironman comps all over the world—'

'But all those excuses were true! I was sweating so hard trying to make my investments profitable while working a month on, a month off at the wretched mines. When I wasn't working I was competing, keeping myself fit for you. Although,' he grinned, cheekily, 'I did lie about the gender-reveal party – fuck that shit!'

He waited for me to be amused, but I wasn't. 'Yet you made time for your motorbike and your music, with that ridiculous guitar of yours. Oh, and art classes, apparently. That's how you met Tish, isn't it? Look, I can see one of your abstract portraits now. No, wait, sorry, that's just a mirror.'

'Okay, I could blame so many things – work pressure, crappy parents, dodgy investment advice, bad luck . . . But the buck stops with me. I know that.'

'Ah, literally. As in – you've stolen *all our money*.'

'If a bloke doesn't learn from his mistakes, what's the point of making them? So, Gwen, sweetheart, how can I make it up to you?'

'You can start by giving back my life savings.'

'You do know that money can't buy happiness. That's why we have credit cards,' Jason winked. When I glared back at him with undisguised loathing, he added, 'You're as hard to hug as a pillow-case full of coat-hangers, these days, Gwennie, do you know that?'

'Can you blame me?' I asked, thin-lipped.

His smile broke on me like a wave on a rock as he covered my hand with his own warm paw. I suddenly felt as though I was looking at things underwater. My thoughts shimmered. A long-forgotten love pang corkscrewed through me. I could never forgive Jason for the agony he'd put me and the kids through – when it comes to the pain and humiliation I have a photographic memory – but one touch of his hand and it was as though I'd forgotten to take the lens cap off.

'Gwendoline.' He leant in and tenderly tucked a strand of my hair behind my ear. My body responded instantly – I was Pavlov's dog waiting for him to throw me a bone. Literally, as Tish would have said.

The thought of Tish pulled me up short. If I'd been in a black and white movie, this would be the time I'd cross my stockings, light up a cigarette, blow smoke in Jason's face and say 'Game's up, big boy' then flash my undercover police officer's badge. Instead, I was struck by the memory of Jason telling me he was taking me to his favourite spot, then flipping me over, sliding a pillow beneath my hips and whispering, 'I think this position hits your spot quite nicely, don't you?'

Taking advantage of what must have been my momentary loss of IQ, he ran his finger softly down my cheek. The gesture imme-diately rekindled the tender sensuality of our former intimacy.

I couldn't help shivering with delight. A wave of tenderness welled up within me, caressing my lips like the carbonated bubbles of the champagne he was pouring into my glass.

When we'd first met, after all those years of widowhood, I'd been so nervous about getting naked in front of a man. Jason's response was to slowly undress me in front of the mirror and show me that my body was beautiful. He'd woken me up from a long sexual slumber – like an erotic prince to my Sleeping Beauty. And then there'd been no time to worry about hiding baby marks or other lumps or bumps, because my whole body was a quivering, orgasmic jelly.

'I still love you,' he said now.

Jason has the charisma of a motivational speaker – and right now he was hellbent on motivating me to love him all over again. He caressed my thigh under the table, and there it was once more – the feeling of liquid gold being poured through my veins. I felt weak-kneed, shin-kicked, sucker-punched, head over hormonal heels. I needed to be lashed to a mast, my ears blocked with wax.

'I had to come back to Oz to tie up a few loose business ends, finalise some contracts, shake a few hands, pat a few backs. All so I could pay you back, sweetheart. I don't care less about the others. Tish, Skye, Carly, Brigitte – they were just a means to an end to make things right with *you*.'

He stroked my leg again, his fingers grazing the top of my inner thigh. His touch was like a low-volt electric charge that hummed against the inside of my spine.

'I'm going to get your money – right now. Meet me at the marina at 5.30. I've rented the last boat moored on pier two: a catamaran named, appropriately, *Aquadisiac*.' He smiled wickedly. 'I'll give everything back to you then.'

247

I shivered but forced myself to remain calm. 'Why on earth would I let you out of my sight? In case you've forgotten, I've just chased you all over the world. Your vanishing act is so good, you should be in the Cirque du Soleil.'

Jason handed me his wallet. I opened it to find three credit cards. He also extracted two passports from his top pocket. 'I'm now your hostage,' he said. Contrition seemed to hit him like a landslide. 'Don't tell anyone. And come alone. If you bring the cops or those other two, you'll never see your savings again.'

'Are you flying the Jolly Roger?'

'Always. We'll take the boat out on a little sunset cruise, maybe throw a line over. I'm still getting the feel for her. But, who knows? Perhaps, if I can win you back, you'll come with me when I sail out of here in a couple of days. Anywhere you want to go. Vanuatu? New Caledonia or Tahiti? We could start over.'

My brilliantly astute psychological acumen and tough negotiation skills became strikingly evident when I looked at him and nodded meekly.

At least that's what *he* thought. In reality, I was a spurned, burnt woman with an empty bank account. If he hadn't been so in love with himself and so persuaded by his own charms, he would have noticed that the look I was giving him was actually reminiscent of a starving dingo giving a lost tourist the once-over.

Then again . . . I watched him wet his lips with his tongue, recalling the way his warm mouth moved down my body. I tried to ignore how his hair smelt like vanilla, his skin of musk. Lust can play havoc with a woman's memory. And morals. And common sense. And plans of retribution.

What I knew for sure is that lust is life's banana skin. And it's so, so easy to slip . . .

27

The *Aquadisiac* bobbed in the water at the far end of the quay.

Jason whipped off his Ray-Bans and zapped me with a smile as he met me at the entrance to the marina. 'Thank for you giving me a second chance.' We walked down to pier two and he stretched out his hand to help me aboard the boat, like a gallant knight of yore. 'I did it all for you, you know, Gwen – to get back your money which I lost. Hopefully this will make up for the shit I've put you through.' He pointed with his bare brown foot to a canvas bag lying in the aft cockpit. 'In there is what I owe you. All of it. Plus interest.'

'I can think of other ways to pay me back,' I said in my flirty voice, which sounded rusty from disuse.

He gave me that smoky look which always meant mischief then gestured towards an esky. 'I brought martinis – your favourite. Let's go for a little sail and talk about the future . . . I've missed you so much, Gwennie. I've made so many mistakes. Can you really forgive me? I just can't imagine my life without you in it. It's like . . . well, it's like a world without Shakespeare.'

I canted a brow, replying breezily, 'Think about it. *Titus Andronicus*? Would that be such a loss?'

Jason laughed. 'Ah, that dry wit again.' He looked at me for a moment, his eyes bright and beguiling, just as I remembered them, and winked – a wink as dirty as those pre-mixed martinis. Then he unzipped the canvas bag, and all I could see were hundred-dollar bills. I reciprocated, handing back his wallet and passports, smiling until my cheeks cramped and my lips went numb.

Jason went to the flybridge console and turned the ignition, clearly enjoying the virile baritone roar of the engine. As he steered the boat out of the marina, I sat on the white leather seat in the aft cockpit, watching the foam curdling against the boat as it churned through the sea.

Once we were out of the harbour, Jason cut the engine and soon the mainsail was set and flogging in the wind. The other sails also puffed up like cheeks as our plucky little catamaran turned through the eye of the wind. And then we were flying. It was as though our boat had snorted cocaine. Skimming over the shimmering silver sea, Jason was winding winches as the wind dictated.

'Get ready to tack!' he called. The boat gave a lurch and my face was spritzed in spray as it heeled over. A pod of dolphins leapt into the air, their precise aquatic choreography reminding me of an Olympic synchronised swim team.

We sailed north, past rocky outcrops cantilevered over crystal-clear lagoons teeming with stingrays. Skirting the edge of resinous rainforests we inhaled a cornucopia of exotic aromas. Before long, an 80-metre-high bank of vibrantly coloured sand came into view, towering over a long pristine white beach. I had my bearings – this was Rainbow Beach, with its seventy-two different hues, from custard-yellow to ruby-red. The geographical layers had been forming since the last Ice Age as a result of iron oxide and leached vegetable dyes.

'Look!' Jason pointed. 'A dugong. Sailors thought they were mermaids.'

'Which showed how long they'd been at sea!' I bantered.

After yet more heaving and ho-ing we finally dropped anchor in a little cove, a crescent moon of deserted white sand fringing the turquoise sea beneath the big blue generous sky. Jason lowered the sails and the anchor, then he leapt down to join me in the cockpit. I watched as he broke out the martini shaker from the esky and poured out two cocktails. The setting sun began to wrap the lush, tropical coastline in crimson gossamer and the inky gauze of early evening started to settle on the sea. A cooling rainstorm was in the air. Jason popped in an olive and passed the chilled martini glass my way.

I could see he was just about to propose a toast when the stowage locker hatch banged open. We both turned around to see . . . Tish, halo-ed in sunlight.

'Don't move, you slimy sonofabitch! I wanna forget you exactly as you are now.' Tish's basso profundo reverberated around the boat.

In general, I find that a husband's opinion of his wife is greatly influenced by whether or not she is pointing a gun at his head.

'A Smith & Wesson .38 calibre – that thing packs a punch,' Jason said, the calm in his voice belying his furious expression. He didn't look remotely frightened, which was profoundly annoying. 'Put it down before someone gets killed.'

'You're wrong, matey. Guns don't kill blokes. A wife who discovers her hubby's run off with all her money is what kills blokes.' Tish berated Jason with a string of explicit curses exclusively insulting a particular part of his anatomy.

'Come now, Tish. You mustn't put Jason down too much to his face. I mean, we're talking about the man he loves,' I said as equably as I could manage under the circumstances.

Wife Number Three then launched onto the deck like a human distress flare. 'Shit. You too?!' Jason yelled at Skye. He wheeled around to me. 'So much for no lie ever passing your lips.'

'I talked through my nose,' I said coolly. 'Did you honestly think I'd abandon my friends? Yes, you've given me back my money,' I indicated the canvas bag, 'but what about the life savings of my pals?'

After I'd surreptitiously texted Tish and Skye from the hotel bar, warning them to vacate Jason's room, we'd regrouped in the hotel's latticed gazebo – used for waterfront weddings, ironically. They reported that Max hadn't had time to crack Jason's computer security code so they'd taken his laptop. When I told them the arrangement Jason and I had made, rather than rely on Max to break into Jason's computer, we concocted our strategy to stow away and simply get our lying scumbag husband to do it himself.

'I thought you still loved me?' Jason asked me in a wounded voice.

'Our love for you is as dead as you'll soon be, you poxy prick,' Tish spat out, 'unless you tell us the passwords to your bloody bank accounts.'

'For a smart man, you really are quite stupid,' I said. 'Anyway, I know now that you only ever loved me for my money. Our wedding ceremony should've been conducted by an accountant.'

'Of course, we'll happily divorce your sorry arse,' Skye enthused, brandishing a speargun, 'but not till we get custody of the cash. Gwen, get the laptop – it's in my pack over there.'

When Jason saw me extract his laptop from Skye's backpack, his face furrowed with furious frowns. 'How the hell . . . How dare you break into my hotel room!'

'How dare you break my heart,' Tish spat back. 'Bigamy? I mean, really? How the hell could you do that to me? To us?! Plus you sneakily remortgaged my house!'

'Girls, be reasonable.' Jason opened his arms in a welcoming gesture. 'I just needed your seed money as fertiliser. And it worked. I've grown a whole hedge fund in the last couple of months alone. All so I could pay you back. Let's just share out the money and bury the hatchet.'

'Surrrrre,' Tish crooned. 'As long as it's in your head!'

'You're not listening. I've finally cleared my debts, so you can have your money, with interest. I'm making a killing with this cryptocurrency caper.' Jason said these last words in that lilt I'd once found so fetching but now just sounded pathetically staged and annoying.

'We should be celebrating,' he went on.

'Hmmm . . . what do you give a man who's had everyone?' Tish mused sarcastically.

'I'd like to take you out for a celebratory dinner, I really would,' I played along. 'But you know what they say – never eat on an empty wallet.' I watched the hamsters in Jason's brain huff and puff as they raced to their wheels to crank up the old bullshit generator even higher. Sure enough, he started spluttering out justifications and apologies.

'Just spit out the passwords and we'll leave you in peace.' Tish waved the stubby-barrelled gun in his face.

'Go to hell!' Jason's tone turned now from wheedling to enraged defiance.

'If it means not spendin' any more time with you, I look forward to the trip.'

'Do you know how hard I've worked to pull off this scheme?' His chin quivered, but the emotion didn't quite reach his eyes.

'Don't play the victim,' Skye hissed. 'By the way, are there any more wives you've forgotten to tell me about?'

'Bloody oath,' Tish agreed. 'You get married so friggin' often you should hold all your weddin' ceremonies in a revolvin' door.'

'Have you seriously forgotten how you tried to ruin my life?' Skye persisted.

A film of indifference settled over his eyes. 'No. But given time, I'm sure I will.' Then, as though a pin had been pulled from a grenade, he made a lunge for Tish and knocked the gun out of her hands. As the revolver skittered across the wooden deck she ducked like a boxer, drove her clenched left fist hard into Jason's abdomen, then uppercut his chin with her other fist. This was followed by a snap kick to his knee, a karate chop to his neck and her elbow to his throat. Not what you'd expect from your average fifty-year-old mum of two.

'My advice is never to hit anyone below the belt, particularly a black one earnt in taekwondo,' she told her ex, whom she now had in a neck hold.

'You're a black belt in taekwondo?' I asked amazed. 'You kept that quiet.'

'I'm in a band. How else does a gal keep her roadies in line?'

As I retrieved Tish's revolver and returned it to her, Skye handed me the speargun and proceeded to treat Jason like a pinata. I was so bamboozled by the surreal situation in which I now found myself that at first I couldn't remember which end of the speargun to point at the victim. With his head wedged under Tish's arm, a speargun and revolver trained on his torso and a Kiwi geologist aiming a kick at his nuts, there was little Jason could do. A film of sweat like oil glistened on his tanned face. 'For god's sake!' he whispered. 'Go easy.'

'Will you give us the passwords?'

'Yes!' he bleated, defeated.

'And the authentication key-code device?'

'Yes,' he yipped once more.

Skye stopped whacking and Tish released her grip. She lined Jason up in her sights, Annie Oakley-style. His designer jeans were stained where Skye's wet shoe had kicked him in the crotch, and his shirt had a tear at the elbow. He looked more like a crazed inventor than a shrewd international businessman and professional scammer.

Jason, trying to buy time, reminded us that daily limits wouldn't allow him to transfer the large amounts we were demanding. Skye calmly reminded him that he'd insisted when they married that they set up an account under another name for tax purposes; a prior arrangement with the bank meant he could transfer the whole amount to her immediately, no questions asked. She then sat down at the starboard dinette and opened Jason's laptop, her head tilted attentively his way.

Jason had slumped into a silent sulk.

Tish cocked her gun. 'Dyin' is a very tedious ordeal, Jase. My advice is to not go anywhere near it. Don't forget I worked as a roo shooter's assistant, so my aim's spot on. I know how to slit animals' throats, and gut 'em too.'

'Just tell us the passwords, Jason, so we can crack open a nice bottle of schadenfreude,' I suggested.

In the distance, dark clouds roiled like a haemorrhage, and the wind was picking up. I could see the tadpole tail of a storm on the evening horizon. It matched our mood.

When Jason folded his arms and jutted out his chin, Tish squeezed the trigger. A bullet whizzed past his ear and thwacked impotently into the ocean. I nearly dropped the spear gun in shock.

'Skye reckons we get reincarnated every 100 to 500 years, 'cause one must rest and grow spiritually between incarnations. So, after I feed you to the fishes, you'll have plenty of time to think over how much easier it would've been if you'd just given us your bloody passwords.'

Jason cursed, then spat out his codes. Skye typed in all the various passwords and her own account details, authenticated the transfer and moments later told us that the money had abracadabra'd out of Jason's account and into hers. When she closed his laptop with a triumphant shout, Tish handed her the martini Jason had poured for himself earlier, passed me the second glass, before swigging her share straight from the cocktail shaker with a jubilant glug.

'To the Three Muffkateers,' she said, wiping her lips.

I was elated and overawed in equal measure. Standing on the deck, sipping a chilled martini, watching the horizon bleed away with the last of the sunlight, I couldn't believe we'd fulfilled our quest. We'd successfully tracked down our husband and retrieved our money, and now he sat cowed in the cockpit corner. A few moments ago, pretty well all we'd had in the world was Tish's Smith & Wesson and a rusty speargun. The range of sound effects available to me as a human seemed inadequate and I wished I were a kookaburra so I could tilt back my head and cackle with joy.

'So, ladies, now we're even, let's just call it quits, shall we?' Jason was still trying on his smarmy act. 'In this life, you're either the predator or the preyed upon. All those years of hard work, and I was still at the bottom of the slag heap. I wanted more out of life. Yachts. Ski holidays. Globe-trotting. "Economy" should only refer to a country's fiscal arrangements; not to the farty end of the aeroplane.'

'Well, sorry, but you'll just have to start all over again at the bottom, buddy, as you're now officially broke.' The lovely fuzzy buzz from the martini was taking effect. Oh, this felt good. I couldn't comprehend why people say that revenge is a dish best served cold. Vichyssoise is a dish best served cold. Revenge needs to be served steaming hot, garnished with tonsil-shredding amounts of chilli.

'Okay, let's tie up this mongrel, lock him below decks and get back to port,' Tish said.

I looked at her with amazement. 'You can skipper a boat as well?'

'Yeah. Sure. Can't you?'

I thought back to my one previous attempt at sailing, on a trip to the Hawkesbury with Jason, which had ended in an unfortunate call to the marina to alert them to the fact that their wharf had hit my boat. 'Gosh, Tish. Kangaroo culling, jazz singing, sailing-boat skippering . . . Is there anything you *can't* do?'

'Well, my interpretive dance and yodellin' needs a little work,' she winked. 'Now, who's got some rope?'

'Wait,' Skye said. 'Is getting our money back enough?' There was a moment of sombre reflection, as she kept the speargun aimed at Jason's groin.

'Are you suggesting we find a way of making him a less prolific groom?' I inquired tentatively.

'It would be nice to take him out of the marriage – and baby – market for good,' Skye toyed with the speargun.

'Yeah, let's neuter him.' Tish cracked open the second cocktail shaker, took a hefty slug and passed it to Skye, then me. 'No gal would want him then.'

The boat bobbed around in the swell. I began to feel a bit seasick – that queasy feeling you get right after a bad batch of prawns. I swayed sideways.

Jason's eyes were on me, watchful, wary.

I was in a cold sweat all of sudden. A Frankenstein-type flash of lightning scissored through the sky. Or was I imagining it? Terror didn't engulf me in one bite but crawled along my spine like a slow paralysis.

Skye's hand chilled my arm in a death grip before she reeled and keeled over onto the deck, accidentally firing the speargun as she fell. The spear hit the rubber duckie with a hiss.

Tish wheeled, as if to charge, before snorting twice and sagging to her knees like a wounded buffalo, her head coming to rest by Jason's feet.

'What's happening?' I managed to croak out. I was crouching now in the cockpit. Next to me was the canvas bag. I lurched sideways, knocking it over, and it yawned open. A thin layer of bank notes fluttered deckward, revealing what lay beneath: rope, electrical tape, gags.

Jason chortled – a dry little chuckle. He prised the gun from Tish's clammy hand and loomed towards me, his voice softly sinister. 'Enjoying your martini, Gwen?'

Another lightning bolt corkscrewed across the dark sky. Panic rolled in and pulled me under. My befuddled mind flitted back in time to that disastrous school camping trip I'd once led into the Blue Mountains. On the first night I'd fried up various mushrooms we'd foraged in the forest, and pretty soon the whole class was hallucinating and had to be rushed to hospital. It had turned out to be a very different kind of 'school trip'. Well, I hadn't felt this stoned since then.

As I lost consciousness, my only thought was, is it too late to escape to a witness protection program?

The last thing I remember is everything on the boat quietening, except for the weird sucking sound of its bilge pump, which sounded like a woman choking.

28

Somewhere in the semi-darkness a woman whimpered. A moment or two later, I realised it was me. I tasted salt air on my tongue – the sharp tang of it woke me with a start. My eyes flipped open. My mouth was sour, my throat scratchy. I felt a jolt of panic. Where was I? When things get dangerous, I like to think with my legs . . . Except they were tied up. As were my hands. Besides the thud of my heart pounding, all I could hear were the clicks and ticks and hisses of the sailing boat.

I discerned another whimper and turned to see Tish was slumped next to me, her hands also tied in front of her body and her legs shackled to the boat railings.

'Tish, are you okay? Wake up.'

She lifted her head, glanced around to get her bearings then said, 'Ugh. Bummer.'

'Um . . . We've been drugged and bound by our deranged psycho husband and that's all you can say? That's like watching a tsunami approaching and saying, "Oops".' There was an edge of hysteria in my voice. There was also a nasty welt on my thigh and an eggplant-coloured bruise on my shin where I'd no doubt collided with the deck. I could feel a throbbing near my temple. 'Do I have a bump on my forehead?'

Tish squinted at me through blurry, heavily made-up eyes. 'Yep. A beauty.'

I examined Tish, who appeared unscathed. 'You don't.'

'Yeah, well, clearly my eyelashes broke my fall,' she said. 'See? I've been tellin' ya to wear more make-up.'

Another groan alerted us to Skye's presence. She was off to our right, similarly trussed up like a turkey. Wide-eyed, wild-haired, the normally perfectly groomed geologist looked like a hair-care-magazine reject, or the 'Before' photo in a makeover feature.

I tried to keep calm. It helped to think that somewhere far away quokkas were contentedly canoodling by a billabong and dugongs were cavorting in the deep without a trouble in their watery world. It was a beautiful morning, and ours was the only boat in sight. As the sun shone onto the thickly forested hills, the wind whispered across the water and the kangaroos bounded along the beach, all we could hear was Jason's rod whipping though the air then landing with a little plop.

Five minutes later he panthered, barefoot, from the boat bow and threw a freshly caught fish onto the deck, where it gasped and squirmed. I knew just how it felt. 'Well, girls, the fish are really biting today.'

'I thought you preferred to fish for compliments?' I said with a bravado I didn't feel. Jason's hair, wet with spray, was brushed straight back like a car salesman or a Mormon preacher or, more aptly, a Mafia hitman.

'That's about 1.2 kilos of prime grouper there, ladies,' Jason boasted, ignoring my barb.

'No doubt it'll be five bloody kilos by the time you get back to the marina,' Tish said, with as much insouciance as a brain haemorrhage would permit. 'When are we headin' to town, by the way?'

'Do you know what you call someone who lies about the size of the fish he's caught? A fisherman.' Jason gave a nonchalant chuckle. 'But you girls took the bait nicely.'

'What do you mean?' Skye said, groggily. She was coming round. I noticed that her white linen trousers were torn, revealing a knee festooned with angry red contusions.

'Did you honestly think I didn't know you'd bring your posse, Gwen?' Jason's voice boomed triumphantly. 'Or that I meant anything of what I said to you? Not only are you insanely loyal but you wouldn't have the guts to track me down by yourself. That's more Tish's style – charging ahead, all bull-in-a-china-shop. I needed somewhere to get the three of you together, alone, so I played along. Just like I played that fish there.'

He looked at the grouper squirming near our feet, then clubbed it over the head. I watched as a trickle of blood oozed from its poor gaping maw.

'I gave you my bank passwords so you'd have something to celebrate. I knew Tish couldn't say no to a martini. And that she'd make sure you joined in the toast. How are you all feeling, by the way? Librium induces fatigue, headaches, dizziness, muscular pain and deep sedation. Alcohol compounds the effects. Too much leads to coma and then death. Although, I'm sure it's a tranquil way to go,' he added, consolingly. 'You wouldn't be aware of anything. Just like this grouper here.'

A shudder went through me. I'd suspected that this outlandish odyssey of ours would require endurance and sacrifice, but I wasn't expecting death. Jason was showing the compassion of a cornered jackal.

'Bigamy's having one wife too many. But surely monogamy's the same thing.' His cruel laughter crashed like a hailstorm onto the deck. 'I just made a second mistake before correcting the first,' he said, looking at me.

My stomach curdled. The sensation was much worse than seasickness or the drug-laced martini nausea – it was a visceral disgust. I thought back to the efforts I'd made on his behalf. I'd plucked and shaved and had bits and pieces of me waxed, and buffed up my skin till it glowed, moisturising every inch with mango-scented aphrodisiacal body cream.

'I married you for your money, Gwendoline, and believe me, I earnt it. That weird son of yours. And that pain-in-the-arse bossy daughter ... Although your layabout brats are no better, Tish. And as for all those vagina-scented candles and yoni egg workshops on the yoga deck, Skye. I mean, what's with all that hippy shit? You're a geologist, for god's sake. Speaking of which, thanks for all the contacts. The three of you did teach me a lot. Gwen, you opened my eyes to history and literature; Tish to music, and we had some fun with those motorbikes, didn't we?' He pointed to her abdomen, where her shirt had ridden up. 'I'm pleased to see you still have a tattoo of my name. A life-long reminder of our love,' he sniggered. Tish swore but no amount of wriggling and squirming succeeded in lowering her top. 'And Skye, I learnt more than I expected to from you about minerals, holotropic breathwork and harnessing the power of talismanic healing stones – what a crazy combo. You girls were my finishing school. You educated me enough to try out my new smarts on richer and richer women. Oh yes, there are bigger female fish to fry out there!' He chucked the grouper corpse into the ice box, then set about winching up the anchor.

The clouds had dispersed and the sun beamed down onto Jason as though it were an interrogator's spotlight.

'Women aren't complicated – you're pathetically simple, actually. You just tell the sexy ones they're brainy,' he said, looking at Tish. 'And the brainy ones they're sexy,' he said, looking at me. 'And the younger ones?' He tucked a strand of Skye's hair behind her ear, the very same intimate gesture he'd used on me in the bar. 'That you'll father their children. I started as an amateur with you, Gwen, but quickly found my calling. What can I say? Women just fall at my feet.'

'But only if you drug them first,' I replied, tartly. I looked up at him with revulsion. The man was seldom over-burdened by self-doubt, but his vanity had now kicked up into megalomania.

'You were the easiest mark, Gwen. Phrases like "I just want happiness" make you older chicks melt. It was textbook stuff. All I had to do was ask a lot of personal questions, make you feel special, spoil you in every way, especially in bed. Then exploit the emotional investment you had in me, to make you invest in my financial schemes.'

He started up the engine and gently nosed the boat into deeper water.

'Tish, you needed to feel desirable. Once I'd showered you with compliments in bed, you willingly gave me access to your bank accounts, transferring money, asking for investment advice, giving me copies of all your personal documents – passport and driver's licence. It wasn't hard to get together the paperwork to remortgage your house and you signed it with barely a murmur.

'With you, Skye, well, I had to start putting on a different game, selling you dreams of us having children one day. I told you everything you wanted to hear until you fell in love.'

Skye's face crumpled like a soggy soufflé.

Tish gave a bitter chuckle. 'Hey, dick breath, why don't you just eat dirt and die, yer lyin' sonofabitch.'

'And what about Carly? Did you also sucker her in by telling her lies she wanted to hear?' Skye lowered her head onto her chest as though trying to protect herself from a body blow.

The cords in Jason's neck stood out like cables. 'Leave Carly out of this. I really did love that girl. It broke me, her death . . .'

'And . . . were you going to have a baby with her?' Skye's voice trembled.

'Yeah,' Jason said wistfully. 'Carly would have made a wonderful mother.'

Skye's head jerked upwards as though a rod of iron had been inserted into her neck. 'And I wouldn't have?!' Her sob was so strangled that it sounded almost animal.

'That diving accident wouldn't have happened if you maniacs hadn't upset her. I blame all three of you bitches.' Jason's fury was intense, shimmering off him. 'So, just give me your fucking banking password, Skye, so we get all this over with.'

I felt as if a spike of ice had just been hammered into my spine. Get *what* over with? Jason's anger was scary, but what frightened me the most was the accompanying gelid calm in his eyes. I could see that my accomplices were thinking the same, hence the muted messages now being conveyed by our darting eyes and sky-high brows.

Jason's rod in the gunwale suddenly juddered. As he calmly walked over to it and played his catch, reeling it in, letting it go, tiring it out, he continued bragging about the thrill of baiting a new woman, hooking her in with lines, pretending to be empathetic until she was lured into his net. 'Along with her net worth,' he punned, pleased with himself. 'That's how I'm setting up my cryptocurrency company.'

'The preferred tender for scoundrels,' I muttered.

Jason cursed as his fishing line went slack. I silently cheered for the fish – at least one of us had got away.

'If you want to steal money, it's so much easier to set up a bank than rob one. Those banker wankers manipulate commodity prices, water down stock issues, trade bonds with privileged info gained at some absurdly overpriced titty bar. The equivalent activities when you're poor are called "stealing". But when you're rich, it's just called "business". "Business, bling, luxury" – that's my new motto.'

The catamaran was coasting along at 10 to 12 knots, zigzagging back and forth, waiting for the fish to come up from the depths into the sun-warmed surface waters. Jason cut the engine. All was silent as the sleek yacht bobbed on the briny.

'Lot of tuna and bait fish about,' Jason said, conversationally, chumming the water with a tote of freshly netted whiting. He draped a good-sized squid onto the hook, cast off and placed the rod back in the gunwale.

'I'm going to be so rich that even my butler will have a butler. I'm going to hire a professional hair trimmer for each nostril. Money can't buy you love but it certainly puts you in a better bargaining position.' He rummaged through our backpacks and casually extracted the last remaining cash from our purses. 'I'm going to own an island, with a beautiful girl on every beach. You see, I'm not against tying myself to one woman, I'm just against cutting myself off from all the others.'

'It must be hard to be humble when you're as awesome as you are,' I said. My only plan now was to keep him talking.

Jason shrugged. 'Like I said, in life you're either the prey or the predator.'

Tish enunciated a gaseous torrent of obscenities then spat in his direction. 'As I've told the girls many times, I look forward to runnin' into you again one day, Jason, preferably when you're joggin' and I'm drivin'; drivin' an armoured tank.'

Jason cast an icy look her way. 'Oh, I don't think we'll be running into each other again,' he said ominously. 'I don't know what I'm going to do without you, but I'm going to give it a try. Gee, what am I going to do for chum when I run out of this whiting?'

Mimed messages were once more conveyed between we captives with darting eyes and WTF eyebrows.

'So, what happened to Tish Delaney?' Jason said, in mock concern. '"Oh, didn't you hear? She died from a combination of old age . . . and a speargun through her head."'

'Oi! I'm *not* old!' Tish retaliated.

'And Gwendoline? "Well, Your Honour, she was attempting a long-distance swim. But she had some trouble with buoyancy."'

I was seriously starting to think I'd prefer death to another minute in the company of this treacherous torturer.

'And Skye. Did I tell you about the best way to get rid of a dead body? Wrap it in chicken wire and weight it down, so it sinks to the bottom of the sea. Then the fish destroy all evidence by simply nibbling the flesh off the bones. You're big on recyling, right?'

Jason began to hum. I couldn't make out the tune at first, then I realised it was 'Staying Alive' by the Bee Gees.

'But if you tell me the password I need, Skye, I'll drop all of you on that beach over there. By the time you get back to civilisation, I'll be long gone. And with no money left, your stalking days will be over, too. You ruined a sweet situation in the Loire by the way. Brigitte didn't even want a pre-nup – then you Three Stooges turned up. Password?'

'This is very bad karma, Jason,' Skye said sternly.

Jason formed a pistol out of his forefinger and thumb and pointed it at her temple. 'So's this,' he said.

I threw Skye an urgent look to tell her to do as he said. Tish also nodded. Skye's face pinched into a mask of concentration as she reluctantly spelt out her password.

Jason had just cracked open his laptop and started snouting around his online banking when the rod whirred and the line spooled outwards at pace.

He sprang up and grabbed the rod in his big hands. 'Wow! Think I've hooked a swordie!'

I'd fished with Jason enough times to know that anglers find it hard to believe their eyes when they see a swordfish leaping out of the water, silhouetted against the big, blue sky. They mistake it for sailfish or marlin. But swordfish have an additional battery of strength in their tail base, which propels them upwards. When the big fish breached again, there were the tell-tale sickle fin and magnificent tail.

'Hey! She's, like, 150 kilos!' Jason let the line spool out as the fish sped off across the sparkling sea. He gave a few turns on the handle and the fish broke the water's surface once more, breaching in all her purple-tinged, electric-blue glory. The swordfish had taken the bait and was now skittering across the waves at high speed. Jason reeled until the line pulled taut, then set the hook with one quick jab. Planting his feet like a wrestler, he prepared to fight the primitive strength of this marine gladiator. Legs braced, shoulders squared, his biceps bulged until it looked as though he had two rockmelons sewn into his upper arms.

But surprisingly the fish didn't make another run. She tossed her head a few times, changed course and torpedoed directly towards the boat. I watched in amazement as she leapt out of the sea in a silvery arc. Her muscular body flexed and arched as she hurtled right over our vessel. Her lance shimmered in the sun . . . before harpooning Jason in the chest.

The force behind the spiked bill of an immense swordfish swimming at 60 or 70 kilometres an hour is vast. As the aquatic javelin struck, the impact propelled Jason backwards. The weight of the fish and gravity dislodged the spike, so that the magnificent creature thudded to the deck. But not without tearing a huge hole in Jason. His arms windmilled frantically as he fought for balance, before tumbling over the side of the boat and into the sea.

The swordfish lay dazed near Skye's feet, her silvery flanks quivering. Skye, thinking quickly, leant forward and used its long, razor-sharp, serrated snout to saw through the ropes shackling her wrists. She cut the main rope tethering all three of us to the railing, freed her feet and sprang to the side of the boat.

Wrists still tied, I pushed myself up into a kneeling position, jack-knifed to standing and also catapulted to the boat's side, as did Tish. Jason's hadn't been a fatal blow, but blood was pumping from his chest wound. The boat swung on the anchor rope further away from him, forcing him to try to swim back to the ladder. But Skye grabbed the boat pole and used it to push him away.

'Stop it!' he yelled.

She whacked him twice on the head as well.

'For fuck's sake!' I could see Jason's Adam's apple hopping up and down in his throat as though on a miniature trampoline.

'In life you're either the prey or the predator,' Skye called out to him with chilly composure.

'Help me back onto the boat or I'm gonna kill you!' Jason's voice was failing him but the savagery of his tone was unmistakable, as was the renewed vigour in the Ironman's stroke. I started worrying about how we could contain him when he made it back on board. Then I saw the fin. For an illogical moment I thought it was the telescope of a submarine. But of course Jason had been baiting the water with burly and chum. His fresh blood in the water had done the rest.

'Quick! Toss the life ring!' I barked.

When Skye didn't move, I tried to dislodge the buoy myself, but it was impossible with my hands tied. I could see the grey fin circling closer. 'Hurry up, for god's sake.' I tried in vain once more to dislodge the floatation device. 'Just use the boat hook, Skye. Pull him in!'

'Get the gun and shoot the fucker!' Jason yelped. Terror and blood loss made him appear mottled and goggle-eyed, just like the grouper he'd clubbed earlier.

'Well, I could, but . . . I don't know . . . Did you throw *me* a lifeline?' Skye said with unruffled thoughtfulness. 'No. You went off to have a baby with a woman ten years younger than me.' She gave him another whack on the head with the boat hook to emphasise her displeasure. 'You stole my money, broke my heart and threatened to kill me. And worst of all, you killed my hopes!'

I'd always imagined the music would let me know if a shark was on the attack, but in real life it's a quick and quiet affair. The fin sliced through the water, the huge shark flashed its monstrous gills in a menacing way, sneered through serrated fangs, the jaws gaped – and then Jason was gone.

The Three Muffkateers stood speechless on the deck until Skye finally spoke. 'Vengeance is mine, sayeth I. An eye for an eye, a tooth for a tooth.'

Tish and I looked at Skye in amazement. No sign of her Life-Optimising Moon Juice now.

'Déjà bloody vu!' a stunned Tish finally exclaimed.

'It's poetic justice,' Skye said. 'I warned him about the bad karma.'

'Well, yeah.' Tish put out her hands for Skye to untie. 'One thing we wives can agree on is that sometimes it's simpler when the "Till death do us part" vow takes on a . . . *shorter* connotation. Right?'

'Right. Especially when there's already a death certificate,' Skye added, practically.

As she unbound my wrists, I couldn't suppress the thought that I'd abetted murder. I started going over aliases I could adopt, other cities I could live in, in between wondering if my life would have been better if I'd joined a Trappist Tibetan retreat as a teen.

I was jolted from my shocked reverie by a flapping sound. I spun around, half-expecting to see Jason crawling back on board, like one of those horror-film creatures from the Black Lagoon that refuses to die. But it was the giant swordfish waking from its daze, gulping for air.

'Quick!'

It took the three of us to drag the fish's majestic body to the duckboard at the back of the boat and nudge her into the water. She floated on the surface. My heart sank – were we too late? Had the poor creature expired? But suddenly she shot down into the deep with a flick of her muscular tail, as if in thanks for saving her life.

I stood staring at the sea. The streaming golden rays made the water sparkle with a frenzied gaiety. The breeze from the shore was sweet with frangipani and eucalyptus oil, and a faint moon swam in the blue sky. I looked back to where I'd last seen Jason.

The water was implacably smooth. Now the wind had dropped, the ocean had a look of blank innocence. Waves lapped at the side of the boat. We hugged, then stood stock still and listened to the sea's complicit promise of silence – *shh, shh, shh*, as ripples caressed the sides of the boat. The water had covered and erased all trace of our husband, the terror and horror of the last twenty-four hours assuaged. I knew then that the surface of our daily lives would similarly soon close over us – looking untroubled and innocent again.

And nobody but us would know what lay beneath.

29

'How's the fishin'?' asked a salty old sea dog who was peeling prawns into a tin bucket. Moments earlier Tish had manoeuvred the catamaran back into its place on the far end of the marina, Skye lassoing the rope over the mooring with the very hook she'd used to clock our ex-husband on the head in the high seas. Watching her wield the hook, I realised with a shudder that Jason really *was* my ex-husband now. I made a cursory stab at feeling guilty – but didn't. At all. In fact, it was only now, as the weight of despair and anger lifted that I realised how heavy the burden of his existence had been.

'The fishin'? Pretty bad,' Tish bantered with gruff good humour. 'So bad, in fact, that not even the liars caught any fish.' She chuckled and Skye and I joined in uneasily.

The first thing we did was check in to the posh Seabreeze, where we requested a suite.

'This is our first hotel room in a while where it doesn't matter if one of you flushes the toilet while I'm in the shower,' I thrilled.

'Shit, yeah. The bathrobes are so big and fluffy I can hardly close my suitcase,' Tish joked.

The second thing I did was ring Max.

'I see from Jason's bank details that it's mission accomplished,' he said by way of greeting.

'Thanks to you, darling.' In truth, the mission I'd most cared about accomplishing was reconnecting with my son – another mission I had thought impossible until now.

'And Jason?'

I paused, not ready to open this industrial-size can of worms. 'Let's just say, he won't be a problem from now on.'

'Copy that.'

'Love you,' I added.

Now it was Max's turn to pause. 'Ditto,' he said, which was the equivalent in Max-speak of a Shakespearean love sonnet.

Sinking into a bubble bath in a marble bathroom overlooking the sapphire sea, I felt giddy. Relief was exploding in me like champagne – the champagne I was drinking an hour later in a beachside bar.

I felt a fizz not just on my tongue but in my brain too; an effervescence that our crazy quest was accomplished. If Einstein had busted relativity on the very same day that an apple had clunked Sir Isaac Newton on the head, Archimedes had run naked down the street hollering 'Eureka!' and women had got the vote, you'd be getting close to how I felt. I leant across the table, glass raised, to make a toast, but Tish beat me to it. 'May this day become a person so I can take it to Las Vegas and marry it,' she said. She lifted her glass and clinked it with mine. 'Here's to friggin' fabulous us!'

Skye's glass clinked ours simultaneously. 'I want to thank you both for helping me avenge the man who broke my heart.'

I felt like a superhero who's just discovered her power.

'Shouldn't we be given some kind of cape or something?' I said.

'We should! I mean, look what we achieved. The sisterhood really is powerful!' Skye poured more champagne into our glasses.

'I'd be happy to start wearin' my undies on the outside of my clothes, except, after all this celebratory bingein', I'm pretty sure none of my clothes will fit anymore!' Tish tugged down the legs of her leopard-skin shorts, which were riding high on fishnetted thighs.

Skye asked the waiter for another bottle of champagne – 'Vintage, this time, 'cause we can bloody well afford it!' Tish thumped the wrought-iron table so hard that it shook.

I'd just raised the paper-thin cut-glass flute to my lips, when Skye said, 'Speaking of which . . .' She picked up her phone. 'I need your bank details to transfer your money. I emptied out Jason's accounts, as agreed. We'll split the spoils three ways. Ping me over your deets.'

I felt the vintage champagne dancing on my tongue. It tasted like carbonated money.

'So, what next?' Skye asked.

'Back to school, I suppose,' I said, between sips.

'Really?' Skye asked. 'You're not tempted to resign and spend all the money you now have?'

'Hmm, I'd rather save it for a rainy day,' I said, cautiously. Truth be told, my teaching life, with all its petty staffroom spats, might as well have been in another universe. I thought of having to listen to whiny parents judging me on the quality of their monosyllabic offspring's misinterpretations of 1788 and groaned. Until you've attended a Year 8 classroom, you have no idea of the insectine attention span of your average teen. I shuddered involuntarily and shelved my misgivings. 'What about you, Tish?'

'I'm gonna pay off that second mortgage, see a tattoo remov-alist' – she gave us another quick peek at Jason's name, inked onto her abdomen – 'Then I guess I'll have to get back to singin' with my band. Or maybe I'll do a solo show – a one-woman show, with one woman too many!' Her tone was sarcastically upbeat, but her expression reminded me of someone waiting in a theme park queue for a terrifying ride they didn't really want to go on.

Skye was gazing up at the afternoon moon, which looked like a pocked golf ball that had been putted into the sky.

'What's next for you, kiddo?' Tish probed.

'I need to get back to Cairo. I have a dig to go to in Syria. And I haven't got long to find Mr Right so I can finally try for a baby. I can't believe I gave up another year of possible child-bearing to that phoney.'

'Yeah, I need to get back on the old datin' market before I get too old. Witches, warlocks, werewolves – they could all go to a fancy-dress party as me,' Tish said. 'Mind you, on Halloween I can just go out as myself. Saves a fortune on costumes, I s'pose.'

It made me sad to hear Tish talking herself down. 'Do you *have* a mirror? You're lovely, Tish.' It was true. I looked at her closely in the late afternoon sun. When Tish smiled it was as if someone had turned a light on. 'And I know I'm a bore, whereas you ooze personality.'

'That's bullshit! I hate to say this, but you're bloody brainy, Gwendoline. But you don't make enough of your looks. Would a bit of lippy kill you?'

'I don't really like make-up. I mean, must you slap that crap on your face day in, day out? You're so naturally pretty, Tish, if only you'd let your skin breathe. Do you know that more money is made from make-up than munitions? And that's what make-up is, really – ammunition in the sex war.'

'Jay-sus,' Tish whacked her palm to her forehead. 'I take it back. You *are* a bore.'

'Ladies,' Skye laughed. 'No more quarrelling. We won! And do you know why? Because we stuck together. So, here's to the sisterhood! In fact, to honour that . . .'

Skye placed a velvet pouch on the table and opened it gingerly. Inside lay two rose-quartz crystals shaped like flat hearts. She handed one to each of us. 'As a sign of our ever-lasting friendship, wear this next to your heart, for positive energy and to protect your love aura.'

'You and your hippy-trippy gobbledegook.' Tish eye-rolled, but she tucked the heart-shaped crystal into her bra.

'Thank you, Skye,' I kissed her cool, pale cheek and pocketed my present.

'I know we're going our separate ways, but I want you to know that I'll never forget you both. And I couldn't have done it without you. Here's to living our best lives.' Skye raised her glass in a toast.

Beside our table, a row of fleecy, flowering gums foamed their white pearls. The sun's warm rays felt like kisses on my upturned face.

'I'll drink to that,' Tish said, glugging down a draught.

A few minutes later a live band started to play; their first song was by the Grateful Dead: 'Friend of the Devil'.

'How friggin' appropriate.' Tish laughed so loudly that she sprayed my face with her happiness. Which made Skye laugh, a guffaw as merciless as a nose-blowing. Which set me off too – until we were all chortling and snorting while harmonising to the band.

Things got more and more blurry after that, but I recall Tish getting up onto a table to sing, winning rapturous applause from the crowd; also, that we smoked a joint with a bunch of sailors, during which Tish somehow flambéed an eyebrow.

Later, in the dolphin-grey hour before sunrise, we pinballed our way down various streets back to our hotel. I'm not sure how we made it back, but there was more singing in the foyer and then somehow or other we were standing outside our suite trying to get the key into the lock.

'Give it to m– m– me, Tish,' I slurred.

'No, I wanna do it.'

'Well, let me just steady your hand . . .'

'My hand is fine. Can you just steady the hotel?'

Skye finally confiscated the key from us, got the door open and we fell into the room.

'I think you're right. I have drunk too much,' I admitted as my nose grazed the shagpile.

'What makes you s– s– s– say that?' Tish hiccoughed.

''Cause I'm beginning to see the writing on the floor.'

We cackled with delight at our sumptuous surroundings. I could finally say for sure that things were looking up – and not just because we were flat on our backs on the hotel carpet.

Gazing up at the moon shimmering across the sea, I realised that Skye was right all along – there really *is* an after-life: after your husband dies.

PART EIGHT

30

I was woken by bubbles of laughter floating up from the pool. A faint citrus light, grapefruit and orange, was seeping into the hotel room from the warm tropical day outside. I'd somehow made it into one of the bedrooms, where I'd fallen asleep fully clothed. The day had started without me. I felt brutally hungover but relaxed, vaguely aware that something momentous had happened, then remembering that our long, crazy ordeal was over.

While waiting for Tish and Skye to wake and for my brain to de-fog, I started reorganising my backpack in preparation for my return journey to Sydney. It was time to admit that it was going to be very hard to go back to normal life after the events of the past month. I felt groggy and disorientated, like a scuba diver leaving the bed of a spectacular ocean. All those countries and landscapes we'd seen. I began to wish I'd kept a diary. Then I remembered I did at least have some GoPro footage. Where was the camera? Turned out I'd buried it in a deep subterranean pocket of my rucksack. I dug it out, puffed up the pillows and lay back on the bed while the recording rewound to the beginning – the glory of the Maldives underwater world.

I was marvelling afresh at the majestic grace of the giant whale shark as it glided past the fluorescent coral flower beds, when something else snagged my attention. What was that, way in the background? At first I thought it was two stingrays fighting, or maybe mating. I zoomed in. Was that Skye in the murk? I stabbed at the zoom button till the lens had focused in as tightly as it would go, and lightened the screen. There was another figure with what appeared to be a ponytail floating around her. Carly? My feeling of wellbeing teetered. What was happening? I did a double take. I pressed replay. Again. And again. And then I stared slack-jawed at the screen.

It was taking me a while to understand exactly what I was looking at – my brain could not compute the messages relayed by my optic nerves. The footage seemed to show one of the figures, who I was convinced was Skye, ripping the regulator out of the other figure's mouth – surely Carly – and holding it out of her reach. Carly's body flailed and fought, and finally went limp. Then Skye swam back to her and wrenched something from around her limp neck. I tried to keep calm and cast my mind back to that afternoon in the Maldives. What was round Carly's neck after she'd pulled on her wetsuit? Eventually I realised: the safety deposit key.

The images sent a bolt up my spine. My heart was galloping and my stomach curdled. I dropped the GoPro as though it were radioactive. Life had suddenly swerved back into the runaway-truck lane. All I could do was put my head between my legs and adopt the brace position. Brace! Brace! Brace! I exhaled with an urgent gasp. I hadn't even realised I'd been holding my breath.

Blundering blindly into the sitting room, I prodded Tish awake. She was lying supine on the couch, a pillow over her head.

'Bugger off,' she growled.

'Emergency!' I ripped open the curtains and light poured in. 'Look at this!'

Cursing, Tish levered open her eyelids, which were matted together with mascara. I was too traumatised to even mention her missing eyebrow. 'Glasses,' she grumbled. 'I've lost my glasses.' She squinted at the screen I thrust in front of her eyes. 'And I can't find 'em . . . till I've found 'em, if ya know what I mean.'

Her glasses were on the side table. I handed them to her and hit play. Her voice stopped abruptly. I rewound and pressed play again. There was the sound of a jaw dropping open and eyeballs springing out of their sockets, going *'Cuckoo! Cuckoo!'* Facts that would normally have reached Tish's brain stem in a millisecond got sidetracked into a befogged swamp of hungover synapses. She asked me to rewind so she could take another look before, it seemed, her subconscious could absorb the full horror unfolding on my GoPro.

'What the *fuck*?' she finally exclaimed, which summed up my feelings exactly. We were in cognitive quicksand, with each passing second bogging us down more deeply.

'Do you remember Skye got hysterical and had to be taken back to the hotel before us? And by the time we got back, the safe had been cleaned out?' I asked.

'Yeah . . . and she'd somehow convinced the Hideaway receptionist to give her Jason's hotel bill,' Tish said.

'And when we were looking for Jason in Paris, while you were ménage-ing, she tricked that hotel concierge into believing that she was expecting his baby to convince her to help us track him down,' I recalled. Sure, I'd found talking to Skye calming, but, looking back, her answers were always pat. In hindsight, it was like talking to one of those computer programs that mimics human responses. 'She never told us anything about herself,' I continued tautly.

'Yeah, she'd just spray that bloody mist all over us and bullshit on about crystals.'

'Maybe she's not even really a New Zealander?'

'Yeah, you're right. Most Kiwis are so cuddly.'

'And . . . yesterday. The way she kept hitting Jason over the head with the boat hook, again and again. Without a qualm? While a shark circled?'

I could see in my mind's eye Skye staring at me with those big blue, impenetrable eyes and her Sphinx-like smile.

'And, wait a minute. Oh god.' I put my hand up to my mouth like a silent movie heroine who's about to be tied to the railway tracks. 'Jason transferred all of our money into *her* account.'

Tish catapulted up from the couch as though she were on springs and flung open the door to the adjoining bedroom. Empty. The bed – unslept in. We stood, transfixed, the only sound our own rapid breathing.

So, Jason had indeed found his perfect match – someone as ruthless and duplicitous as him. New-age Skye was a little love, light and peace . . . but a lot more 'go fuck yourself'. She was Iago in a pashmina; Lady Macbeth with a mindfulness jar. She had achieved something even one of her gurus would envy: she'd managed to be reincarnated while still alive.

With shaking hands we logged on to our accounts. No money transfers.

Tish began to shuffle groggily around the room looking for any trace of our third Muffkateer, but Skye's clothes, make-up, toiletries and backpack were gone. Harmless, artless, caring, sharing Skye Cavendish had used us to get her revenge on Jason. Her motto? To double-cross that bridge when she came to it.

31

'What now?'

'I dunno. My brain's emptied faster than a fart-laden lift.' Tish launched a halo of blue vape smoke ceilingward.

'It all makes sense now,' I post-mortemed, pacing the hotel suite. 'Skye used us to help track down Jason, killing her love rival en route, then finally she was able to prevail over Jason *and* get away with all our money. She arranged things more carefully than a newsreader's comb-over. I think perhaps the time has come to call the police,' I concluded, in an anaemic murmur.

Tish shot me a scalding look. 'And say what exactly? Oh hi. Yeah, well, we killed our husband, a bigamist, who was already dead, weirdly . . . Our accomplice, oh, who just happens to be a murderess . . . helped us find him and his money, returned it to us – it was ours all along, by the way – stole it back again and then buggered off.'

It sounded not just ludicrous but also incriminating. '*Yes, officer, we are just back from a little pleasure trip . . . feeding our husband to a man-eating shark.*'

'If we go to the cops, it'll mean years of legal wranglin' and I doubt very much it will help us get our dosh back. No. We need to find that New Age dipshit ourselves.'

'Really? Who are we, exactly? Cagney and Lacey?'

'Let's get to Brisbane Airport pronto. We can still catch that hypocritical hippy traitor to the sisterhood if we put our skates on.' Tish started throwing her clothes into her backpack, then paused. 'Nah. Forget that. Skye knows that's the first place we – or the cops – would look.'

'Maybe she's hired a car to escape across the border?'

'Risky – traffic police, road blocks . . .'

'Lying low in town then?'

'Let's go find out.' Tish lifted a duvet in the corner of the room with her purple painted toenails. Much to my surprise, a man was lying under it, face down in his marijuana stash, a Tally-ho paper stuck to his forehead.

'My roadie. Drove up from Brizzy yesterday with the band.'

'Wait. Is that what you meant when you said you were having one *for the road*? You meant your actual roadie?'

'Jeezus, no! He just came back for his gun. And *you*, apparently, you hornbag. Doan cha remember snoggin' him in the lift last night?'

I cringed, watching as the snoring bloke worked a last sinew or two of meatpie from his mossy molars. 'Oh good god! I certainly do not.'

'Just joshin'. The day Ms Gwendoline Goody Two Shoes snogs a random stranger is the day I yodel in my undies, balancin' two teaspoons on my tits.'

Tish excavated the car keys out of the man's pocket and left a note saying he was too stoned to drive so she was removing the temptation.

The lift disgorged us into the foyer. Tish was striding towards the hotel's revolving doors when the receptionist beckoned her over to the desk.

'You were amazing last night!' the young woman enthused.

'Oh, thanks, but ... what happened last night?' Tish asked tentatively.

'You were singing, here in the foyer. Janis Joplin. Joni Mitchell. Dolly Parton. You've got some lungs on you.'

'Um, no memory of that, but good to know ... Hey, the woman we were with? Blonde, with a haircut so sharp you could shave your legs on it?'

'All dressed in white,' I added, fumbling in my bag for my phone and flashing up Skye's image.

'Oh yes. She left early this morning.'

Yes, with all our money, I thought bitterly. 'Do you know where she was heading?'

'No. But she caught a taxi ... Actually, my boyfriend took her. He's driving cabs while working on his album. Do you want a demo?'

In exchange for us taking the demo for Thrusting Groins and the Throbbing Gonads, the receptionist rang her musical beau, who said he'd driven Skye to Brisbane and left her at the cruise ship terminal.

'A cruise ship. Clever.' Tish peered over the top of her heart-shaped shades. 'I'd never have thought of that.' If she'd had any eyebrow left, it would have arched.

Pulling out of the hotel car park in Tish's roadie's old banger, I prepared for our usual divergence in what she and I found acceptable in road rules. For example, I would say that an orange light is a signal to slow down, not speed up, and that the use of the rearview mirror is to aid traffic visibility and not solely for the purpose of downward angling for make-up application. Driving our hire car from Brisbane Airport to Noosa, two days earlier, a particularly tricky mascara manoeuvre had meant that we'd nearly collected a pedestrian on the roo bar. Terror-stricken, I'd had to grab the wheel to steer us back into our lane.

'J'mind?' Tish had fumed. 'I'm at a friggin' crucial stage of the second coat. Oh, thanks! Now I've blobbed.'

She'd blobbed and I blubbed all the way up the Sunshine Coast.

But much to my amazement, Tish was now driving south with caution. After a sedate 10 kilometres I checked my watch. 'Um, don't you think you'd better step on it a bit?'

'Jesus, that's rich comin' from you, kiddo. I'm tryin' to be more considerate of your friggin' nerves.'

'Oh, right,' I said, astounded. 'Thanks.'

Two uneventful hours later we reached the cruise terminal. Tish made a slow roll past the boom gates before circling the block in search of a parking spot.

'This is hopeless!' I said, on our third circumnavigation, once more glancing at my watch. 'Why don't we just pull into the disabled spot?'

'WHAT?' It was now Tish's turn to be amazed.

'Well, marriage to a con man did leave us both emotionally crippled and mentally crushed.'

Tish laughed. 'Ain't that the bloody truth,' she said, and swerved into a No Stopping zone.

Striding into the terminal we quickly ascertained that the docked ship, the *Rhapsody of the Sea*, was leaving at sunset, bound for New Zealand, via Sydney. There were available berths aboard. Only one problem: money.

'What now?' I asked Tish. 'Our bank accounts are emptier than a supermodel's pantry.'

'Hey there! You girls!'

We swivelled as one to see a six-foot hulk in a dazzling white seafaring uniform bearing down on us. His bullet-headed baldness further enhanced a faint aura of menace. He'd no doubt seen us parking illegally. Tish was just getting ready to tell the interloper to go fuck himself, repeatedly and without lubricants, when the giant fell to his knees before her.

'Oh babe. Can you forgive me?' The man extended forearms splotched floridly with sunburn, huge as cudgels. He appeared to have put in some serious gym time and was wearing his clothes a size too small to showcase the results.

'Whatcha on about, numb nuts?' Tish demanded, suspiciously, fists clenching.

'What a voice! Wow! I've been thinking about you all morning. Thought I'd never see you again.' He pointed sheepishly to Tish's missing eyebrow. 'Please, tell me how I can repay you.'

'You can start by telling us who the hell you are,' Tish said sharply. Then her eyes narrowed. 'But yeah, there might be something you can do for me. Are you on this ship?'

The big guy nodded, pointing to his name tag. 'Chook Fowler. Cruise director.'

A beam spread across Tish's face. Five minutes later we had obtained free passage to Sydney in exchange for Tish agreeing to sing with the ship's band. Turned out this was the man who'd accidentally singed off her eyebrow during an over-exuberant spliff ignition.

The only downside of the deal was that before I could jump in and explain that we actually needed his help because we were in pursuit of a ruthless sociopath who'd drowned a love rival and then fed her own husband to a shark, Tish, in exchange for a better cabin, had also volunteered me to give a talk on Australian history to the passengers. Fowler referred to it as an 'enrichment lecture'.

'You have lectured before, right?' he asked as he gave me a sceptical once-over – possibly because I was looking like a finalist in a Fixed Smile competition. 'I mean, I don't want any trouble.'

Tish raised her one remaining brow at me. I swallowed my fear and tried to neutralise my inflection. 'Of course,' I said.

I had a feeling that this last leg of our journey would turn out to be an experience we'd always remember – or one we'd never be able to forget.

32

During check-in, Tish casually inquired about a dear friend of ours who was also aboard – a New Zealander called Skye Cavendish. She mentioned Skye's geology profession, but tactfully left out the fact that in her spare time this particular Kiwi suckled demons at the bidding of the Dark Lord.

Skye's name was not on the passenger list, Chook Fowler informed us, so we knew she was travelling under an alias. The muster drill seemed our best chance to find her. Having cruised to Fiji, New Caledonia and Vanuatu with my children before I'd met Jason, I knew that a muster drill is that time in shipboard life when passengers realise they paid no attention to where their lifeboat station is. But today I was fully focused.

The ship had just left port when the tannoy summoned passengers to the evacuation points. Fowler ticked off our names with a wink, freeing us to scuttle around the ship's other assembly points in search of our kale-juice-quaffing Judas.

'I can't be held responsible for what I'll do when I see that tapeworm with tits. I'm warnin' you that I may go off my rocker.'

'You? Lose your temper. Gee, imagine that,' I said, but I too was fantasising about tossing Skye into a jacuzzi of battery acid.

It took us a while to spot her – at the Deck B muster point – because she had swapped her trademark white attire for a flowing frock so golden-yellow it looked like a sunbeam. I froze, stiff as an accountant at a swingers' party. Tish yanked me down out of sight behind a lifeboat and we waited, then trailed Skye back to her state room. (Yes, a state room no less.) 'Ah,' Tish punned, 'the suite smell of success.'

Darting behind the maid's trolley, Tish flattened herself against the corridor wall and whispered, 'I'm so friggin' wired right now, I could power an appliance. I probably don't even need this.' She opened her handbag so I could peek inside.

'A taser? Let me guess, courtesy of your roadie pal?'

'Yup. Smuggled it aboard in my cabin luggage. Chook took one look at my big, pink, solar-powered vibrator, blushed bright red and just waved me through. Ready?' Tish flashed the skeleton pass key she'd just purloined as we walked past the cleaning trolley. Breaking into hotel rooms was becoming second nature to me now. At this rate, I'd be adding it to my CV. The suite door clicked open soundlessly. The living room was dark. Tish and I tiptoed across the carpet as though into a minefield in some war-torn outpost. As we approached the bedroom door, I wished I'd donned some emotional PPE. Tish, fearless as ever and wielding her taser like it was a handgun in a John Wayne Western, flung open the bedroom door.

Skye's yellow dress was hitched up as she squatted over a bowl of steam. We stared, flummoxed, until I realised this must be the mugwort she'd told us about: apparently it maximised one's conception potential. Upon seeing us, Skye's eyes opened wider than a cash register mid-robbery. But she quickly regained her composure. The woman was so poised and pale that she seemed partially drained of blood: the look she levelled at us as she rose to standing could have refrozen a melting polar ice cap.

As she stood, her summer dress swished around her legs. She waved a manicured paw in the air as if shooing away invisible wasps. 'Oh, look what the ship's cat has dragged in,' she said, coolly.

'Yeah, well, we're not exactly shittin' confetti to see you either, vinegar tits . . . We've come for our dosh.' Tish thrust her taser forward as though in preparation for a medieval jousting.

'What dosh?'

I marvelled how once I'd found Skye's voice so soothing. Now it just made me want to punch out a porthole.

'Cut the Mother Teresa act. Your halo's slipped, fuck-face. We know about Carly.'

Skye's eyelids shuttered up and down. She got busy inspecting distant corners of the ceiling. Then a chilly smile chased itself across her face and she said in an acidic tone. 'I don't know what you're talking about.'

'You're fulla shit, d'ja know that? Do the honours would ya, Gwendoline, please?'

I whipped out my GoPro from Tish's bag, turned the screen in Skye's direction and pressed play. As the diving footage began to roll, she looked bamboozled for a moment, blinking to make out what she was watching. Once her eyes and mind had adjusted, her lips began to move soundlessly, like a goldfish bumping up against the glass of its bowl. I hadn't seen anyone this rivetted by screen footage since my primary school class had laid down our pencils to watch Buzz Aldrin's moon landing.

I lowered the camera. My eyes searched her face. 'Why?'

Skye's serene expression melted as a tremor ran through her body and then she erupted Vesuvially. 'When I unlocked Jason's secret phone in my apartment, do you know what I found? Endless sickly sweet messages to that bikinied tart. He really did want to have a baby with her. He told her he had a "few loose ends to tie up" in Cairo and then they'd be together forever. He meant me – *I* was the loose end. Me! The woman who'd given him everything! The woman who'd agreed to postpone being a mother just to keep him! What did Carly have that I didn't?'

'Um . . . a rich daddy?' Tish ventured.

'And her gazillions of eggs waiting to hatch from her throbbing young ovaries. I'm forty! My eggs are fried. Scrambled. Jason not only stole my money, he stole my chance of being a mother. That man broke my heart and betrayed me, and for a . . .' she picked up the next word with invisible tweezers, '*Texan*.' The Kiwi ground her molars ferociously. I couldn't believe a faint pall of blueish smoke wasn't seeping from her mouth as she spoke. I thought of that poor, perky, chirpy Carly with her bouncy ponytail sticking up like a radio aerial – if only she'd been able to pick up our SOS signals to stay away from Jason Riley – and Skye Cavendish, it turned out.

Tish looked unimpressed. 'Yadda, yadda. As deeply touchin' as all this is . . . transfer the friggin' money. Now. Or we call the cops.'

'My relationship with Jason bankrupted me, but not just financially – emotionally, psychologically, physically. To the core. He used me. And for that he had to pay. Carly was collateral.'

My blood ran cold. Skye was starting to make the Wicked Witch of the West look like a kindergarten teacher.

'If Jason hadn't forced me into that compromising position, I wouldn't have had to get the key to the safe to destroy any incriminating evidence.'

Incriminating evidence? Compromising position? There was an unpleasant buzzing in my ears. Standing there under Skye's level, ice-blue gaze, the truth finally clicked into place like the tumblers of a safe. I felt exactly the same kind of buzz I got from solving a cryptic crossword puzzle. 'You helped Jason fake his own death.'

Skye gave that tilted head, pouty, tender-eyed look, that could melt a man at a hundred paces. A sardonic smile played at the margins of her lips. It reminded me of one person – Jason Riley.

She nodded. 'Jason planned it so that we could be together with enough money to start a new life. I loved him. So I skippered a boat for him, near Shark Island, with everything ready . . . fake passport . . . plane ticket. We escaped to Cairo, where he was using my contacts to start up his mining venture – and then, I hoped, a family. We were so happy. And then you bozos turned up. I knew that Jason had one wife, but not two. I had to think on my feet. While you were chasing after Jase, I rushed to our secret rendezvous point, with bags and passports. But he never showed. Nor was he answering my calls. I checked our debit card to try to locate him via any purchases – you know, a coffee or petrol – and that's when I found out he'd betrayed me too.'

'And that's also when you decided to trick us, then ditch us,' I concluded for her.

Skye smiled mirthlessly in my direction. 'Well, I couldn't go to the police. I was an accessory. Jason had all the evidence proving I'd helped him commit fraud. That's what I read on the text messages Jason sent to that bent solicitor of his on his secret phone.'

'Marty Cash?'

'Jason told Cash he'd blackmail me if I threatened to make any trouble for him and Carly, the love of his life. I had to get into that hotel safe to destroy the evidence. And Carly had the key.'

'My heart is breakin', it really is. Your parole officer is gonna need a hanky.' Tish pointed at Skye's iPad with her taser. 'Log on and transfer our money back or that GoPro footage goes straight to the cops.'

Skye sat down on the bed, primly scissored her long legs and ran a pink tongue across her perfect teeth. She cracked open the device, but then looked up at us and said beguilingly, 'You know, crime is such a male-dominated world. Male bosses control their illicit businesses through the threat of physical violence. However, as opportunities for crime have diversified, women are taking over lead roles – especially in white-collar crime. As feminists, I'm sure you're supportive of women using our brains to smash all the glass ceilings – even in the criminal world.'

'Um, I'm not sure that's why Emily Davison threw herself under the King's horse,' I replied, granite-faced.

Skye looked blank, not comprehending my reference. She returned my harsh gaze, unperturbed. 'I now have *all* of Jason's money, which is really quite substantial, plus his cryptocurrency contacts. Why don't we just carry out his well-laid plans? We work so well together. The Three Muffkateers. And we've got so much to bond us – betrayed by the same man. Let's be partners again. Not Robin Hood – but the Sister Hood.'

It was an adroit piece of psychological sophistry – for a psychopath.

'Yeah, you're a great gal to work with – if you like blood suckin' vampire bats.' Tish jabbed the taser close enough to shish-kebab

Skye through the eye. 'Once I've seen you transfer the dosh, I'll give you the GoPro.'

Skye gave a deep moan, which could have been mistaken as either Kama Sutra-related or meditation-orientated to a passing passenger with bionic hearing. 'Your loss,' she laughed, but her eyes were hard, her expression without merriment. She turned the iPad towards us so we could check the transfer amounts and bank account details. After we'd nodded our approval, she said, 'And if I do hit this transfer button, the rest will be our little secret?'

I remembered, the ocean's soothing call for secrecy on the yacht – *shh, shh, shhh*. Tish nodded, but I caught the briefest of winks she sent my way. I nodded too, so that, as usual, no lie passed my lips. I also surreptitiously hit the RECORD button on the GoPro dangling from my wrist. I strained to detect the murmuring *fffttt* of the video whirring into life, hoping it had worked because clearly this would be a moment to treasure forever.

Skye's eyes were fixed straight before her, her lips moved as if reading from an invisible book, her face blank as paper.

'I can't hear you.' I moved a little closer, presuming she wanted to check my account details or maybe even apologise for turning into Lucrezia Borgia in an ethically sourced sundress. Suddenly her whisper turned into a hiss. She now had all the charm of a cornered cobra. Rearing up as if to strike, she came at us, aiming her Psychic Vampire Spray like a gun. She hit the trigger and the vile unguent squirted me full in the face. I felt the sting in my eyes and choked as the mist hit my tonsils. One of Skye's healing gems used to dispel bad vibes whizzed past my ear and struck Tish in the temple. Skye then hurled the vagina mugwort steaming bowl at Tish, who recoiled in pain as piping-hot water seared her arm. Through streaming slits for eyes, I saw Skye lunge at my buddy with a syringe and in the heat of the moment – literally – jab it straight into her heart.

Call me clairvoyant, but I had a strong feeling it wasn't a Vitamin B shot. Tish went down with a thud. I lurched blindly forwards to try to catch her but it was too late – her yelp as her head hit the back of a chair cleaved my cranium . . . except, wait, something was actually cleaving my cranium.

'Is that your vagina egg?' I asked, picking up the airborne missile that had just blindsided me. Skye had told me all about her jade yoni egg and how it and Kegel exercises could harness the power of positive energy. Once the egg was inserted, by squeezing and releasing your vaginal muscles, inner femininity was restored, apparently. Not included in her sales pitch was the fact that, when thrown, a yoni egg can cause concussion. My brain detonated and the world went black.

33

I regained consciousness to a throbbing about the temples and the sight of the foaming, dark sea directly below me. A blinding headache made it hard to open my eyes; when I did, they burnt and my stomach roiled: someone had wedged my torso up over the railing and was trying to lift my legs to follow. The sea churned below, a blanket of black velvet. You could slip down into that dark water and nobody would ever know how you'd disappeared.

Coming to with an electrifying jolt, I braced one foot on the glass balcony and pushed back against Skye with all my might, twisting to wrap my legs around her waist. I grabbed a clump of her hair for purchase and a great hunk of extensions came away in my hands. Staring up into her scowling face in the harsh fluorescent light, I saw for the first time how fake she really was – her 'natural' lips were plumped with hyaluronic acid, her cheeks with silicone and her forehead with botulinum toxin. The look of peaceful serenity I'd always admired on her face, I now realised, was nothing more than ossification.

Skye pummelled me as though I were a human punching bag. I screamed but the sound was lost – drowned out by the ocean rushing by sibilantly below; a churn of white foam against the inky depths. The dark water seemed alive and sinister. Terrified, I squeezed my legs tighter and clung on for dear life. If I was going into the drink, then this duplicitous diva was coming with me.

Balanced there on the ship's railing, I felt the pulse of the boat's engine throbbing through my body. The GoPro, still tied to my wrist, banged percussively on the balustrade.

I detected a flicker of movement out of the corner of my eye. It took me a moment to realise that it was Tish charging like a bull on steroids. I could almost see the cartoon smoke steaming from her ears. Viewed from my precarious position atop a ship's railing, the fracas unfolded with eerie, slow motion inevitability. Bursting onto the balcony, Tish launched herself into the air and tackled Skye at the waist, simultaneously grabbing my shirt in one swift movement – all three of us splattering sideways onto the deck in a tangle of limbs; faces mashed up against the glass.

I was too relieved at being rescued to appreciate the artistry of Tish's manoeuvre – her shove managed to send Skye sideways, without hurtling me backwards into a watery grave.

Skye's mangled form lying stunned on the deck was a thing of beauty and a joy forever. As, of course, was the miracle of Tish being alive, despite her harpooning with a hypodermic syringe.

'You're here! But I saw her stab you. With a needle. Straight into your heart!'

'I know, right.' Tish fished around in her bra and retrieved a heart-shaped rose-quartz crystal. 'I'm still wearin' the same clothes from last night. Remember how Cruella de Vil told us to wear it near our hearts, for positive energy?'

'Ha! Finally something of hers worked! It positively saved your life. And then you saved mine.'

'Fuck a duck. That was bloody close. Were you terrified?'

'No, not much. Only when I saw that bright tunnel with my dead ancestors waving me towards the light,' I said, giddy with relief.

'Okay then, matey,' Tish sobered suddenly, 'let's go kick some serious New Age arse.'

We took an armpit each and, hoisting the dazed Skye upwards, dragged her into her suite and tethered her to a chair by her dressing gown cord.

When Skye started coming around, her voice was sluggish and wet like something oozing down a drain. Tish's eyes, fixed steadily on Skye, were lucid with wrath.

When Skye realised the reversal in her fortunes, her beautiful face contorted into a gargoyle grimace. She flushed red and the lines on either side of her pretty mouth deepened in fury. She half-rose from her chair, hands claw-shaped, but was brought back to earth by her bonds.

'But I stabbed you! With toad poison. What are you made of? Kryptonite?' Her neat blonde bob with its razor-sharp edges was running amok, wisps of hair falling across her furious face.

'Thanks for the rose-quartz crystal.' Tish retrieved it once more from the depths of her bra and waved it in Skye's face. 'You pretended to be prey when all the time you were the predator. And for that you're gonna pay.' Tish retrieved her taser from the carpet where it had fallen and handed it to me. 'Give her a zap or two with this, Gwennie baby. It'll make you feel so much better, *karmically*,' she said, her voice oozing sarcasm.

I recoiled, shaking my head. 'Who am I? Xi Jinping? Alexander Lukashenko? Kim Jong-un?'

'Okay, okay, what about this?' Tish picked up Skye's lymph gland flow brush and handed it to me. 'Give her a whack around the chops. It'll help carry away her toxic thoughts in the most positive fashion,' she said.

I looked at Tish as though she'd asked me to gargle napalm. 'No!'

'Okay, okay. What about beltin' her with crystals. Or, wait. A good whack in the head with her yoni egg would rebalance her energy nicely, I reckon.' Tish tossed the vagina egg from one hand to the other like a baseball.

Skye flared her eyebrows and favoured me with a scalding glare. 'Join forces with me, Gwendoline. You loathe Tish. She's driven you mad since day one. Remember when you were talking about Chekhov and she thought you were a Trekkie? Or when you were comparing our odyssey to Homer's epic poems? You said that Homer reckoned nectar was the drink of the gods and Tish said that Homer only liked doughnuts. The woman's not in our league. Come on. Untie me.'

I noticed Skye's mindfulness jar by her bed – filled with water, dish soap and glitter glue. Skye had told us that the coloured glitter in the jar was a very powerful visual metaphor for being able to express one's feelings. Well, on this the woman was right, because pouring its contents over her head expressed my feelings perfectly. Stalactites of glittery goo glooped down her forehead – *drip, drip, drip* – from her nose and chin and into her lap.

'So, are you living your best life now?' I asked her.

Tish looked at me, incredulously. 'That's *it*? *That's* your revenge? A bit of glittery soap?'

'No,' I said, untying the GoPro from my wrist. '*This* is my best revenge. I turned on the GoPro before Skye attacked us then tried to throw me overboard. It's all recorded here, for posterity . . . oh and the police.'

Skye gave me a venomous look. In my reflection in the ornate, gilt-edged bedroom mirror on the wall behind her, I was wearing the smug expression of a woman who'd lost the most that week at a Weight Watchers weigh-in.

Tish's laughter lit up the room. She picked up Skye's iPad from the bed where she'd tossed it before she'd attacked. Tish re-entered Skye's password, having beadily spied her typing it in earlier, saying sarcastically, '*Archangel*. Really? That's your password? You'd better change it to "*Fallen Angel*" now, fuckface.' She tapped in the authorisation code that pinged onto Skye's phone. And then she completed the transactions. 'Although . . . Wait. I think I'll add a few noughts to the amount.'

Skye's face twisted and bitter tears bit into lines I'd never noticed before; lines etched around her eyes and mouth. The coolest customer I'd ever met had started to sweat more than a menopausal woman in a sauna. It was then that she screamed – the bloodcurdling, bone-marrow-melting howl of a rat caught in a trap.

A few minutes later the suite door burst open and Chook Fowler barged into the room with the cabin steward, who'd heard the scream, noticed his pass key was missing, and had alerted security about a possible emergency in Skye's suite.

'Help! Help! Untie me!' Skye pleaded. 'These lunatics broke into my room. They're torturing me for money.'

'What have you done?' Fowler yelled at Tish, seizing her arm. 'Please don't tell me I'm gonna lose my job over you?' Admittedly, he must have thought this was a lot of payback for one singed eyebrow.

'On no account listen to her,' I commanded Fowler. 'And unhand that heroine. She saved my life.' I fumbled around with the GoPro's buttons, rewound my surreptitious footage, and played it to him.

The cruise director's thatched eyebrows jumped halfway up his forehead. Much goldfish-gulping ensued. 'Holy fucking mackerel!' he said, which aquatically summed up my own seasick sentiments.

Skye looked up at him with her big blue, innocent eyes. 'It's a set-up! Don't believe them.' Her pretty face had the angelic look of the kind of woman who takes orphaned kittens for dialysis on her day off.

Tish and I grabbed an elbow each and steered the cruise director onto the balcony to explain that Skye was unhinged. In stereo, we gave graphic details of how she'd tried to embezzle our money before doing away with us both. When Tish showed him the needle and the spot where Skye had tried to thrust it into her heart, Chook took a moment to put his eyeballs back into their sockets.

Two of your standard shipping-line-issue goliath security guards arrived shortly afterwards and Skye was handcuffed.

'The moral of the story?' Tish high-fived me. 'If you want somethin' fixed, always get a workin' mum. Those bitches get shit done!'

Skye just stared straight ahead, with the bitter pride of a woman heading to her execution. I thought back to when we first met her in Cairo. Her geological profession had surprised me because she seemed to have not a skerrick of actual science in her head, but I'd reminded myself that everyone has hidden traits and talents just waiting to be excavated. Of course, however, sometimes all that slithered out was a worm.

'To the Three Muffkateers!' I saluted her.

'Go to hell!' she snarled.

'Actually, I have plans for today,' I replied. 'And they include living a little longer.'

34

After a long night's sleep and a full breakfast in our lavishly linened beds, I rang Max to suggest he sabotage, by cyber-attack, the seedy Marty Cash and leak details of all his dodgy dealings to fellow solicitors. 'Affirmative,' he said, with pleasure. 'Roger that.'

With relish, Tish and I took a moment to envisage the odious solicitor, his teeth parted in the middle as though by a comb, and so yellow they looked jaundiced, shrieking as his corrupt little empire came crashing down.

I then fulfilled my promise to Chook Fowler and gave a post-lunch history lecture in the ballroom on Australia's First Nations and their strong female networks, segueing to colonial beginnings, Federation and suffragettes – pointing out that it was Australia's progressive stance on female emancipation that had earnt the country the accolade of being one of the most innovative, liberal and modern nations on Earth at the time.

My conclusion was greeted with a susurrus of politely muted appreciation, except for one member of the audience, who leapt up, whooping, wolf-whistling, clapping and stomping her feet. 'Awesome!' she shouted out.

Tish! A truffler of arcania? Seeing Tish in a history lecture was like seeing the Statue of Liberty busting out some disco moves at a backyard barbecue.

I've no doubt she felt the same, finding me in her nightclub audience that night. She strode on stage, her mass of hair swept up into a coiffured meringue. The room throbbed with laughter and gaiety. The band struck up the opening chords of Joni Mitchell's 'Both Sides, Now'. Nobody stopped talking or showed the least inclination to do so. The animated hum of conversation was only broken by the cheery clatter of silverware and china. The glow from the stage lights bathed Tish in crazy colours, making her look like a tipsy pixie. She already looked faintly ridiculous with one singed eyebrow and a slightly scalded arm. My chest tightened with anxiety on her behalf, but then she started to sing. Arms flung wide, hands fluttering, her voice soared up and down the scale in free-form extemporisation – and the room fell silent.

When Tish had finished her set, everyone in the audience was on their feet begging for an encore. She sashayed to a table, where Chook had a bottle of champagne waiting on ice. At the sound of my staccato little gallop her way in clickety high heels, Tish turned and gawped. 'Bloody hell! Are you wearin' *stilettos*?'

'Well, when I was doing my lecture today . . .'

'. . . which was actually kinda *interestin*', by the way.'

'Was it? My heart wasn't really in it. All I could think about was going *dancing*.'

'You? Dancin'? I don't think you've recovered from Skye's whack on the noggin' with her yoni egg.'

'That song. I had no idea you could sing with such heartfelt, haunting, soulful emotion.'

'You have no idea about a lot of things.' Tish pushed a glass of Krug in my direction.

'Well, now I'm keen to learn. So, where shall we go first? Do you feel like the disco or the live band?'

'You know what, I reckon I'd rather have a bit of a natter about those early Aussie suffragettes. What heroines. I'm a heroine addict, after that bloody lecture. Besides, I'm pooped,' she said, kicking off her shoes.

'*You*? Pooped? Um ... I don't think *you've* recovered from Skye's whack on the noggin. Just picture it – in two hours we'll be onto our third pitcher of negronis and about two drinks away from flip, sip or strip.'

'Not tonight. Sorry, Gwennie babe. I've got orgy knee.'

'What on earth is that?' I asked. 'Although, do I even want to know?'

'I wore out my knee on the carpet doin' it backwards at that ménage à trois. It's like tennis elbow of the knees. Have a great night but I'm gonna hit the sack.'

I stared at her amazed. 'That's a turn-up for the books. Are you sure you haven't been kidnapped by aliens and replaced by some kind of pod person?'

She pointed at my high heels. 'You can't talk, twinkle toes.'

'I've realised,' I said proudly, 'that the vital thing to remember, as middle age comes and plonks itself down on you with its enormous backside, is not to grow too cautious and nervous. To seize the day. That's what being dangled over the side of a cruise ship will teach you.'

Tish shook her head. 'That's it. I'm callin' the ship's doctor, pronto,' she laughed, waving me away.

In truth, I'd never felt better.

35

I was woken by a prod. Well, a few prods as I was in a deep sleep – I'm talking a Sleeping-Beauty deep sleep.

A faint chink of light was seeping into my bedroom from a crack in the curtains. Tish whooshed them open and midday sunlight streamed in. Backlit as she was, it took me a moment to realise that her jaw had dropped wide open.

'Gwendoline Brookes. Is that a bloke in your bed?'

I glanced at the pillow next to me and rubbed my eyes. A tousled head of hair, a broad brown shoulder . . . it all came back to me in a glorious rush.

'Well, it was just a drink and next thing I know I'm watching his silver chain slapping against his sweaty, bronzed torso. As I raked an orgasmic scratch down his broad, chiselled back, I found myself wondering if "shagged to death" might be the official explanation on my death certificate,' I said, repeating word for word – I was pretty sure – Tish's words post-bonk in Budapest.

Tish was too amazed to laugh. 'You actually got laid!' Checking that my conquest was out for the count, she flumped down on the bed, hungry for details.

'Middle-aged women are being encouraged not to forget to have sex because it's good for your memory ... Sorry, what was I saying again?'

'Oh ha ha.' Tish picked up the end of the duvet to take a glimpse at the sleeping form beneath.

'Seriously,' I said, propping myself up on my elbows, 'I read some research yesterday in which scientists revealed that females who have sex more often score on average two percentage points higher on cognitive tasks. So, I don't want to be outdone by you, Tish, now, do I?'

'Only *you* would have sex for your mental health. Did you actually enjoy it?'

'Well, I was a bit shell-shocked. At first I couldn't remember which end of the vibrator went where.'

Tish exploded with surprised laughter.

'Shhhh.' I motioned for her to follow me into our adjoining sitting room. Shrugging on a bathrobe and softly closing the door, I continued. 'And of course, young men are uncut. The glans seemed distinctively bigger. It looked like a medieval soldier's helmet, which is called a sallet, in case you're interested, worn most commonly by archers.'

Tish was now bent double with laughter. 'I thought your pudenda was the Greta Garbo of sexual organs? Shy. Reclusive. Inhibited. No sightin's. So, Greta ... opened up?'

'She got very chatty.'

'The sex was good?' she inquired, wide-eyed with a mix of mirth and amazement.

'Oh yes.'

'The earth moved?'

'Good god, I think I moved three time zones in about three minutes. I definitely crossed the International Date Line. You were correct, Tish. Museums and galleries do not compare to a night with an orally fixated love god with gymnastic tendencies. And I was just so relieved to discover he's of legal age, because most of the things I did to him were not!'

I caught sight of my reflection in the gilt-edged mirror. I was smiling like a canary-filled cat. 'What I've realised is that a woman can spend her whole life worrying about what other people will think . . . Or you can ignore them and die with a grin. We have one day left at sea!' I nodded towards the next room. 'I want to make the most of it.'

'I'm gonna loll in bed all day too – readin'. Maybe some Chekhov,' she twinkled. 'And then on to some Homer.'

It was my turn to be amazed now. I also noticed that for the first time ever, Tish wasn't wearing any make-up. 'It's nice to see you without gloop all over your face.'

'And it's nice to see you with it . . . Suitably smeared.'

We smiled at each other with our eyes.

'So, what are your plans once we're back?' Tish asked, getting to her feet.

'Oh, back to teaching. I'm halfway to becoming a principal; in career terms, I'm enjoying the Friday afternoon of my metaphorical week.'

'Good for you. Sounds as though you've got it all sorted. I can't wait to get back into the studio and record some new songs. I've got so much to sing about.'

'That sounds exciting. I'm going to have a much more honest and open relationship with my kids, too,' I said decisively.

'Yeah, yeah, ditto, darl. And I won't be fallin' for any more conmen ever again, that's for friggin' sure. No more men on my menu. Just the boys in the band. It's gonna be so great to get back on stage with those rascals. Once my bloody eyebrow grows back.' Tish made a move towards her bedroom door. 'Okay, time to go slip between the covers ... the book covers, that is,' she winked.

'Hey, not so fast.' I stretched out a hand to the complimentary fruit bowl on the side table, plucked off a fat glossy cherry and popped it into my mouth, whole. 'So, strip off,' I ordered her.

'What?' Her nose twitched. 'Sweet Jesus. You want me to go back in there and join you?'

'No! We're not in Paris now. But don't you remember you said that if I ever had random sex with a stranger you'd yodel in your underwear with two teaspoons balanced on your tits?' I spat the cherry pip in her stunned direction.

'Oh shit. I bloody did, didn't I?'

And with that, Tish stripped off her top and bra, grabbed the teaspoons from the tea console, balanced them on her nipples and let out an exuberant yodel – just as my one-night stand opened the door and sauntered in. He took in the quivering teaspoons and grinned.

'So, I'm not too late for breakfast then.'

36

The behemoth boat docked in Sydney's Circular Quay at dawn and we disembarked shortly afterwards. Standing on the deck of the Passenger Terminal I watched the orange blur of the sun rising across the sequinned harbour, chasing the night westwards and with it all sense of melancholy and anxiety.

My newly discovered penchant for parties meant I'd had to buy a suitcase on board to accommodate the high heels and strappy dresses I'd found in the ship's best boutique. As we waited for our luggage to be unloaded, Tish picked up her hire-car keys from the assigned desk. And then we stood together watching the chirpy green and gold commuter ferries darting like fireflies back and forth across the sparkling harbour.

'Looking forward to seeing your family?' I asked.

'Of course. You?'

'Oh yes. Can't wait. And to get back to work.'

'Yeah,' Tish said, sounding uncharacteristically subdued.

We stood in silence watching the porters decanting the suitcases onto shore. 'I suppose you've missed rehearsing?' I asked conversationally.

Tish took a moment to answer. She took a pull on her e-ciggy, then replied, 'To tell you the friggin' truth – nope. I haven't missed any of those mongrels. Even though I started the band, I know they're gettin' ready to toss me for a younger, hotter lead singer.'

'What? How infuriating,' I commiserated. 'Why is a man our age given the sobriquet "silver fox", while a woman our age is labelled an "old hag" or "bag"?'

'Yeah. Sometimes I think, fuck it. I'm just gonna chuck it all in and become a stripper in a lap dancin' joint. But then I remember that I can't dance and I'm several kilos overweight, and a feminist, so . . .'

'Well, as we're being honest, I'm so sick of clearing a path through Terminology and Advanced Jargon 101 at school meetings that I could shoot myself.'

Tish swivelled to face me. 'You're shittin' me? I thought you loved teachin'.'

'I do. At least I did. But now I think I want to learn about myself for a change. Life can be bloody wonderful,' I paraphrased her motto. 'I don't want to miss it.'

'Well, my ex-hubby Brendan's on a learnin' curve, that's for sure. Left in charge of the sprogs for once. To be frank, I'm in no hurry to go back into Mummy mode. Hey, doan get me wrong. I love my kids dearly . . .'

'Oh yes, me too. Wouldn't be without them. I'm sure children can be a great comfort in your old age . . .'

'Yeah, and they make you reach it bloody faster too!' Tish cackled, sucking on her e-ciggy once more. 'I just wish they weren't so keen to give ya the benefit of their inexperience.'

'Ha! True. By the time a woman realises her mother was right, she has a daughter telling her she's wrong.'

On cue, a horn beep alerted me to the fact that Julia had arrived in her spotless hybrid eco car.

A strange sense of loss gripped me and a small sadness caught briefly at my throat. I turned away from Tish to hide my face. This woman had arrived into my life with a ladder and a getaway car, whisking me away into a world of adventurous escapades. How would I readjust? I'd need a decompression chamber to wean me off excitement and get me used to marking homework again.

What would I do without the daily fix of her crack cocaine company? How would I revert to the friendship equivalent of a half-glass of weekly shandy and sensible spritzer? Clearly there was going to be a degree of cold turkey in the transition.

I tried again to imagine slotting back into my old life but shuddered at the thought of now having to deal with all the bigamy rumours and endless sticky-beaking. The night before, I'd looked at photos of my kids and friends on Facebook. Despite the pain of losing Jack, I'd managed to rebuild a decent life for our little family of three – until Jason had torn at its fabric. And now the pain of his betrayal had finally faded. He'd become no more than a few dark threads in our tapestry.

'Thank you, Tish, for bringing colour back into my world. Too much colour at times. But at least there'll be no sepia grey for me anymore.'

'And no more ironin' tea towels, okay? Ironin' tea towels is God's way of telling you to get a life.' Tish tossed her backpack nonchalantly over one shoulder.

My daughter beeped once more from her double-parked position some way off and gave a friendly wave out the window. I fluttered my fingers in her direction.

'You are actually pretty friggin' fabulous, Gwennie. Keep that shit up, okay?'

My pulse beat with an irrational sense of pleasure. I had never seen myself living a Big Life. I enjoyed my book club, buying fresh coriander at the local farmers market, growing basil, bush walking. But was this life the human version of an orthopaedic sandal – comfy, well-worn and unremarkable? I wanted to feel like a sequinned, spangly, sparkling stiletto.

Soon I'd be letting myself into my house. Yes, it would be joyous to hug my darling Max and thank him for all his hard work. And to apologise to my dearest daughter for the subterfuge and thank her for all her concern. But then what? I felt irrationally worried the house would be steeped in an atmosphere of rebuke, like a possessive lover, welcoming me home with a slightly histrionic, sulky air of having been abandoned. I imagined peering through the windows of the suburban homes in our street and their violet flicker of television sets and sighed. Feeling my old life hardening around me like a habit, I suppressed the disorientating feeling that I'd lost my place in a book. 'Thank you for the adventure, Tish.' I picked up my suitcase. 'It was, well, unforgettable.'

'Yeah, it was a bloody wild ride, wasn't it?' She hoiked up her shirt to reveal her Jason tattoo again. 'I've decided not to get it removed. I'm just gonna turn it into a Pyramid or a Paris café, to commemorate our incredible trip.' She pulled down her shirt. 'See you around, Gwennie.' She squeezed my shoulder and sashayed away, tossing her hire-car keys into the air and catching them with expert ease.

Walking out of the terminal towards my daughter, the breeze ruffling the hem of my dress, I found myself looking back over my shoulder. And suddenly I wasn't just looking, but power-walking – back towards Tish, calling her name. I hardly recognised my own voice. 'You know what sucks?' I said, employing her vernacular. 'Just when you've learnt to make the most of your life, most of your life is gone.'

Tish pivoted around on her brand-new Birkenstock. 'I'm sixty now,' I carried on. 'At best I have only 87,000 hours left before I die. And I don't want to spend any of them being avoidably miserable.'

'I get it,' she said, peering at me over the top of her red, heart-shaped shades. 'Ya doan wanna play the role of wing woman to your own life.'

The morning sun had strengthened and was now blazing across the passenger terminal forecourt, bathing everything in a golden, magical hue, like a Venetian painting.

'Exactly. I want to swim with dolphins, skinny-dip in a rock star's private infinity pool, bonk my brains out with a nice-guy Mr Universe in a champagne jacuzzi . . . instead of re-lining the linen press and de-moulding the shower grout.'

'Yeah? My life wants to take off its bra, relax and take time to think about stuff a bit more.'

'So our aim is the same – to build a life you don't need a vacation from?'

'Yep. That about nails it.'

Julia's horn gave another long honk. When I ignored her, my mobile started to buzz in my handbag like a trapped bee.

Tish cocked her head to one side and gazed my way, intrigued, waiting for me to go on.

'Julia's always telling me all the things I should *stop* doing, like drinking cocktails and eating cake. But I can't stop thinking of all the things I want to *start* doing: sky diving, caving, zip lining. Nothing makes you evaluate your life more than a few near-death experiences, right?'

'So what are you drivin' at? Clearly not home in your daughter's car, where you're supposed to be.'

Tish pointed at Julia, who now had her head out of the window and was hollering, 'Hi Mum! What's going on? Are you okay?'

'If a woman's healthy in middle age, she'll probably live to ninety-six,' I said. 'So there's a hell of a lot of adventures still to be had. Because if I don't start having adventures now, then *when*? I imagine a mobility scooter could seriously cramp a girl's style on a scuba in Cuba.'

Tish took off her sunglasses now and scrutinised me. 'Are you sayin' that you wanna keep on truckin'?'

'Yes. I think I do . . . With you.'

'With me?! You said we're like oysters and custard . . .'

'Yes, but the Venn diagram of what you share as older women is much bigger than what we share when we're young. At that time of life, you're putting yourself first, fighting for your man, your career, your kids. But those days are over.'

'I thought you were savin' your money for a rainy day?'

I looked up at the sky. It was bright blue, with not a cloud on the horizon. 'Hmmm. Raining cats and dogs, I'd say.'

She too looked skywards and chuckled. 'Yep, bloody bucketin' down.'

I rang Julia to say I was so sorry, I loved her dearly, but I wouldn't be needing a lift home after all as there was something I needed to sort out. Nor did I want to do any more dog sitting – not just yet anyway. Nor did I want to spend my spare time buying her pool chlorine from Bunnings. I thanked her profusely for coming to pick me up, and broke the good news that her inheritance was intact. She tried to interrupt but I rushed on, explaining that as much as I adored her, I wasn't coming over to the car for a kiss and a cuddle, because she might talk me out of my crazy impulse.

I vowed to be in touch later, sent my love to Max, then rang off before her Early Warning Parental Anxiety System could activate in full, summoning psychiatrists and paramedics.

I then strode after Tish towards her hire car. 'Do the authorities know Tish Delaney is getting behind the wheel? You really should have your own designated lane at all times,' I teased.

Much to my astonishment, Tish chucked the car keys in my direction. I caught them in one deft movement, just the way Tish had done earlier, and smiled at her.

'So,' she said, sliding into the passenger seat. 'What's our plan?'

'For the first time in my life, I have no plans and no plans to have plans,' I laughed. 'But you always seem to know your own mind and what you want and where you're going, Tish.'

'All bluff, kiddo. To be honest, I'm just wingin' it. Life ... Love ... Career ... Motherhood ... Genital topiary ... Everythin'. But j'know what I'd like to do?' Her voice dropped low as she murmured something almost but not quite inaudible.

I looked at her, flabbergasted. 'Did you just say you want to go to a *museum*?'

'Yeah. Let's start in London! And then maybe a gallery, I'm thinkin' ... the Uffizi.'

'Really? 'Cause I'd like to lie on a deserted Tahitian beach and let my hair down ... on my chin.' I flicked down the visor to check for whiskers in the mirror.

'Don't be a vulgarian, Gwen! Let's do the Hermitage or the Acropolis. Or the Smithsonian,' she enthused.

'Or migrate back to the Serengeti, annually, just like those wondrous wildebeest. But do it slowly this time. Or what about the Galápagos? How refreshing to be in a place where the creatures are even weirder than you are!'

'Than *you* are, you mean! I mean, for chrissake, who the hell *are* you, Gwendoline Brookes?'

'That's what I want to find out, Patricia Delaney.'

'I can't stop thinkin' about somethin' David Bowie once said – that agein' is an extraordinary process whereby you become the person you always should have been.'

'Gap years are so wasted on the young. A gap year, at our age – now, that's better than HRT. I think we've joined the Rare Creatures Club. We're the two-legged version of the duck-billed platypus.'

'Yeah, with a barb in our tongue instead of our foot.'

'So, watch out world . . . Cocktail?'

'What a good idea. Buck's Fizz or Bloody Mary?'

One day later, having hugged kids, sorted mortgages, re-filled dishwasher salt dispensers, watered orchids and re-packed, Tish and I slapped our passports down on the airport ticketing desk behind which sat a helpful-looking young man. 'We want two first-class tickets. Round the world.'

'First class?' I gawped, stunned.

'My pal here used to be terrified of flyin', but it turns out she was just terrified of flyin' friggin' economy with the plebs,' she explained.

'Please ignore my friend. She's uncouth, loud, crass and foul-tempered.'

The ticketing agent looked indignant on Tish's behalf. 'Surely you shouldn't say those awful things about your travel companion?'

'Of course I can . . . She's my best friend.'

'Kiddo, you just made me so happy, tears of laughter are running down my leg!'

I laughed too then. Peal after cackling peal floated up into the cavernous terminal.

As the man began to read out possible itineraries, Tish winked at me. 'And we'll film it all on the trusty GoPro.'

'Plus keep a diary and then write up a story of the trip.'

'Yeah. To inspire other women our age to go forth and be friggin' fabulous.'

'And the last line will read, "And she gave no fucks . . . Not even one . . . And she lived happily ever after. The End."'

Acknowledgements

Thank you for taking this flight of fancy with me. I hope you enjoyed it as much as I enjoyed taking you for a ride.

Thanks to my fabulous flight crew – my dear sisters, Jenny, Elizabeth and Carolyn, who always endure my bumpy first draft; my beloved mum, Val, crossword queen; cherished offspring Jules and Georgie; and my treasured mainstay, Brian O'Doherty.

Thanks also to my perspicacious editorial captain, Catherine Hill, and her creative co-pilots Meredith Curnow and Karen Reid.

Heartfelt thanks to the ground staff, as well: agent Tara Wynne and my aptly named PA Rebecca Helps.

To my super sleuths, the financial crime expert (and Greek love god) Steve York; and the world's best private investigator, Kenneth Lodge, it's so comforting to know that if ever I can't find myself, you boys can.

Finally, this book never would have got off the ground without travel maestros Claire Irvin and Penny Walker. Here's to more adventure before dementia.

And to my dear readers, I look forward to the next exciting escapade in your wonderful company, when we get to re-fasten our psychological seatbelts for another wild ride.

About the author

Kathy Lette is a celebrated and outspoken comic writer with an inimitable take on serious current issues. She is the author of fifteen bestselling novels, including *Puberty Blues*, which was made into a major film and a TV miniseries, *Mad Cows*, which was also made into a film, starring Joanna Lumley, and *How to Kill Your Husband (And Other Handy Household Hints)*, which was staged by the Victorian Opera. She pioneered smart, funny, feminist fiction and has been published in seventeen languages.

Kathy is an autodidact (clearly it's a word she taught herself) but has honorary doctorates from Southampton and Wollongong universities, and a Senior Honorary Fellowship from Regent's University London.

She is an ambassador for Plan International, Theirworld and the National Autistic Society UK. Kathy lives in Sydney and in London, and can often be found at the Savoy Hotel drinking a cocktail named after her. She cites her career highlights as once teaching Stephen Fry a word and Salman Rushdie the limbo, and scripting Julian Assange's cameo in the 500th episode of *The Simpsons*.

Visit her website, www.kathylette.com, to read her blog, follow KathyLetteAuthor on Facebook, @KathyLette on Twitter and @kathy.lette on Instagram.

HRT: Husband Replacement Therapy
Kathy Lette

What do you do when you're told you've got terminal cancer at 50? Take up crochet, get religion and bow out gracefully? Or upend your life and spend every remaining minute exploring new pleasures? Rollicking fun for women of a certain age.

Ruby has always been the generous mediator among her friends, family and colleagues, which is why they have all turned up to celebrate her 50th birthday. But after a few too many glasses of champers, Ruby's speech doesn't exactly go to plan. Instead of delivering the witty and warm words her guests are expecting, Ruby takes her moment in the spotlight to reveal what she really thinks of every one of them. She also accuses her husband, Harry, of having an affair.

Saving the best till last, Ruby lambasts her octogenarian mother for a lifetime of playing her three daughters against each other. It's blisteringly brutal. As the stunned gathering gawks at Ruby, the birthday girl concludes her bravura monologue with the throwaway comment that she has terminal cancer. She has cashed in her life savings and plans on taking her two sisters cruising into the sunset for a dose of Husband Replacement Therapy. Courageous? Or ruthlessly selfish?

But, do they even want to go with her?

Rollicking fun for women, and men who dare.

Paperback: 9781760890131
EBook: 9781760890148
Audiobook: 9781760896676

How to Kill Your Husband (and other handy household hints)
Kathy Lette

From the author of the bestselling *HRT* and *Puberty Blues*.
All women want to kill their husbands some of the time.

Marriage, it would appear, is a fun-packed frivolous hobby, only occasionally resulting in death. But when Jazz Jardine is arrested for her husband's murder, the joke falls flat.

Life should begin at 40 – not with life imprisonment for killing your spouse. Jazz, stay-at-home mum and domestic goddess; Hannah, childless and career-focused; and Cassie, demented working mother of two are three ordinary women.

Cassie and Hannah set out immediately to prove their best friend's innocence, uncovering betrayal, adultery, plot twists, thinner thighs and toy boys aplenty en route. But will their friendship survive these ever darker revelations?

A novel that will strike a chord with women everywhere and ensure that, from now on, they all read the small print on their marriage licenses.

Paperback: 9781761042072
EBook: 9781760145514

The Boy Who Fell to Earth
Kathy Lette

Told with Kathy Lette's razor-sharp wit, this is a funny, quirky and tender story of a mother's love for her son – and of a love affair that has no chance of running smoothly.

Meet Merlin. He's Lucy's bright, beautiful son – who just happens to be on the spectrum.

Since Merlin's father left them in the lurch, Lucy has made Merlin the centre of her world. Struggling with the joys and tribulations of raising her adorable yet challenging child (if only Merlin came with operating instructions), Lucy doesn't have room for any other man in her life.

By the time Merlin turns ten, Lucy is seriously worried that the Pope might start ringing her up for tips on celibacy, so resolves to dip a toe back into the world of dating. Thanks to Merlin's candour and quirkiness, things don't go *quite* to plan . . . Then, just when Lucy's resigned to singledom once more, Archie – the most imperfectly perfect man for her and her son – lands on her doorstep. But then, so does Merlin's father, begging for a second chance.

Does Lucy need a real father for Merlin – or a real partner for herself?

Paperback: 9781761042089
EBook: 9781760145521